CARTOON NETWORK

ADVENTURE TIME

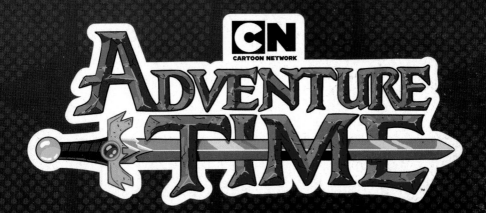

MARCELINE THE PIRATE QUEEN

ROSS RICHIE CEO & Founder
JOY HUFFMAN CFO
MATT GAGNON Editor-in-Chief
FILIP SABLIK President, Publishing & Marketing
STEPHEN CHRISTY President, Development
LANCE KREITER Vice President, Licensing & Merchandising
PHIL BARBARO Vice President, Finance & Human Resources
ARUNE SINGH Vice President, Marketing
BRYCE CARLSON Vice President, Editorial & Creative Strategy
SCOTT NEWMAN Manager, Production Design
KATE HENNING Manager, Operations
SPENCER SIMPSON Manager, Sales
SIERRA HAHN Executive Editor
JEANINE SHAEFER Executive Editor
DAFNA PLEBAN Senior Editor
SHANNON WATTERS Senior Editor
ERIC HARBURN Senior Editor
WHITNEY LEOPARD Editor
CAMERON CHITTOCK Editor
CHRIS ROSA Editor
MATTHEW LEVINE Editor

SOPHIE PHILIPS-ROBERTS Assistant Editor
GAVIN GRONENTHAL Assistant Editor
MICHAEL MOCCIO Assistant Editor
AMANDA LaFRANCO Executive Assistant
JILLIAN CRAB Design Coordinator
MICHELLE ANKLEY Design Coordinator
KARA LEOPARD Production Designer
MARIE KRUPINA Production Designer
GRACE PARK Production Design Assistant
CHELSEA ROBERTS Production Design Assistant
SAMANTHA KNAPP Production Design Assistant
ELIZABETH LOUGHRIDGE Accounting Coordinator
STEPHANIE HOCUTT Social Media Coordinator
JOSÉ MEZA Event Coordinator
HOLLY AITCHISON Operations Coordinator
MEGAN CHRISTOPHER Operations Assistant
RODRIGO HERNANDEZ Mailroom Assistant
MORGAN PERRY Direct Market Representative
CAT O'GRADY Marketing Assistant
BREANNA SARPY Executive Assistant

Created by Pendleton Ward

Written by **Leah Williams**
Illustrated by **Zachary Sterling**
Colors by **Laura Langston**
Letters by **Mike Fiorentino**

Cover by **Sara Kipin**

Designer **Chelsea Roberts**
Assistant Editor **Michael Moccio**
Editor **Whitney Leopard**

With Special Thanks to Marisa Marionakis, Janet No, Becky M. Yang, Conrad Montgomery, Kelly Crews, Scott Malchus, Adam Muto and the wonderful folks at Cartoon Network.

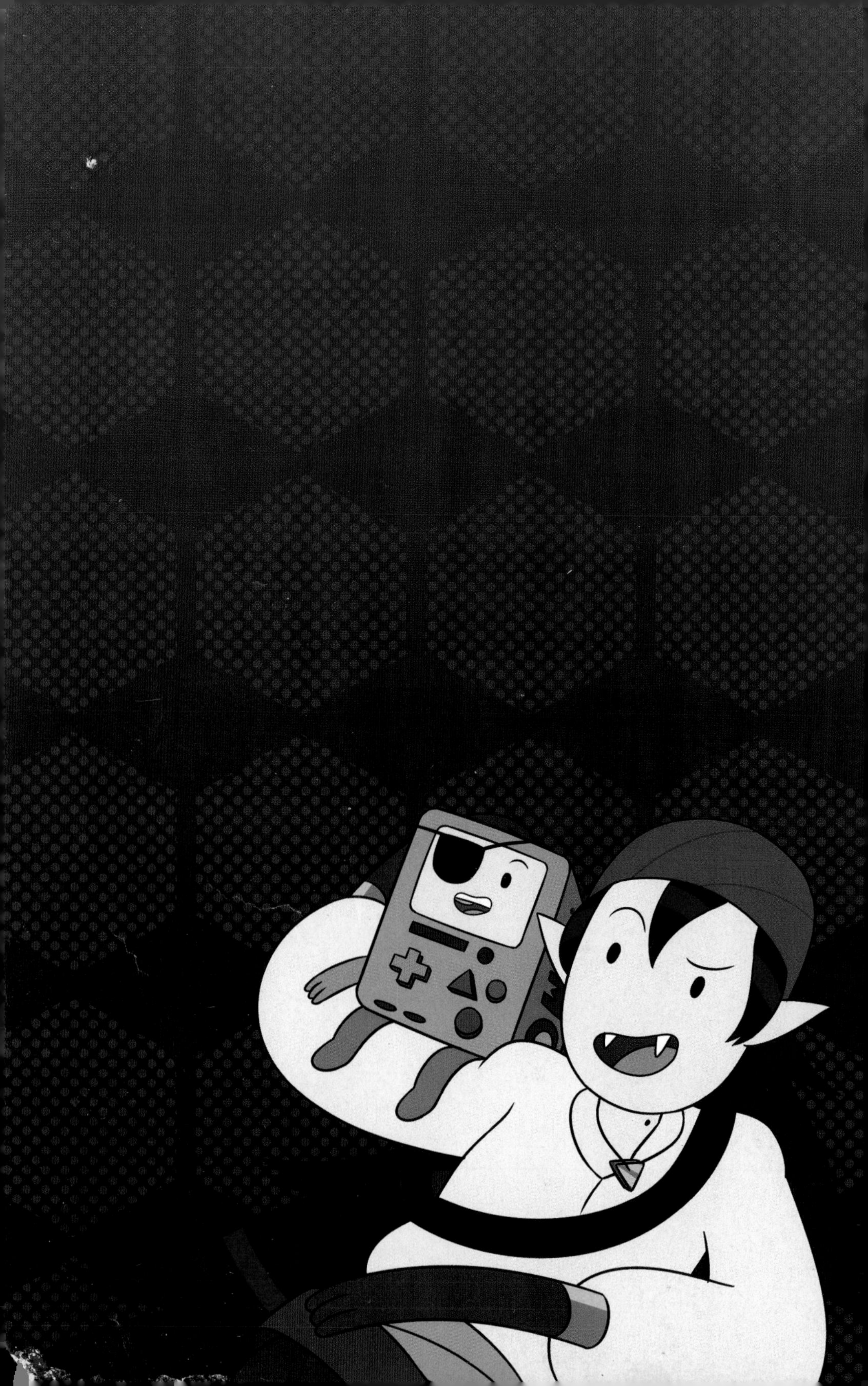

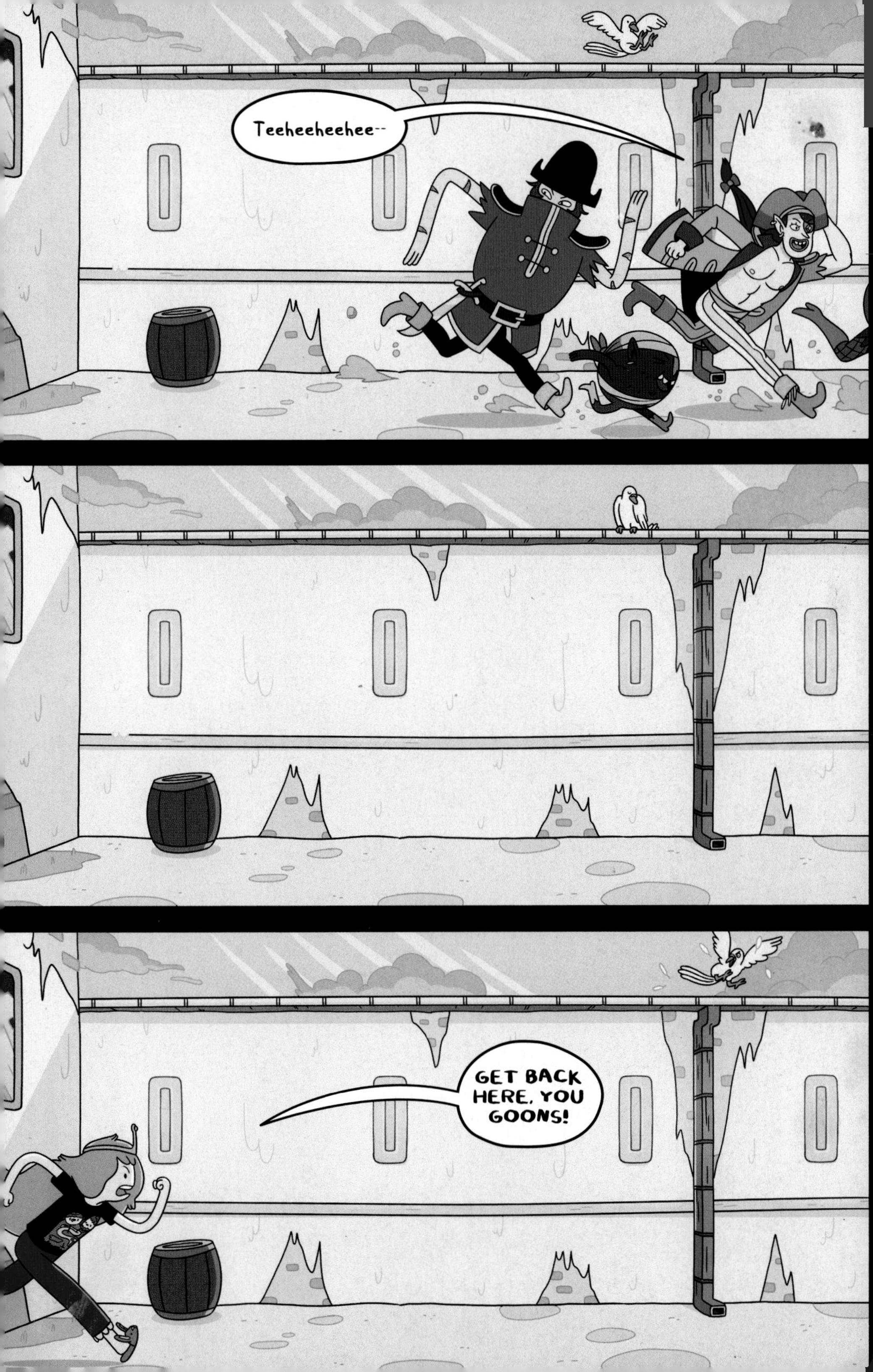
Teeheeheehee--
GET BACK HERE, YOU GOONS!

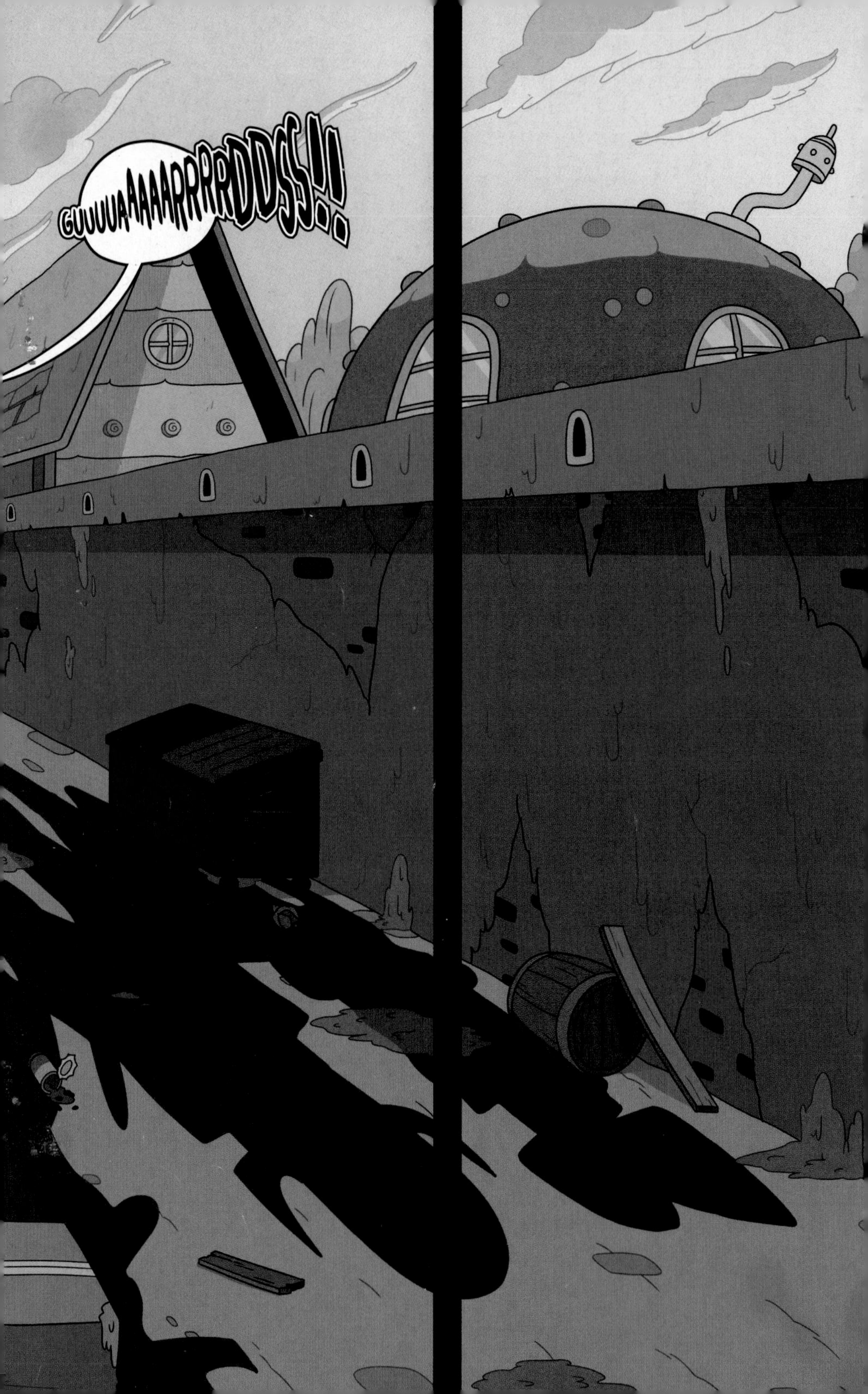
GUUUUAAAAARRRRDDSS!!

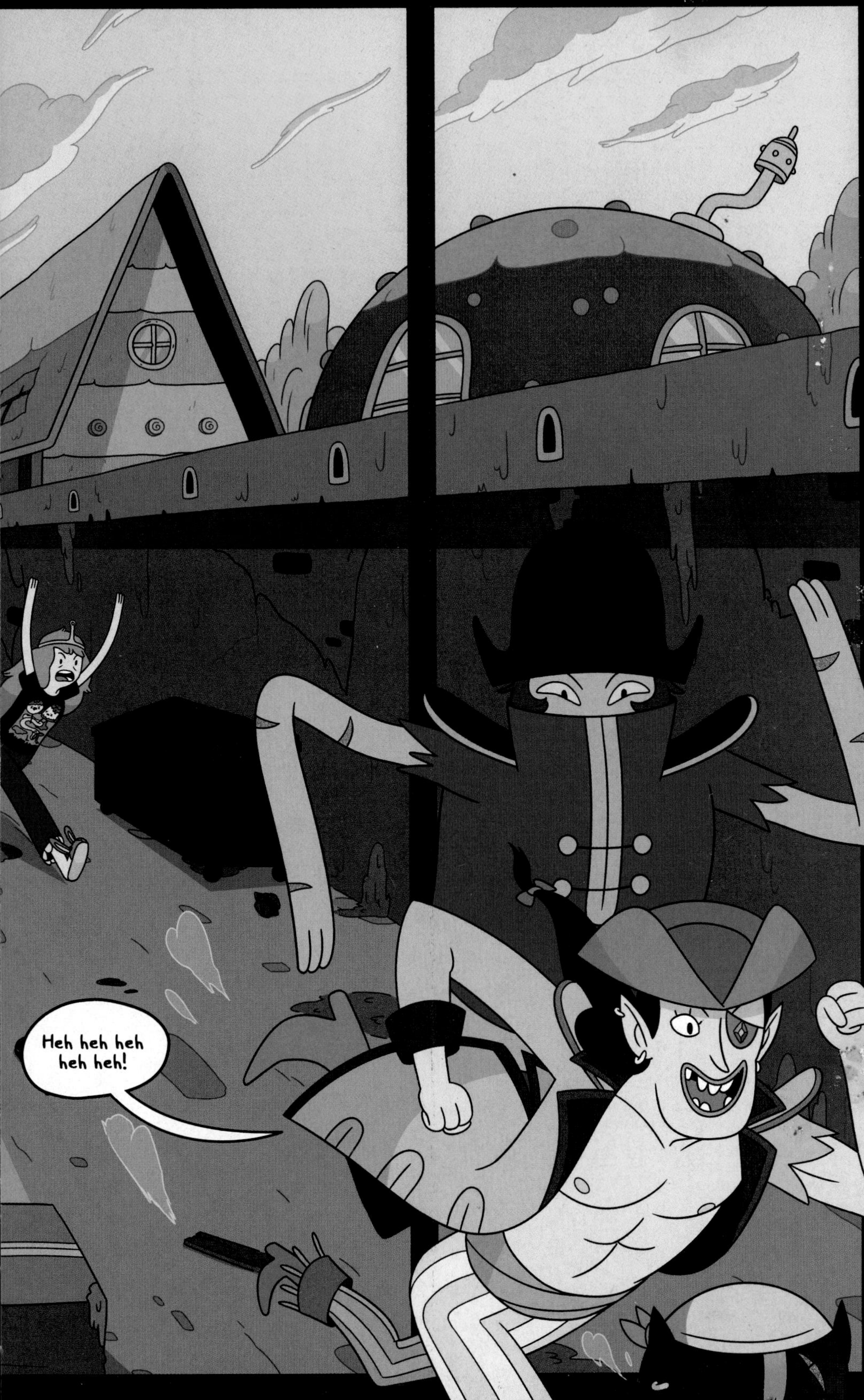
Heh heh heh
heh heh!

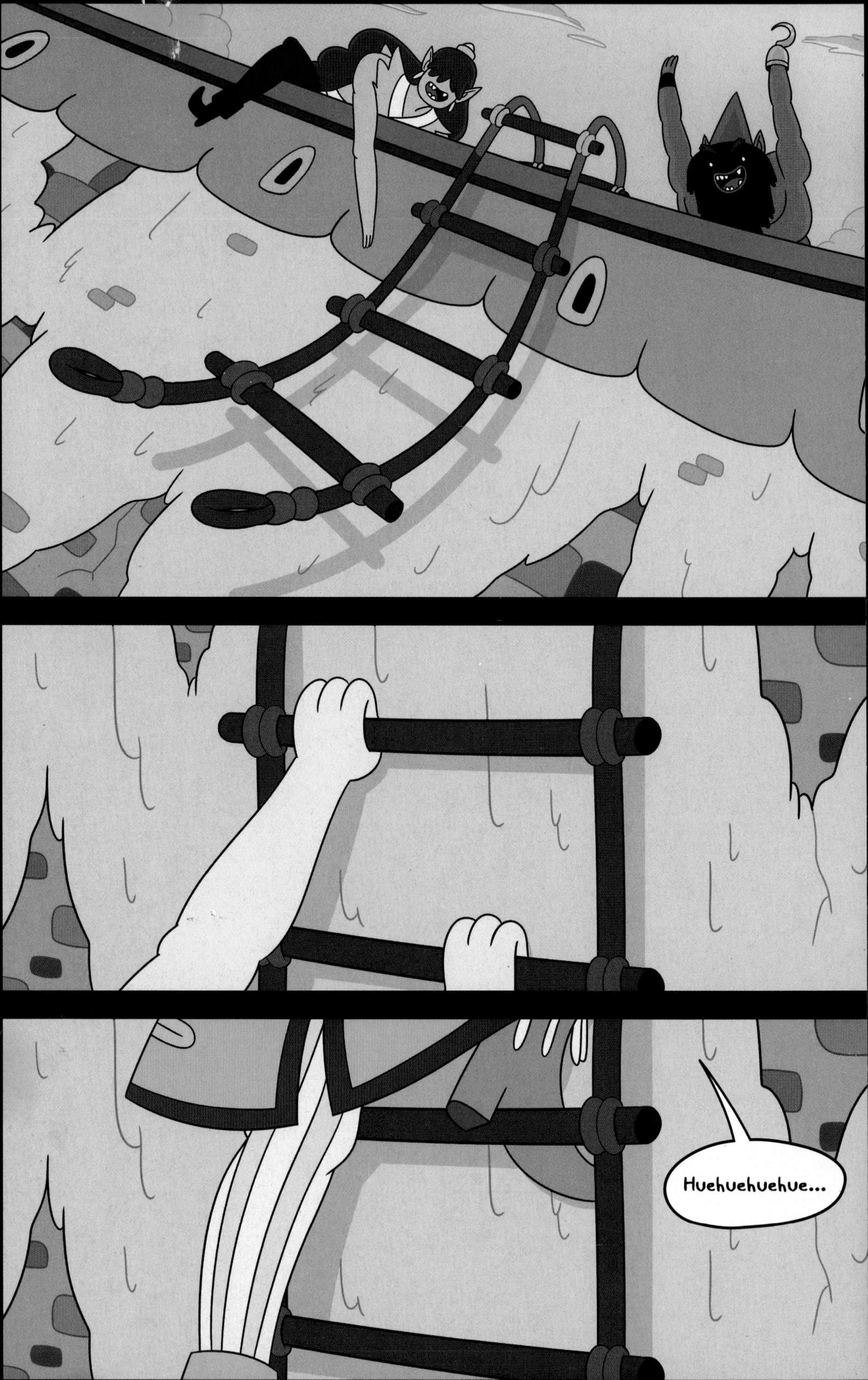
Huehuehuehue...

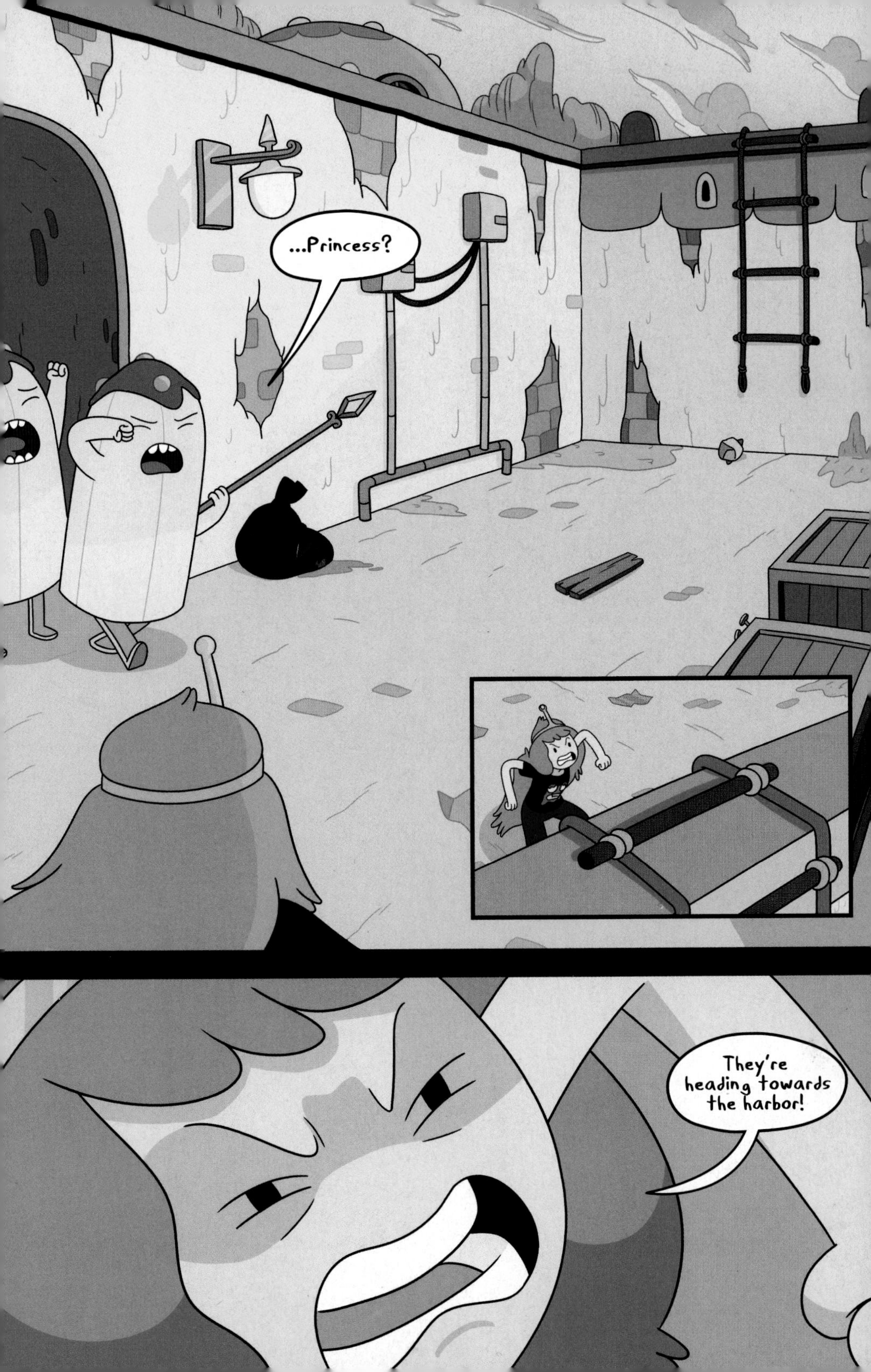
...Princess?
They're heading towards the harbor!

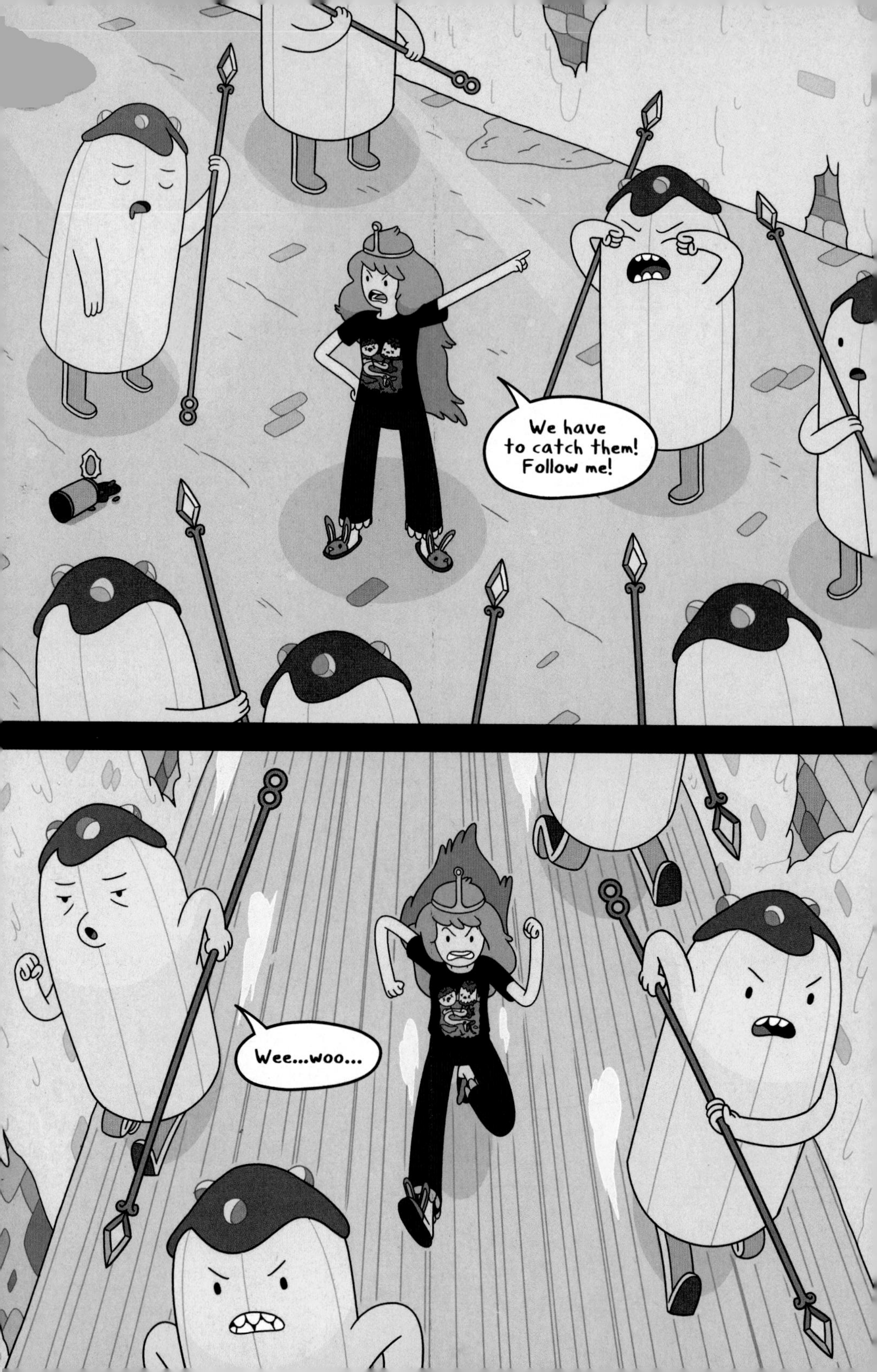
We have to catch them! Follow me!
Wee...woo...

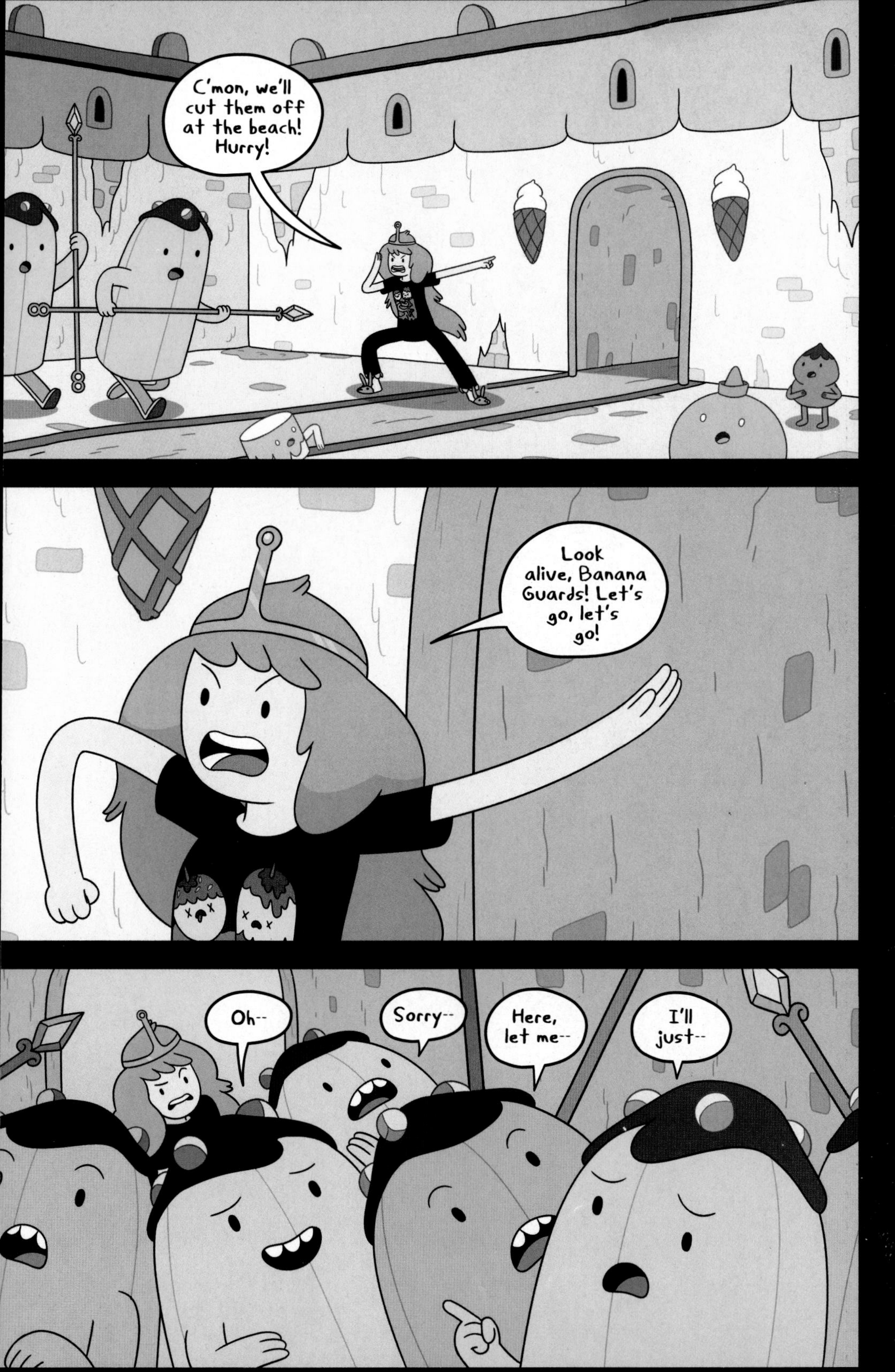
C'mon, we'll cut them off at the beach! Hurry!
Look alive, Banana Guards! Let's go, let's go!
Oh--
Sorry--
Here, let me--
I'll just--

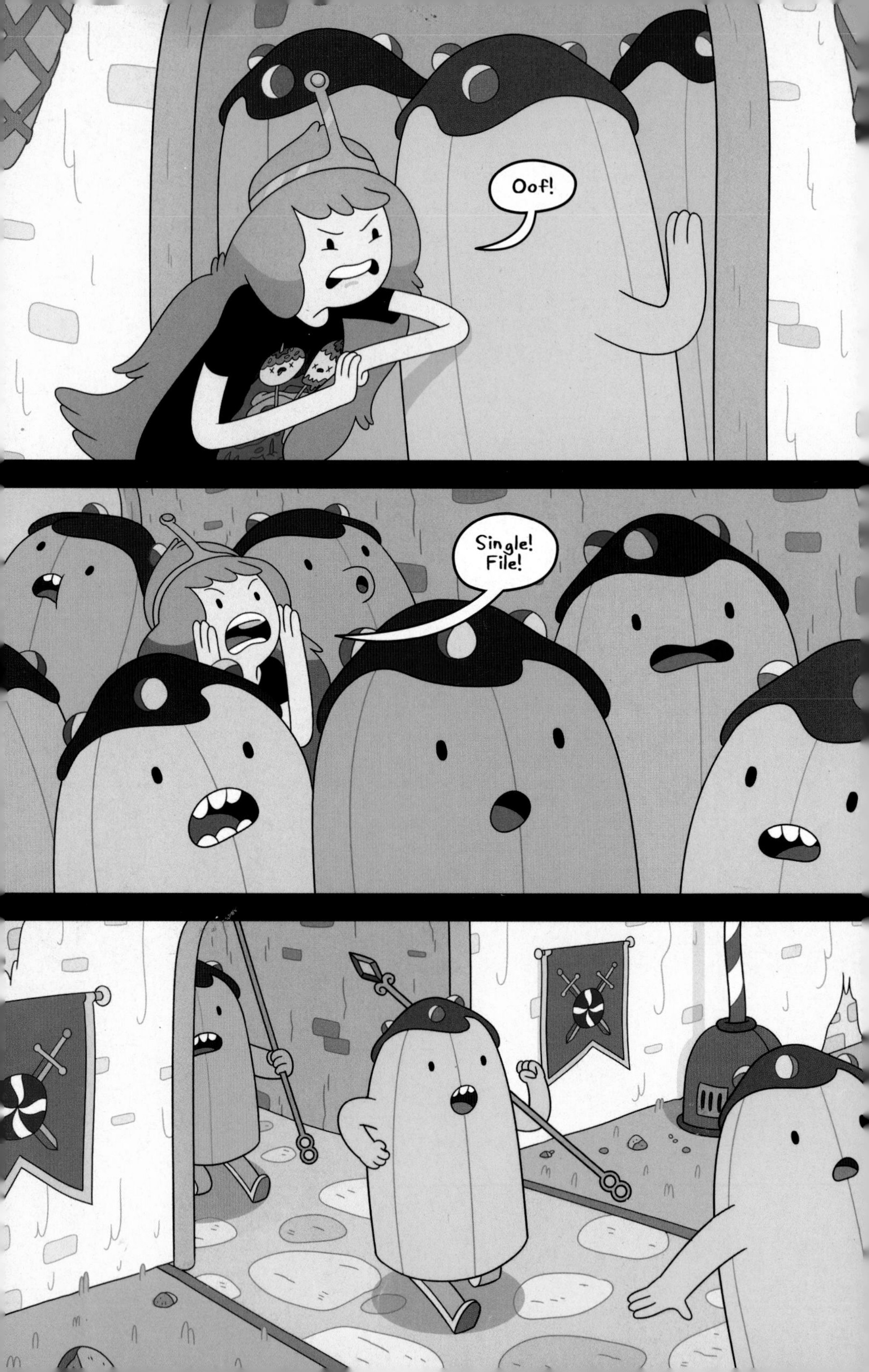
Oof!
Single! File!

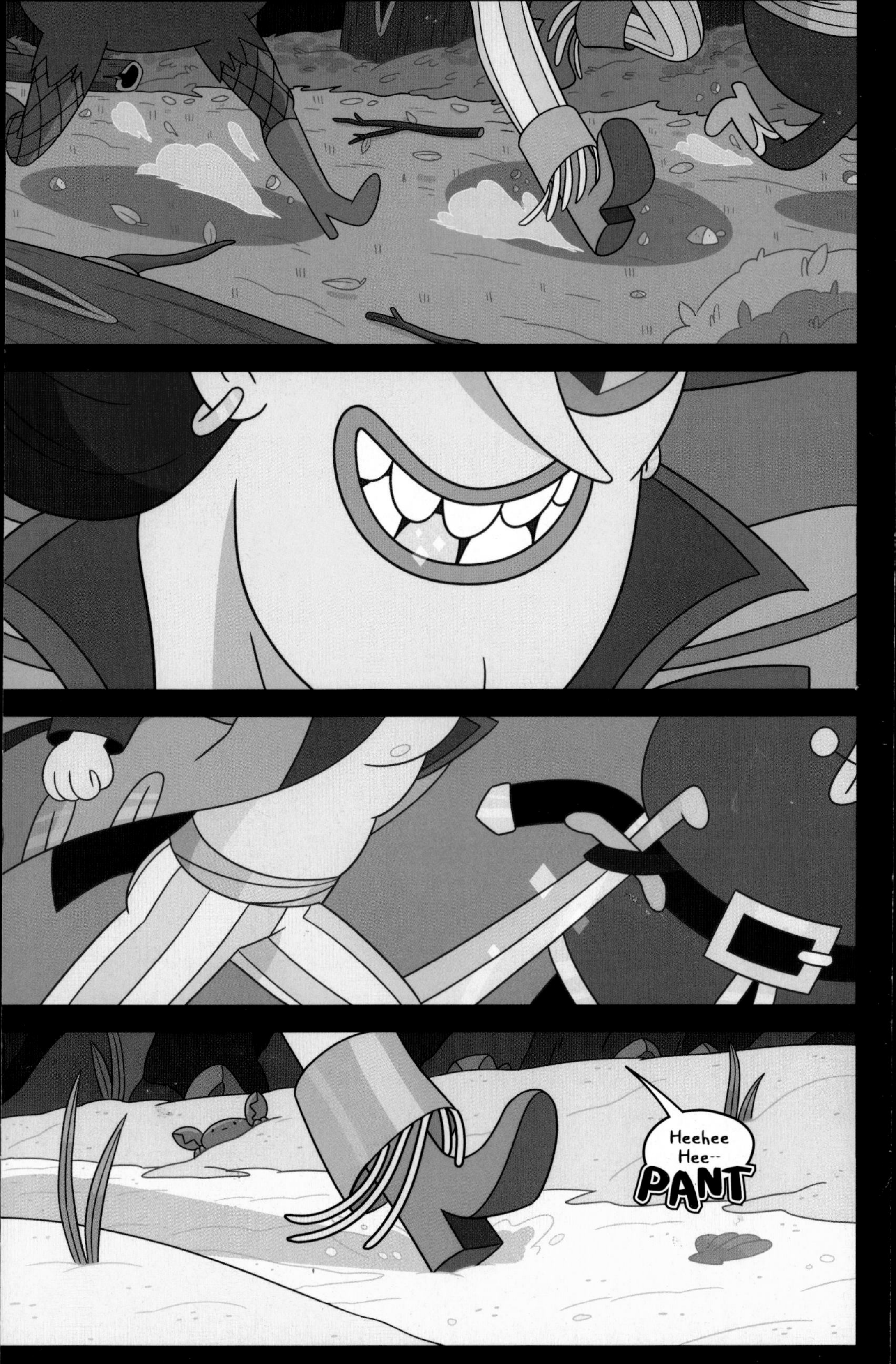
Heehee
Hee--
PANT

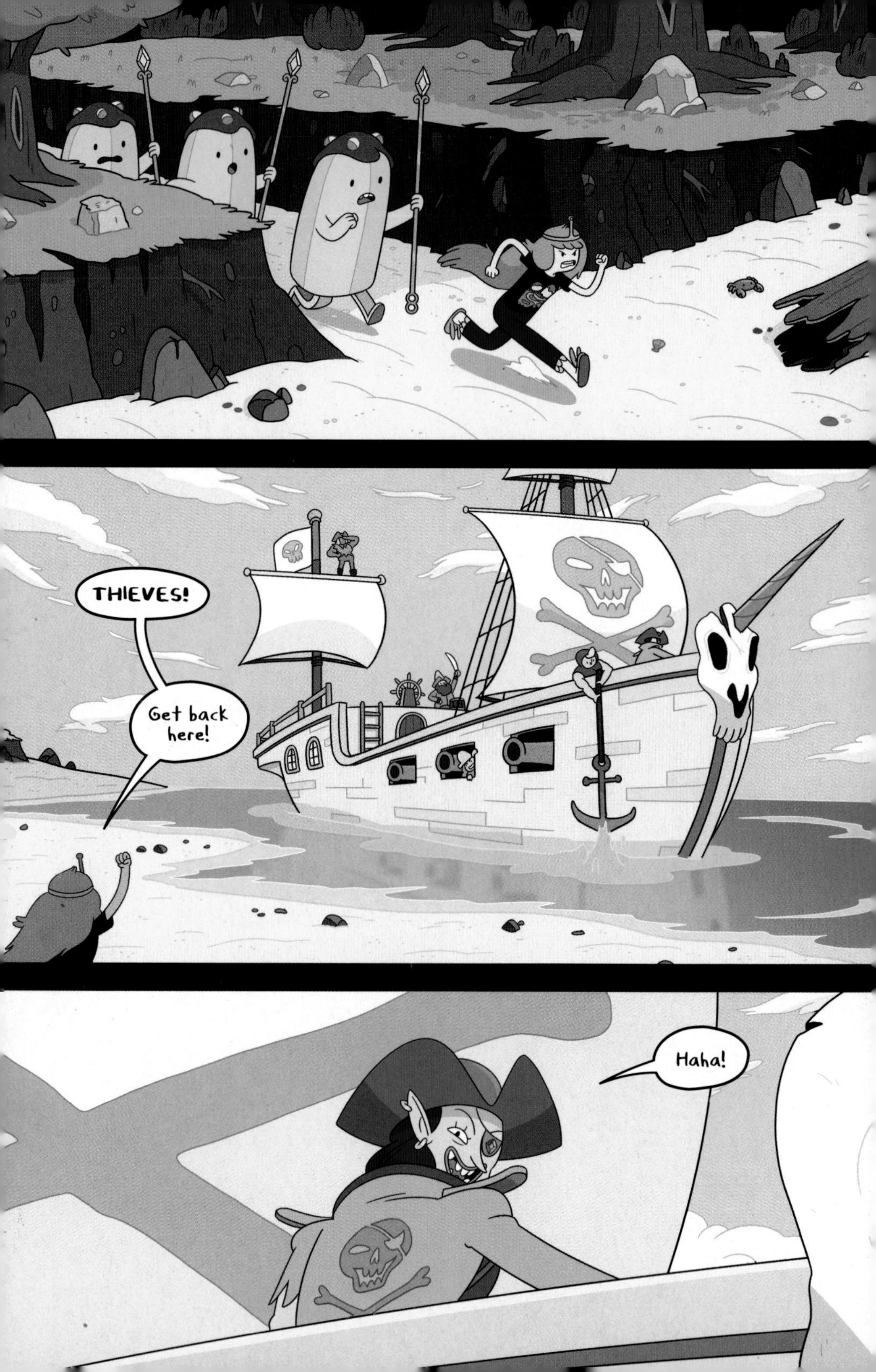
THIEVES!
Get back here!
Haha!

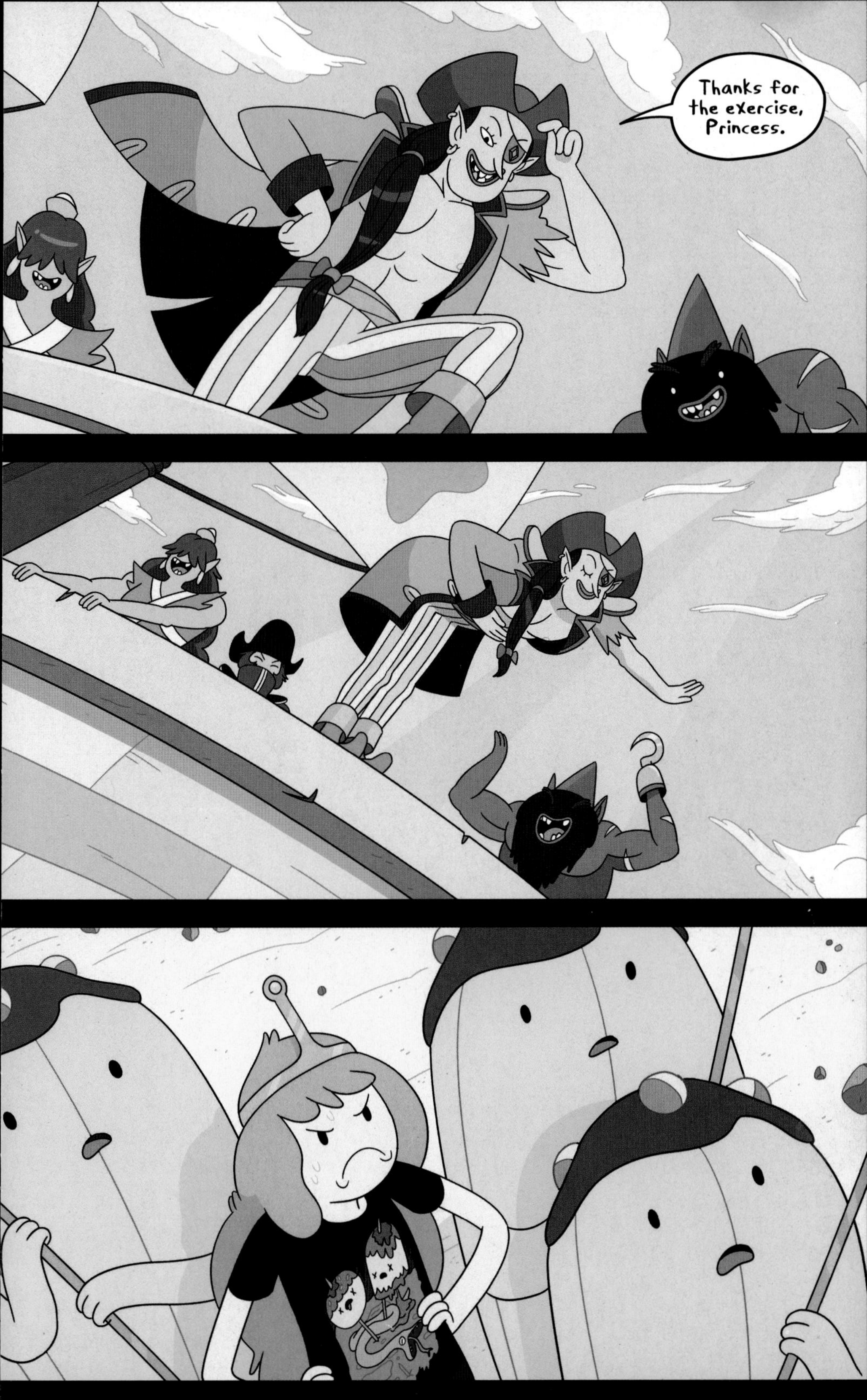
Thanks for the exercise, Princess.

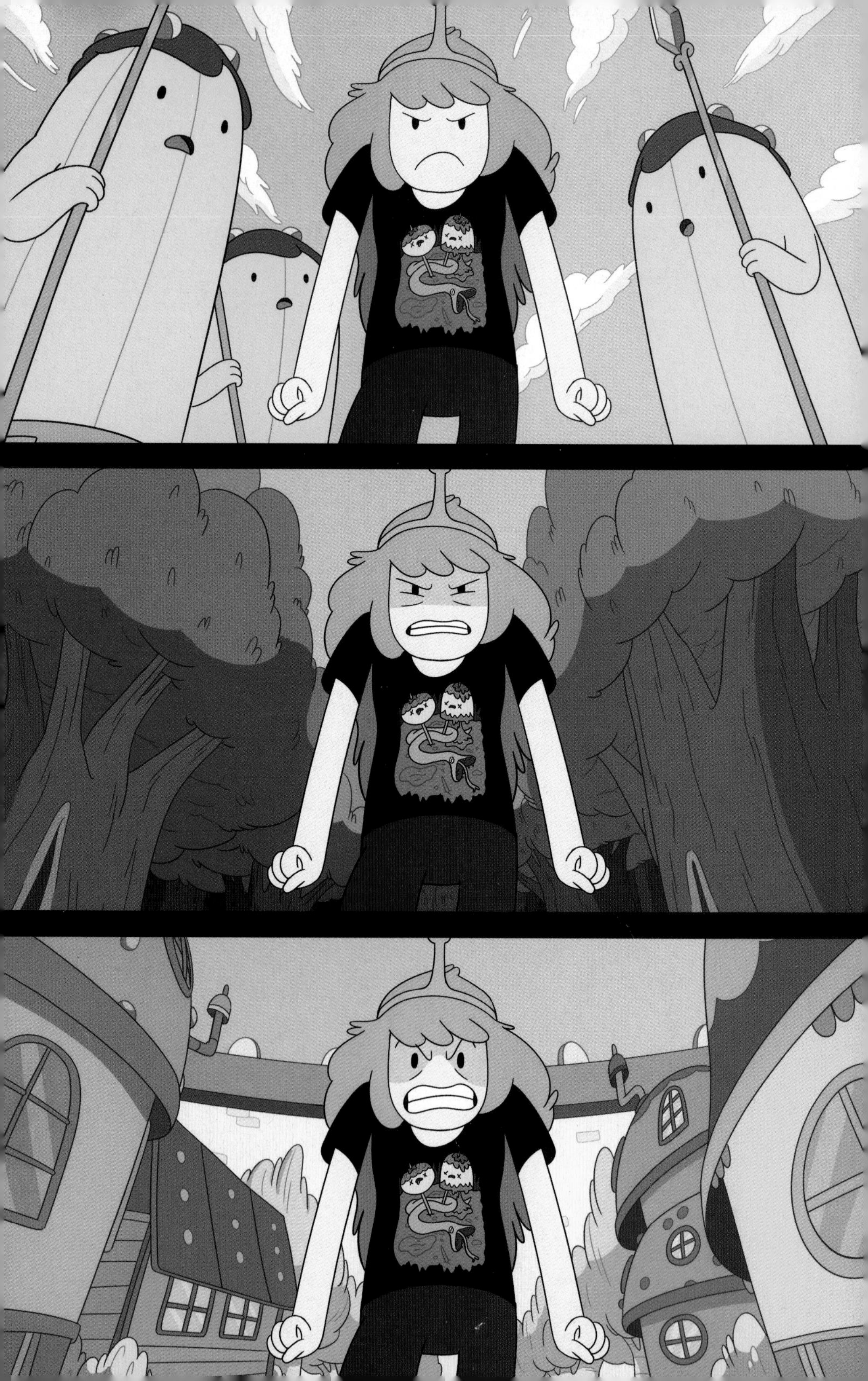

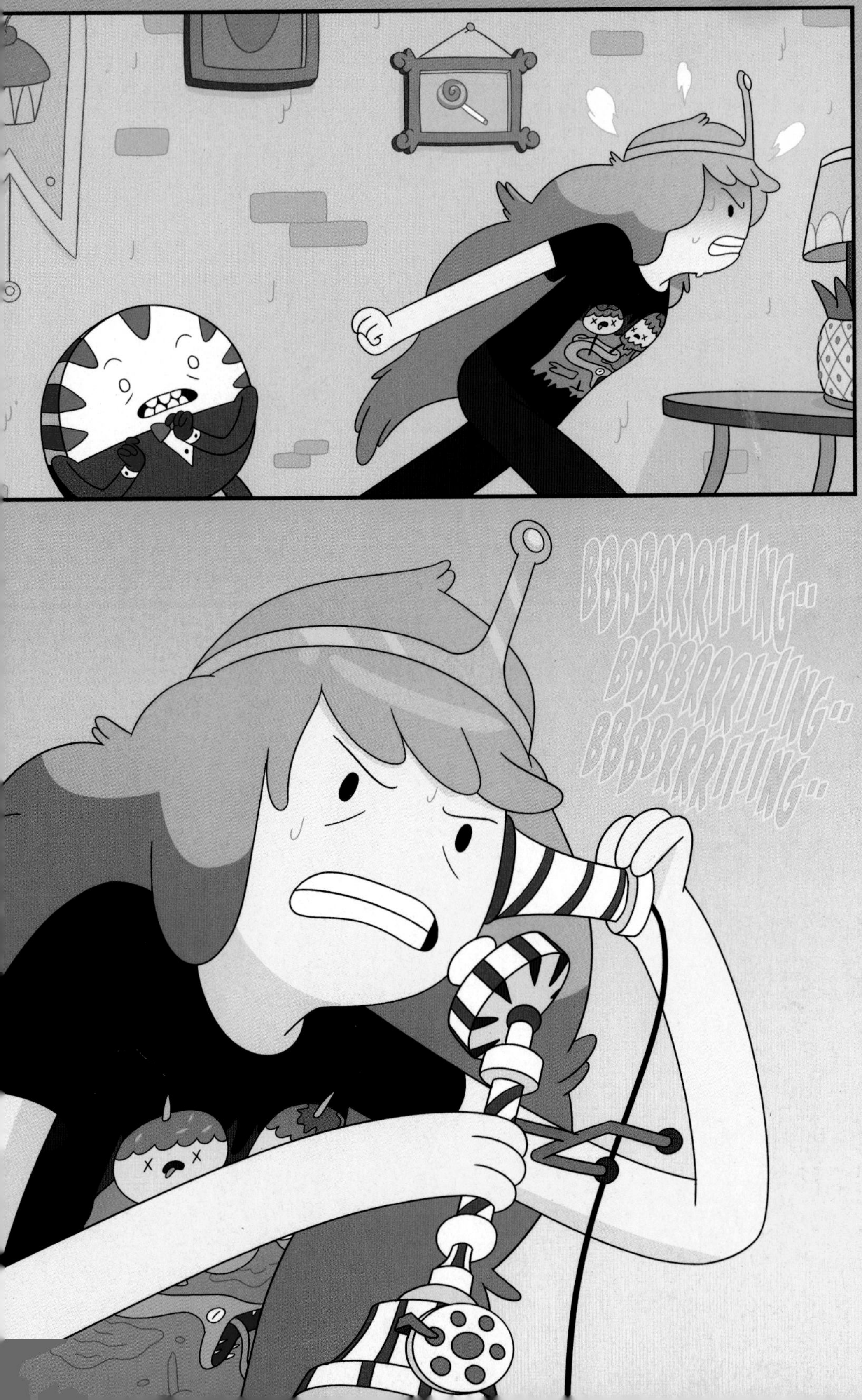
BBBBRRRIIING..
BBBBRRRIIING..
BBBBRRRIIING..

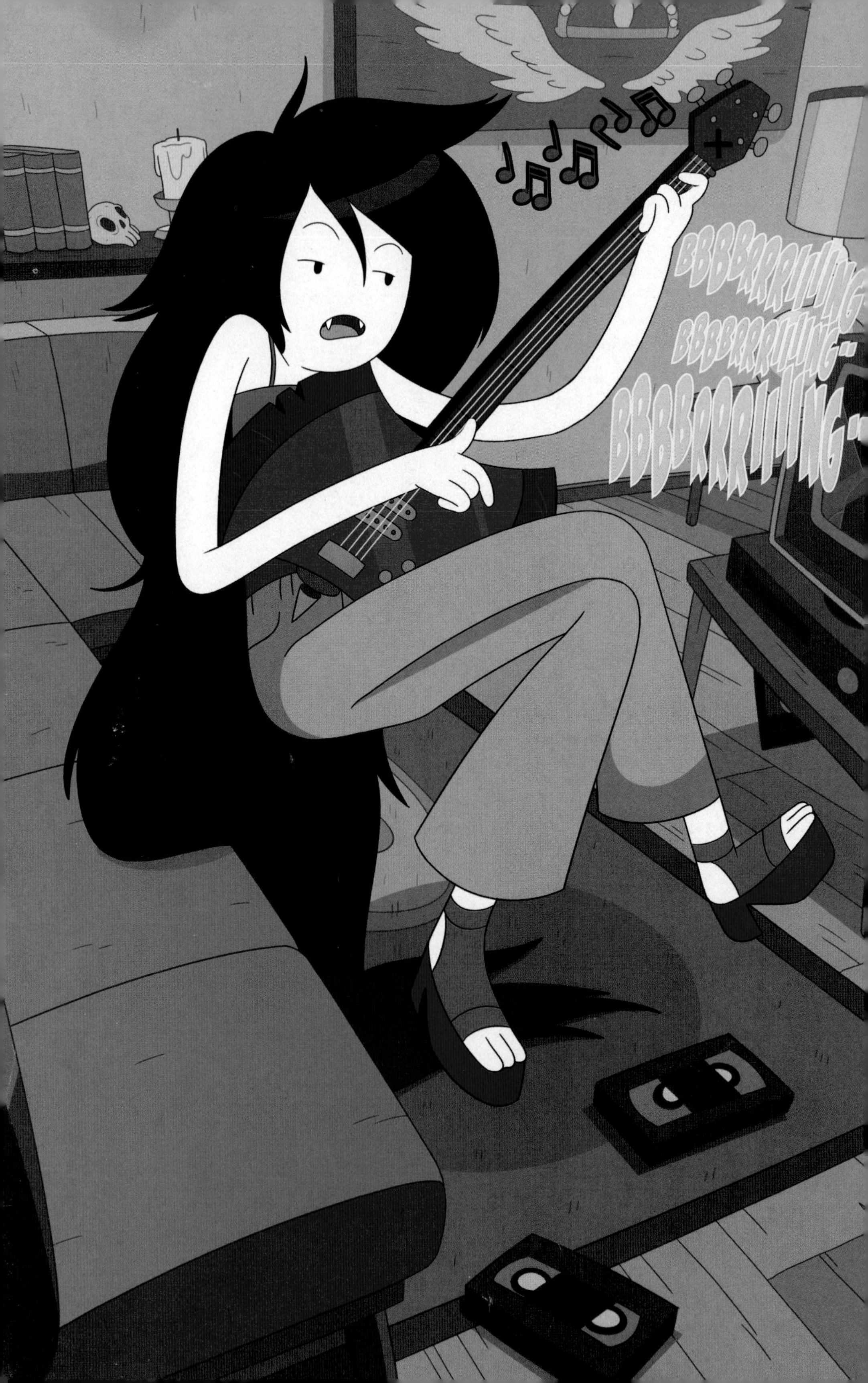
BBBBRRRIING
BBBBRRRIIING--
BBBBRRRIIIING--

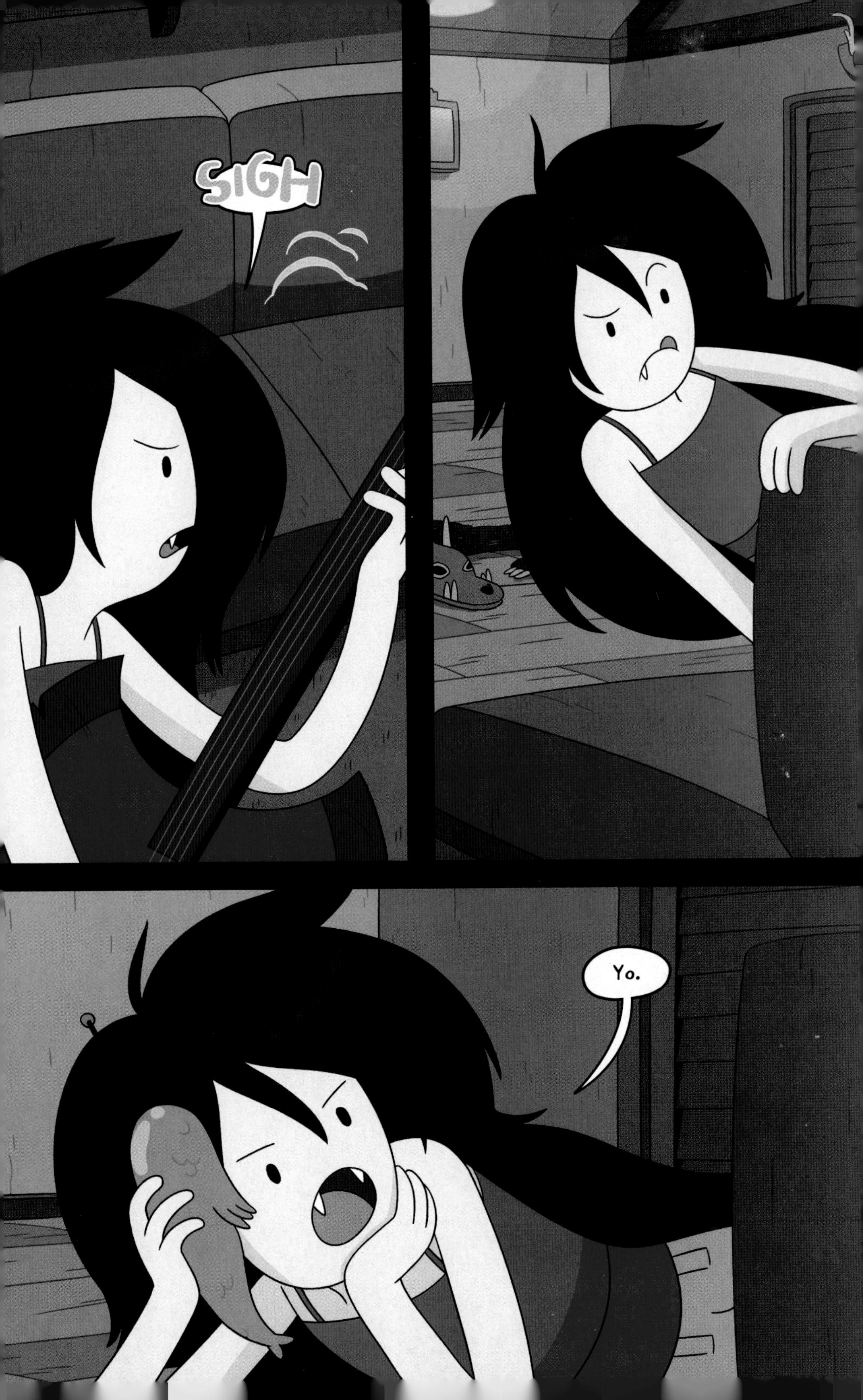
SIGH
Yo.

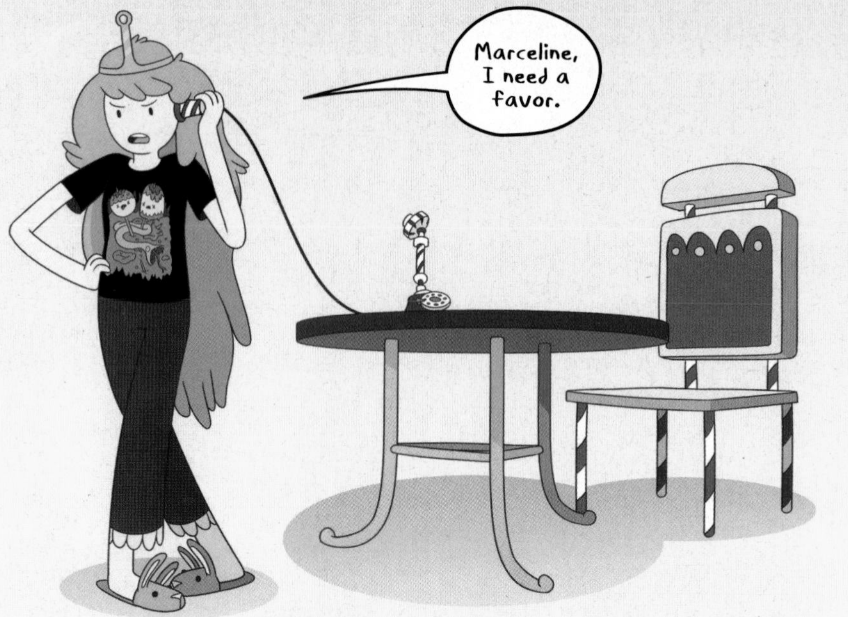
Marceline, I need a favor.

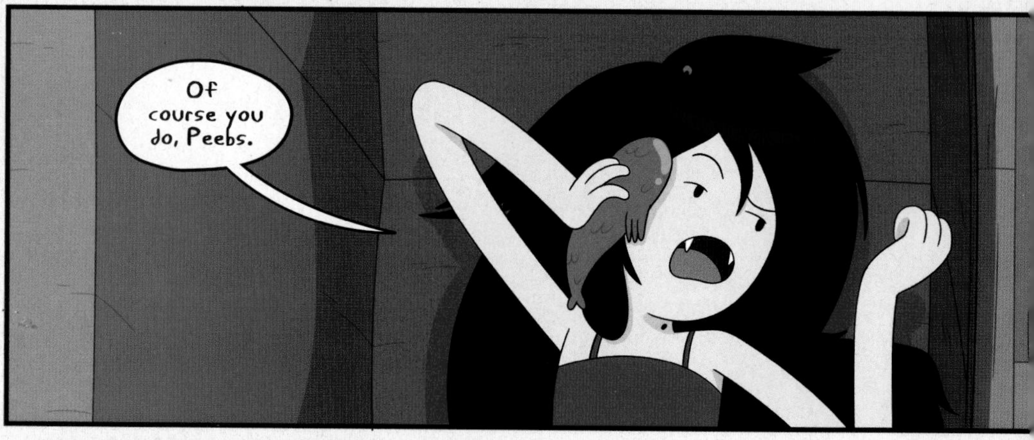
Of course you do, Peebs.

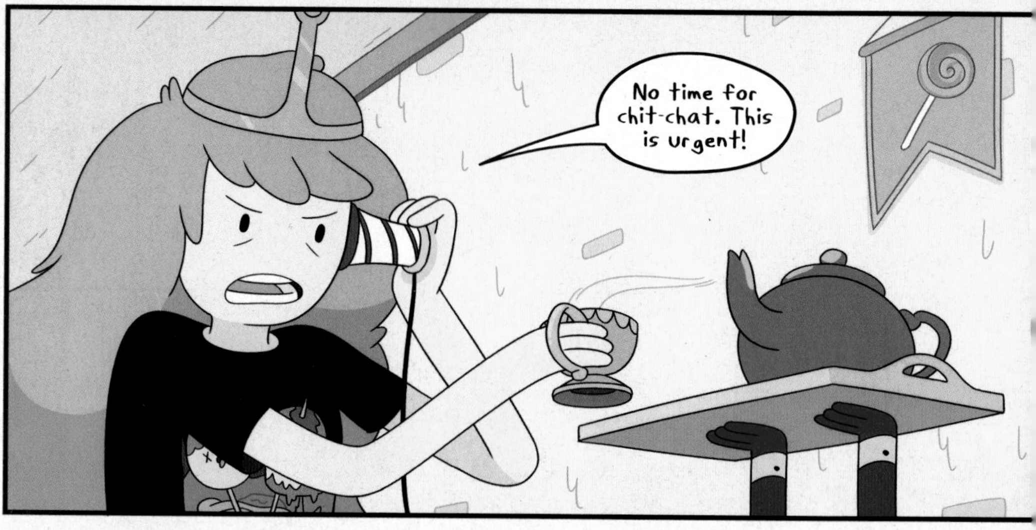
No time for chit-chat. This is urgent!

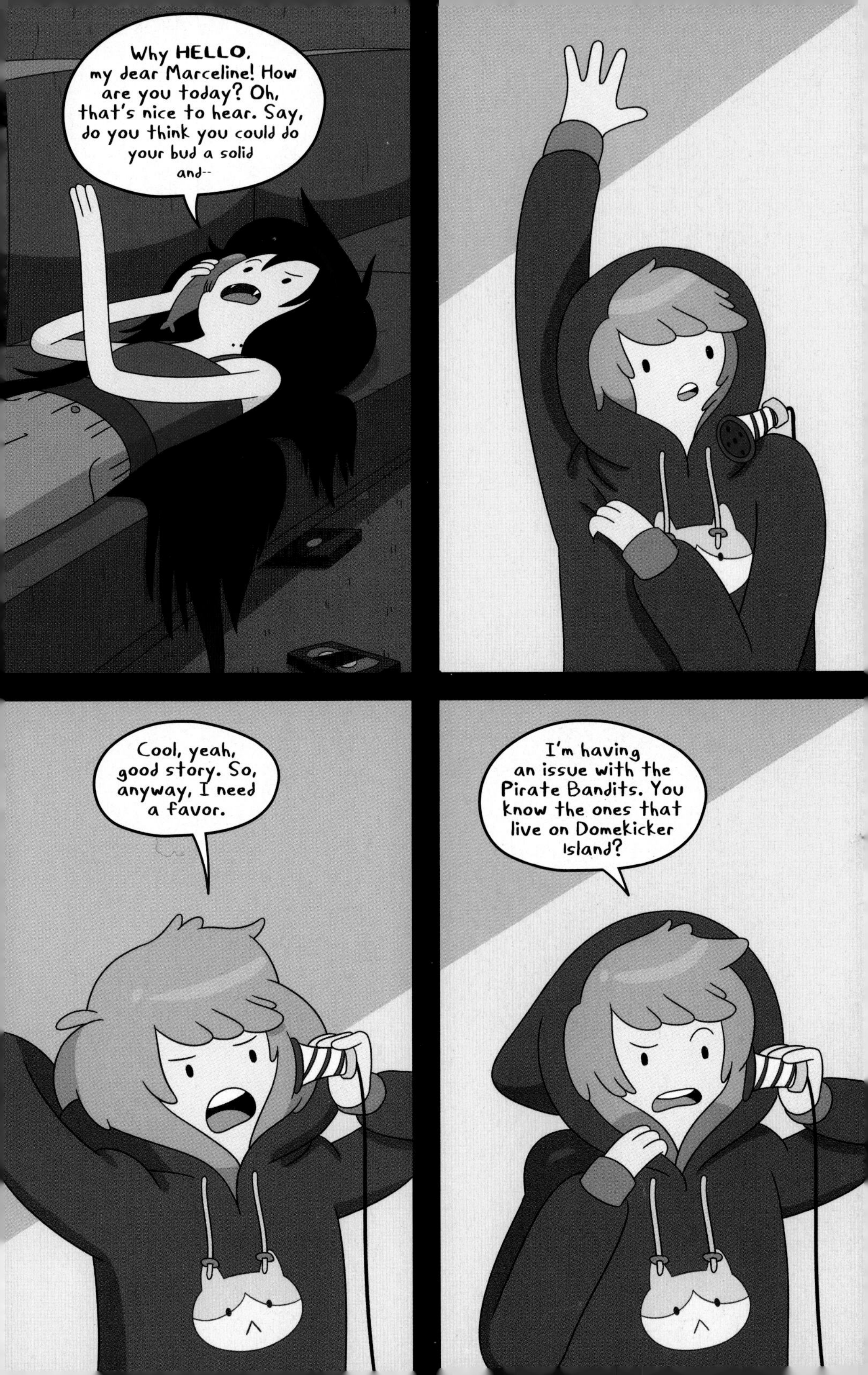
Why HELLO, my dear Marceline! How are you today? Oh, that's nice to hear. Say, do you think you could do your bud a solid and--
Cool, yeah, good story. So, anyway, I need a favor.
I'm having an issue with the Pirate Bandits. You know the ones that live on Domekicker Island?

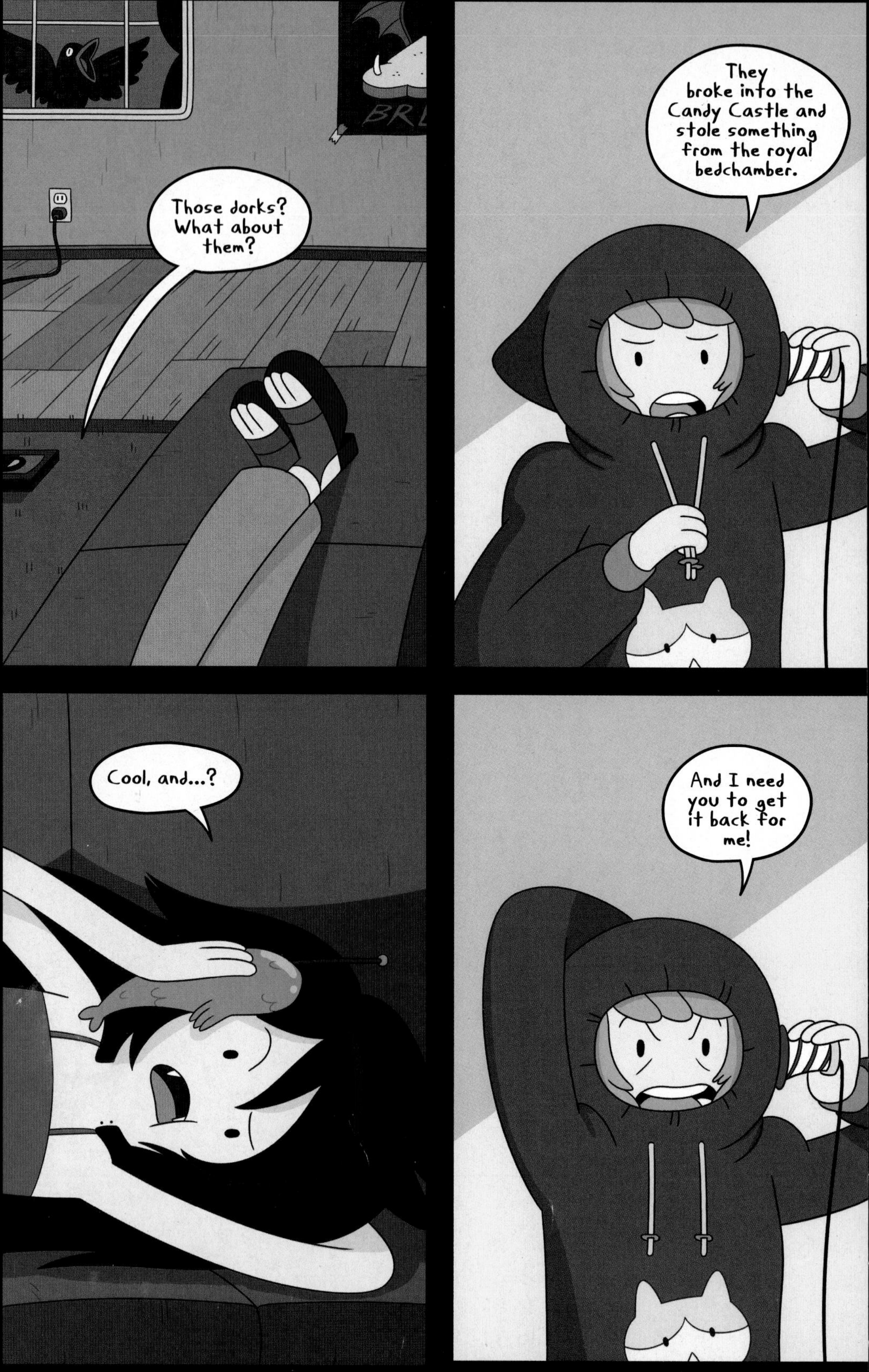

Those dorks? What about them?
They broke into the Candy Castle and stole something from the royal bedchamber.
Cool, and...?
And I need you to get it back for me!

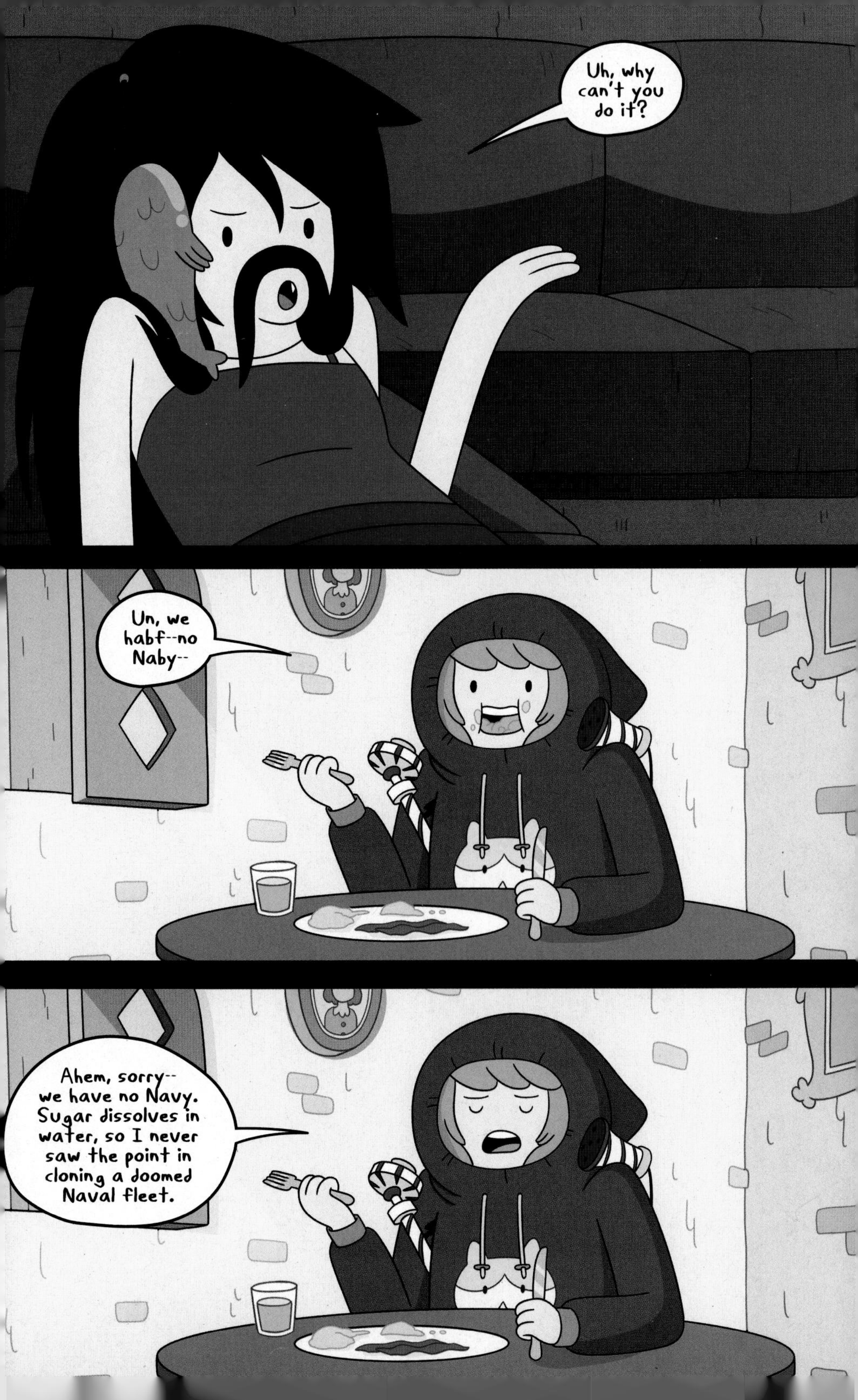
Uh, why can't you do it?
Un, we habf--no Naby--
Ahem, sorry-- we have no Navy. Sugar dissolves in water, so I never saw the point in cloning a doomed Naval fleet.

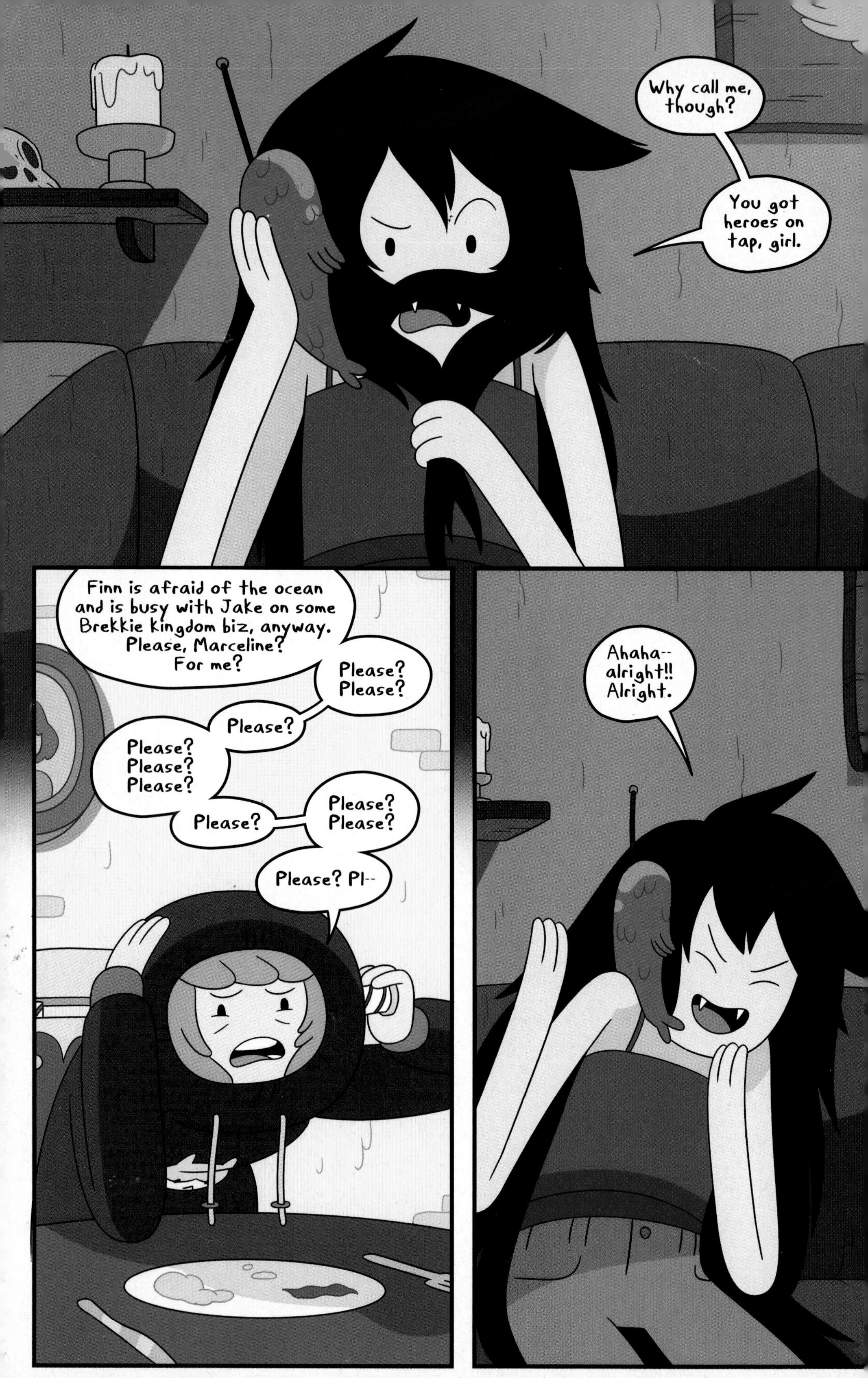
Why call me, though?
You got heroes on tap, girl.
Finn is afraid of the ocean and is busy with Jake on some Brekkie kingdom biz, anyway. Please, Marceline? For me?
Please? Please?
Please?
Please? Please? Please?
Please?
Please? Please?
Please? Pl--
Ahaha-- alright!! Alright.

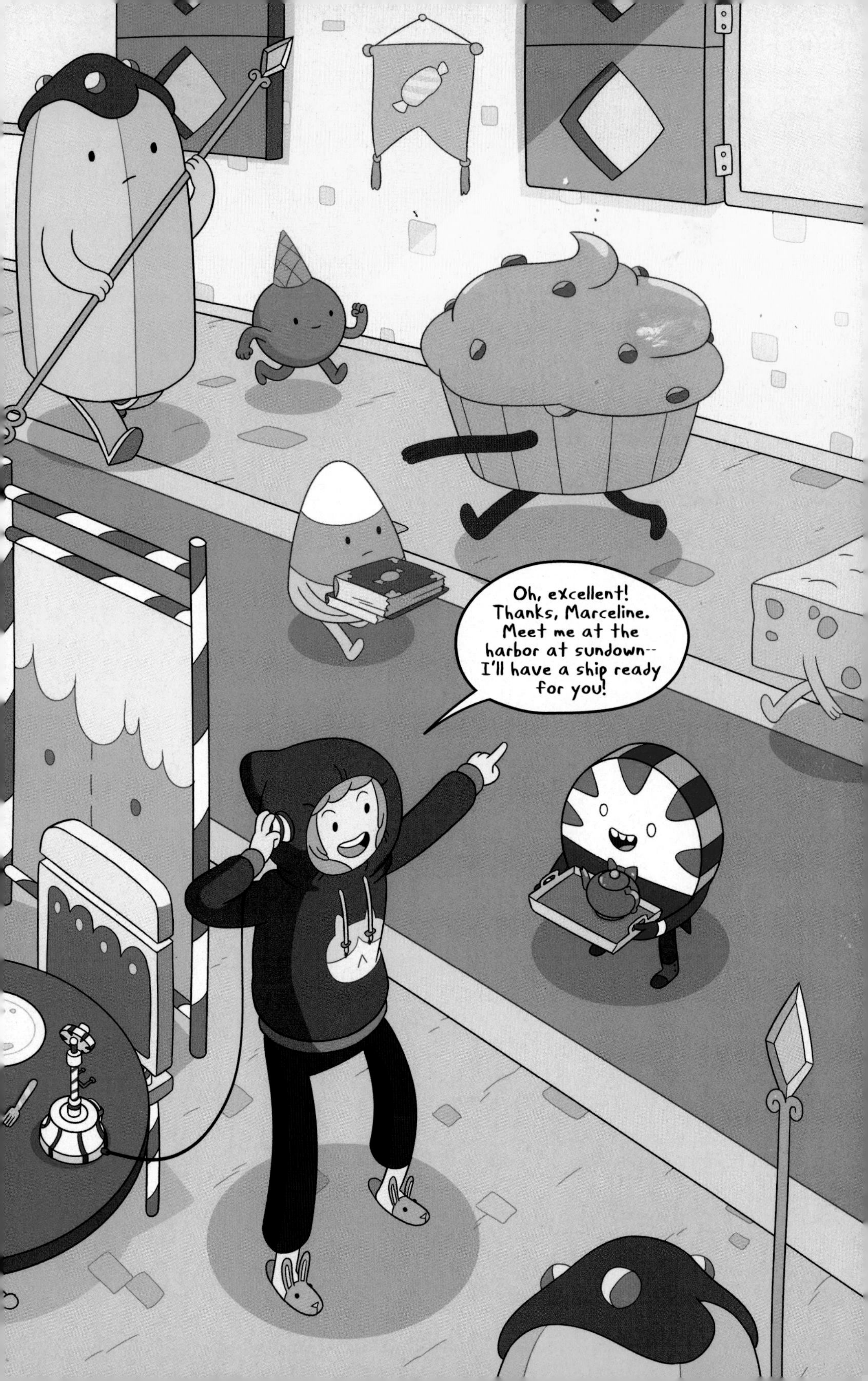
Oh, excellent! Thanks, Marceline. Meet me at the harbor at sundown-- I'll have a ship ready for you!

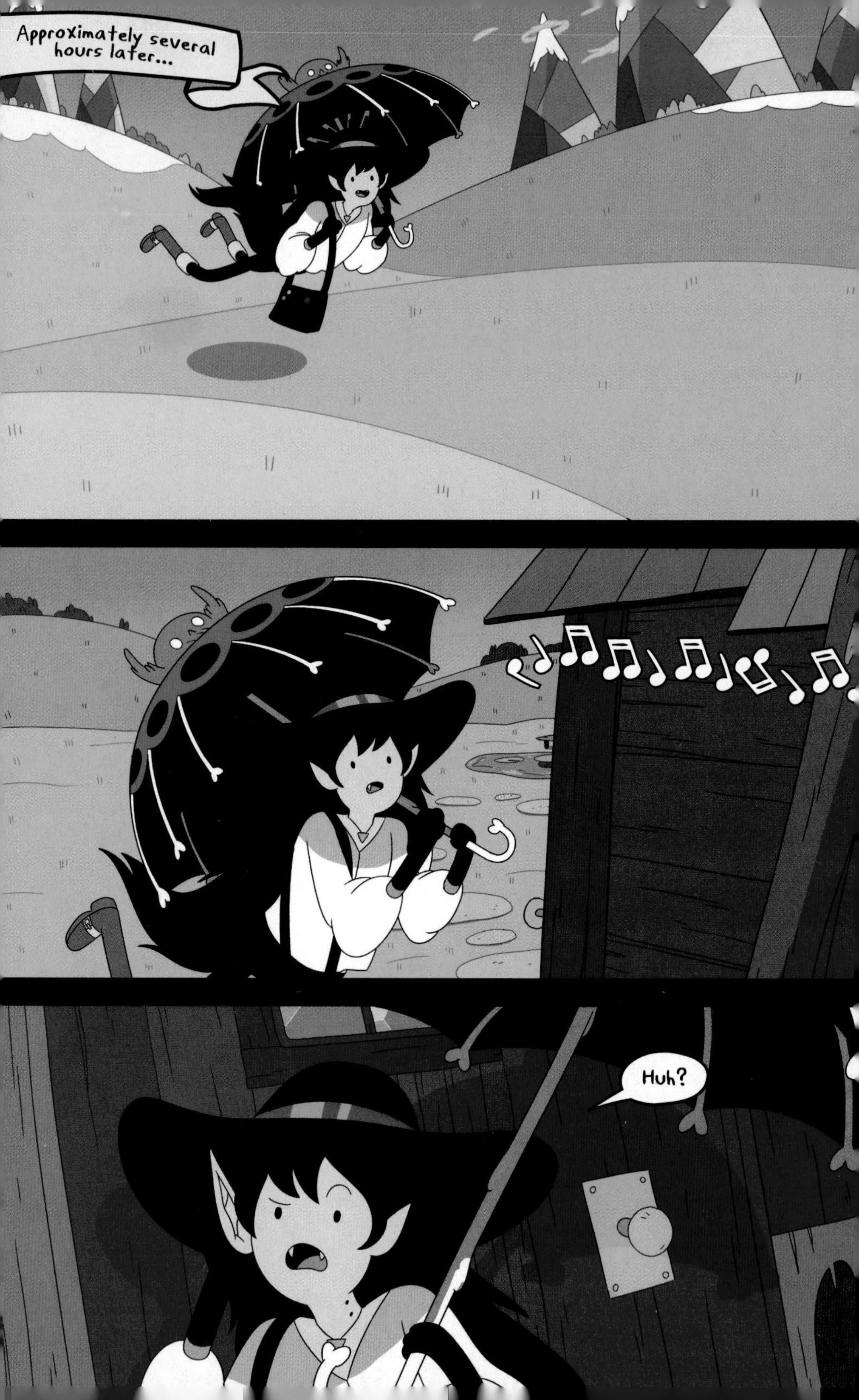
Approximately several hours later...
Huh?

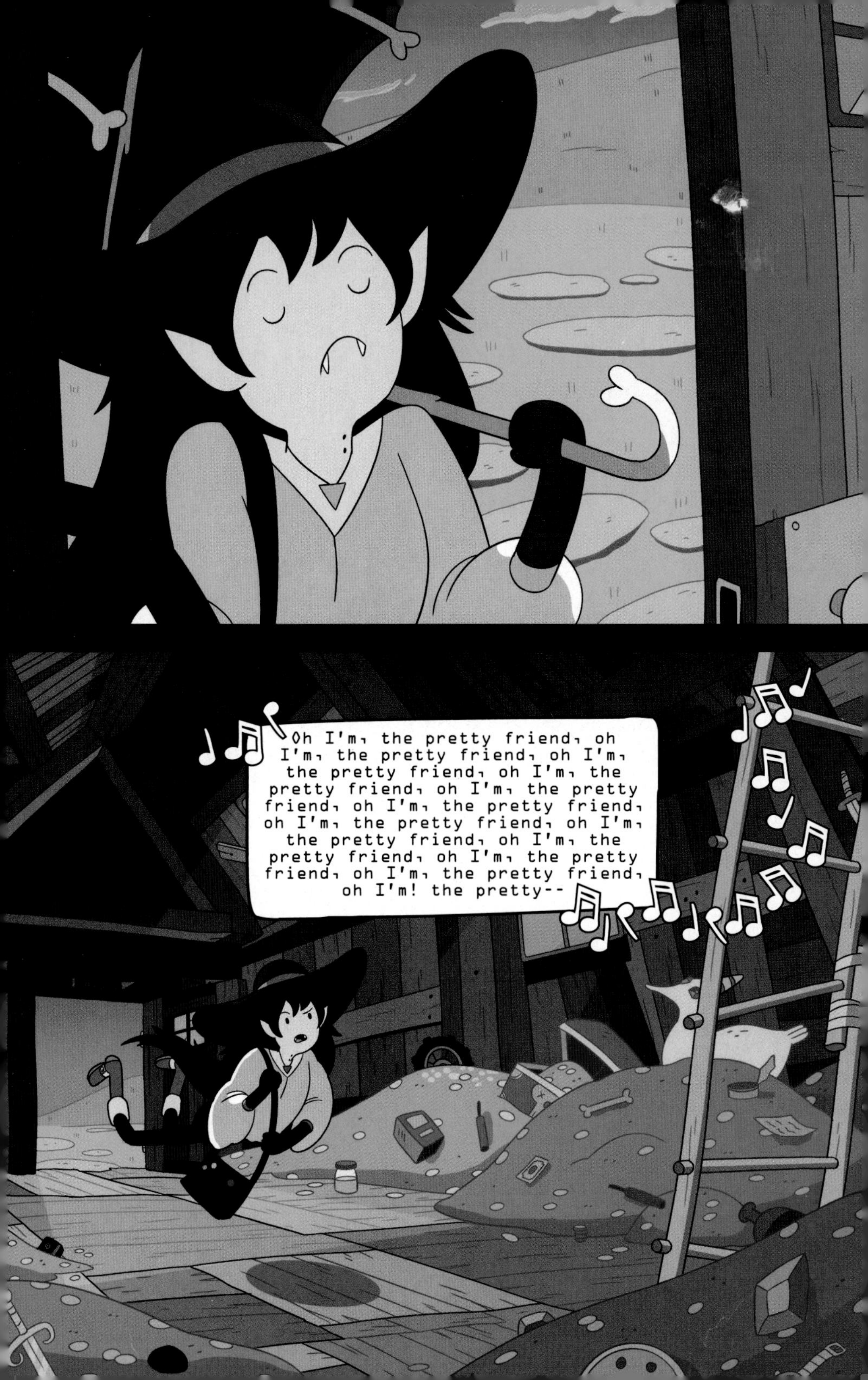
Oh I'm, the pretty friend, oh I'm, the pretty friend, oh I'm, the pretty friend, oh I'm, the pretty friend, oh I'm, the pretty friend, oh I'm, the pretty friend, oh I'm, the pretty friend, oh I'm, the pretty friend, oh I'm, the pretty friend, oh I'm, the pretty friend, oh I'm, the pretty friend, oh I'm! the pretty--

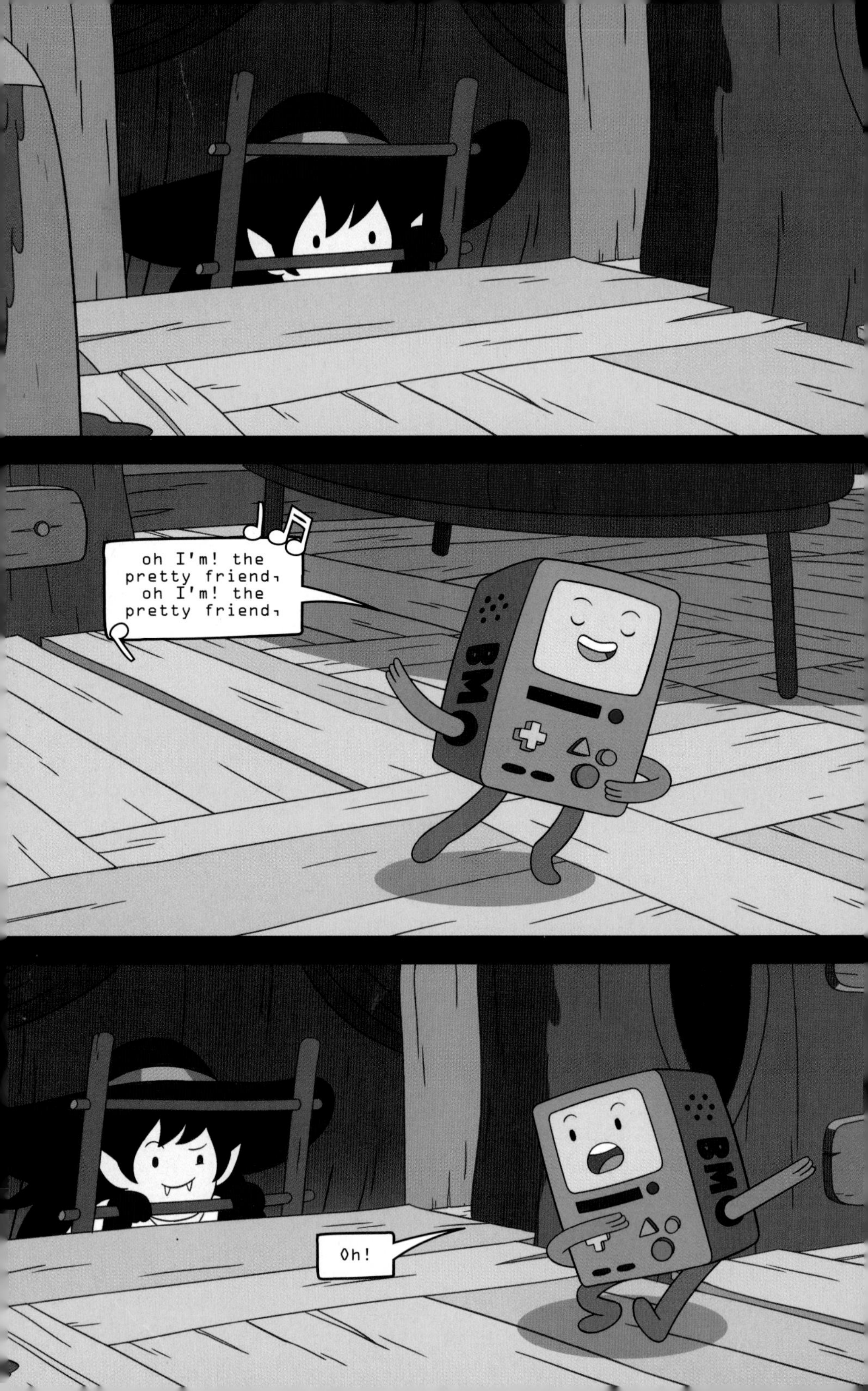
oh I'm! the pretty friend, oh I'm! the pretty friend,
Oh!

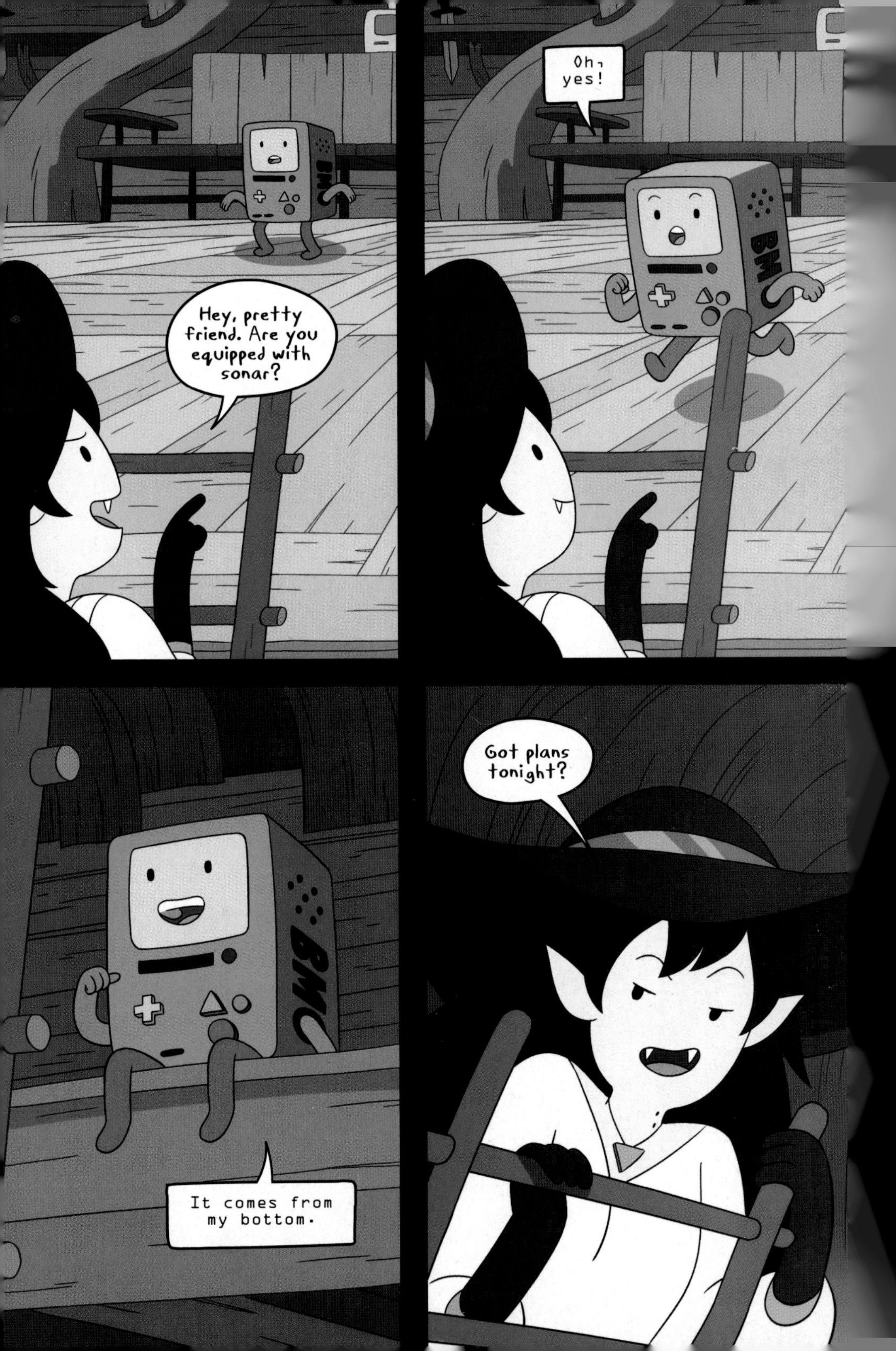
Hey, pretty friend. Are you equipped with sonar?
Oh, yes!
It comes from my bottom.
Got plans tonight?

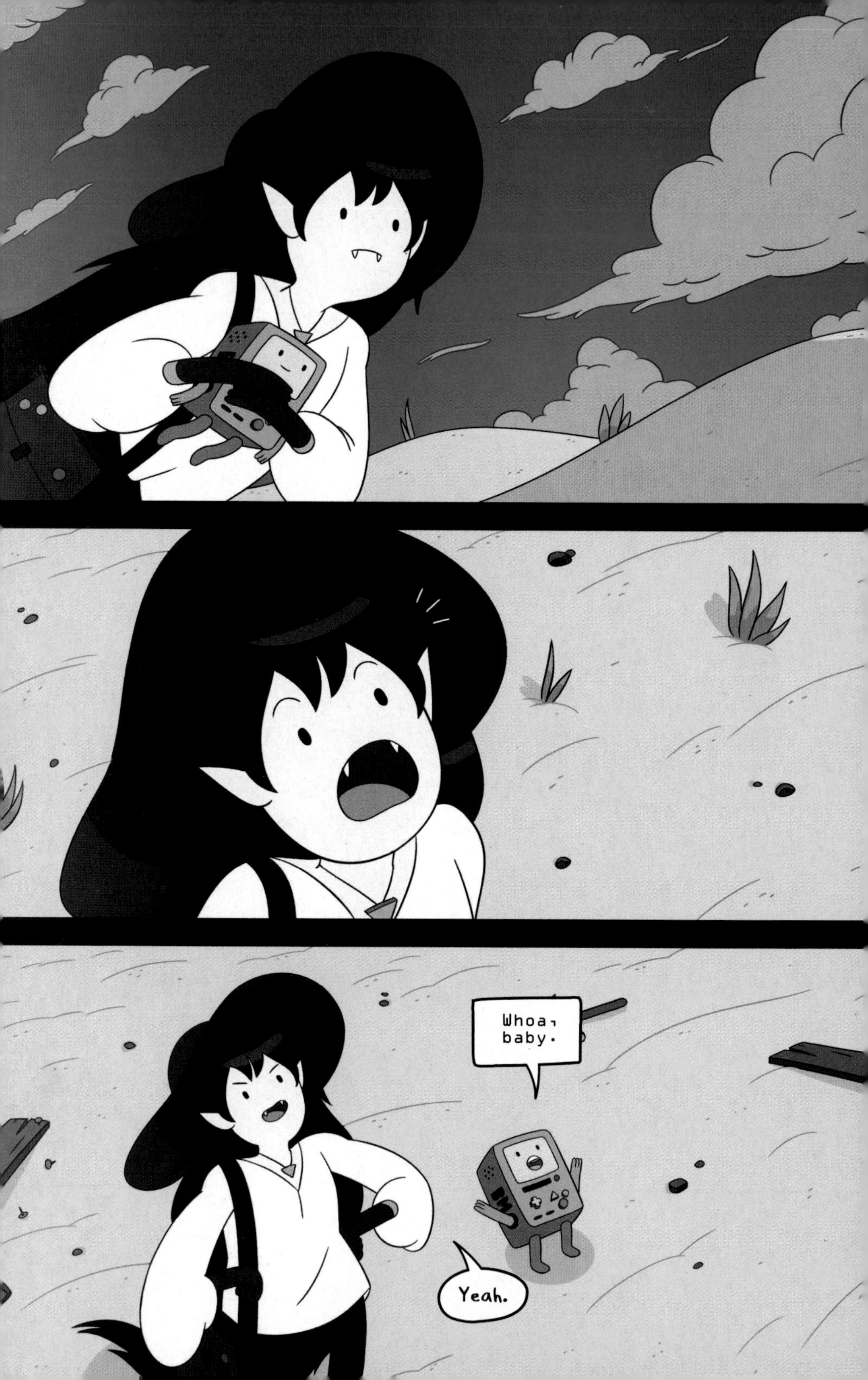
Whoa, baby.
Yeah.

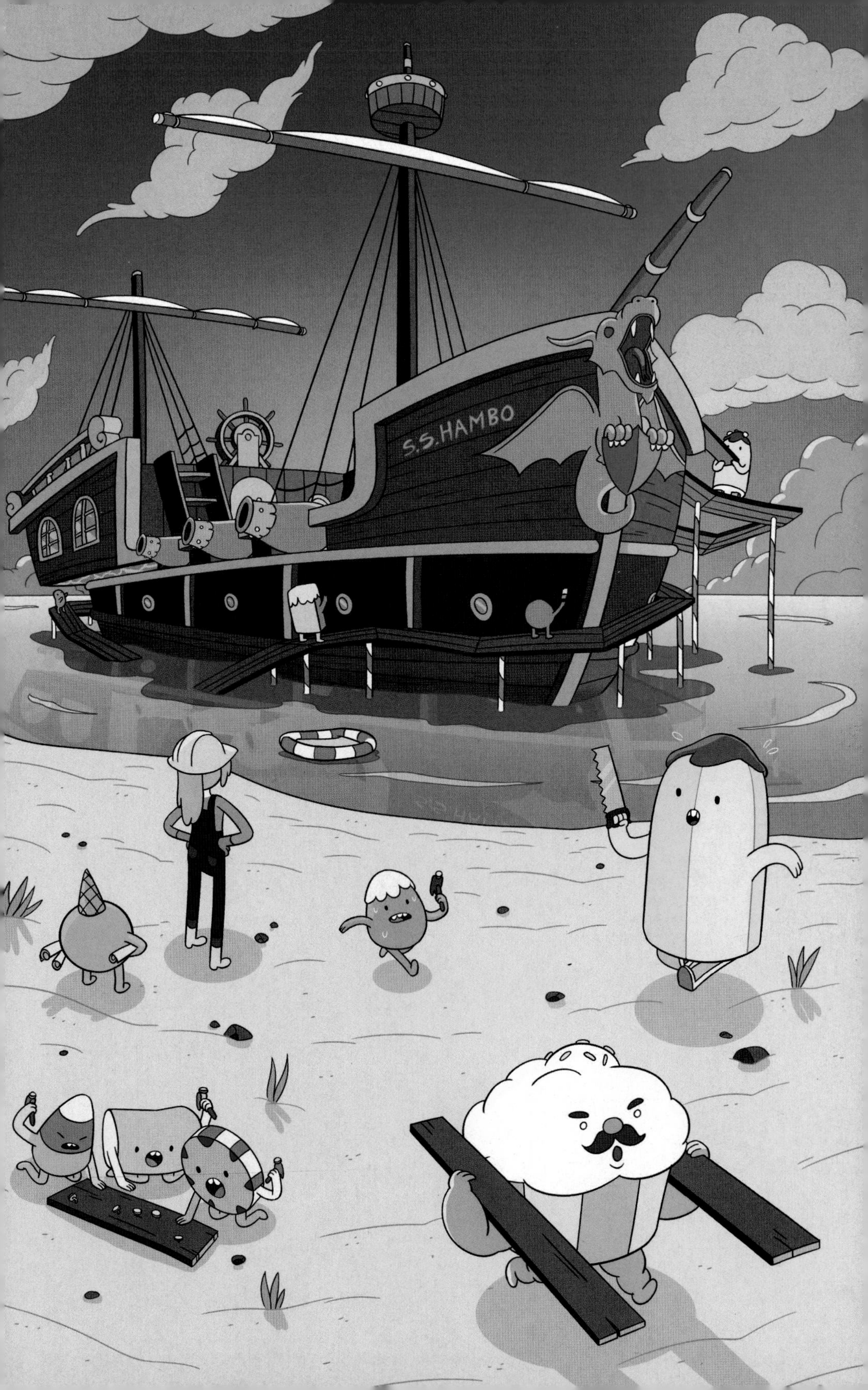
S.S.HAMBO

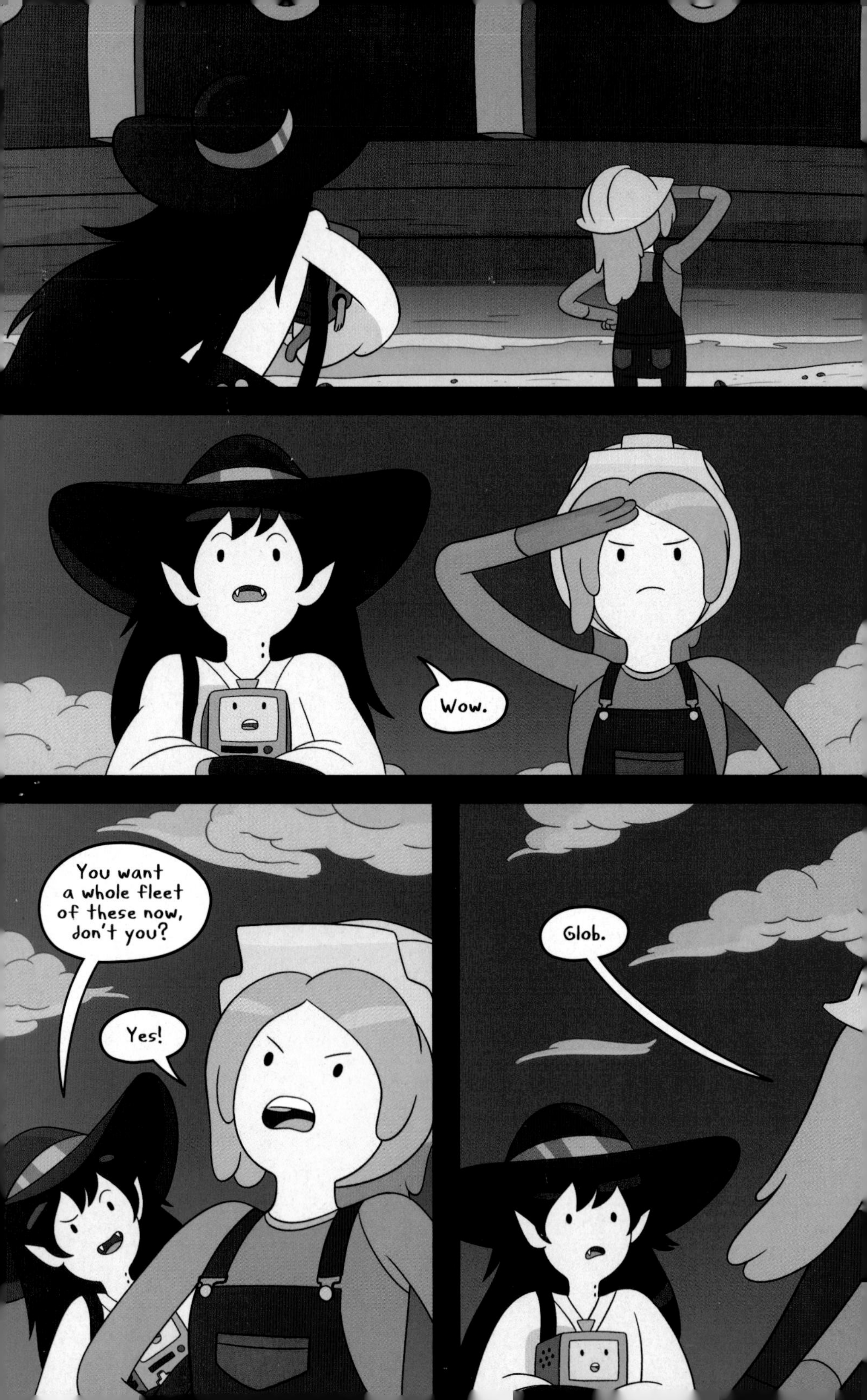
Wow.
You want a whole fleet of these now, don't you?
Yes!
Glob.

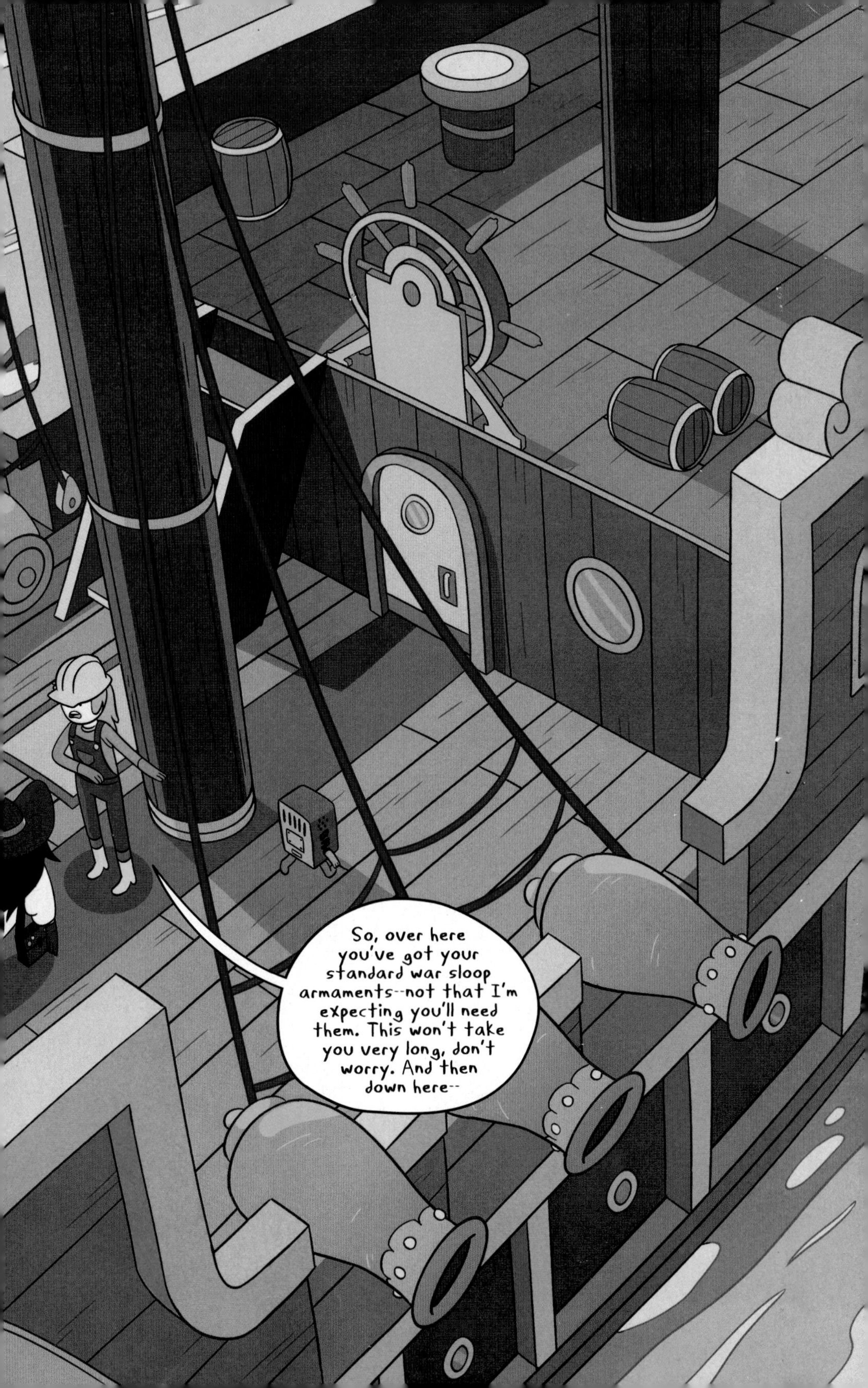
So, over here you've got your standard war sloop armaments--not that I'm expecting you'll need them. This won't take you very long, don't worry. And then down here--

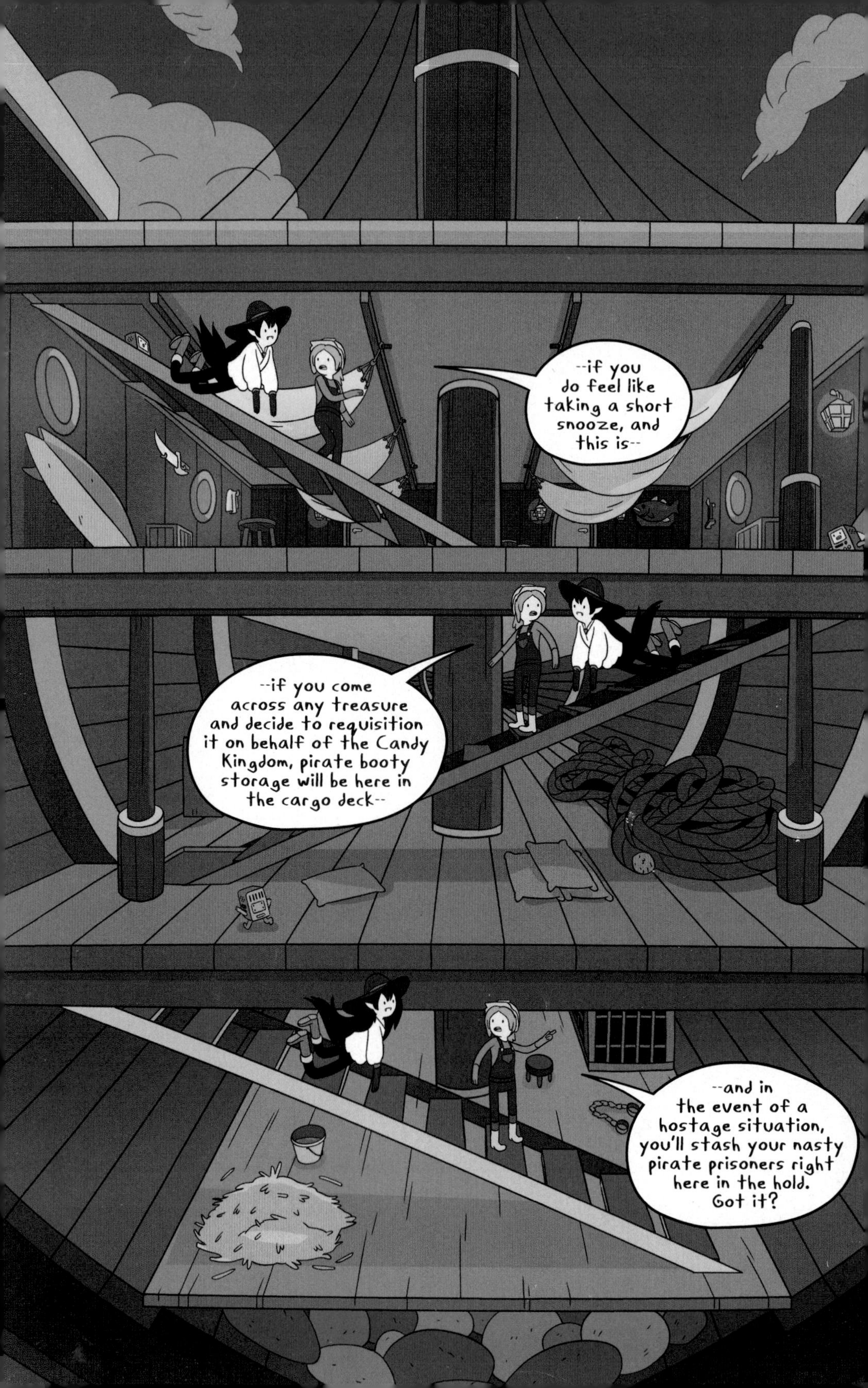
--if you do feel like taking a short snooze, and this is--
--if you come across any treasure and decide to requisition it on behalf of the Candy Kingdom, pirate booty storage will be here in the cargo deck--
--and in the event of a hostage situation, you'll stash your nasty pirate prisoners right here in the hold. Got it?

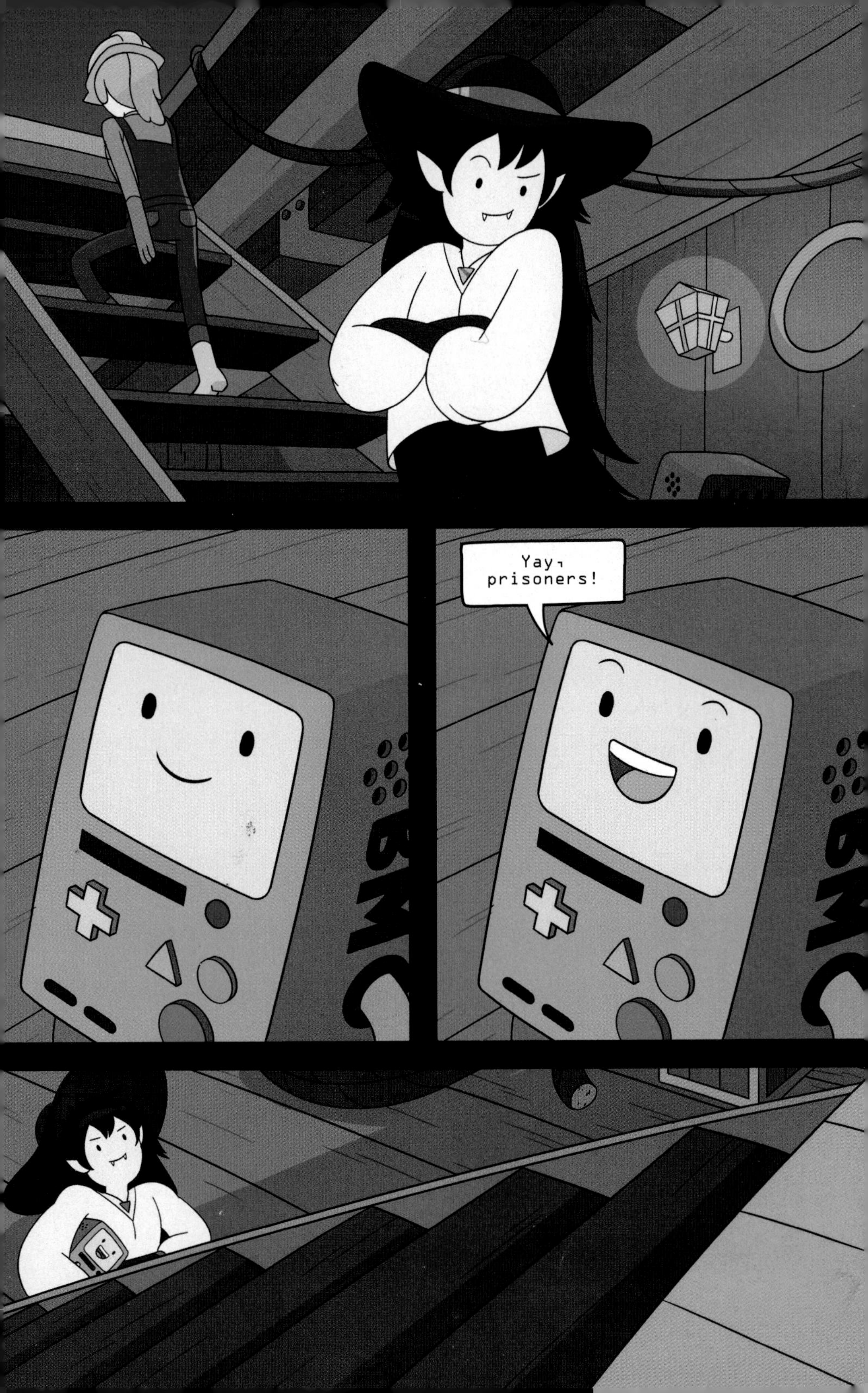
Yay,
prisoners!

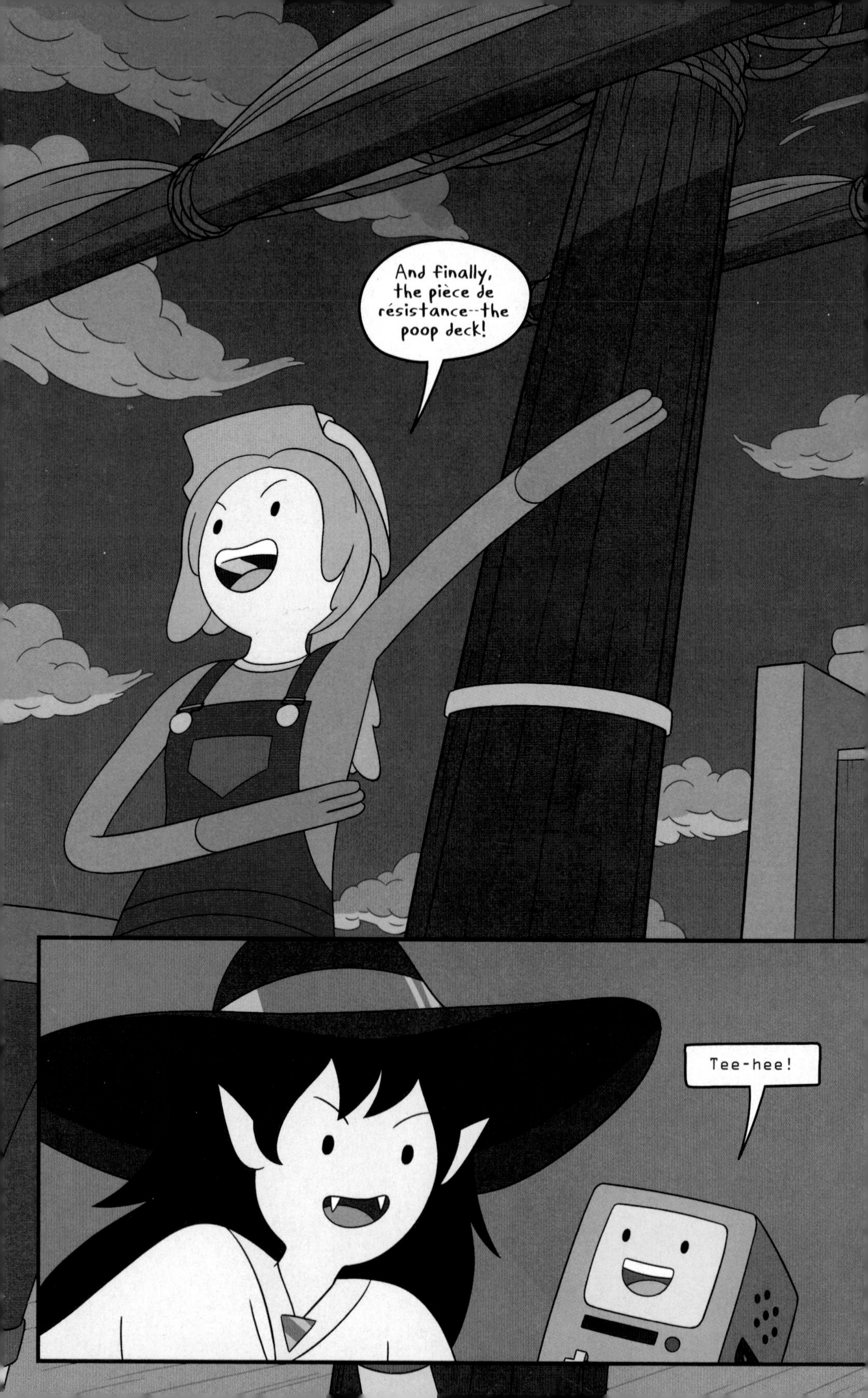
And finally, the pièce de résistance--the poop deck!
Tee-hee!

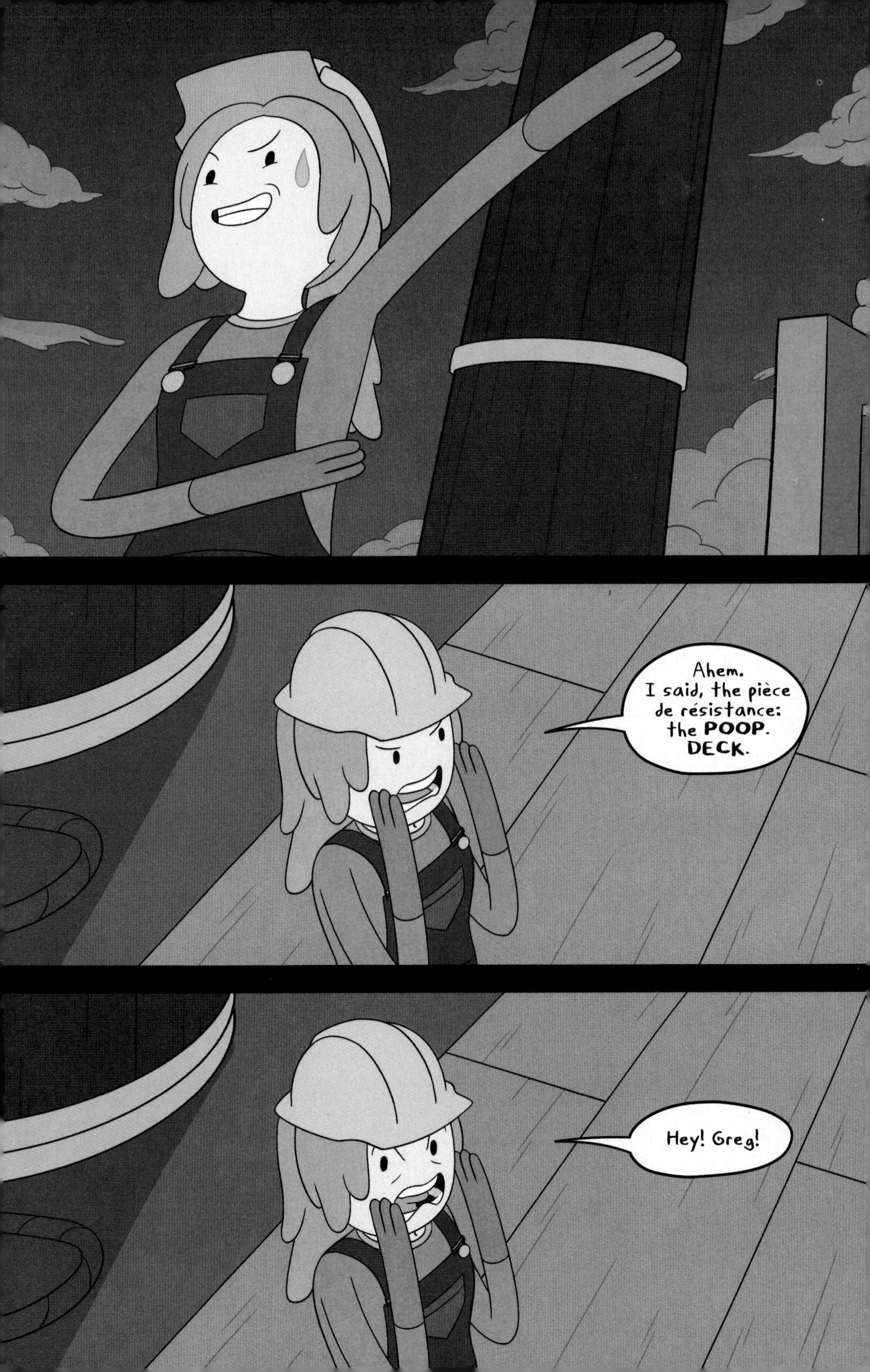
Ahem. I said, the pièce de résistance: the **POOP. DECK**.
Hey! Greg!

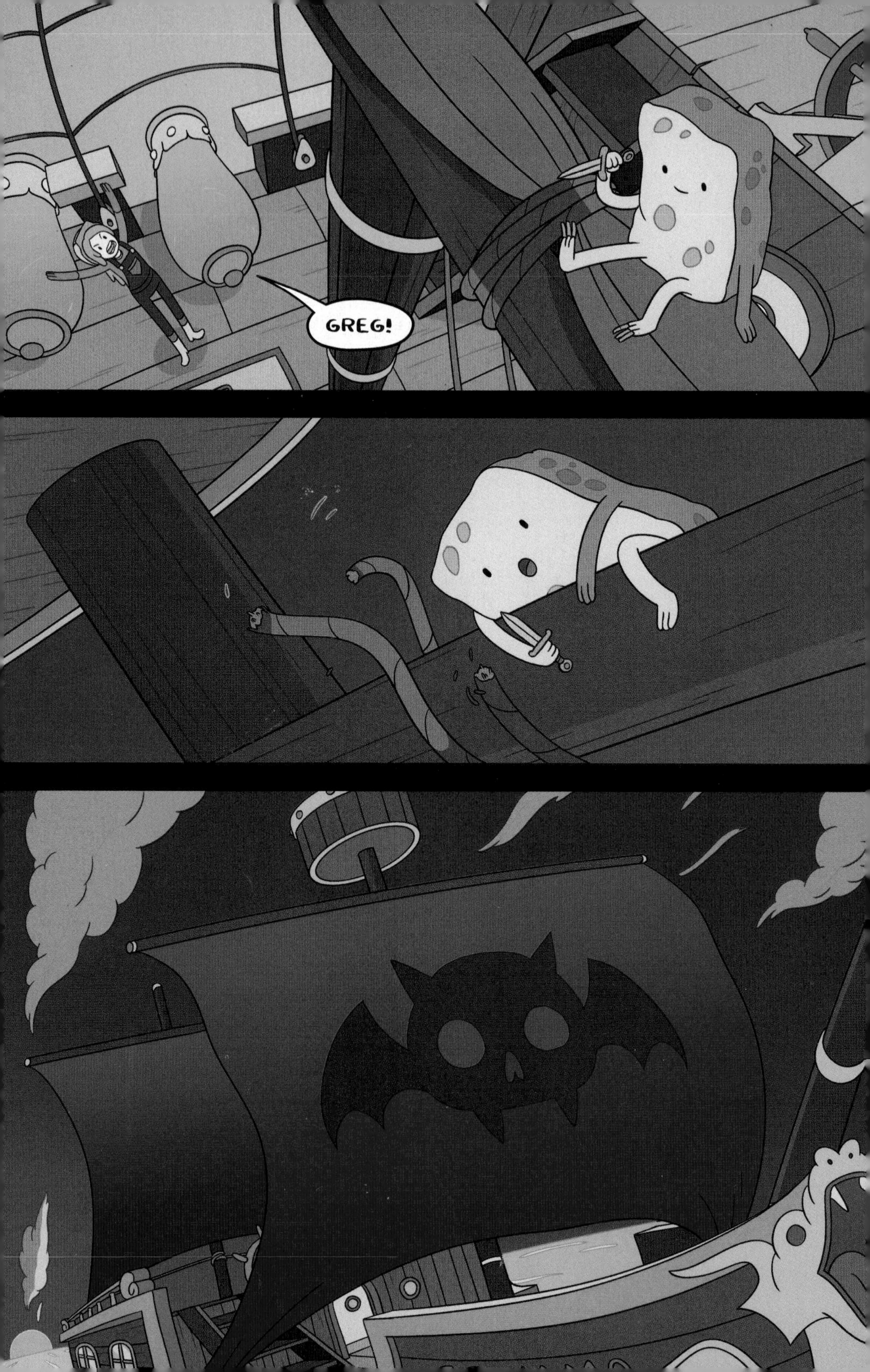
GREG!

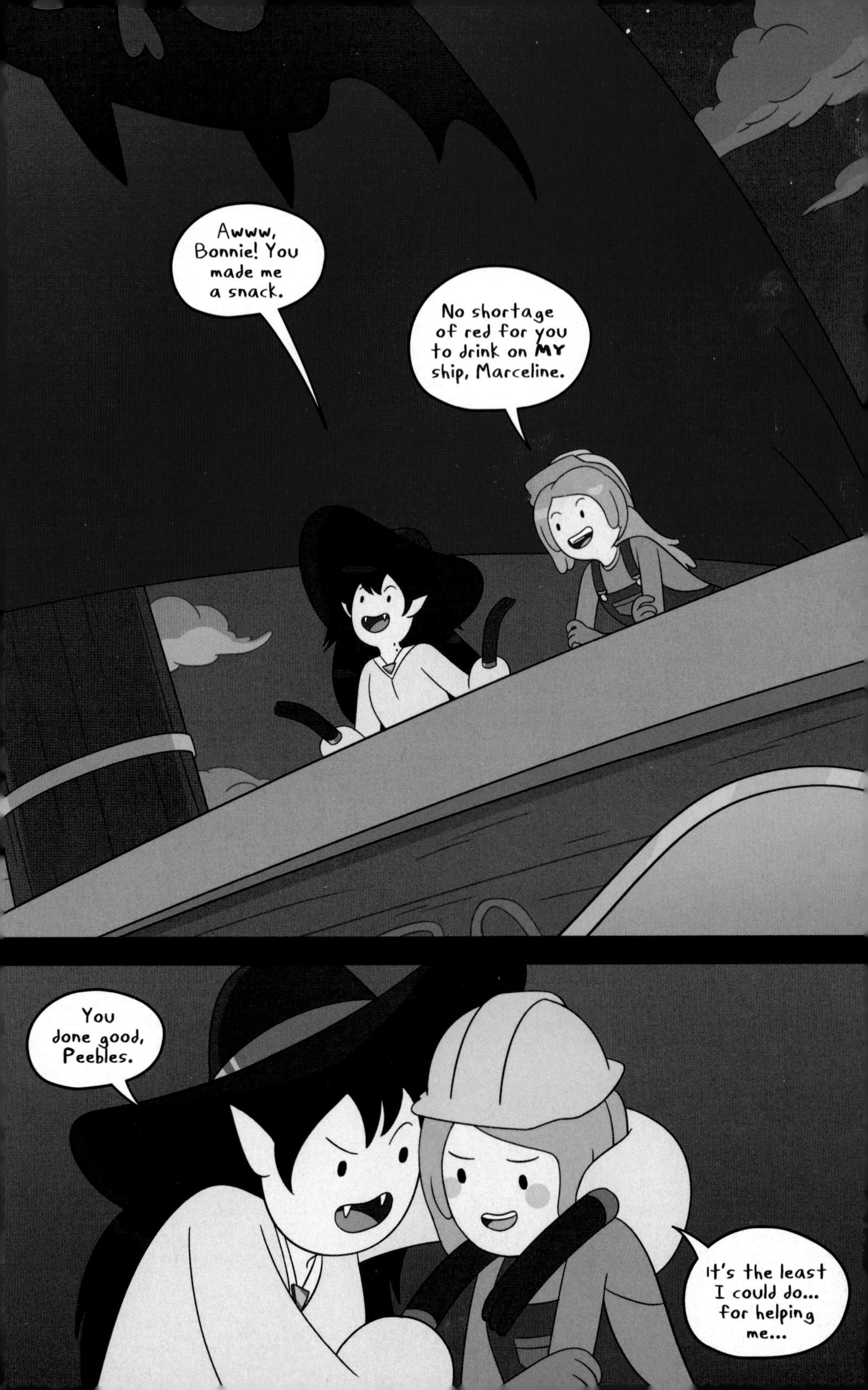
Awww, Bonnie! You made me a snack.
No shortage of red for you to drink on MY ship, Marceline.
You done good, Peebles.
It's the least I could do... for helping me...

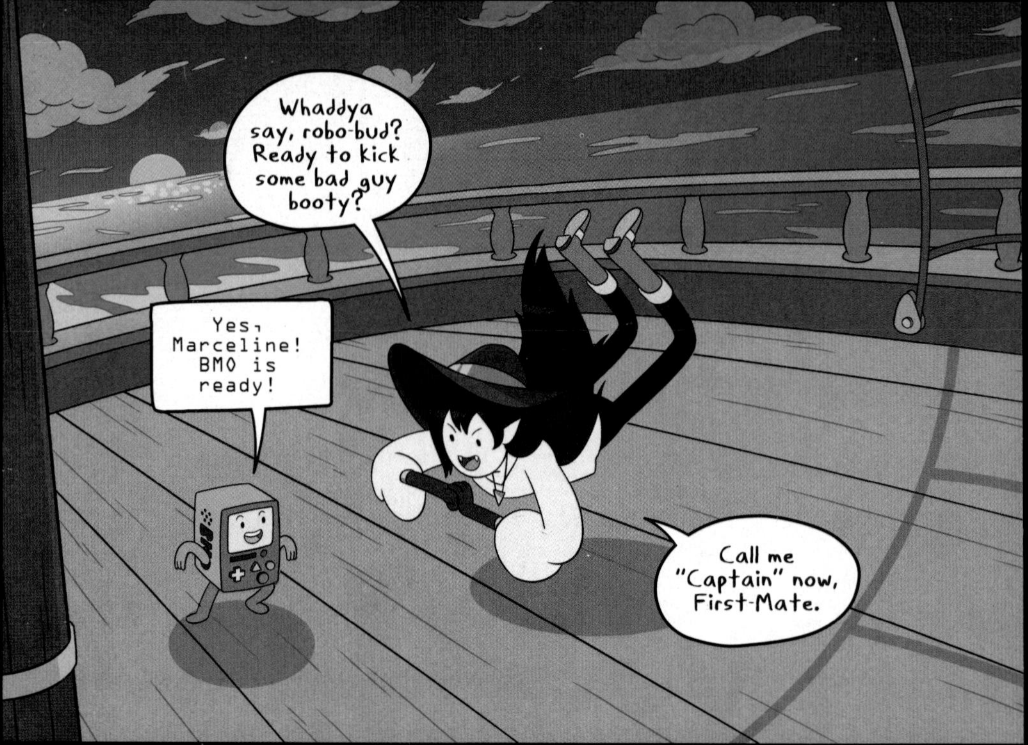
Whaddya say, robo-bud? Ready to kick some bad guy booty?
Yes, Marceline! BMO is ready!
Call me "Captain" now, First-Mate.

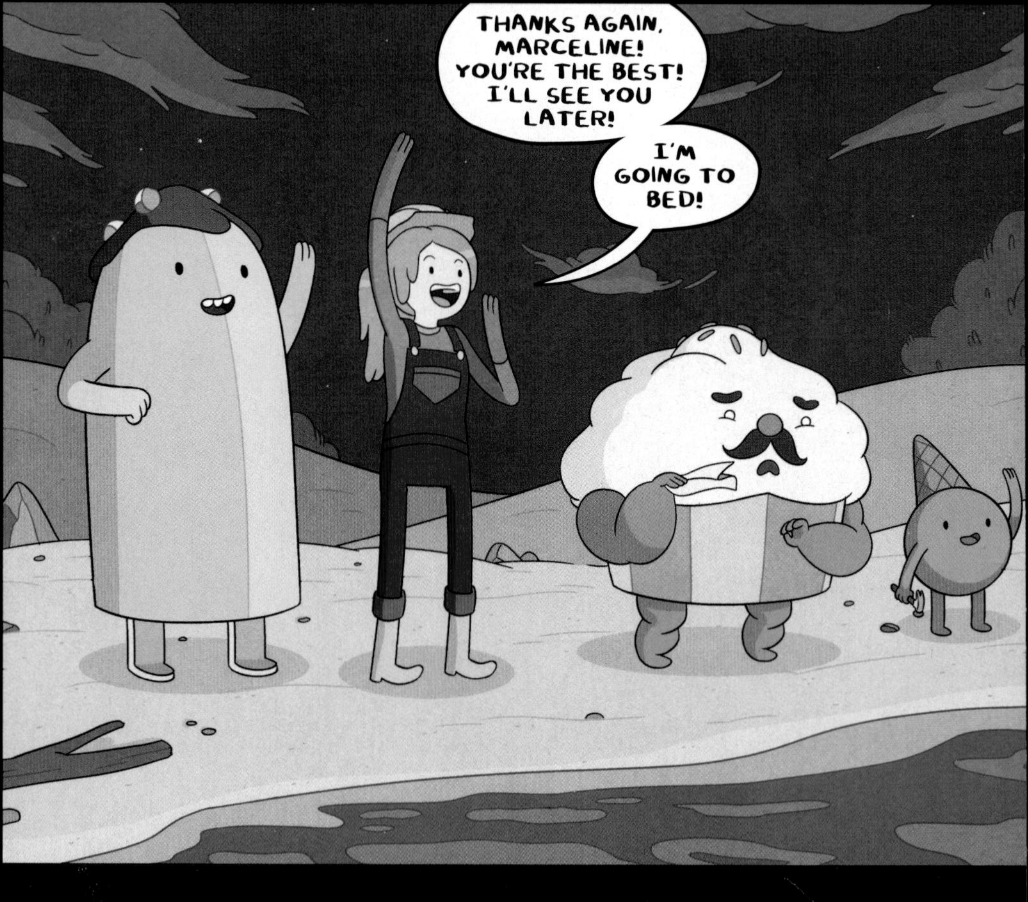
THANKS AGAIN, MARCELINE! YOU'RE THE BEST! I'LL SEE YOU LATER!
I'M GOING TO BED!

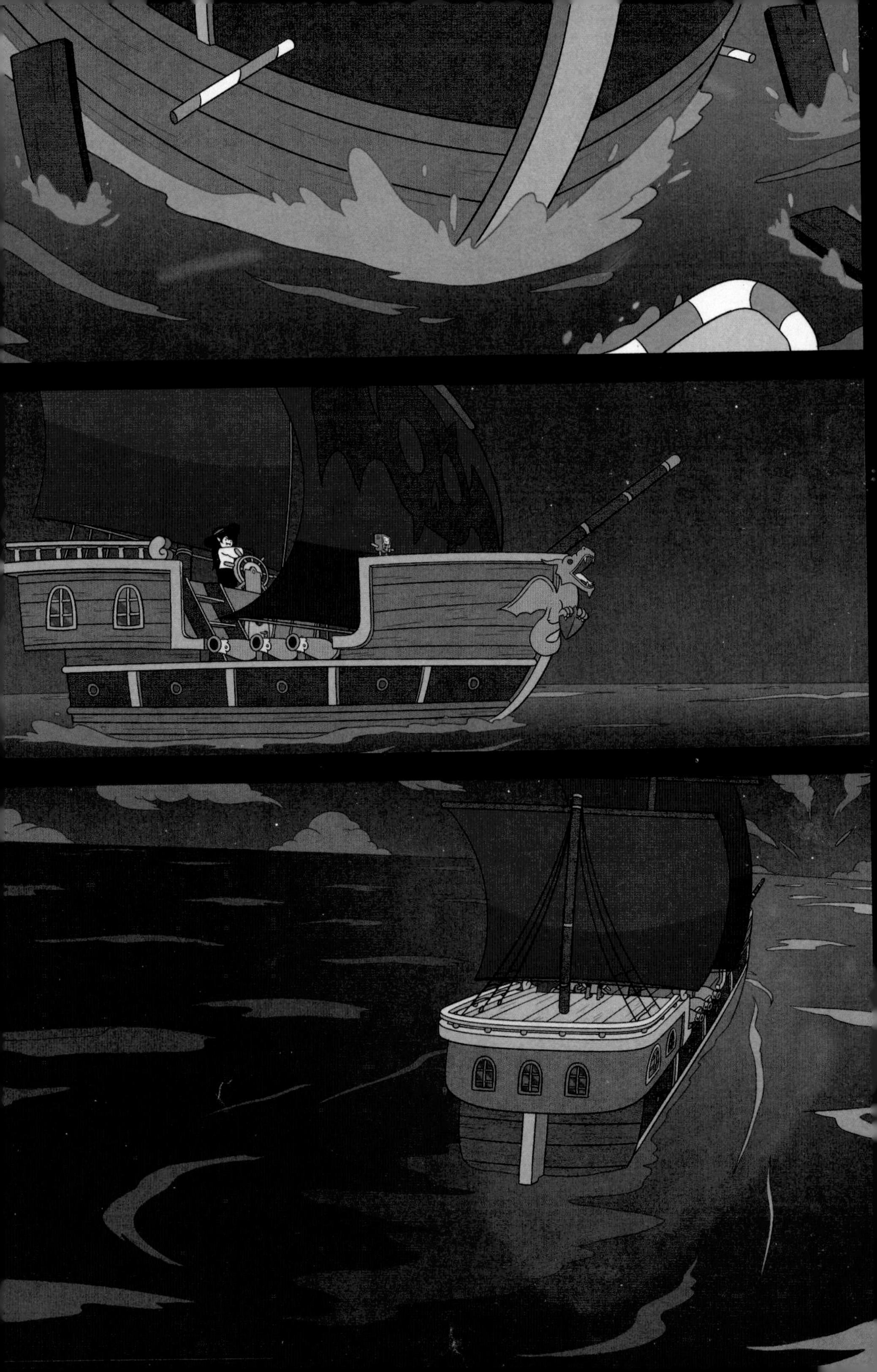

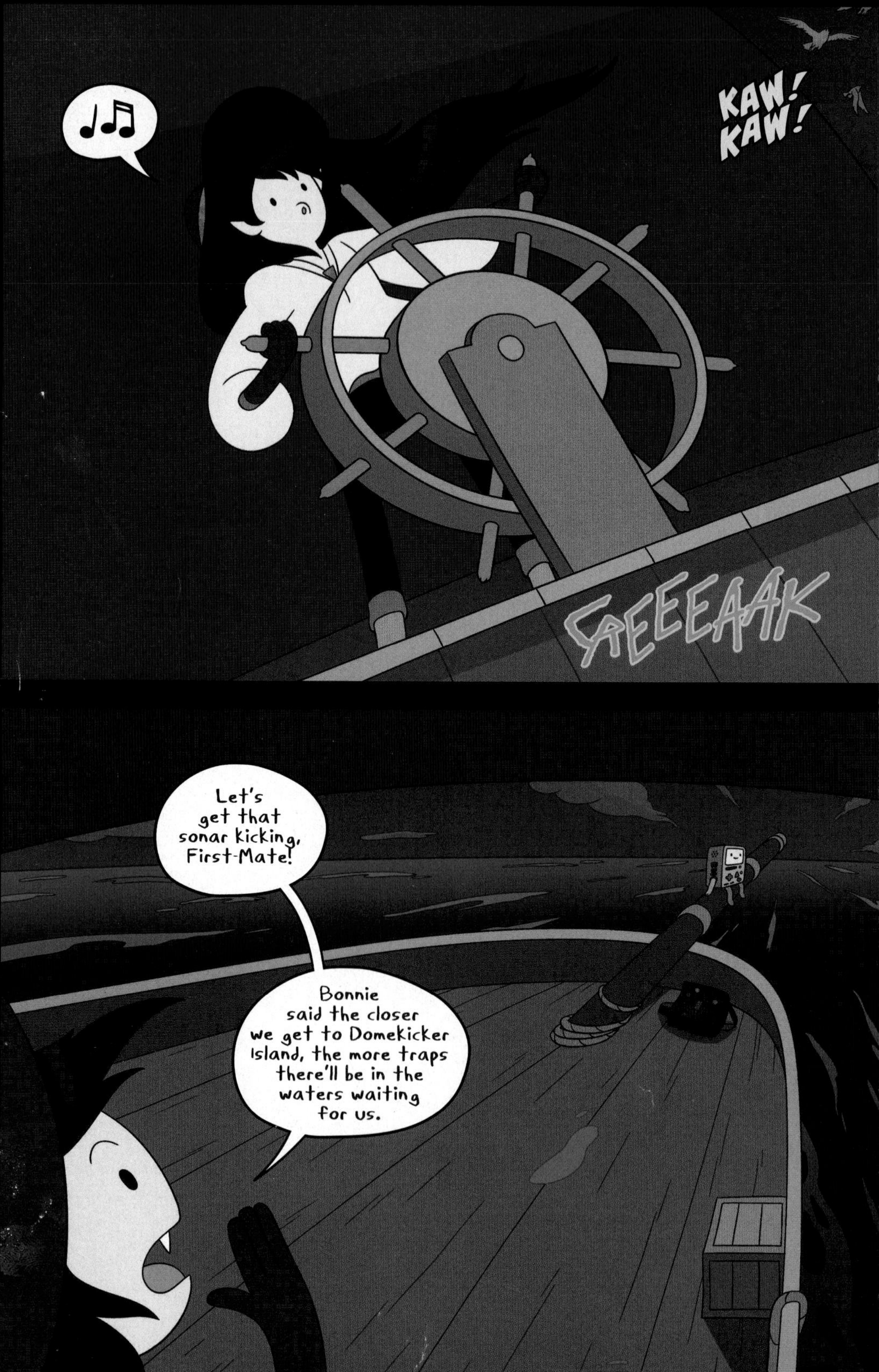
KAW! KAW!
CREEEAAK
Let's get that sonar kicking, First-Mate!
Bonnie said the closer we get to Domekicker Island, the more traps there'll be in the waters waiting for us.

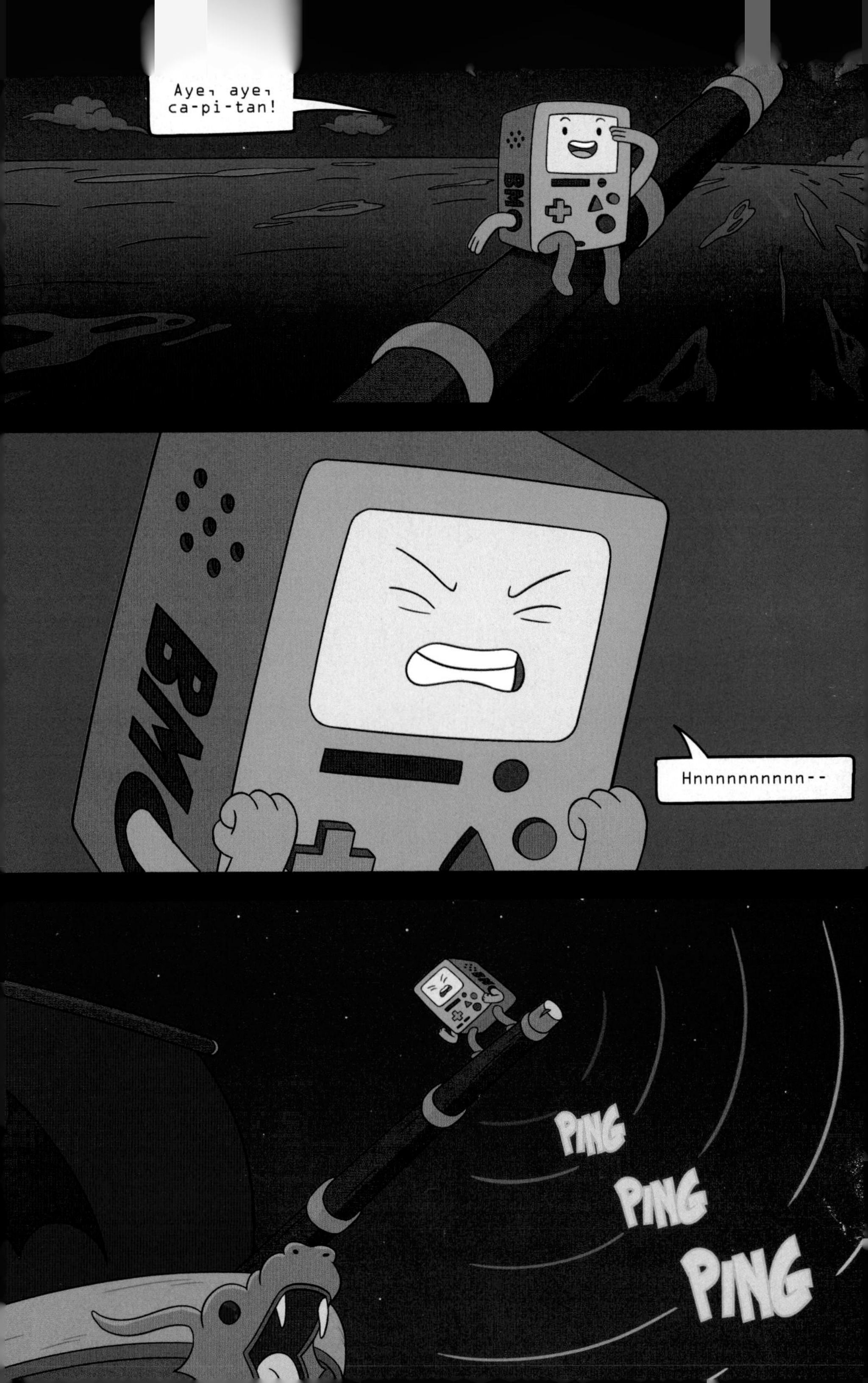
Aye, aye, ca-pi-tan!
BMO
BMO
Hnnnnnnnnnn--
PING
PING
PING

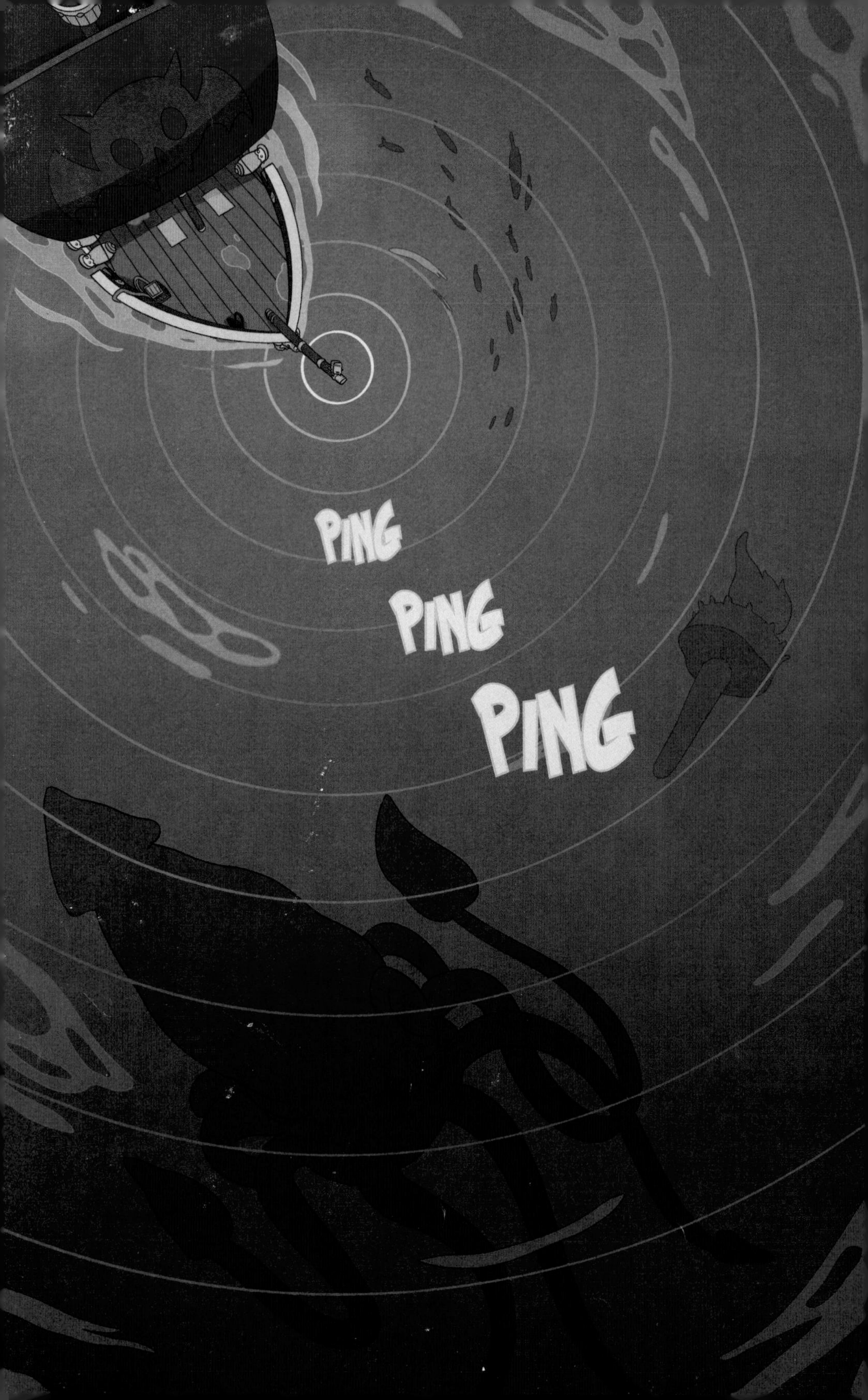
PING
PING
PING

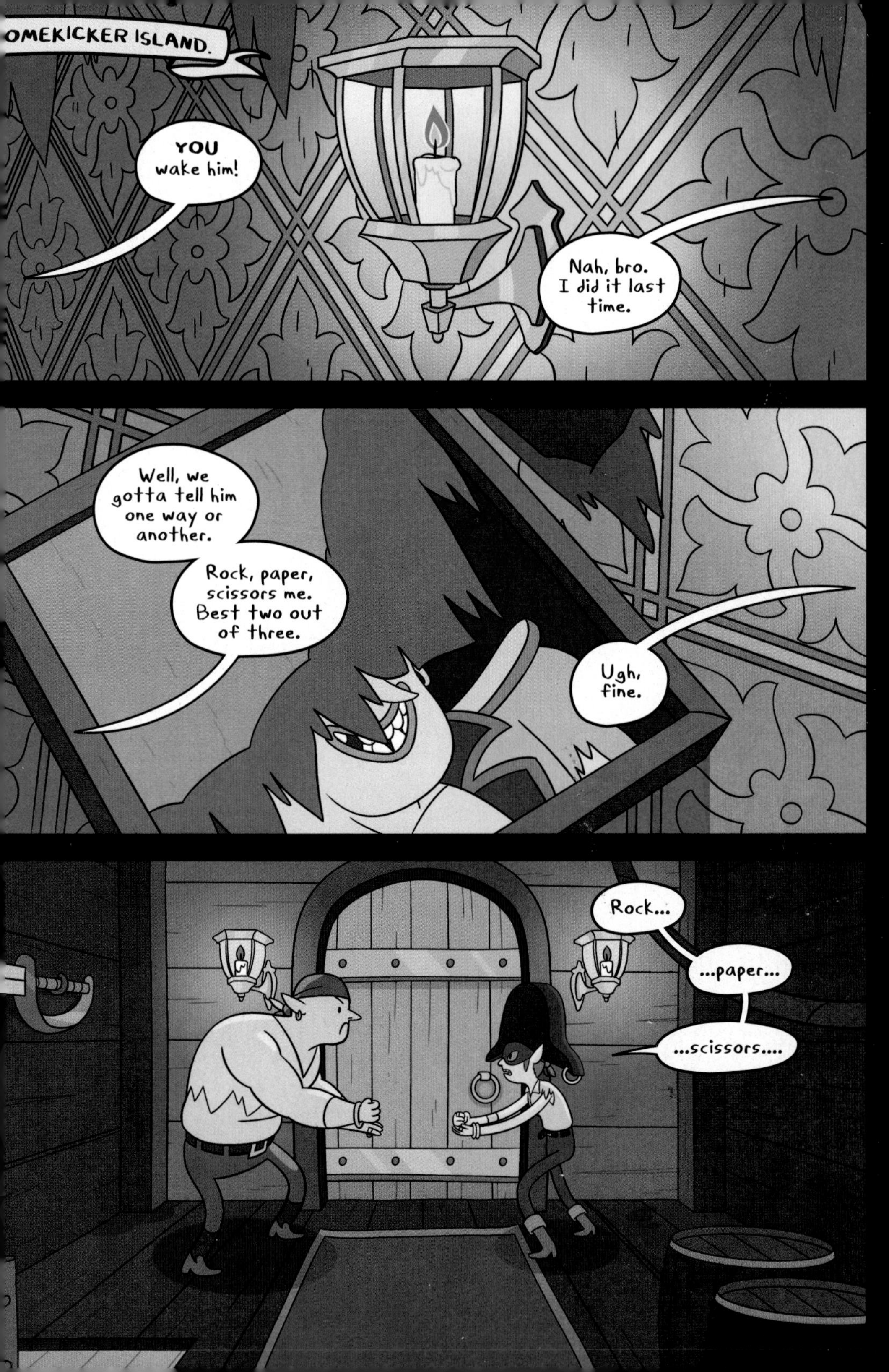
OMEKICKER ISLAND.
YOU wake him!
Nah, bro. I did it last time.
Well, we gotta tell him one way or another.
Rock, paper, scissors me. Best two out of three.
Ugh, fine.
Rock...
...paper...
...scissors....

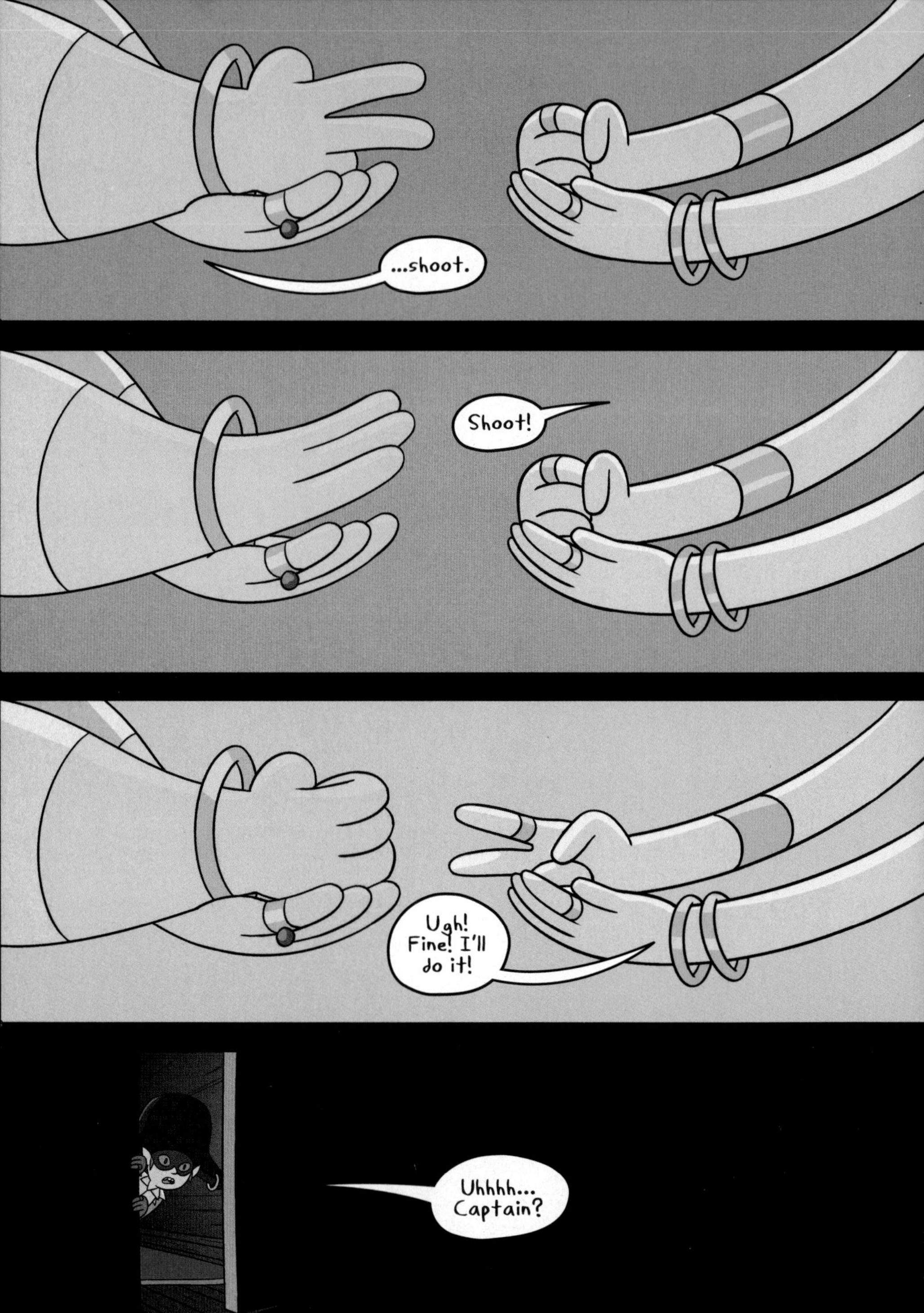
...shoot.
Shoot!
Ugh! Fine! I'll do it!
Uhhhh... Captain?

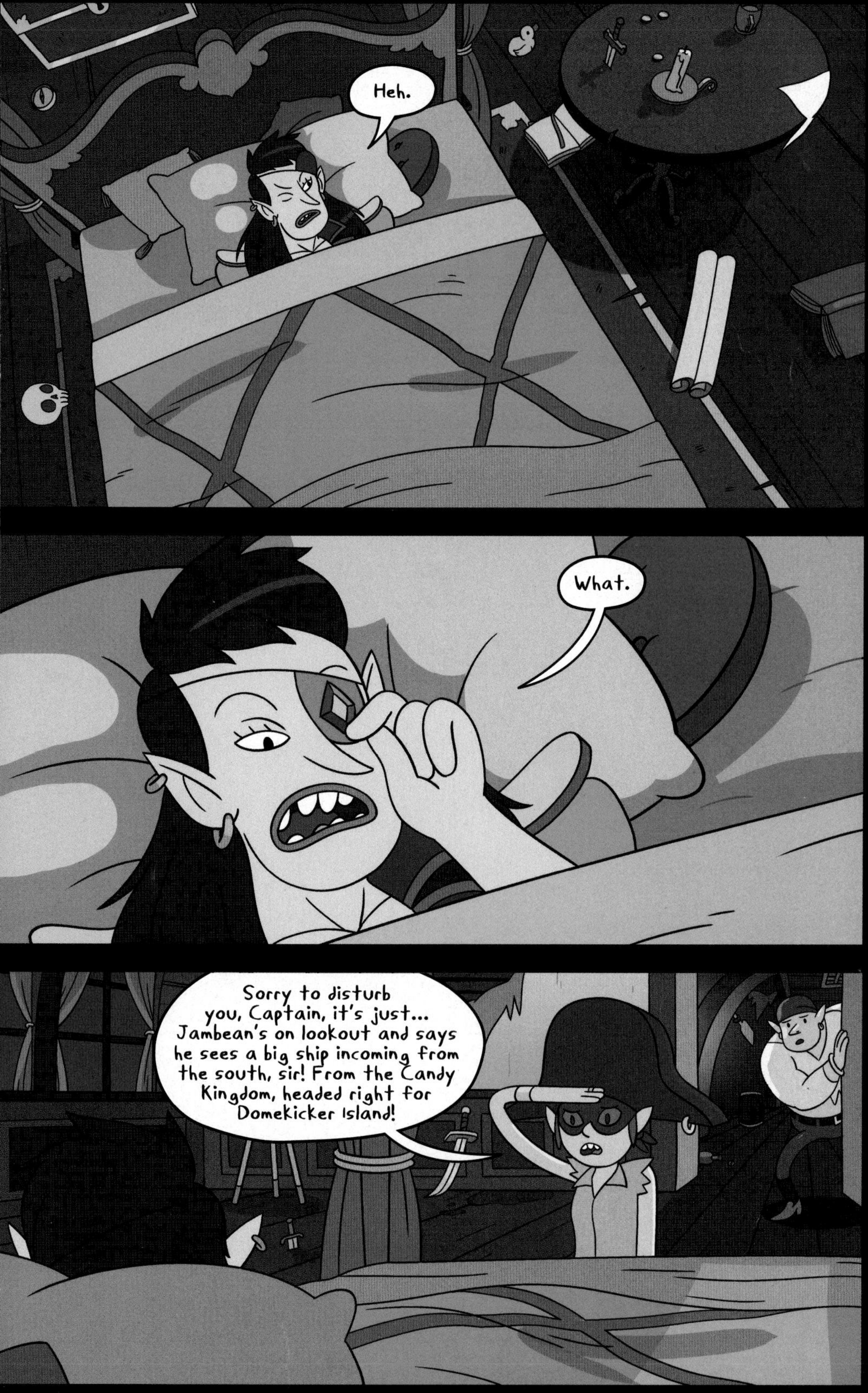
Heh.
What.
Sorry to disturb you, Captain, it's just... Jambean's on lookout and says he sees a big ship incoming from the south, sir! From the Candy Kingdom, headed right for Domekicker Island!

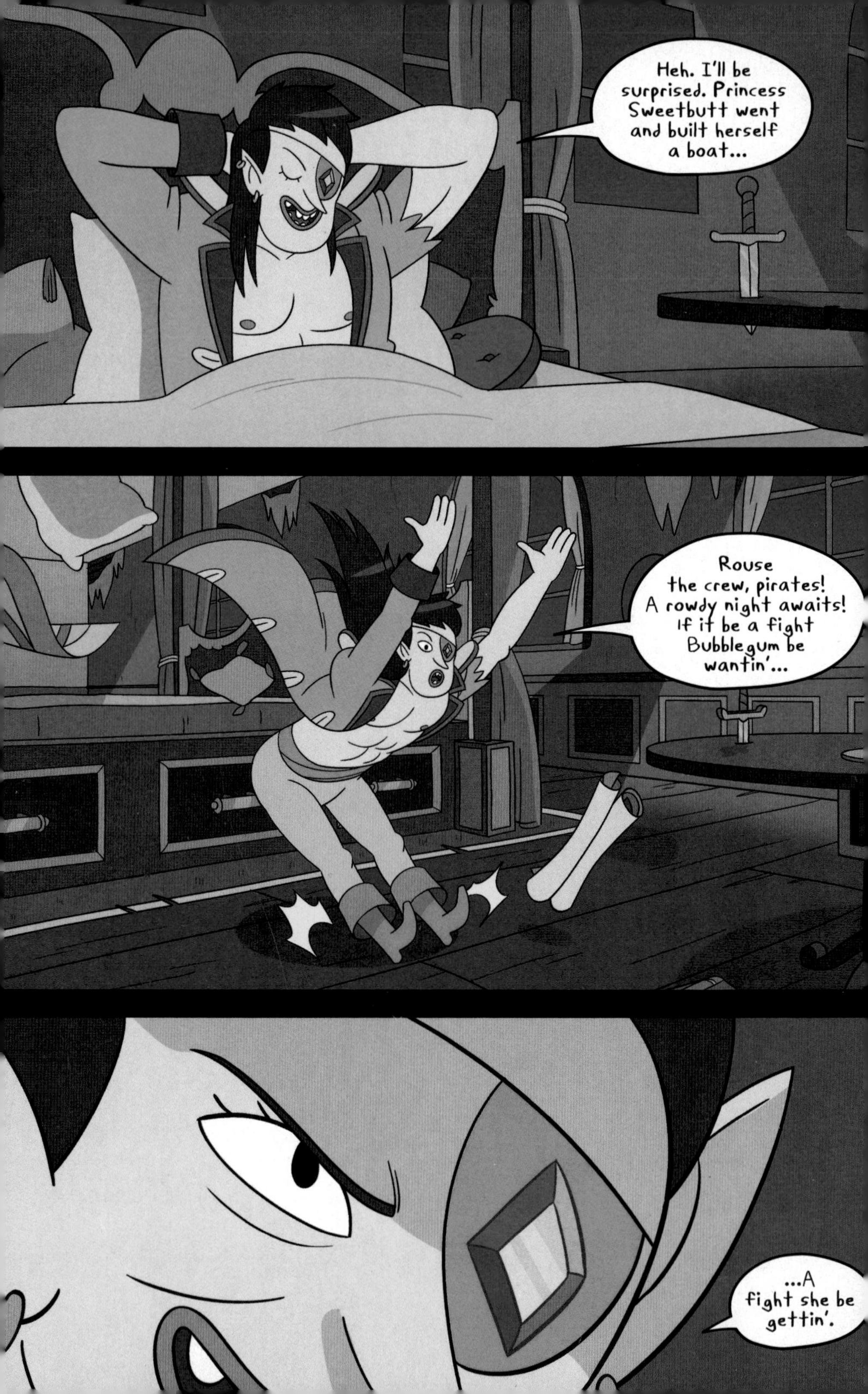
Heh. I'll be surprised. Princess Sweetbutt went and built herself a boat...
Rouse the crew, pirates! A rowdy night awaits! If it be a fight Bubblegum be wantin'...
...A fight she be gettin'.

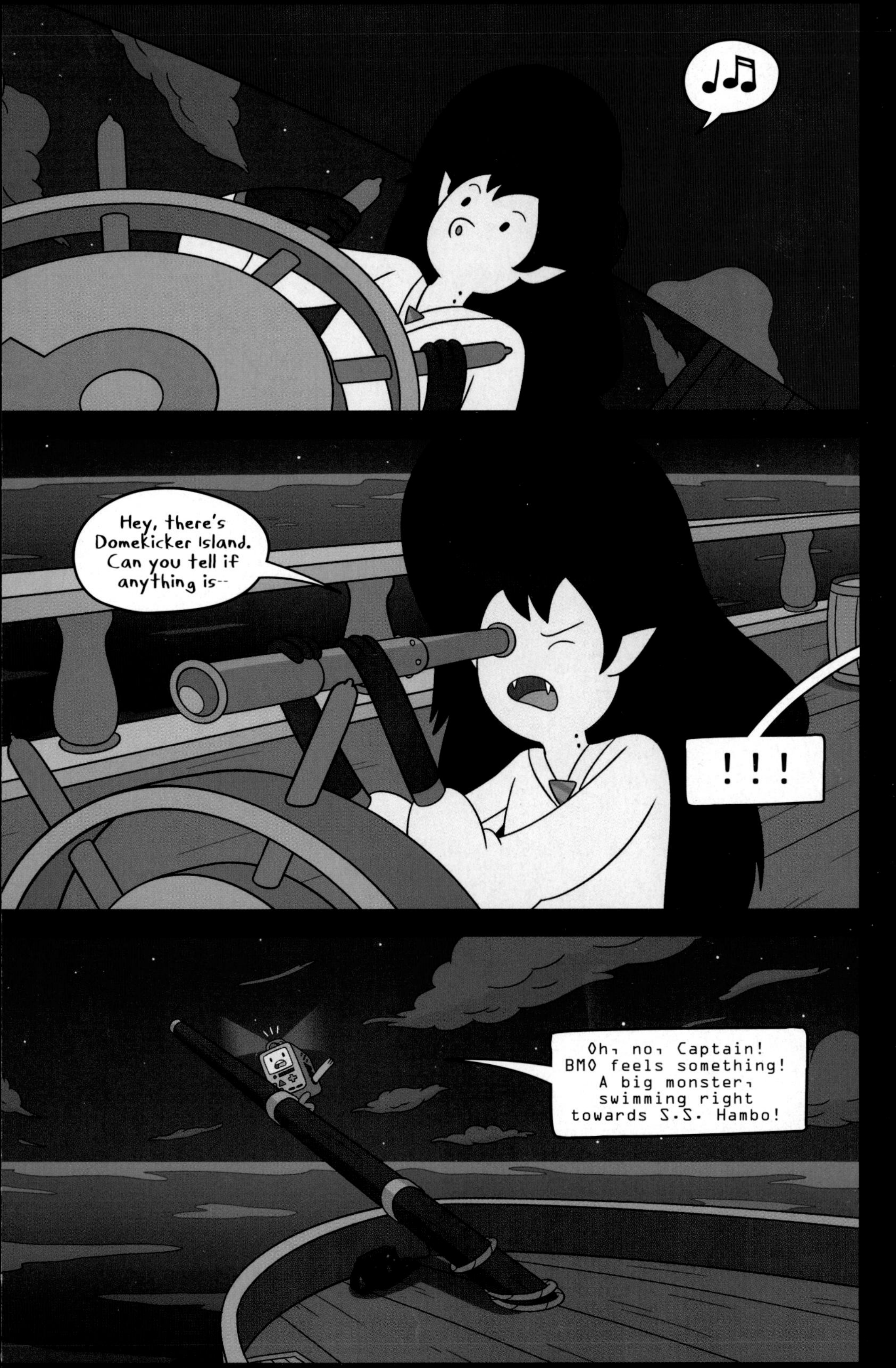
♩♫
Hey, there's Domekicker Island. Can you tell if anything is--
!!!
Oh, no, Captain! BMO feels something! A big monster, swimming right towards S.S. Hambo!

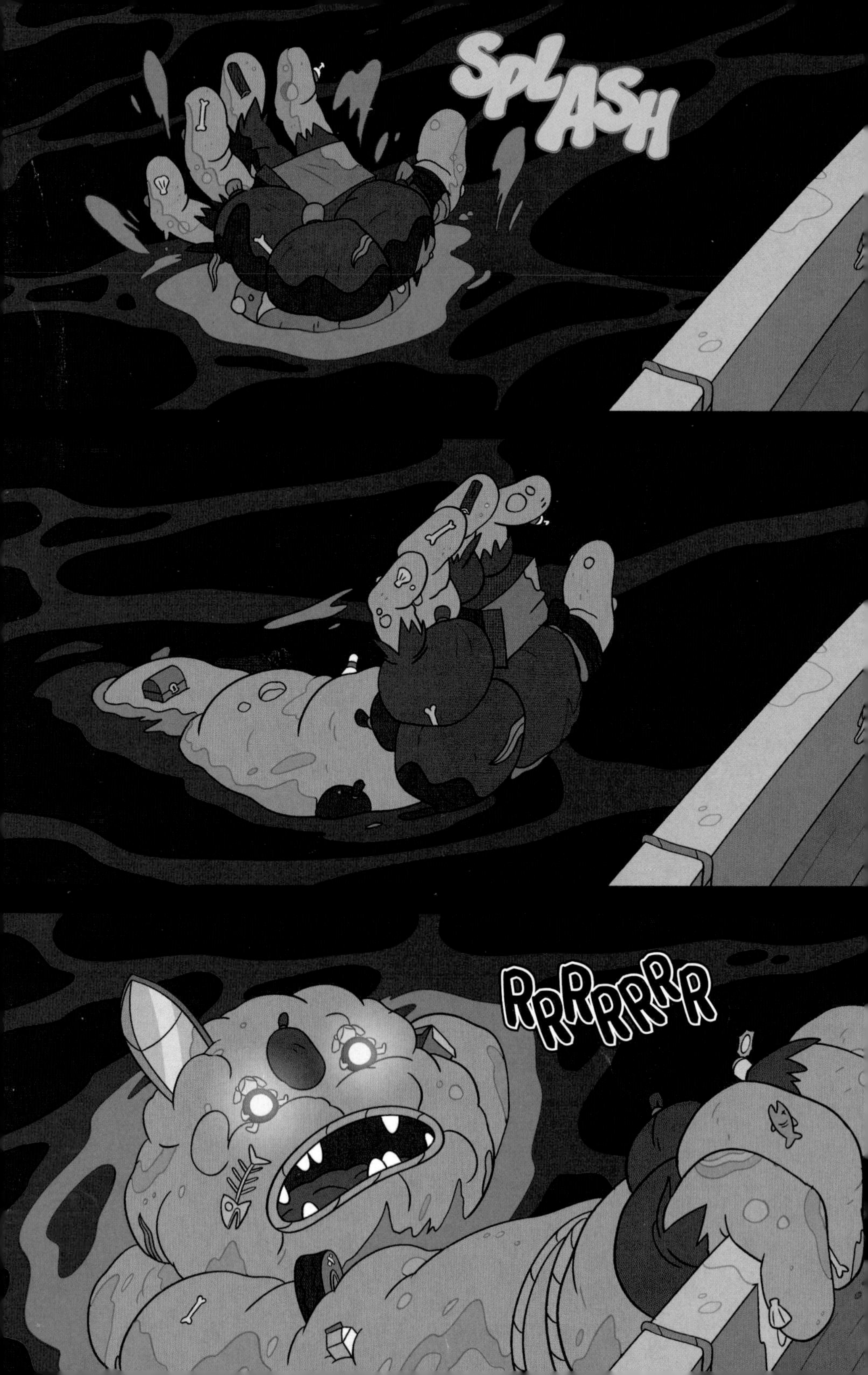
SPLASH
RRRRRRR

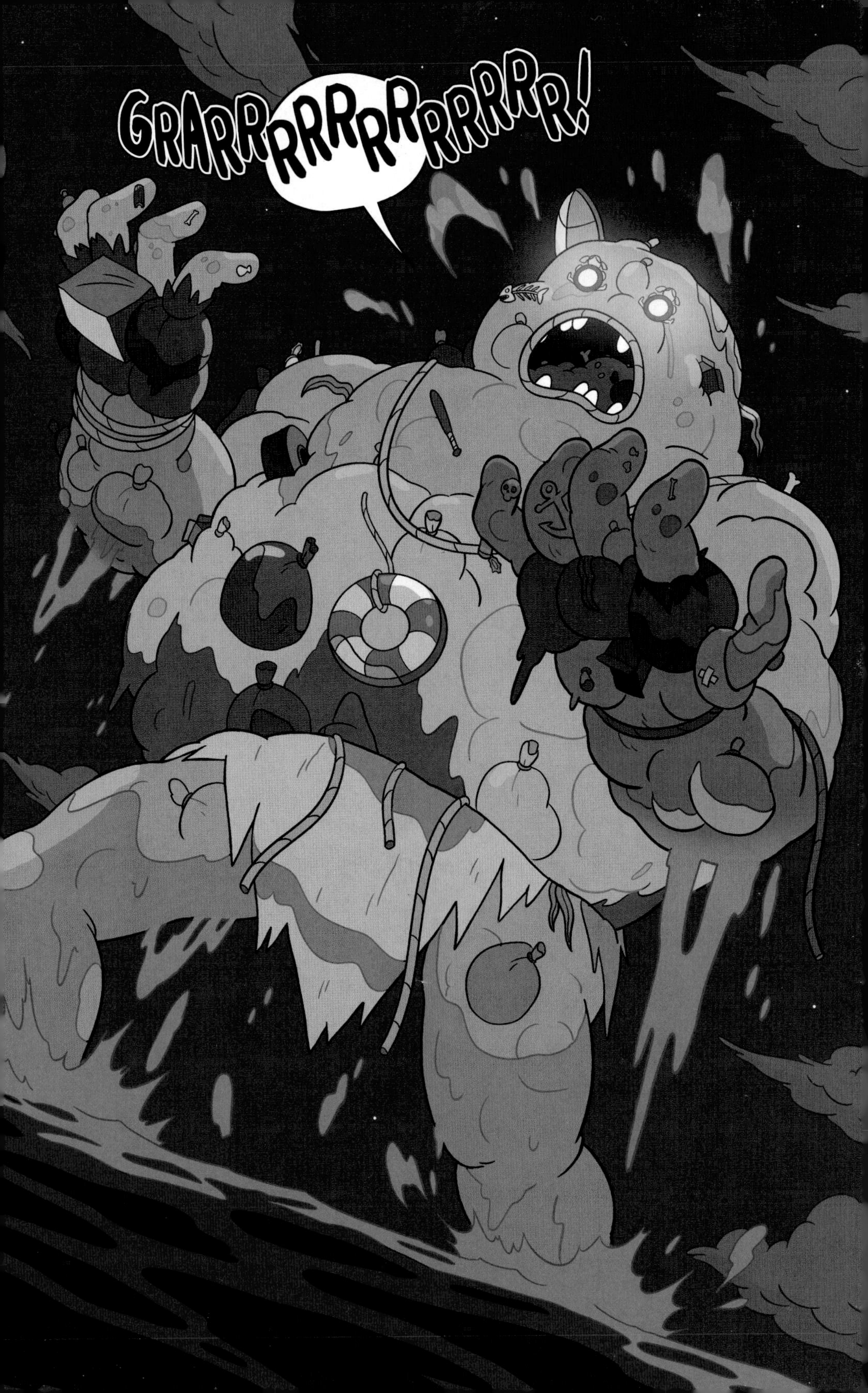
GRARRRRRRRRRRRRR!

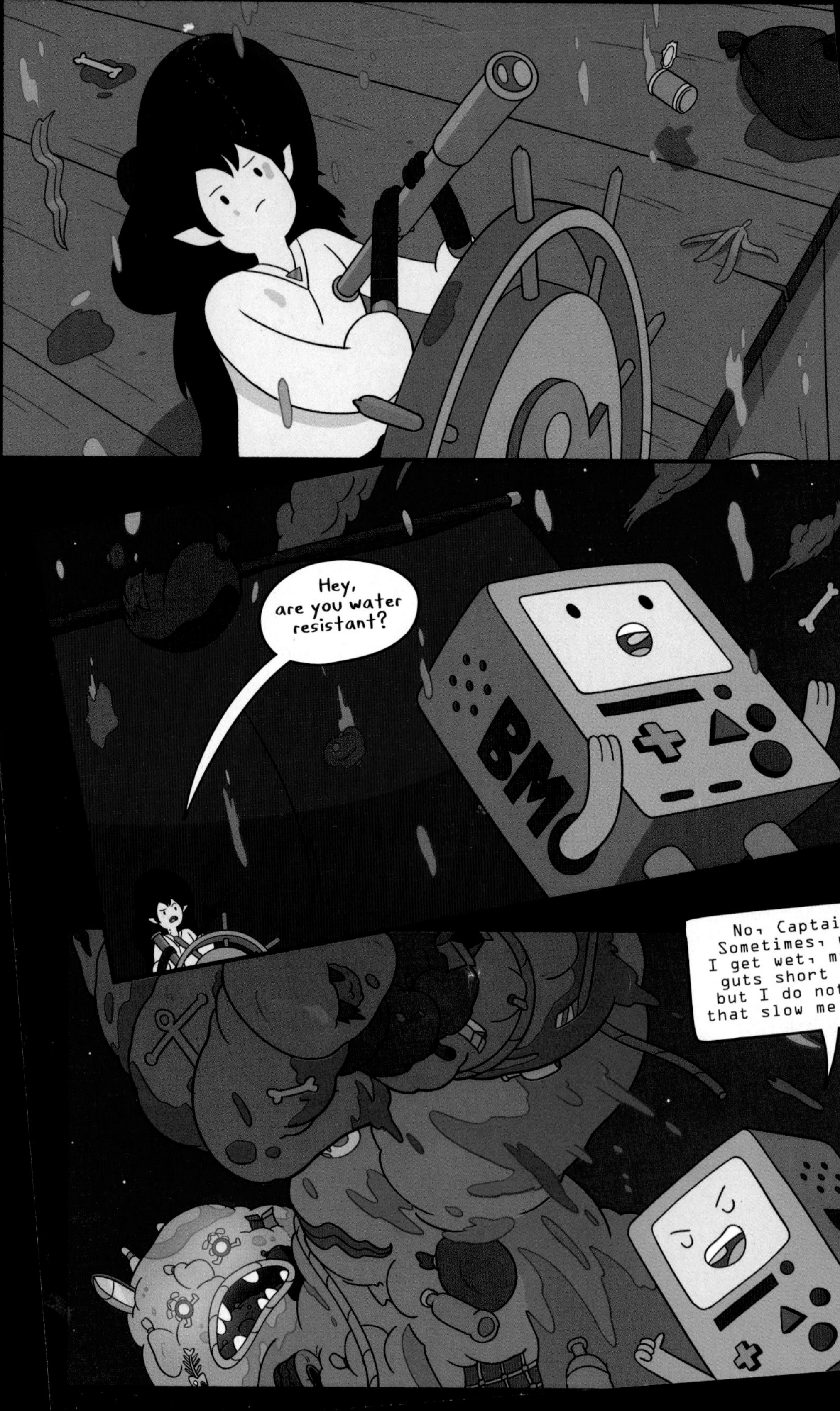
Hey, are you water resistant?
No, Captain! Sometimes, when I get wet, my BMO guts short out, but I do not let that slow me down.
BMO

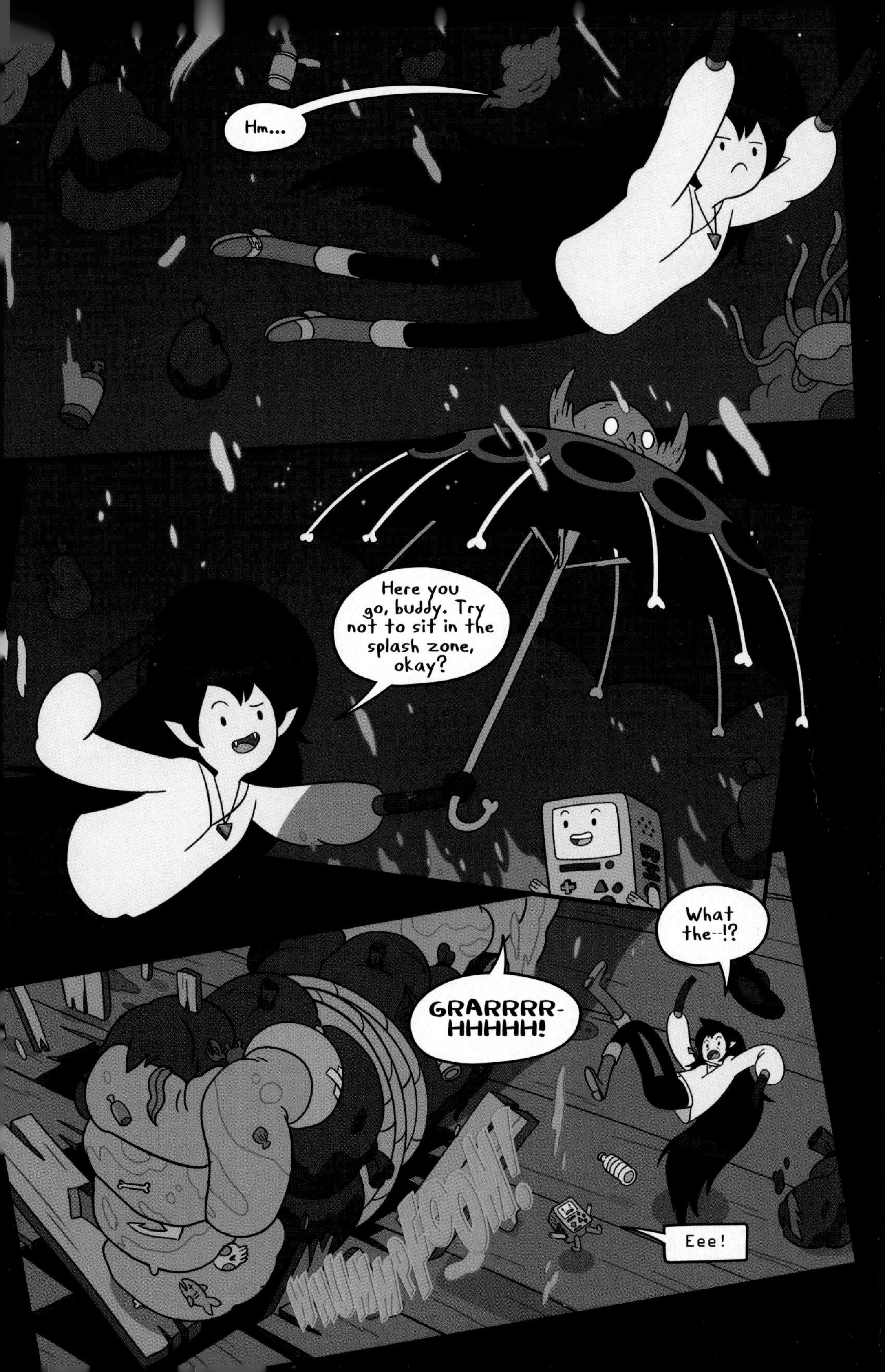
Hm...
Here you go, buddy. Try not to sit in the splash zone, okay?
BMO
What the--!?
GRARRRR-HHHHH!
WHUMPFOOM!
Eee!

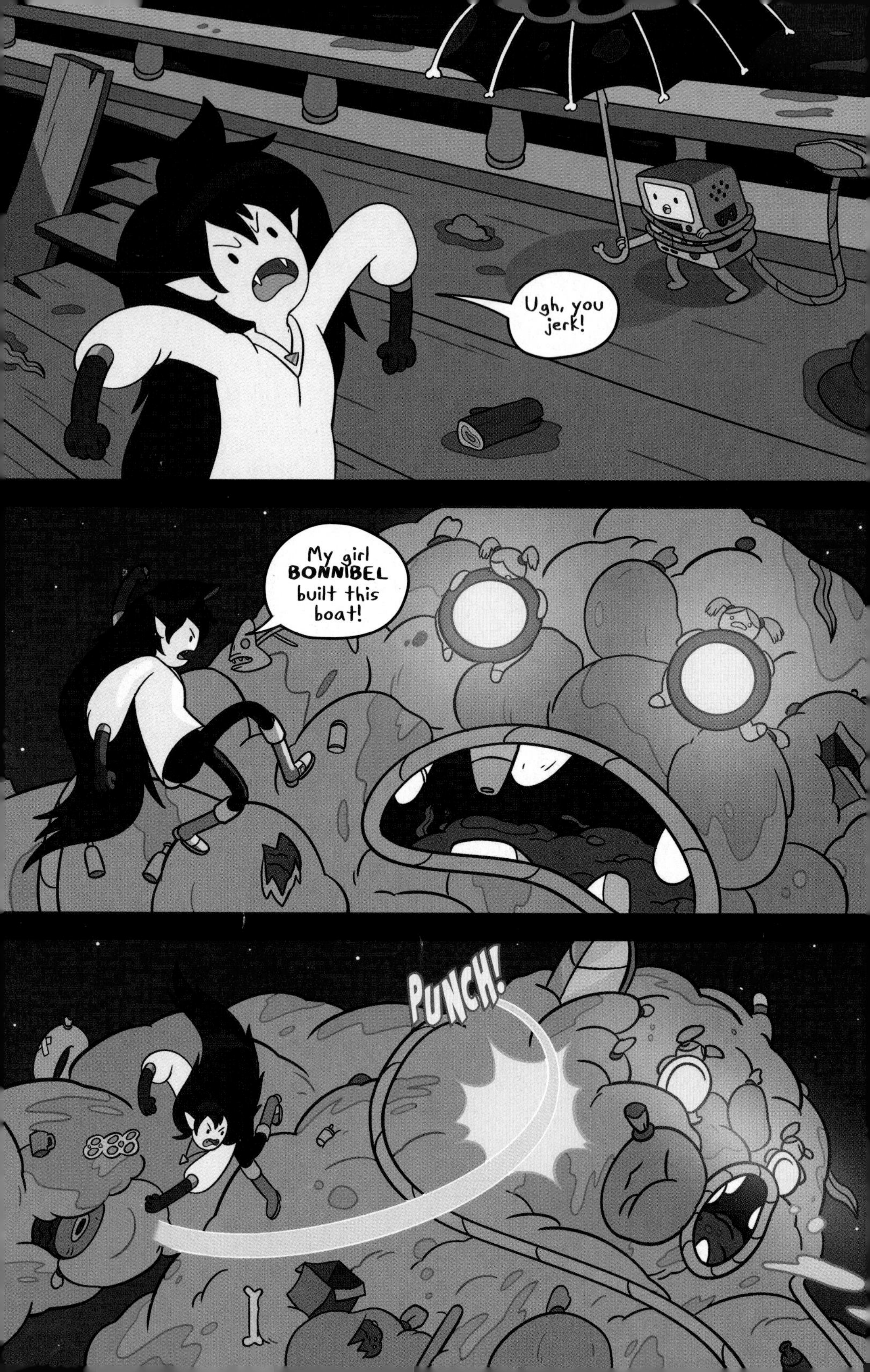
Ugh, you jerk!
My girl BONNIBEL built this boat!
PUNCH!

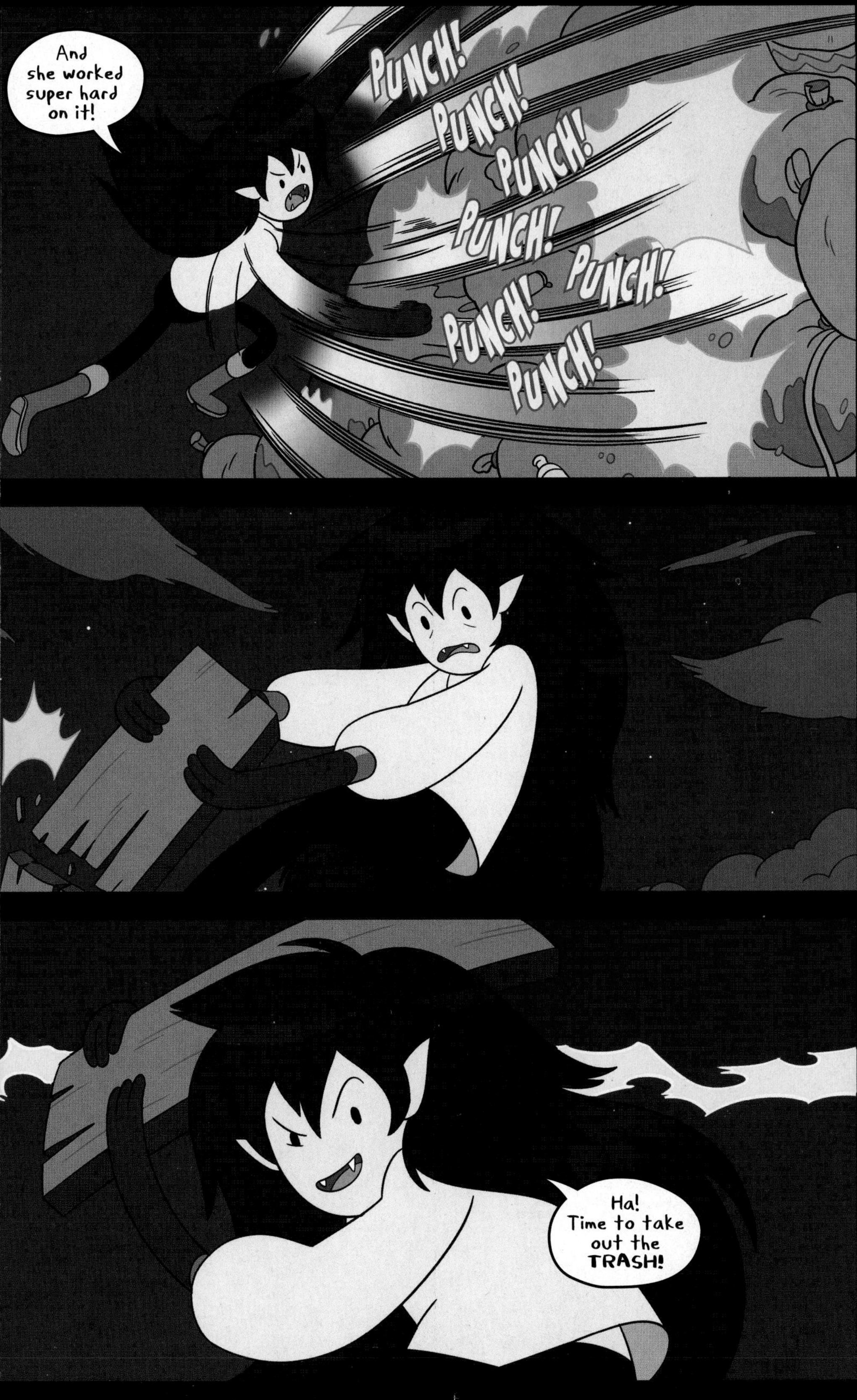
And she worked super hard on it!
PUNCH! PUNCH! PUNCH! PUNCH! PUNCH! PUNCH! PUNCH!
Ha! Time to take out the TRASH!

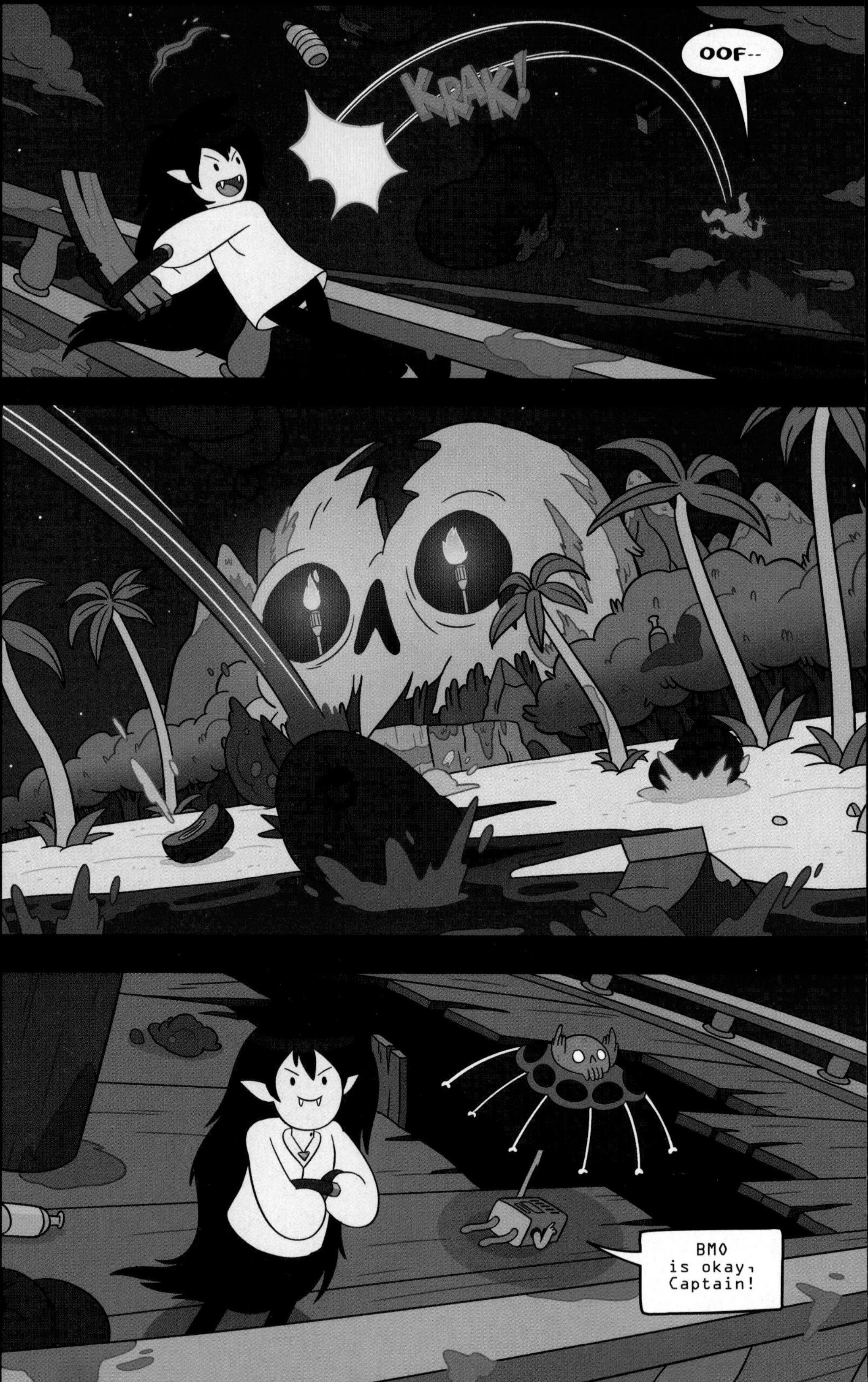
KRAK!
OOF--
BMO is okay, Captain!

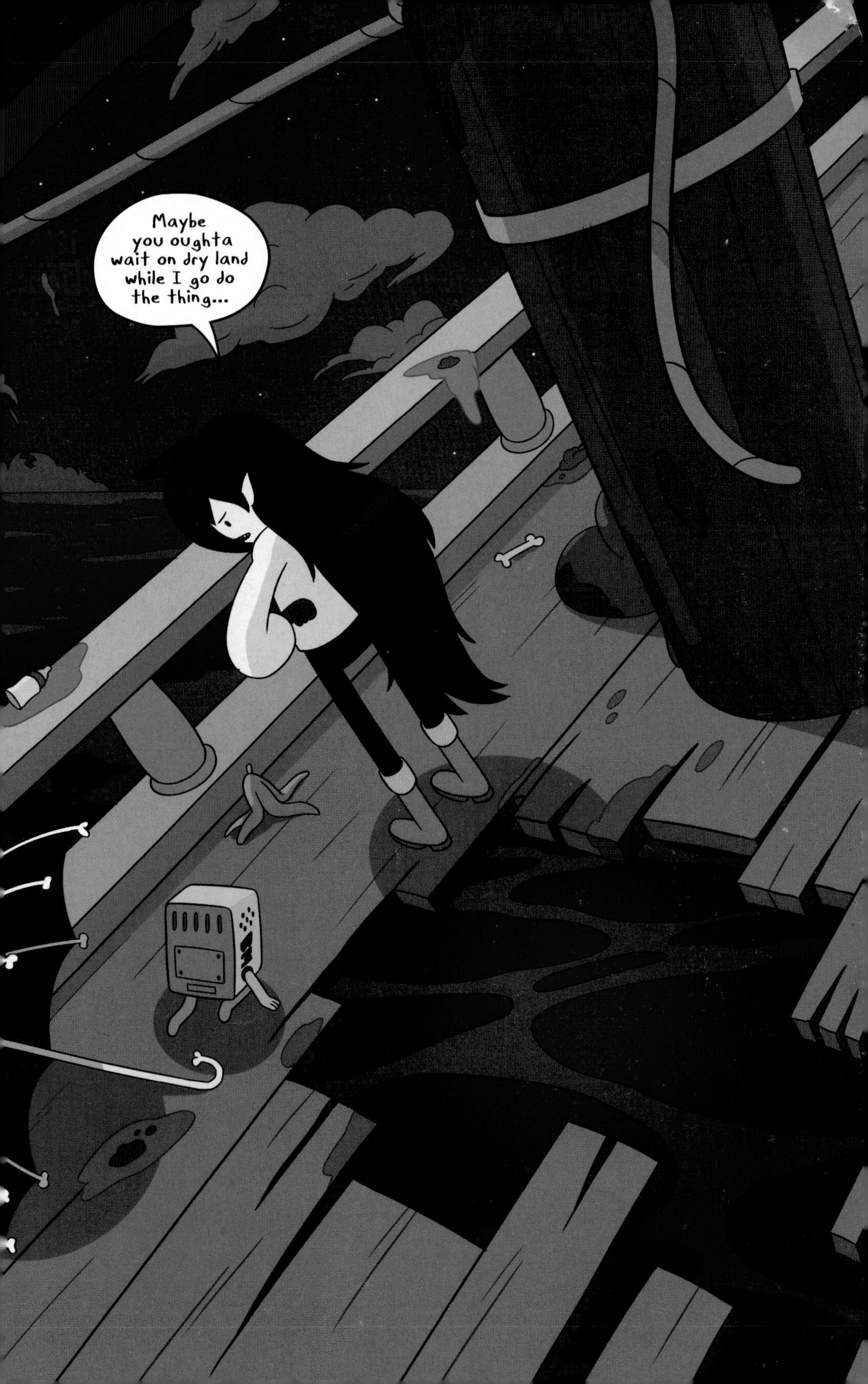
Maybe you oughta wait on dry land while I go do the thing...

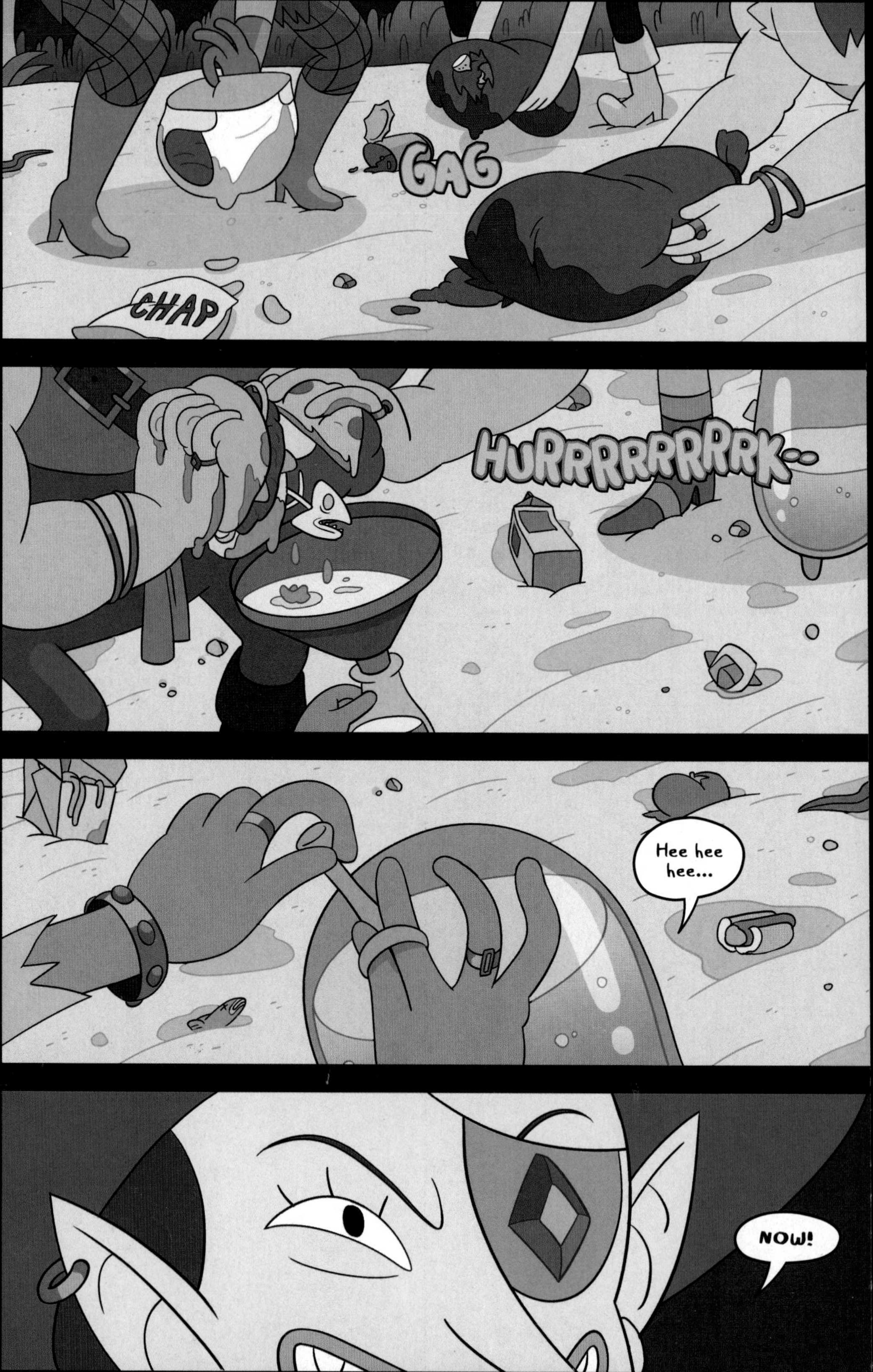
GAG
CHAP
HURRRRRRRRK--
Hee hee hee...
NOW!

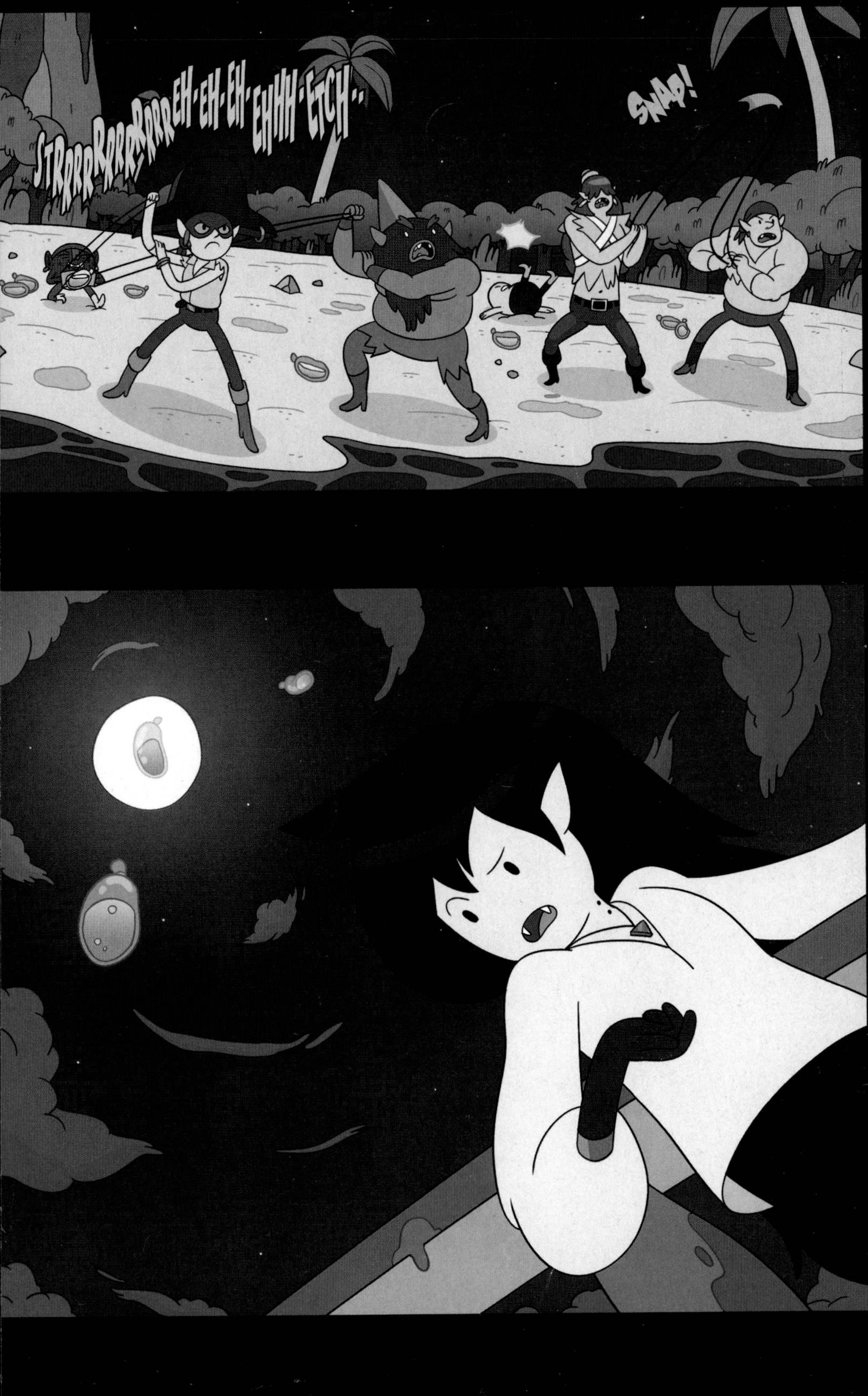
STRRRRRRRRRREH-EH-EH-EHHH-ETCH..
SNAP!

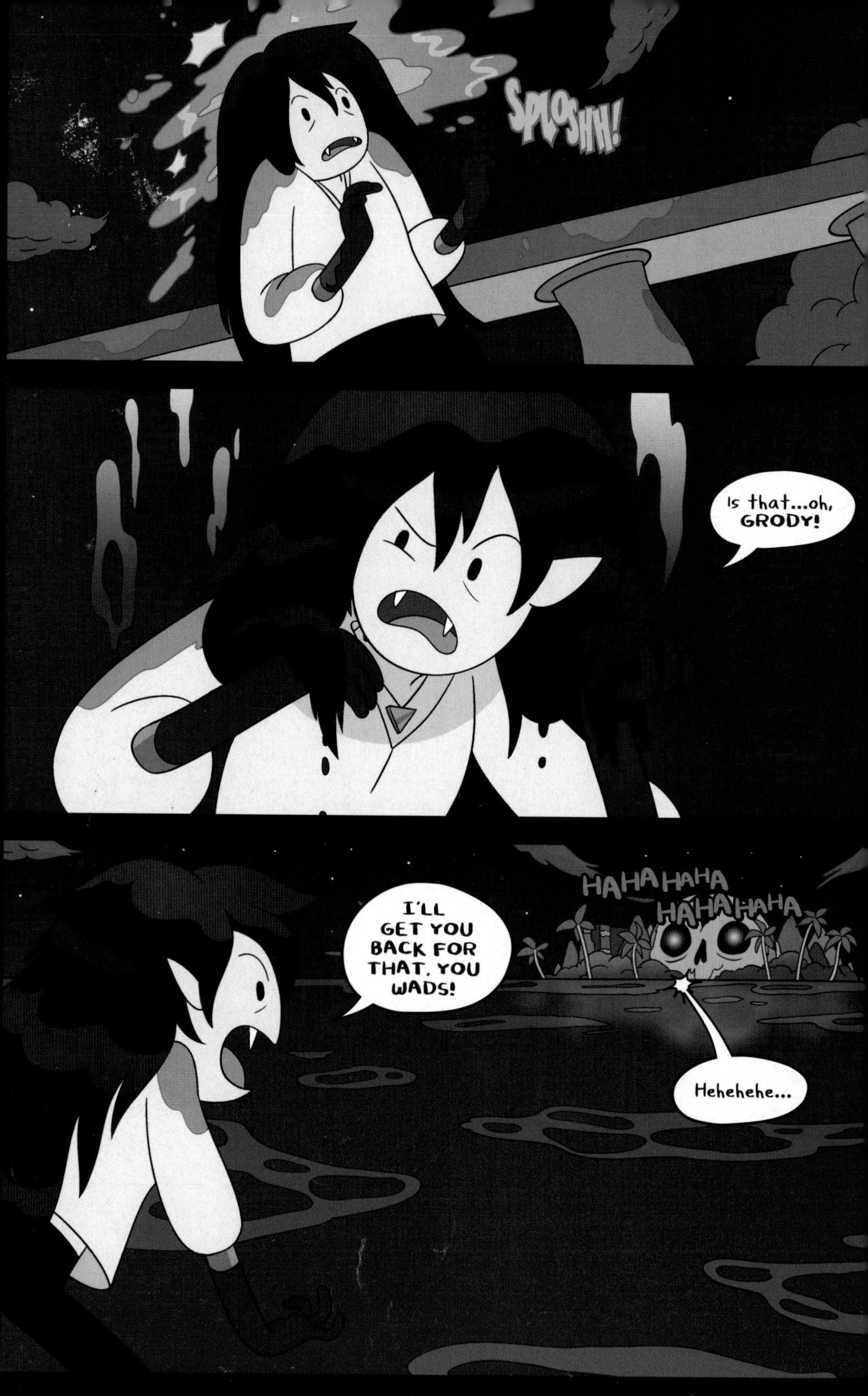
SPLOSHH!
Is that...oh, GRODY!
I'LL GET YOU BACK FOR THAT, YOU WADS!
HAHAHAHA HAHAHAHAHA
Hehehehe...

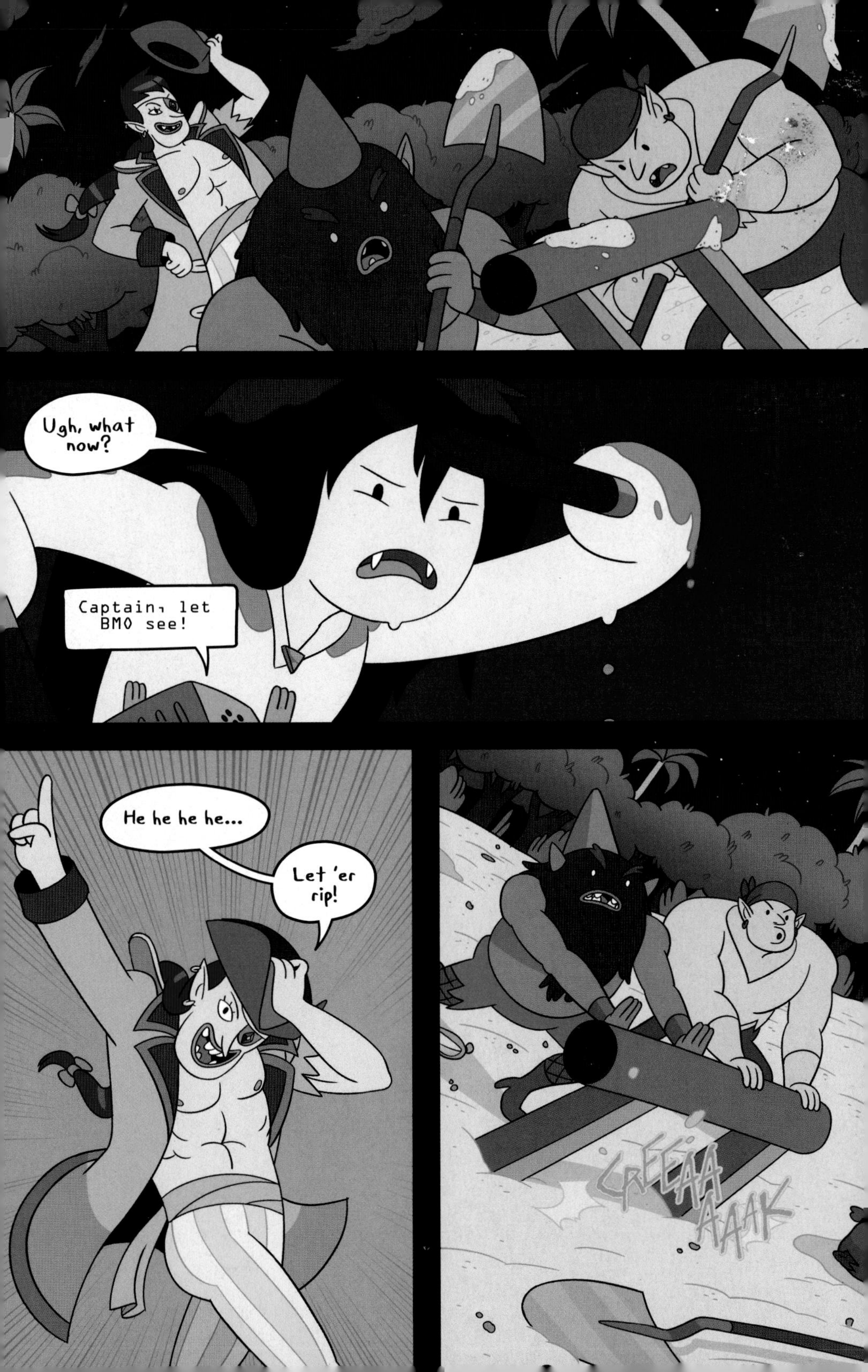
Ugh, what now?
Captain, let BMO see!
He he he he...
Let 'er rip!
CREEAA AAAK

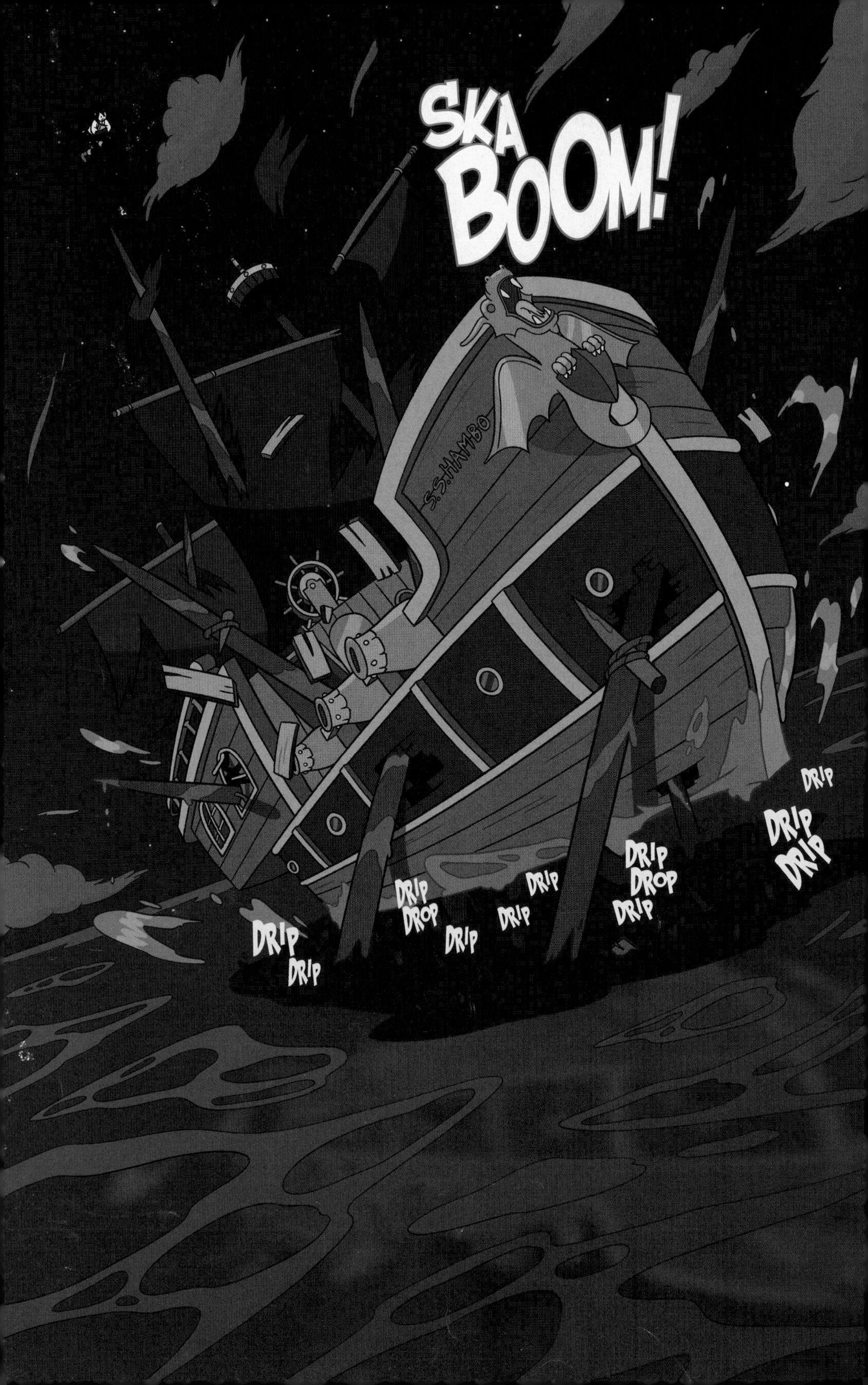
SKA BOOM!
S.S. HAMBO
DRIP DRIP
DRIP DROP
DRIP
DRIP
DRIP
DRIP DROP DRIP
DRIP
DRIP DRIP DRIP

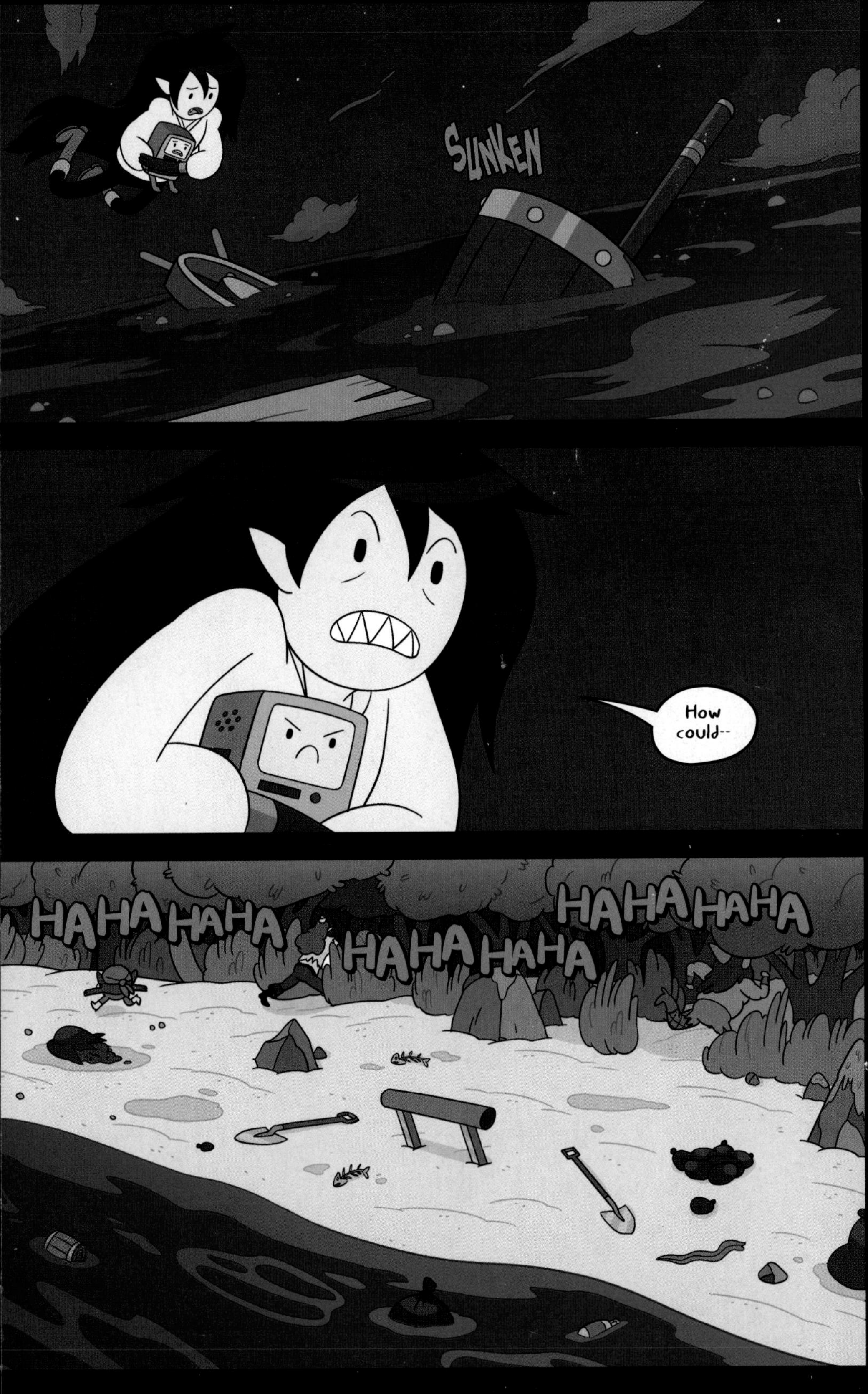
SUNKEN
How could--
HAHAHAHA
HAHAHAHA
HAHAHAHA
HAHAHAHA

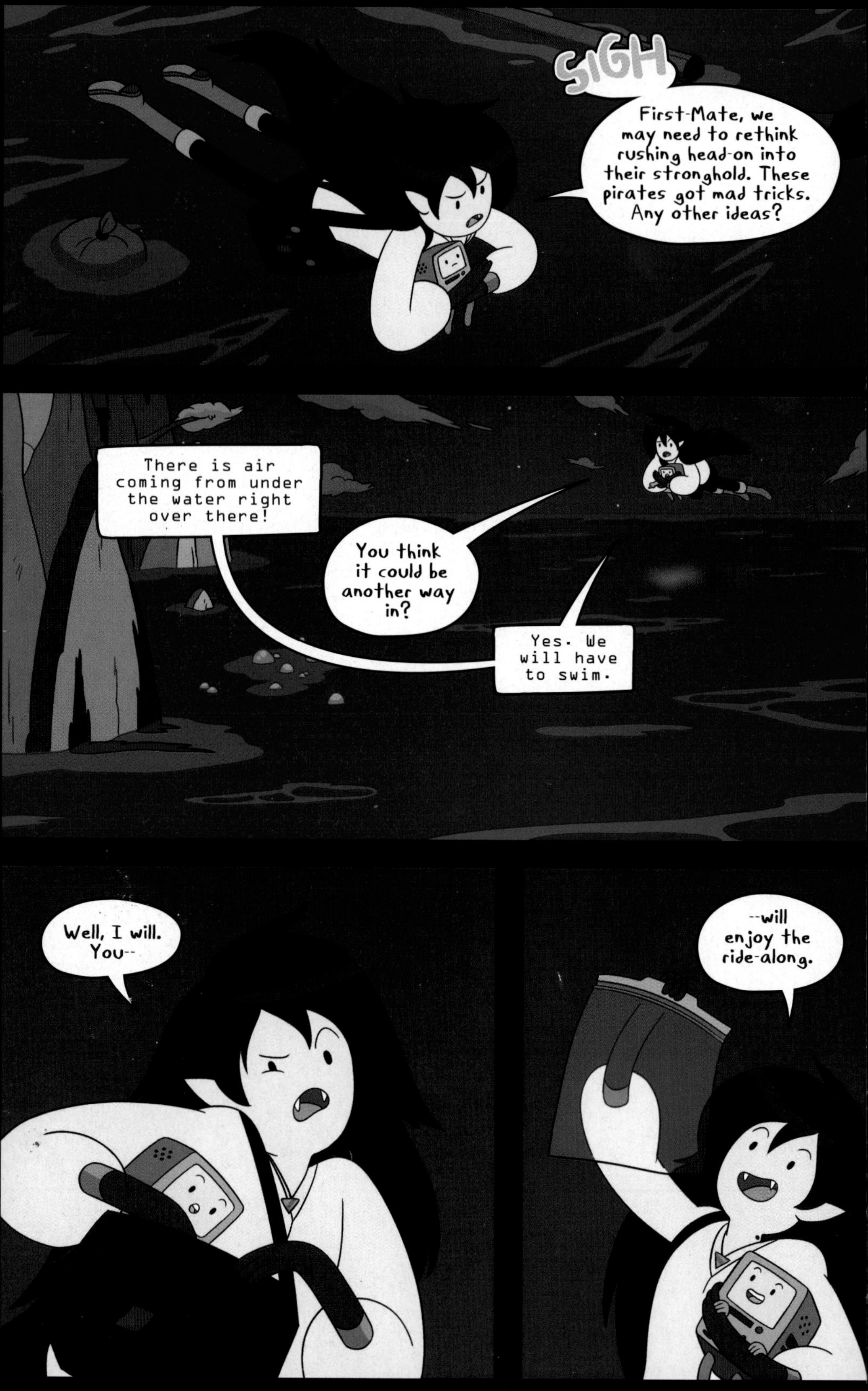
SIGH
First-Mate, we may need to rethink rushing head-on into their stronghold. These pirates got mad tricks. Any other ideas?
There is air coming from under the water right over there!
You think it could be another way in?
Yes. We will have to swim.
Well, I will. You--
--will enjoy the ride-along.

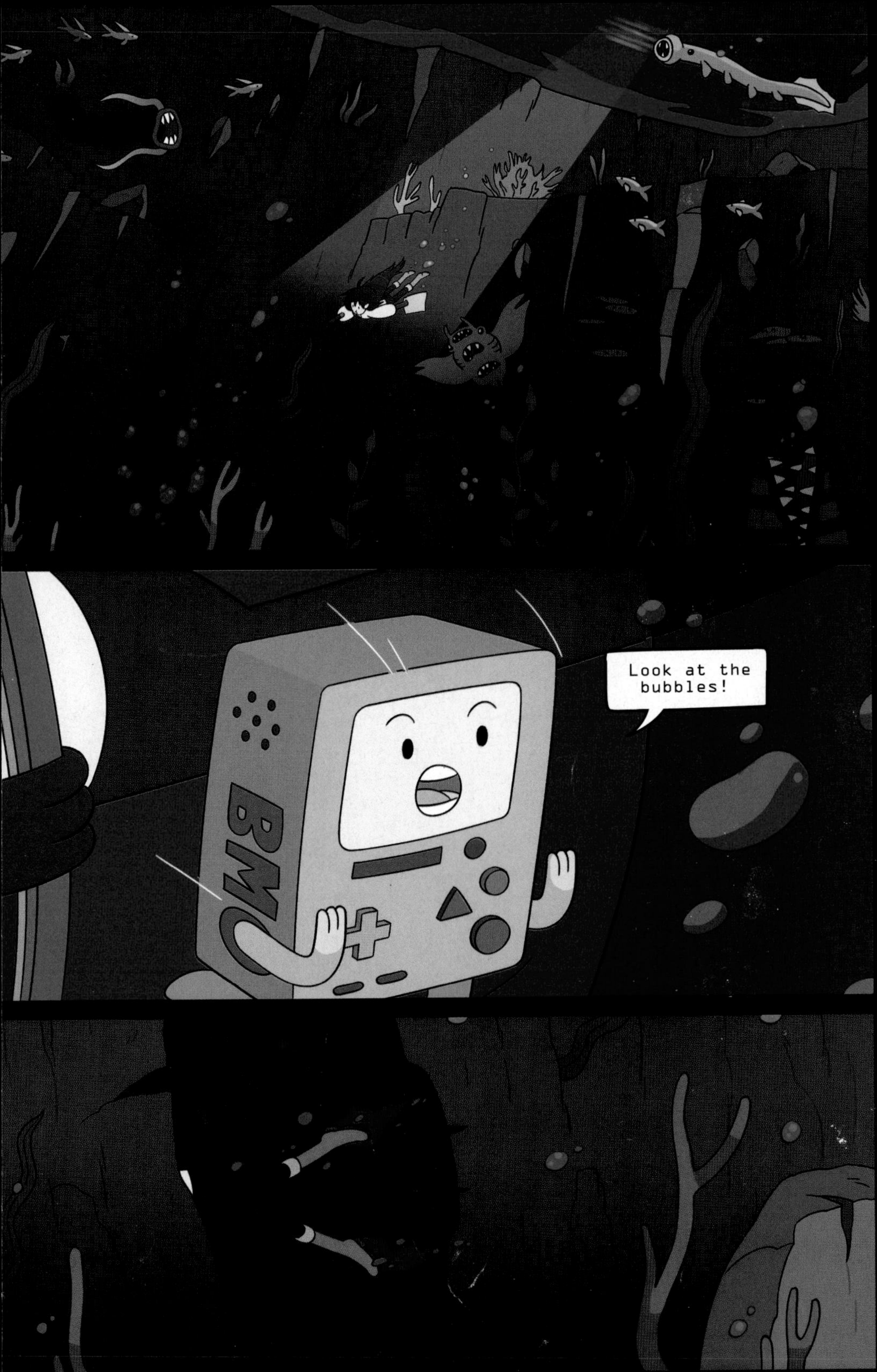
Look at the bubbles!

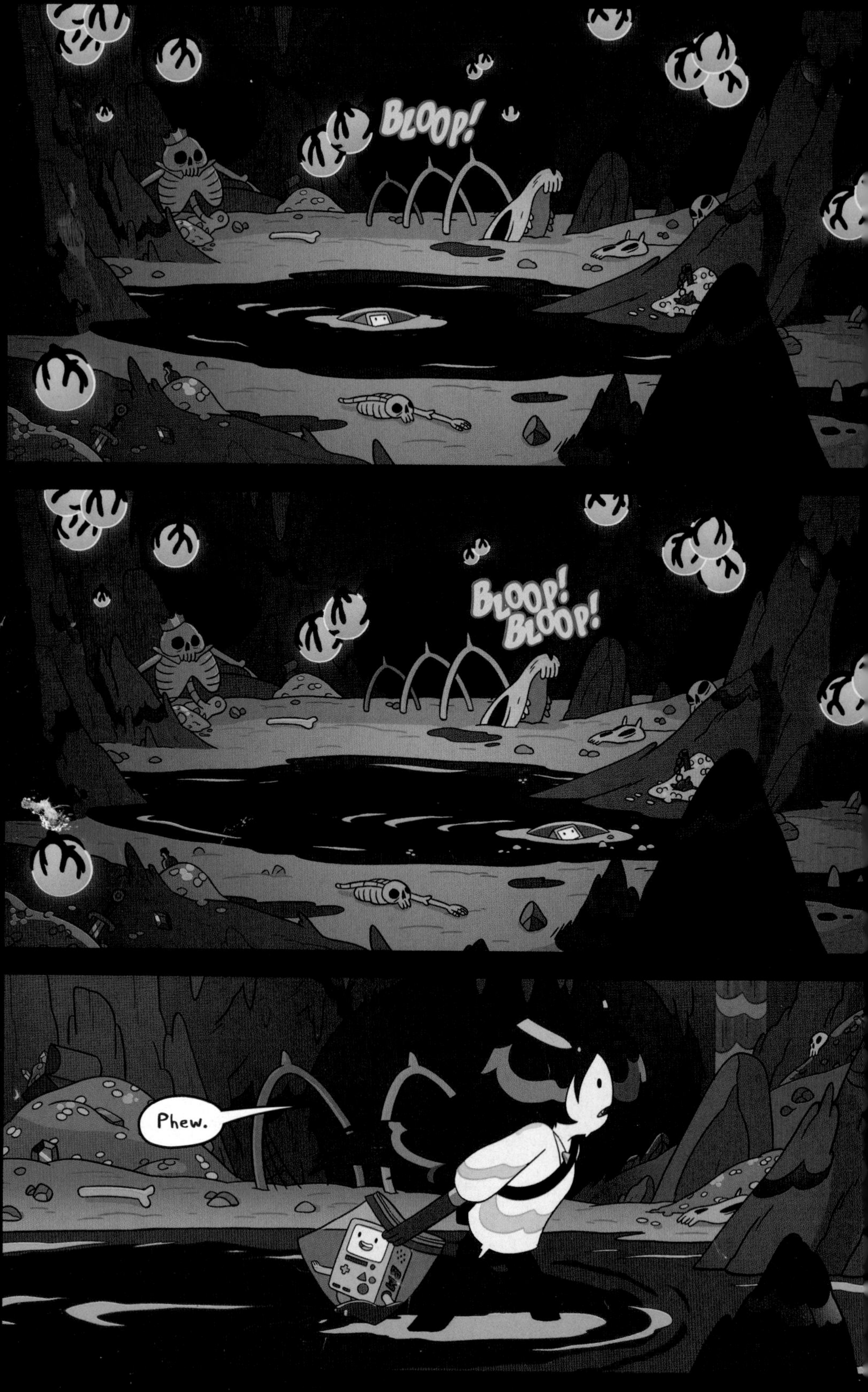
BLOOP!
BLOOP! BLOOP!
Phew.

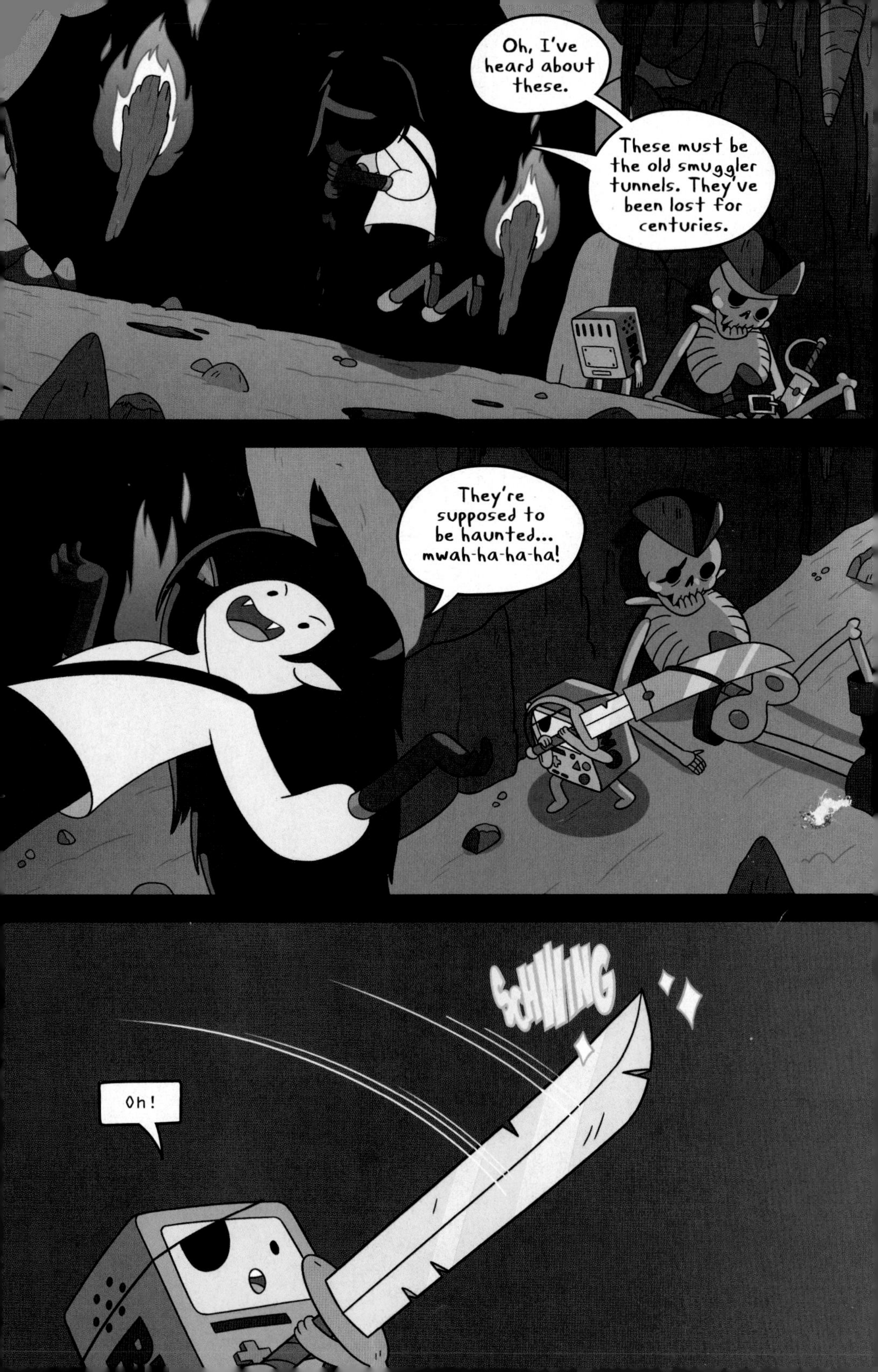
Oh, I've heard about these.
These must be the old smuggler tunnels. They've been lost for centuries.
They're supposed to be haunted... mwah-ha-ha-ha!
SCHWING
Oh!

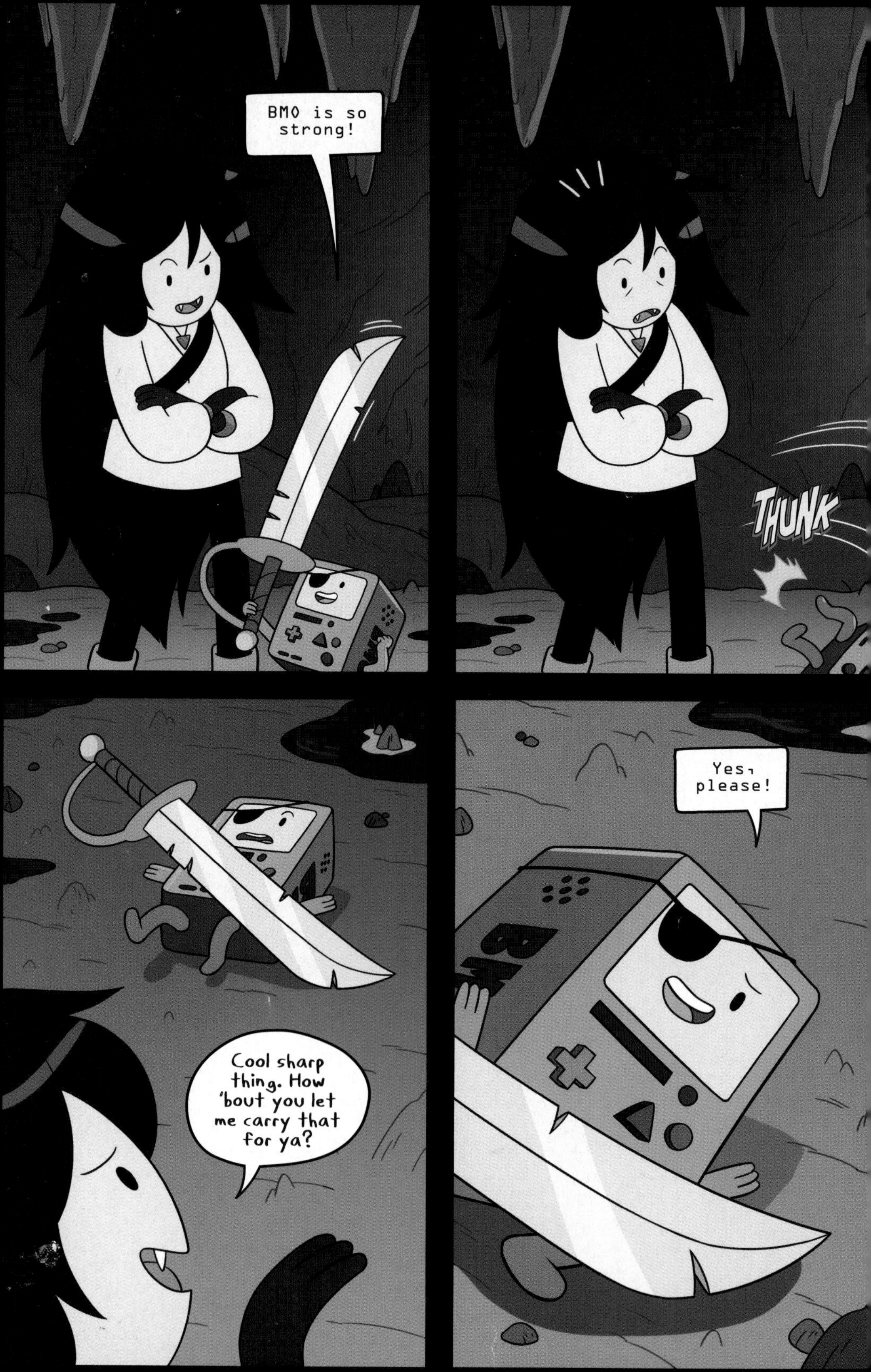
BMO is so strong!
THUNK
Cool sharp thing. How 'bout you let me carry that for ya?
Yes, please!

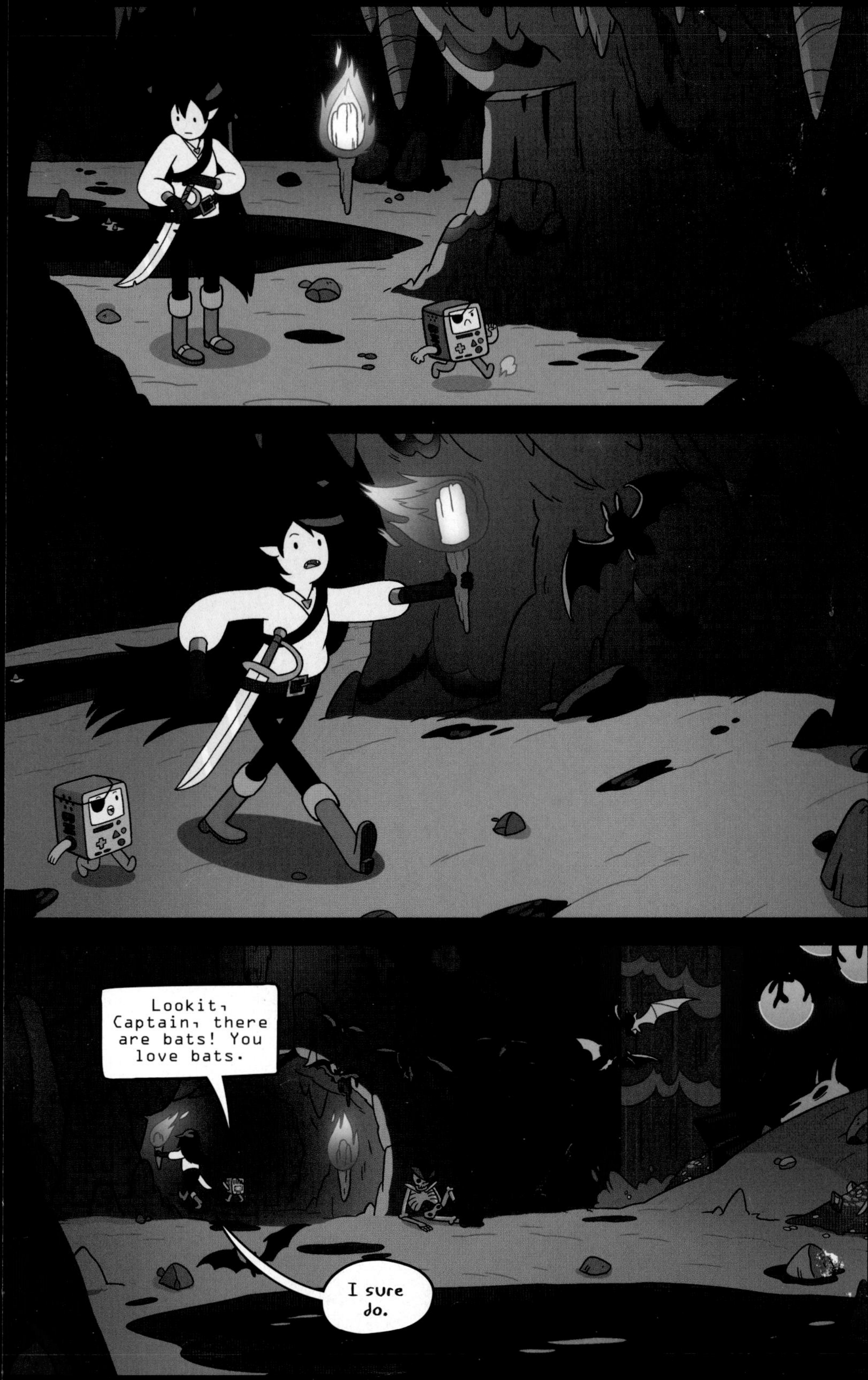
Lookit, Captain, there are bats! You love bats.
I sure do.

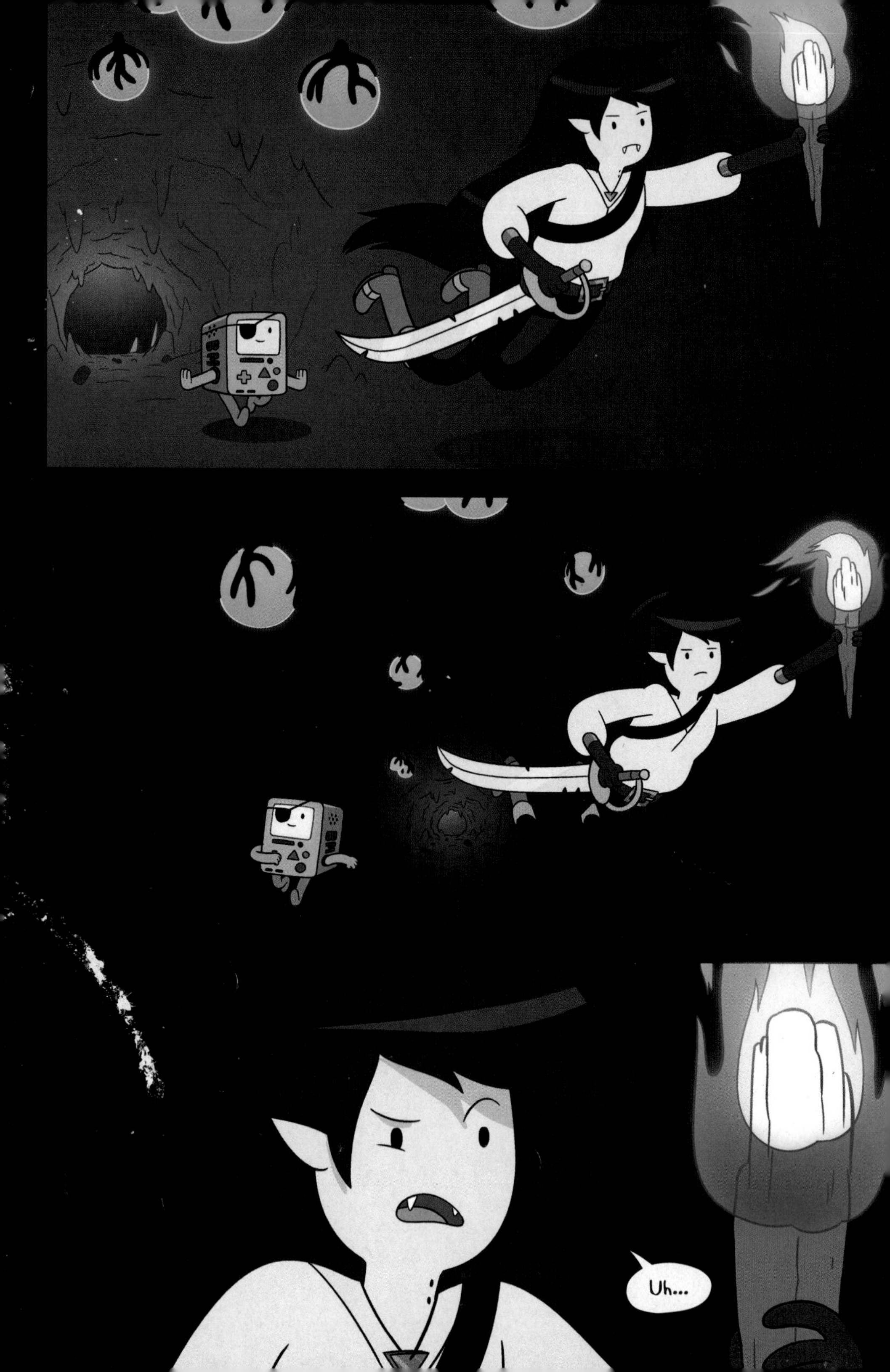
Uh...

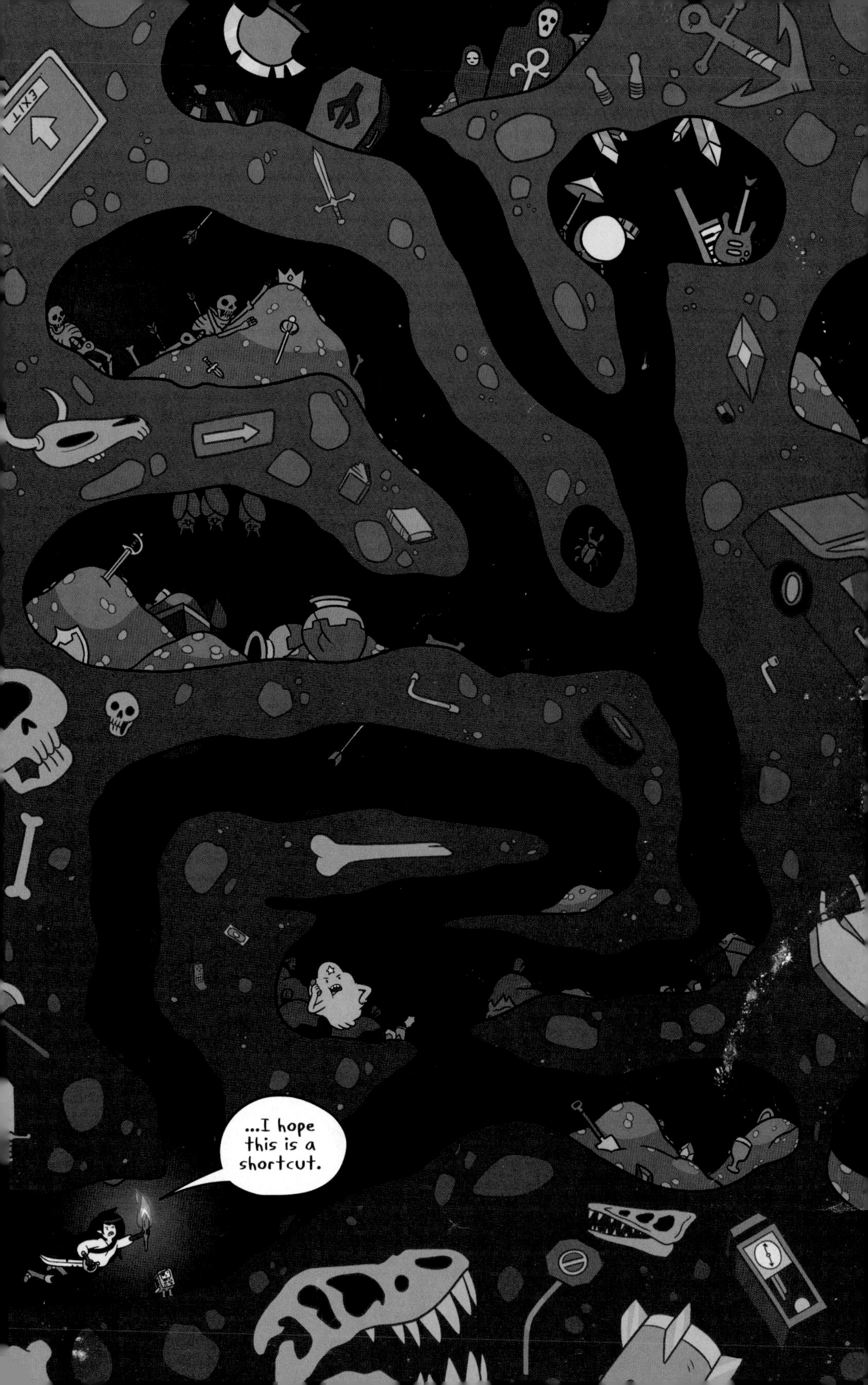
EXIT
...I hope this is a shortcut.

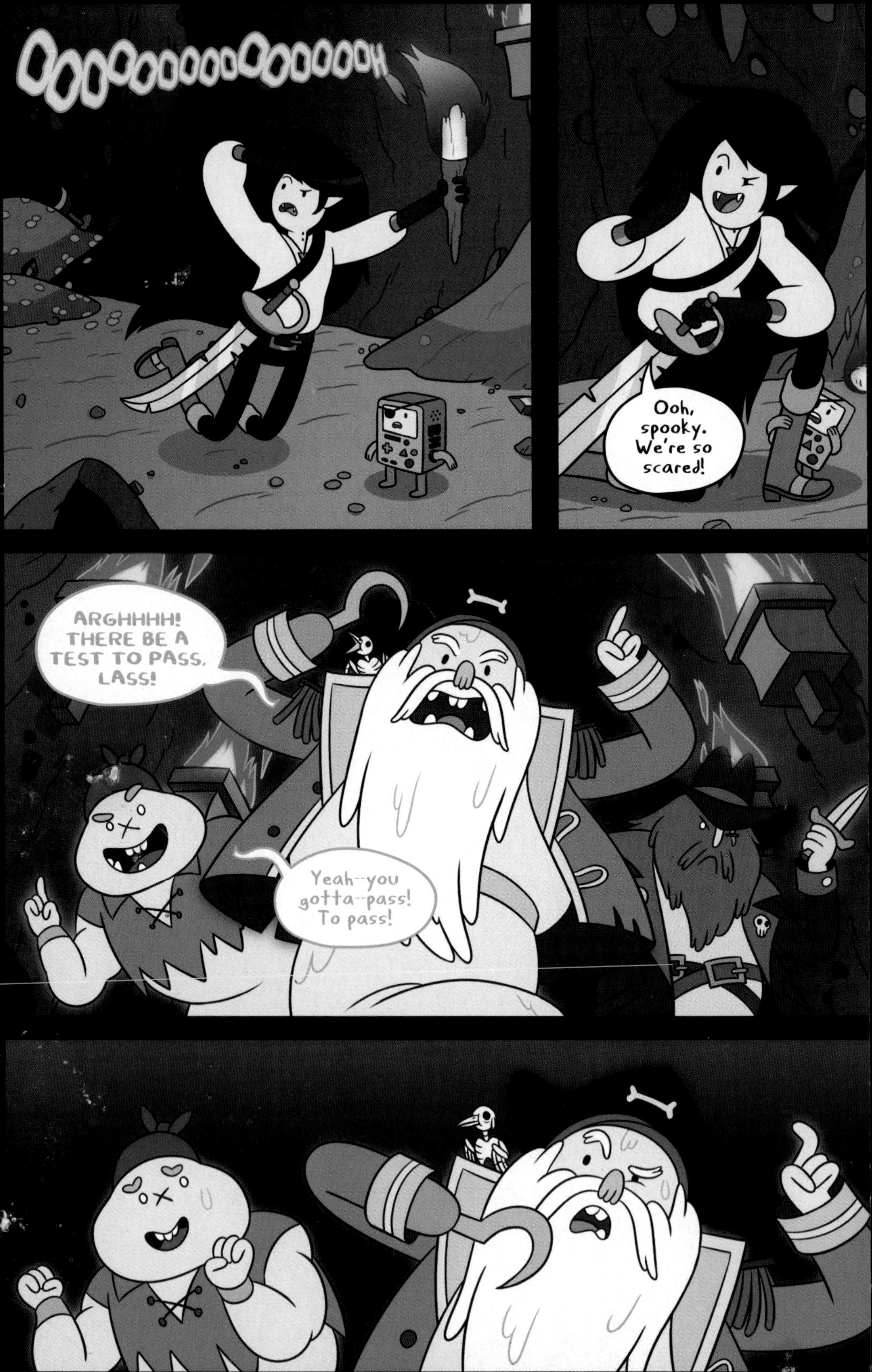
OOOOOOOOOOOOOOOOOH
Ooh, spooky. We're so scared!
ARGHHHH! THERE BE A TEST TO PASS, LASS!
Yeah--you gotta--pass! To pass!

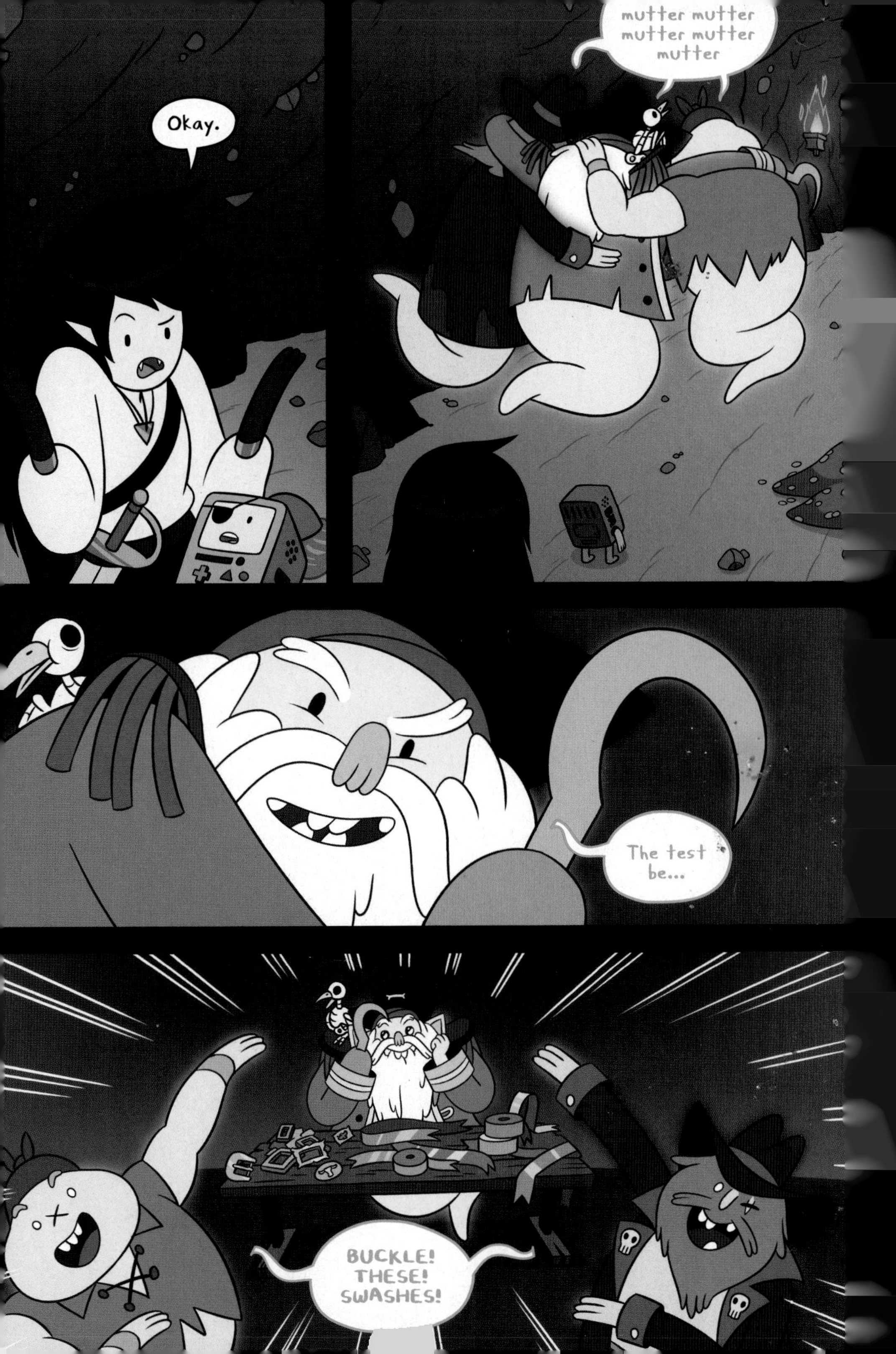
Okay.
mutter mutter
mutter mutter
mutter
The test be...
BUCKLE! THESE! SWASHES!

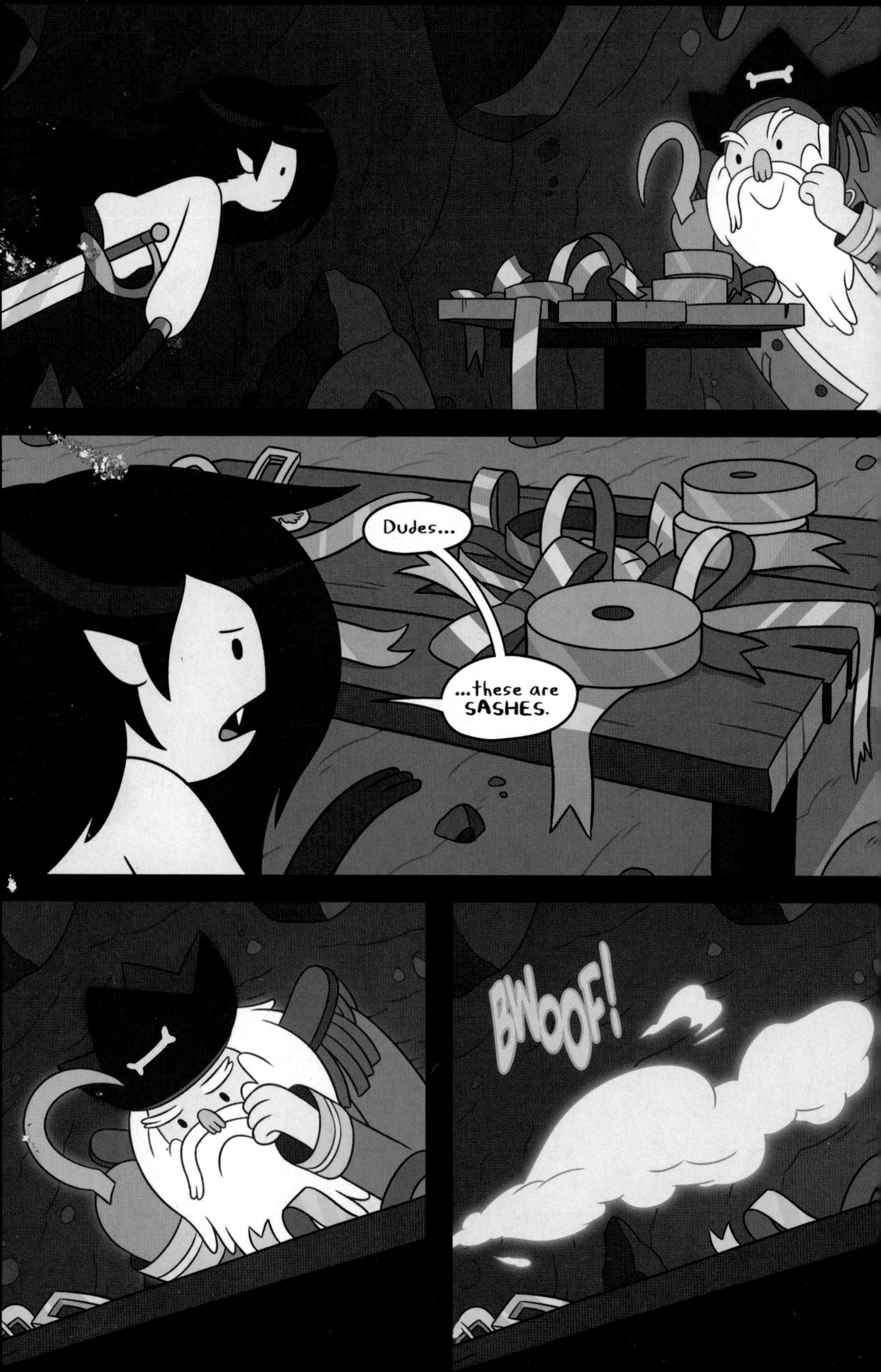
Dudes...
...these are SASHES.
BWOOF!

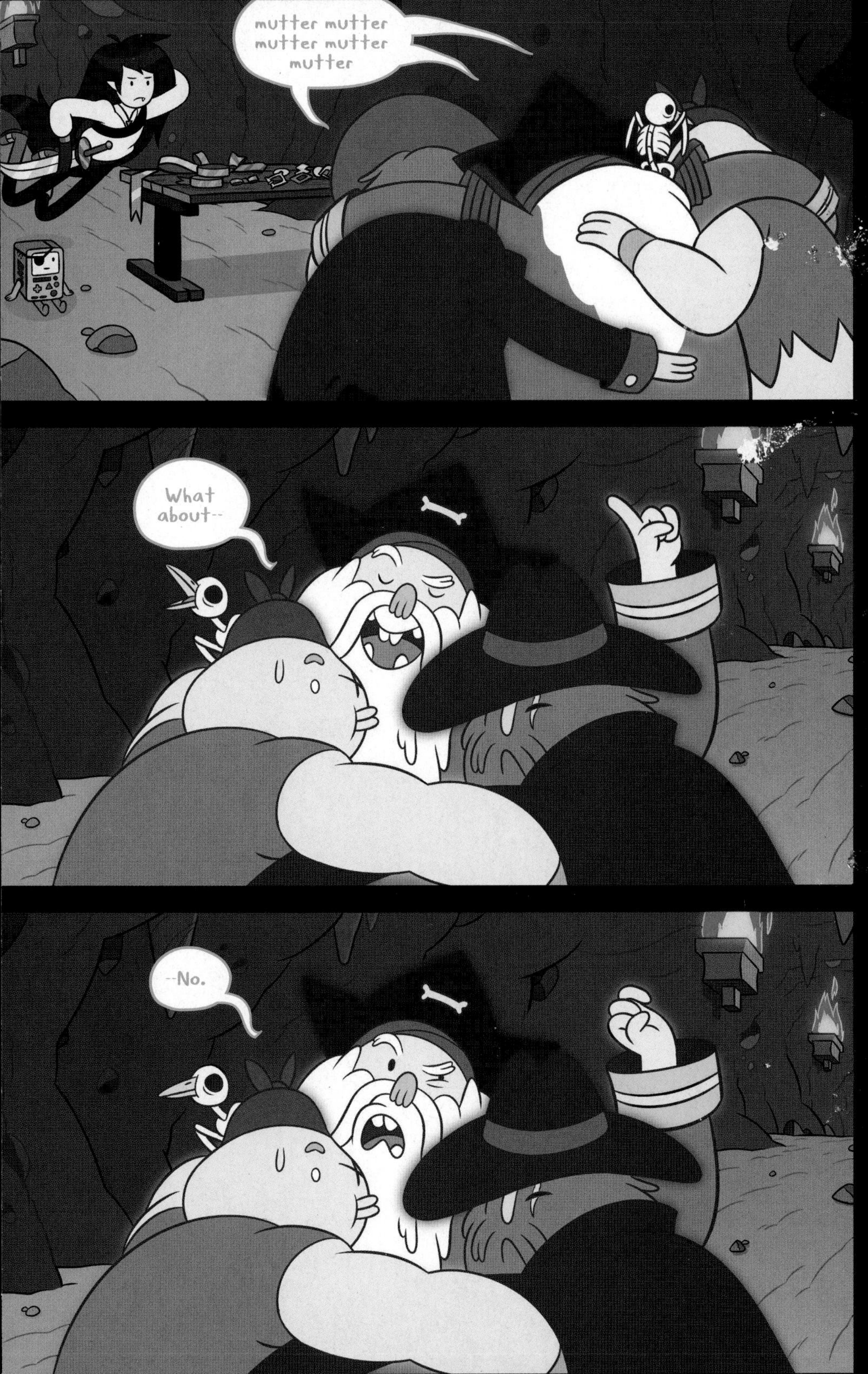
mutter mutter mutter mutter mutter
What about--
--No.

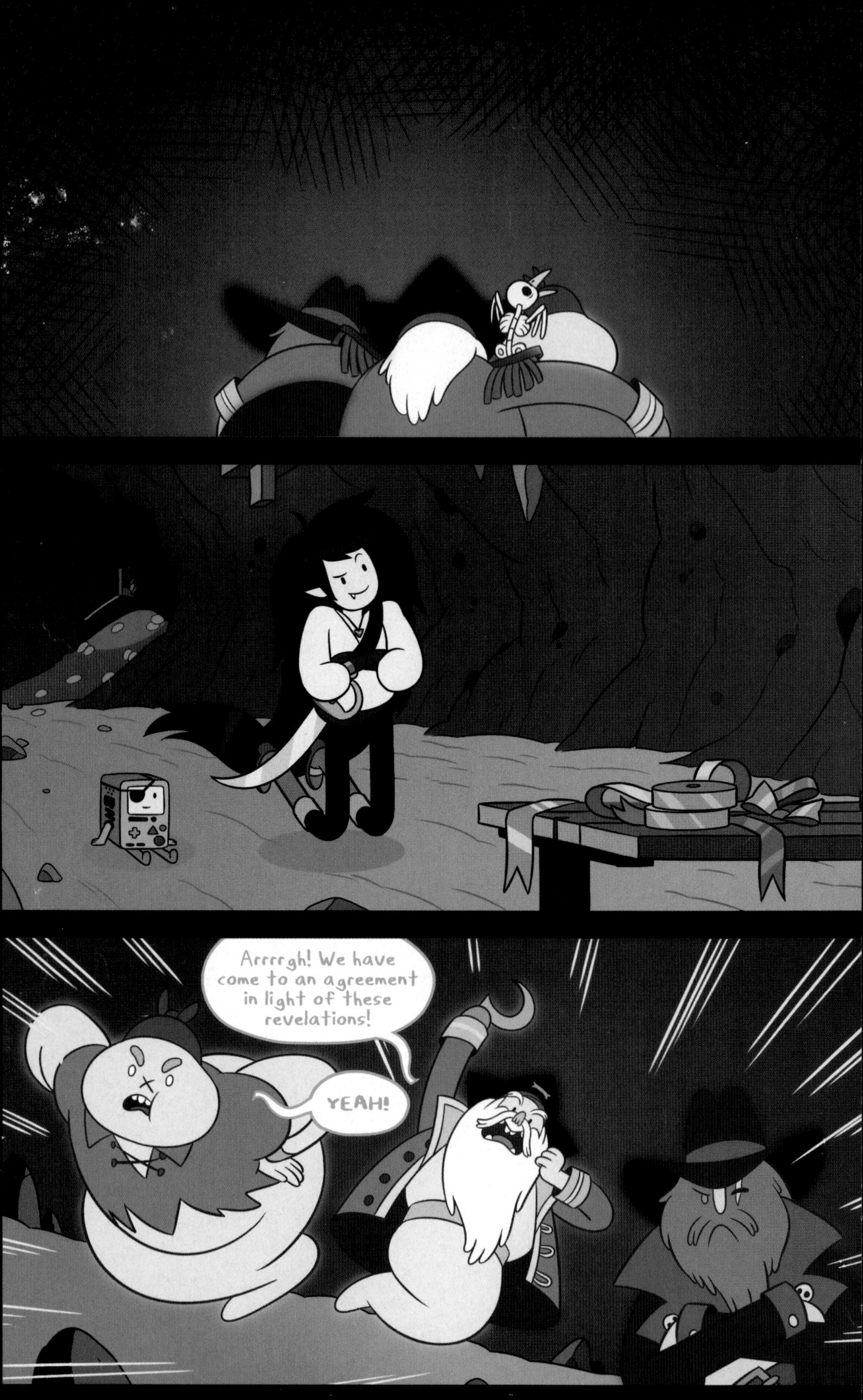
Arrrrgh! We have come to an agreement in light of these revelations!
YEAH!

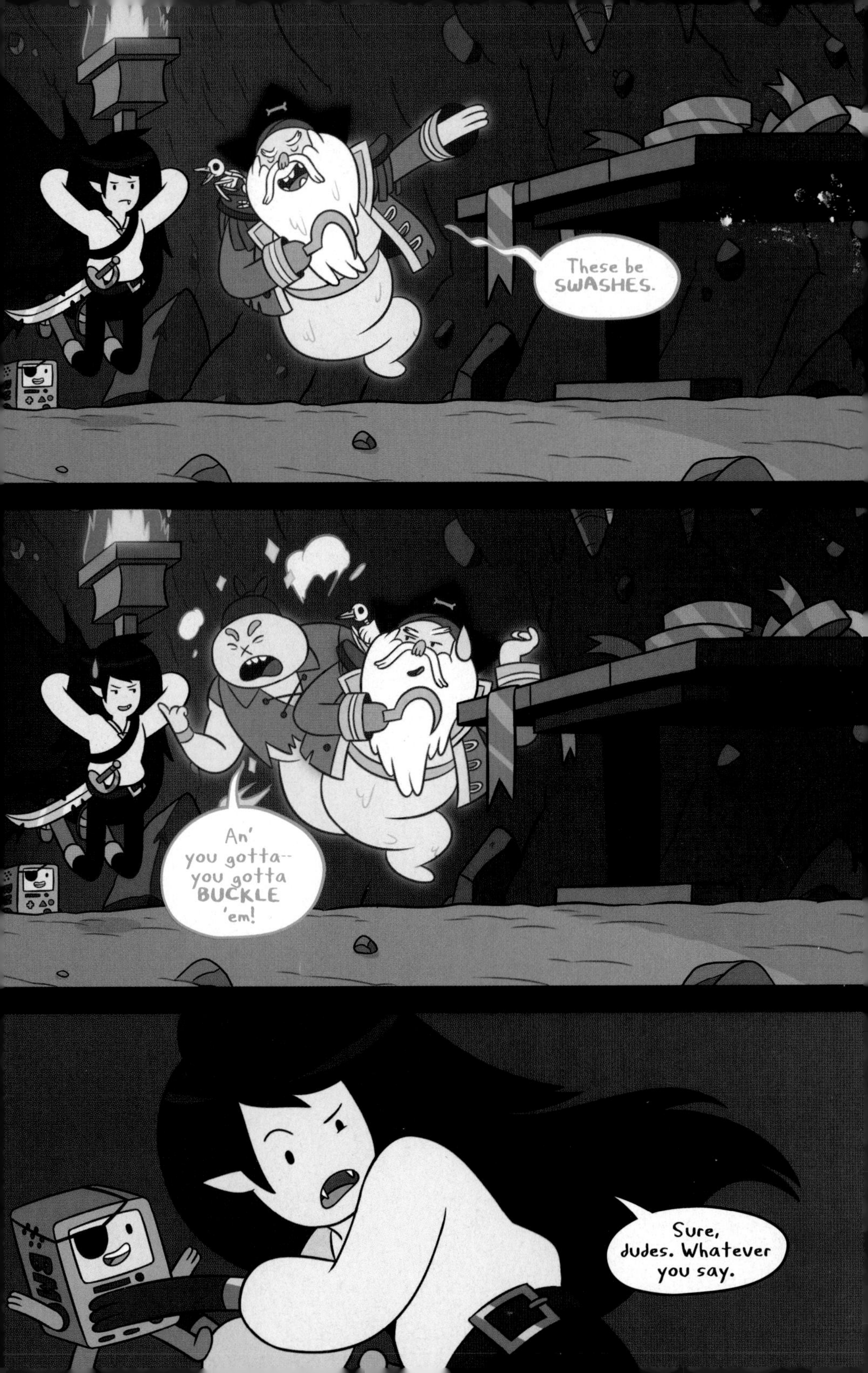
These be SWASHES.
An' you gotta-- you gotta BUCKLE 'em!
Sure, dudes. Whatever you say.

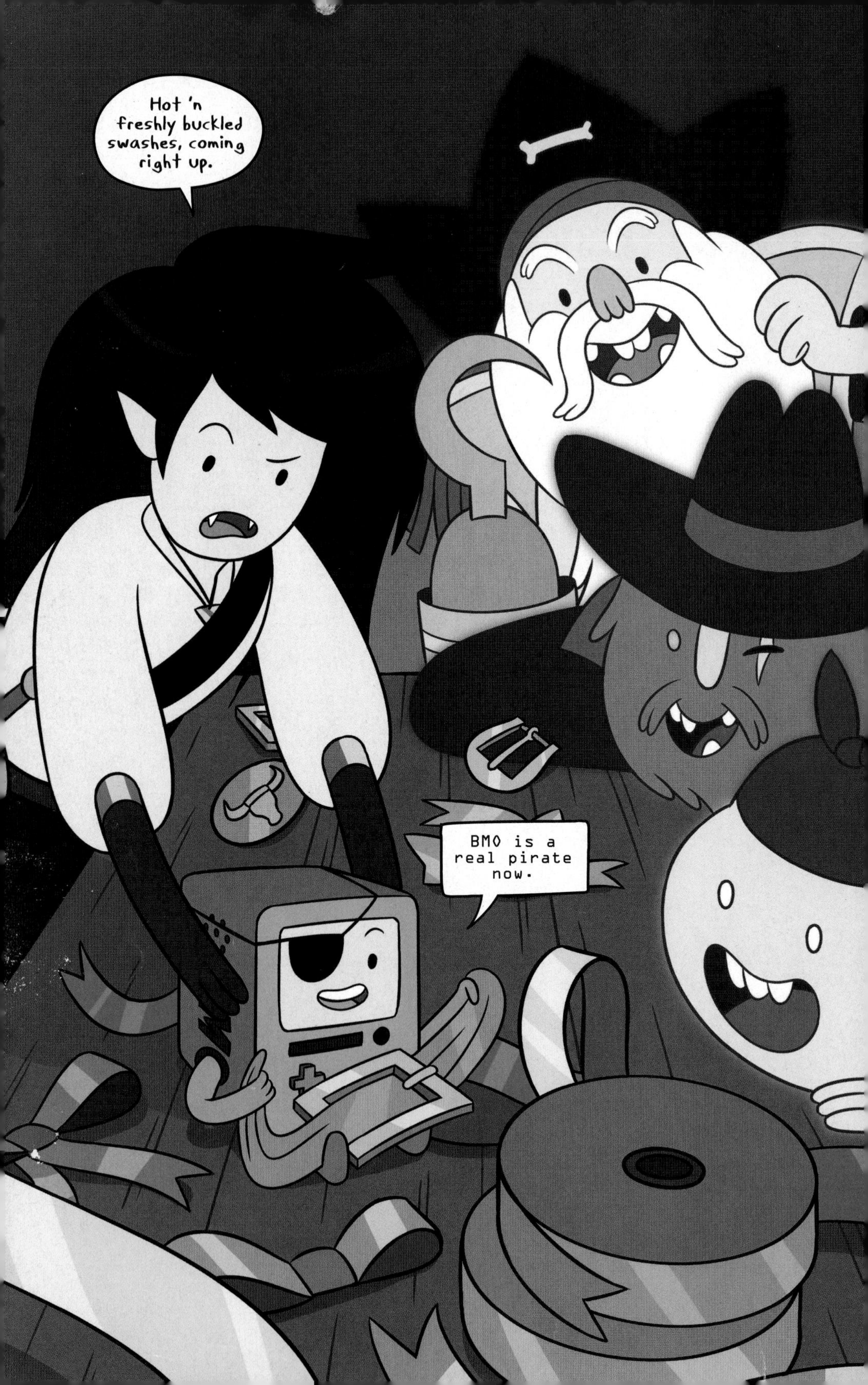
Hot 'n freshly buckled swashes, coming right up.
BMO is a real pirate now.

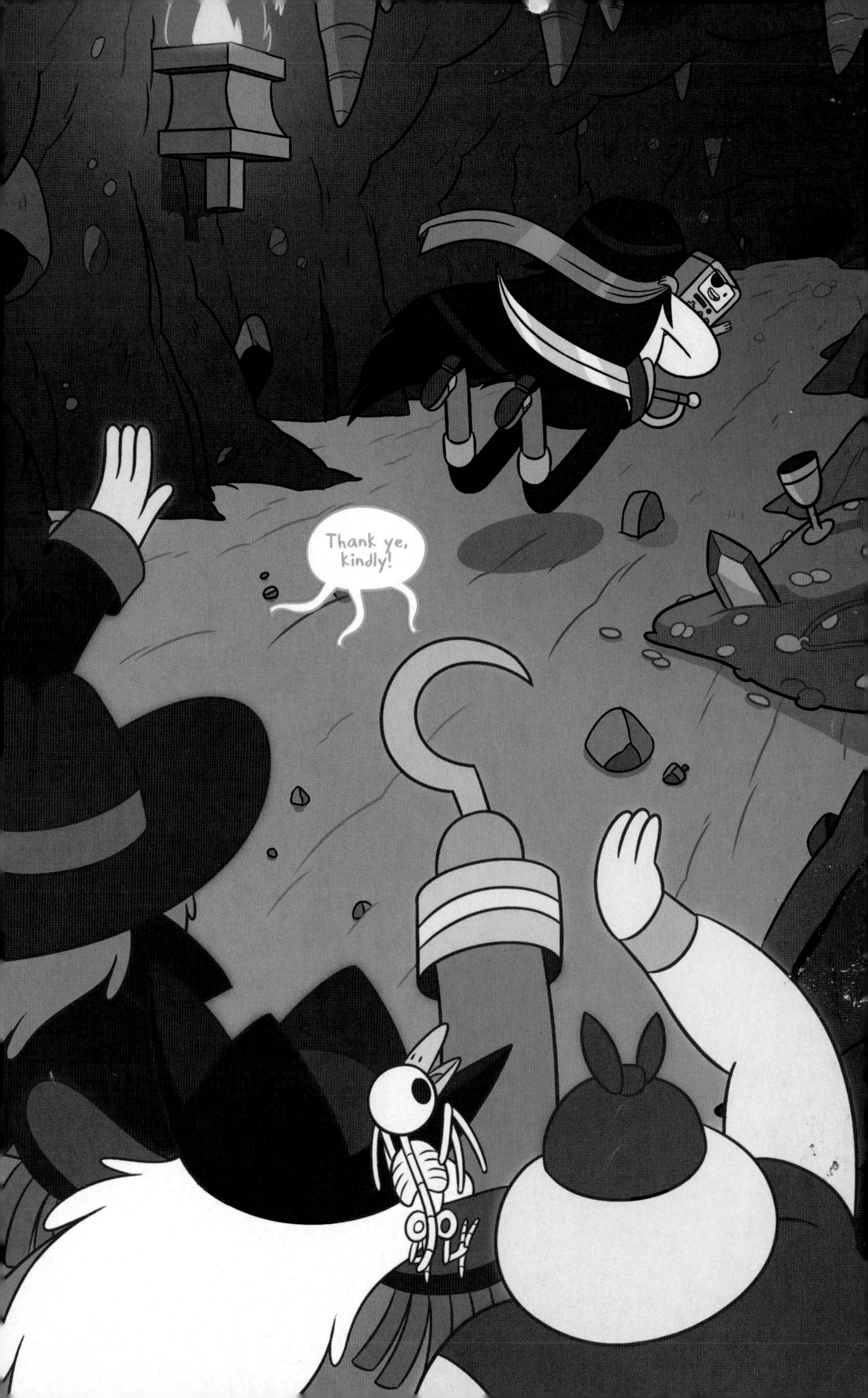
Thank ye, kindly!

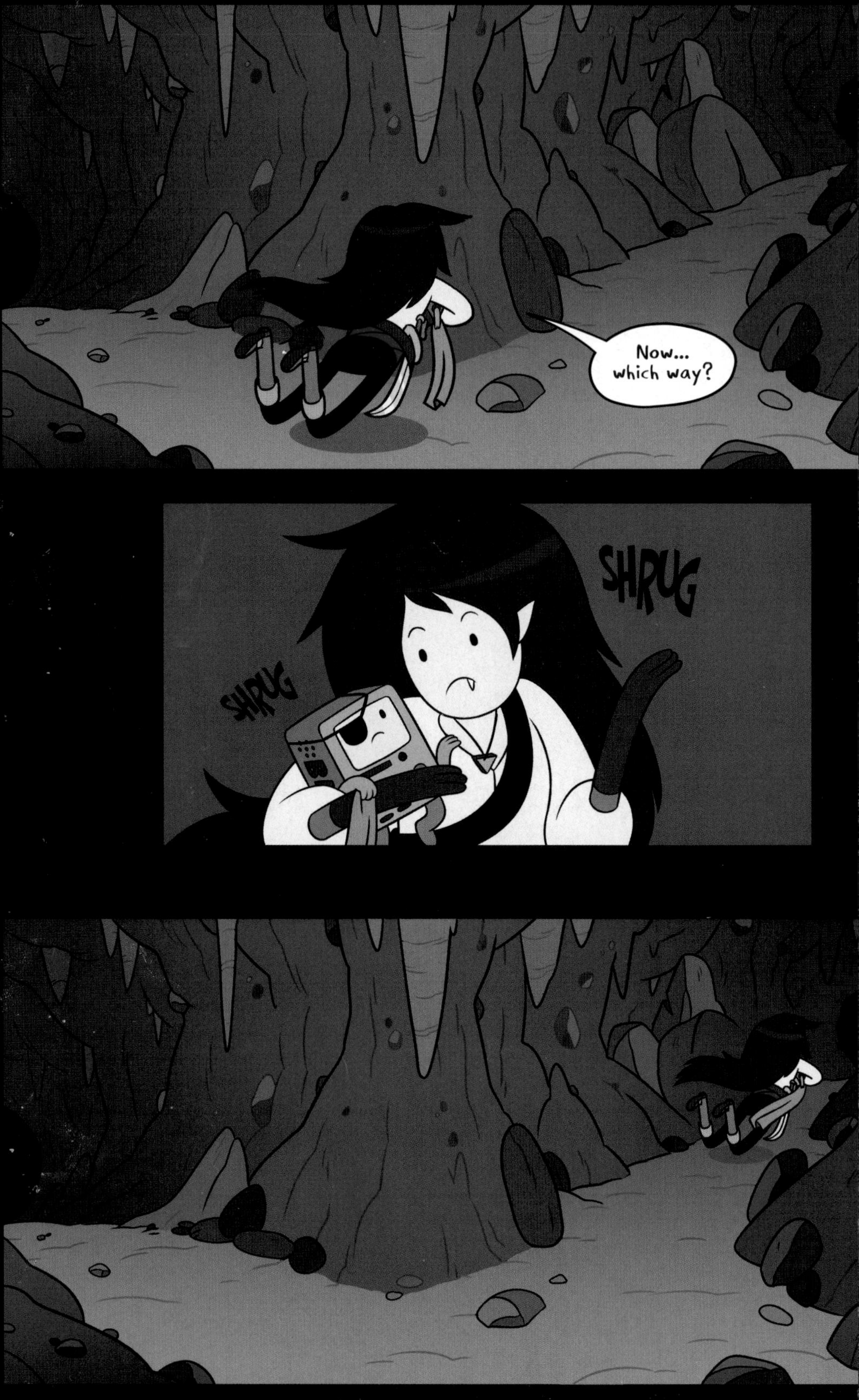
Now...
which way?
SHRUG
SHRUG

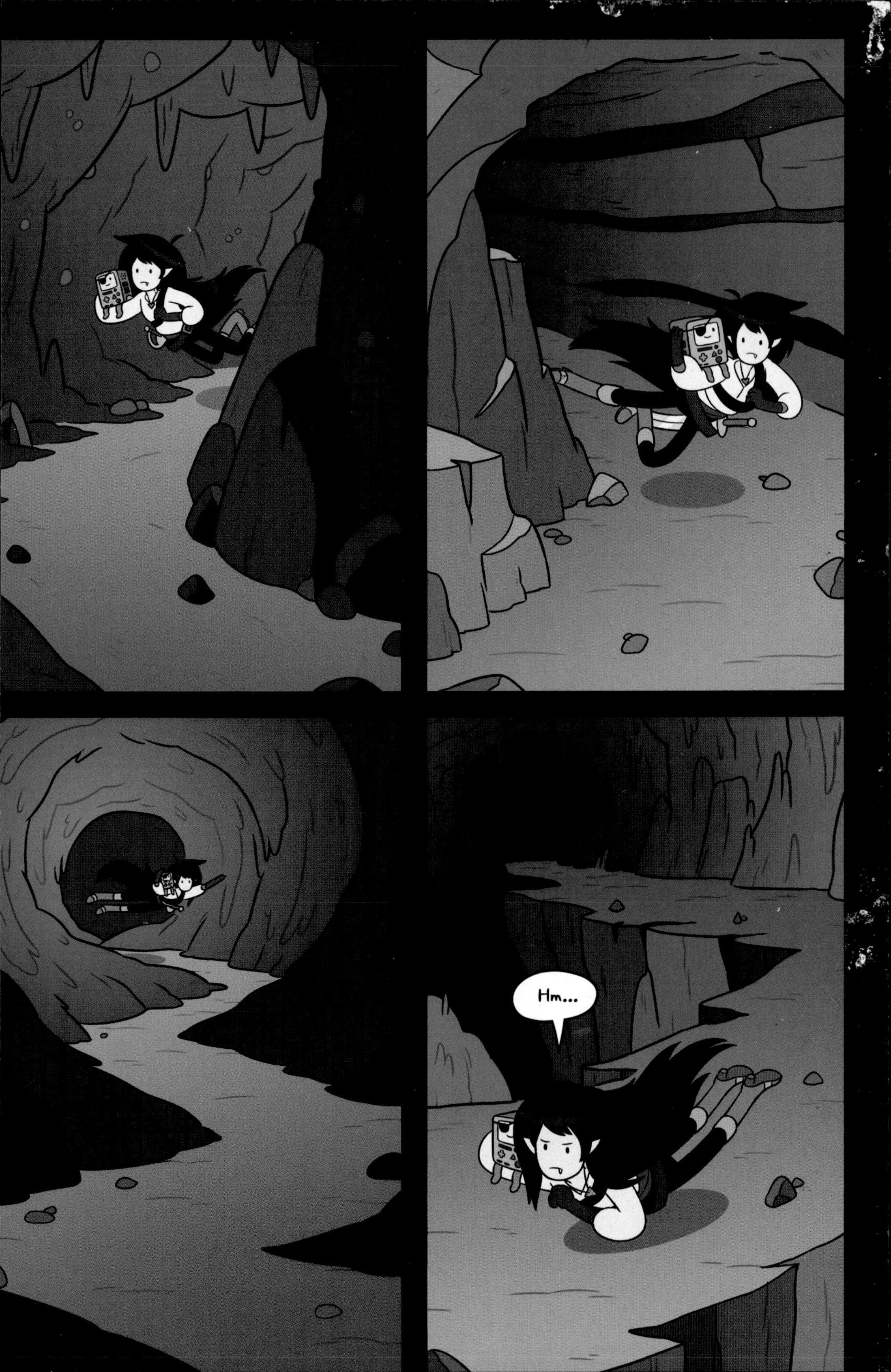
Hm...

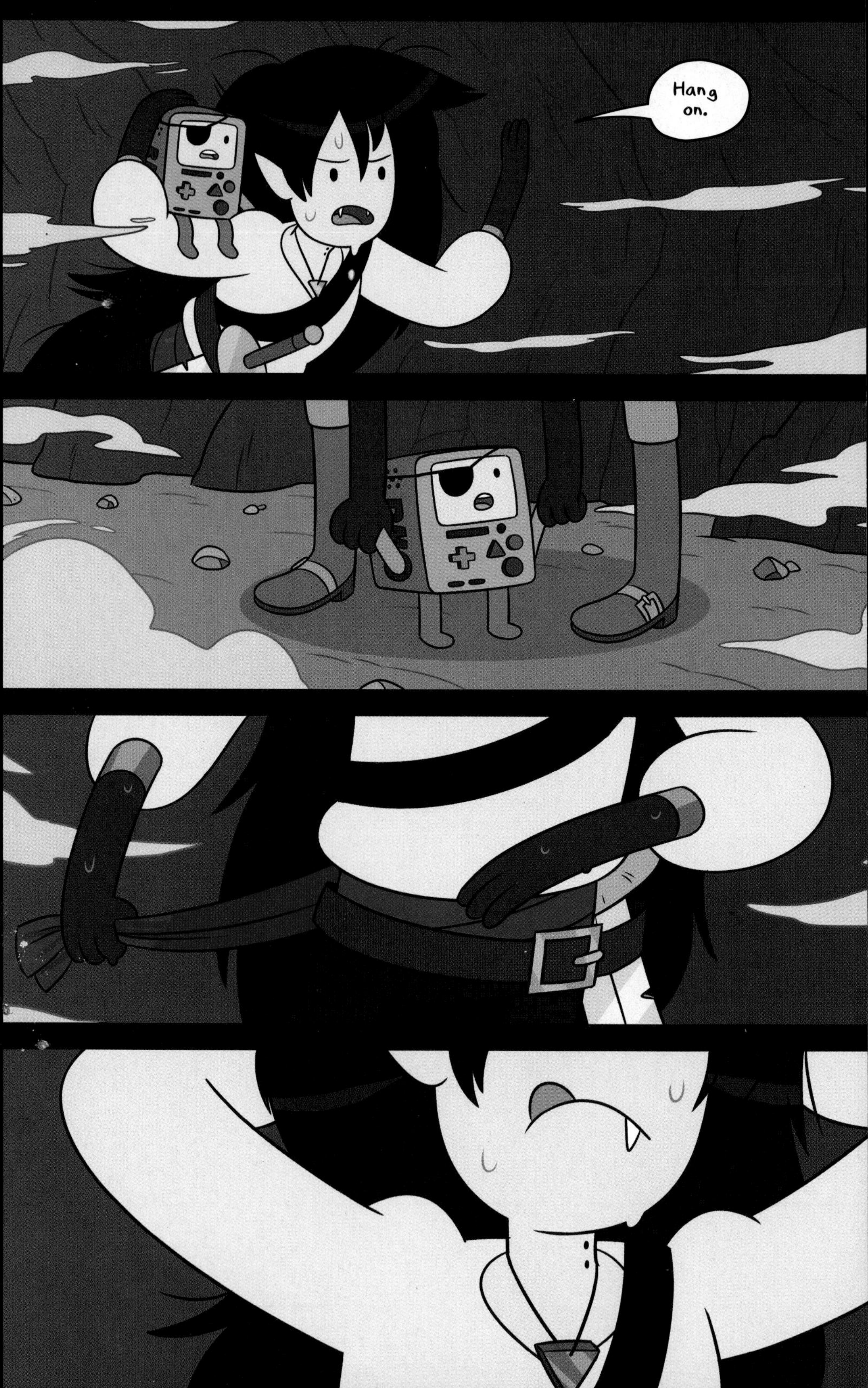
Hang on.

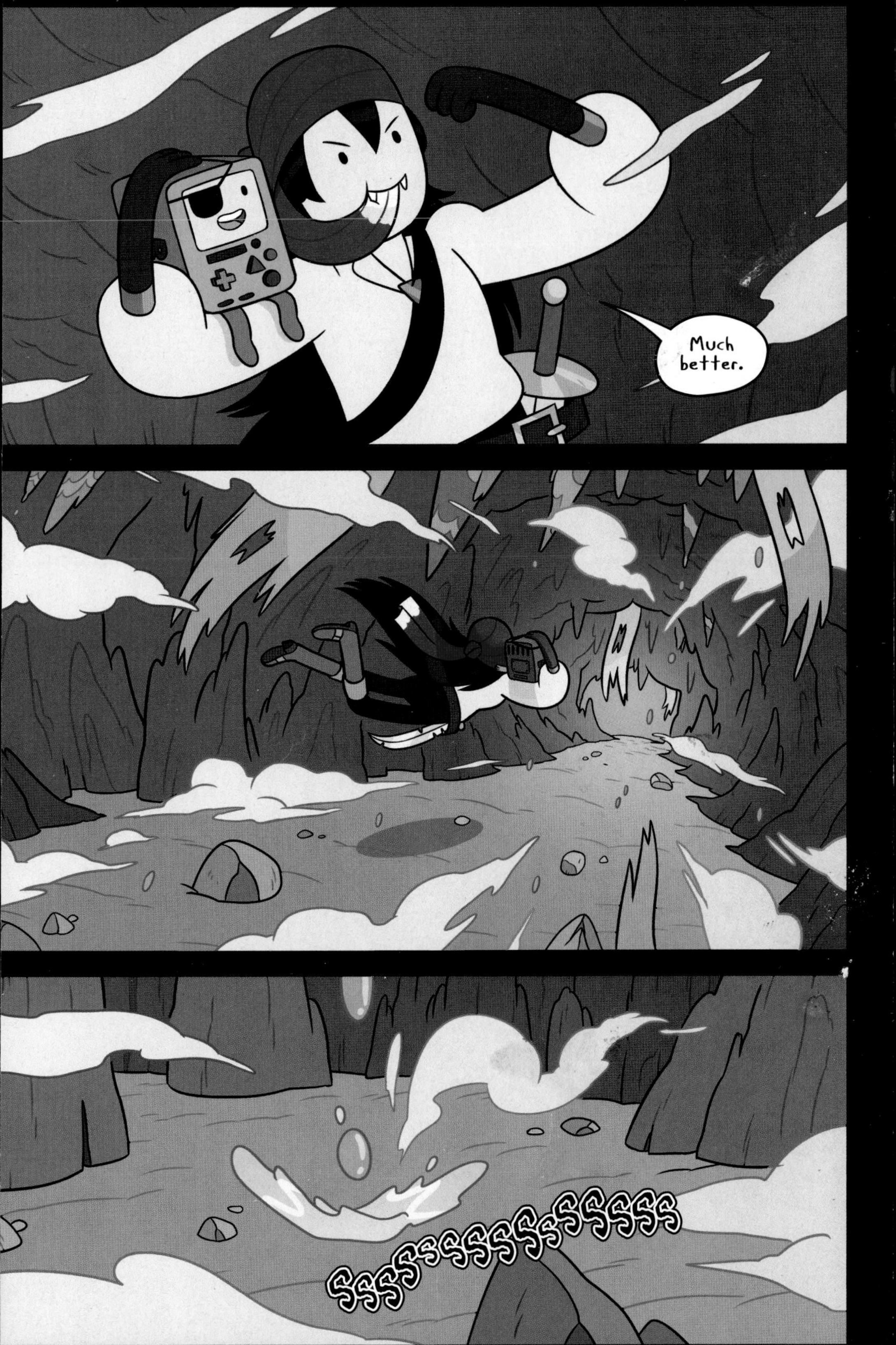
Much better.
SSSSSSSSSSSSSSSSSS

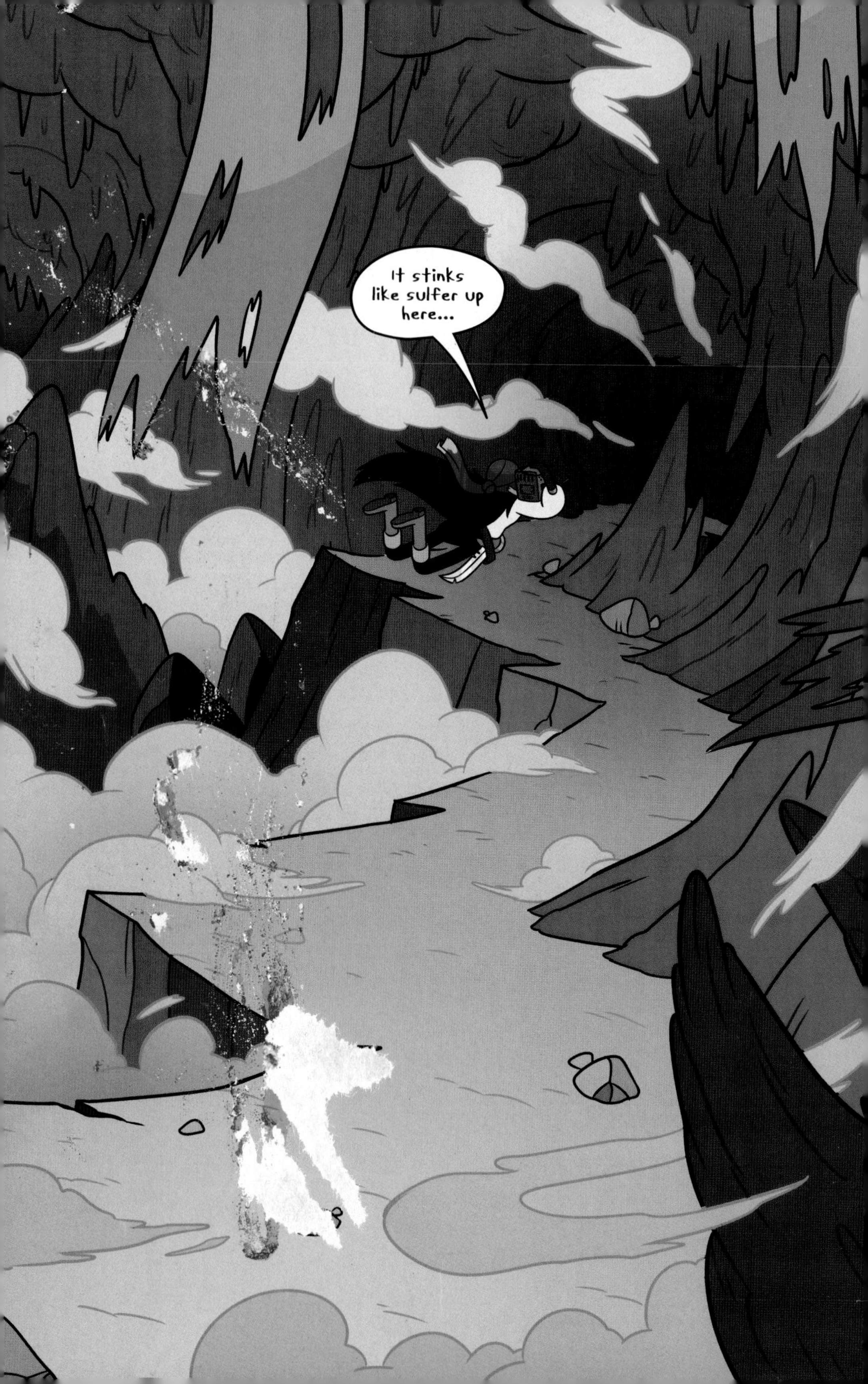
It stinks like sulfer up here...

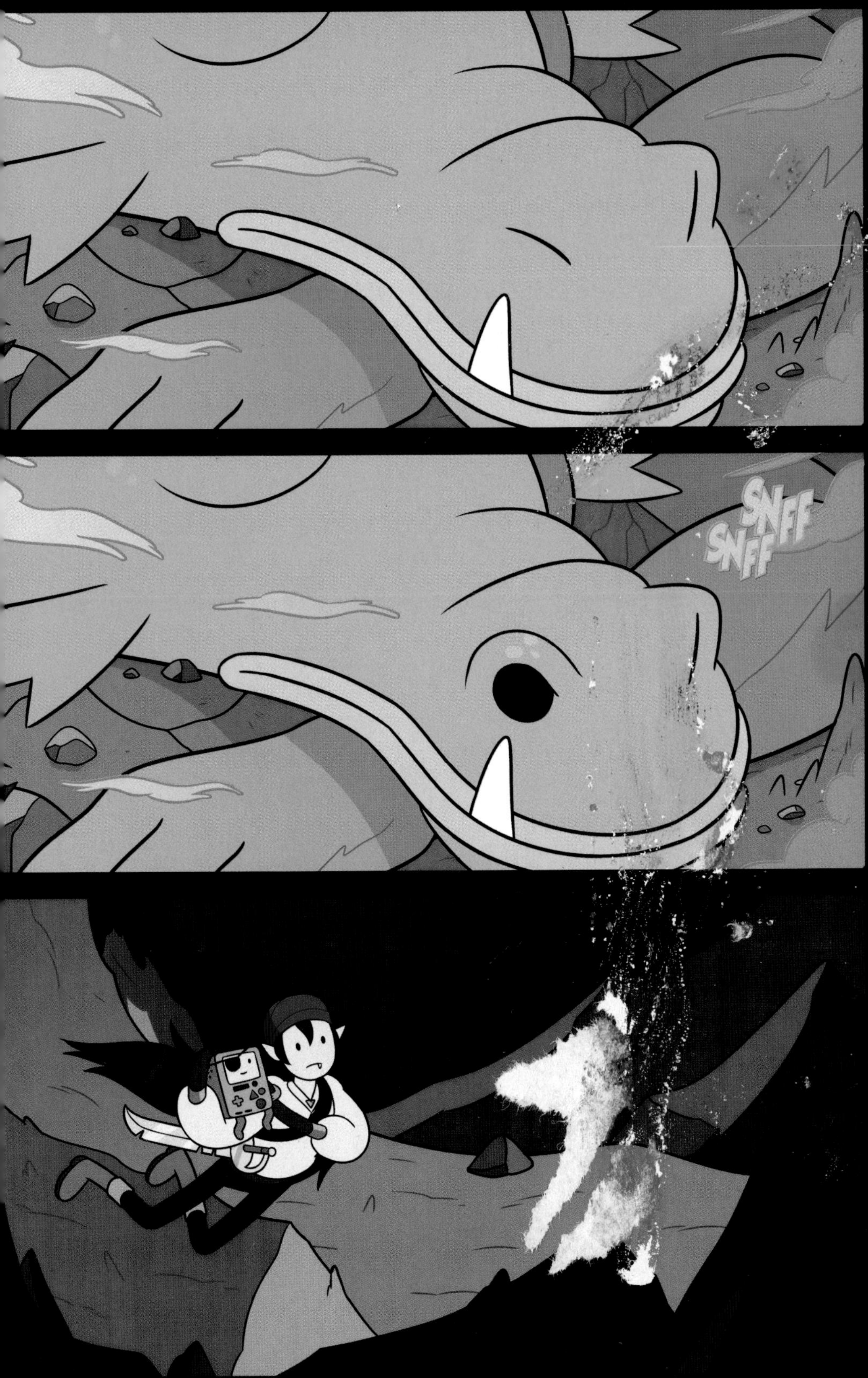
SNFF
SNFF

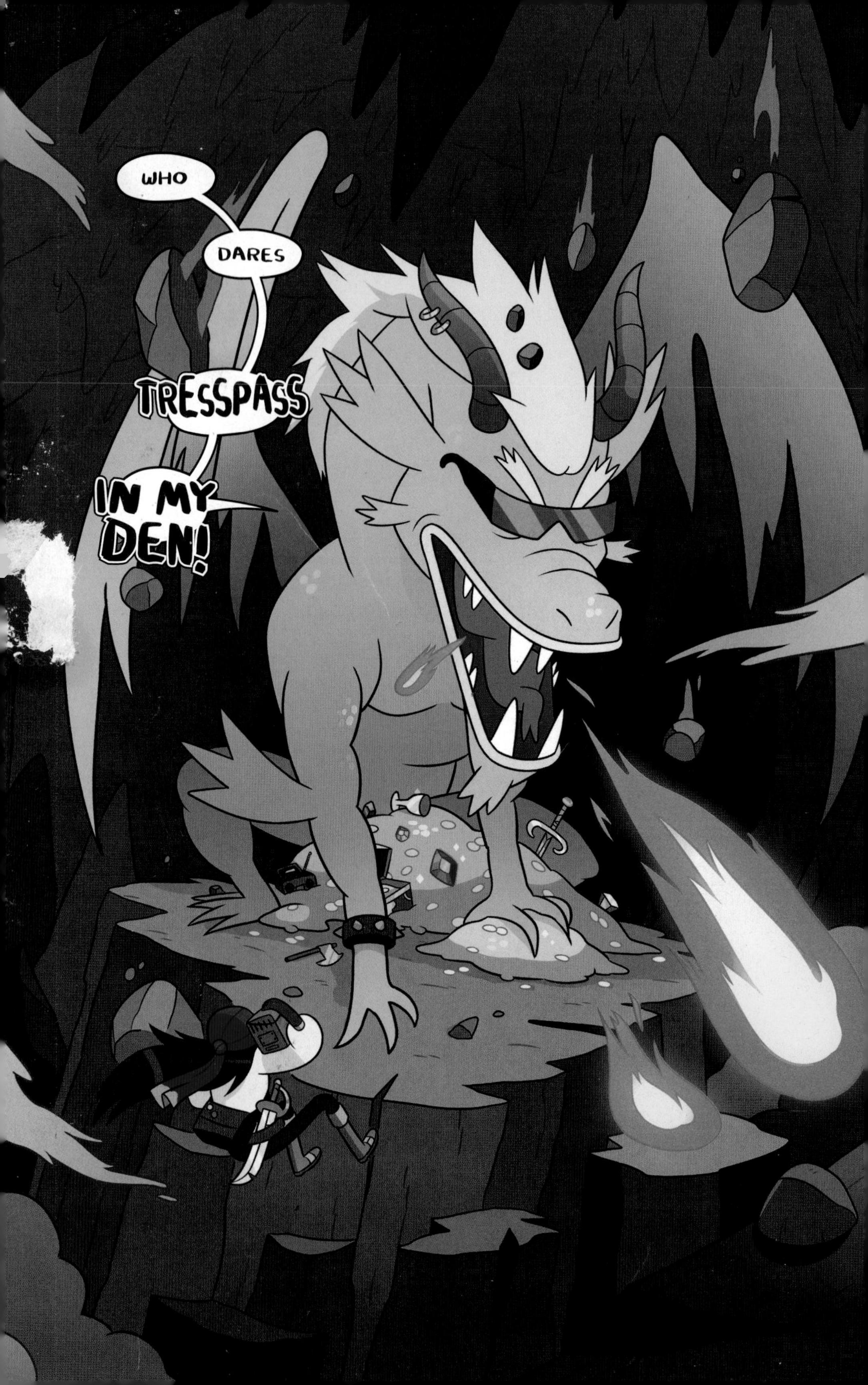
WHO
DARES
TRESSPASS
IN MY DEN!

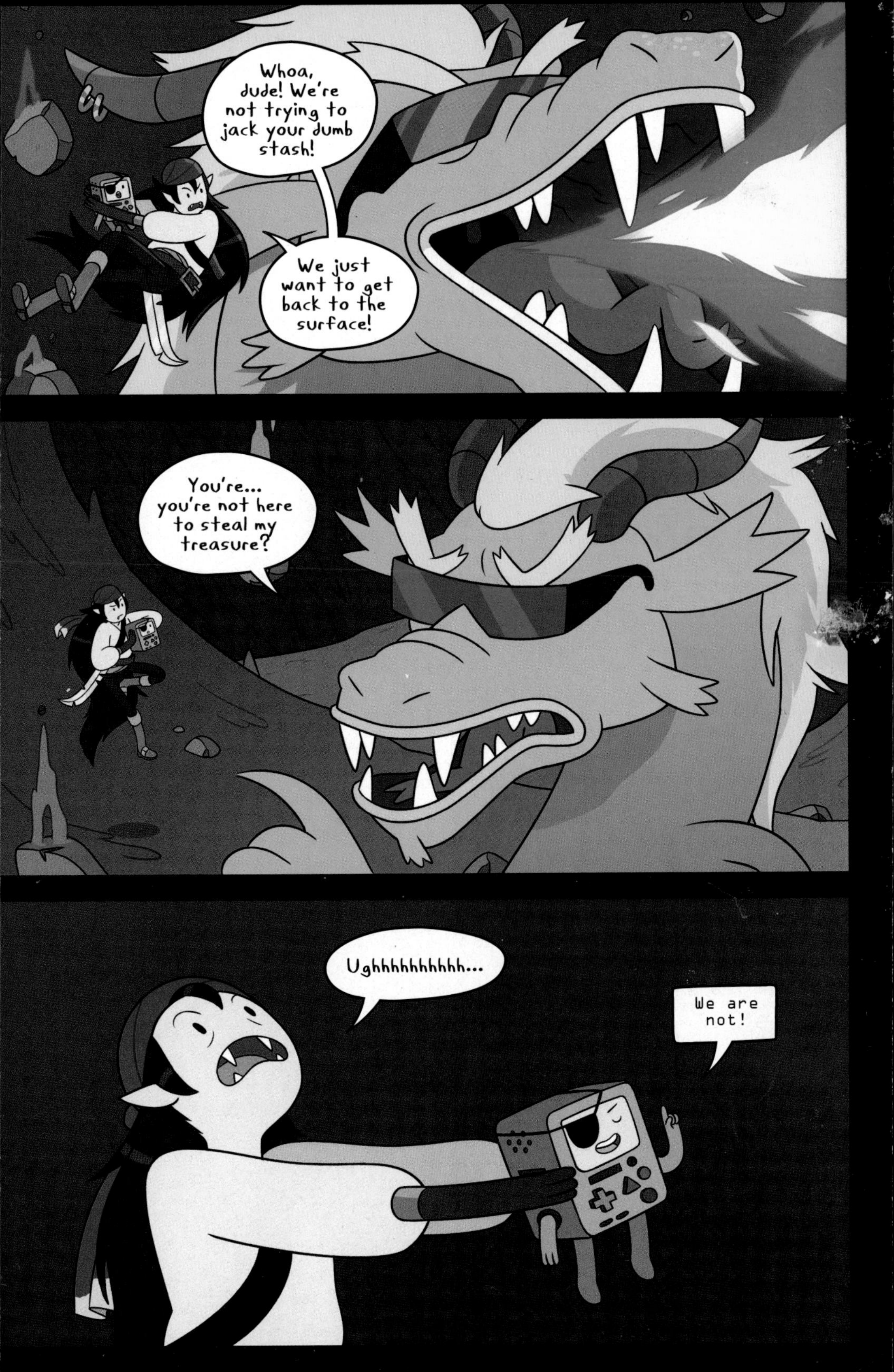
Whoa, dude! We're not trying to jack your dumb stash!
We just want to get back to the surface!
You're... you're not here to steal my treasure?
Ughhhhhhhhhh...
We are not!

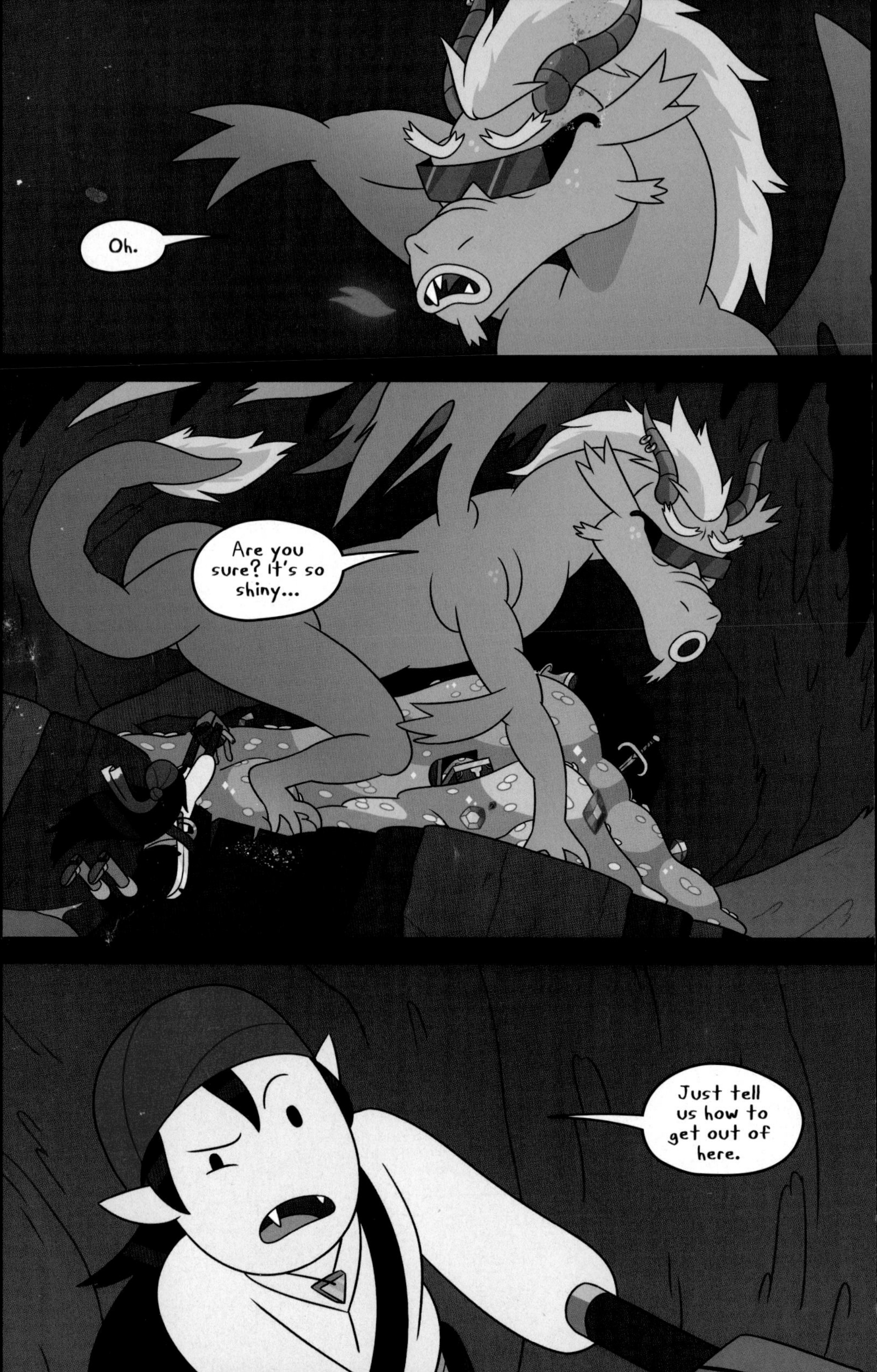
Oh.
Are you sure? It's so shiny...
Just tell us how to get out of here.

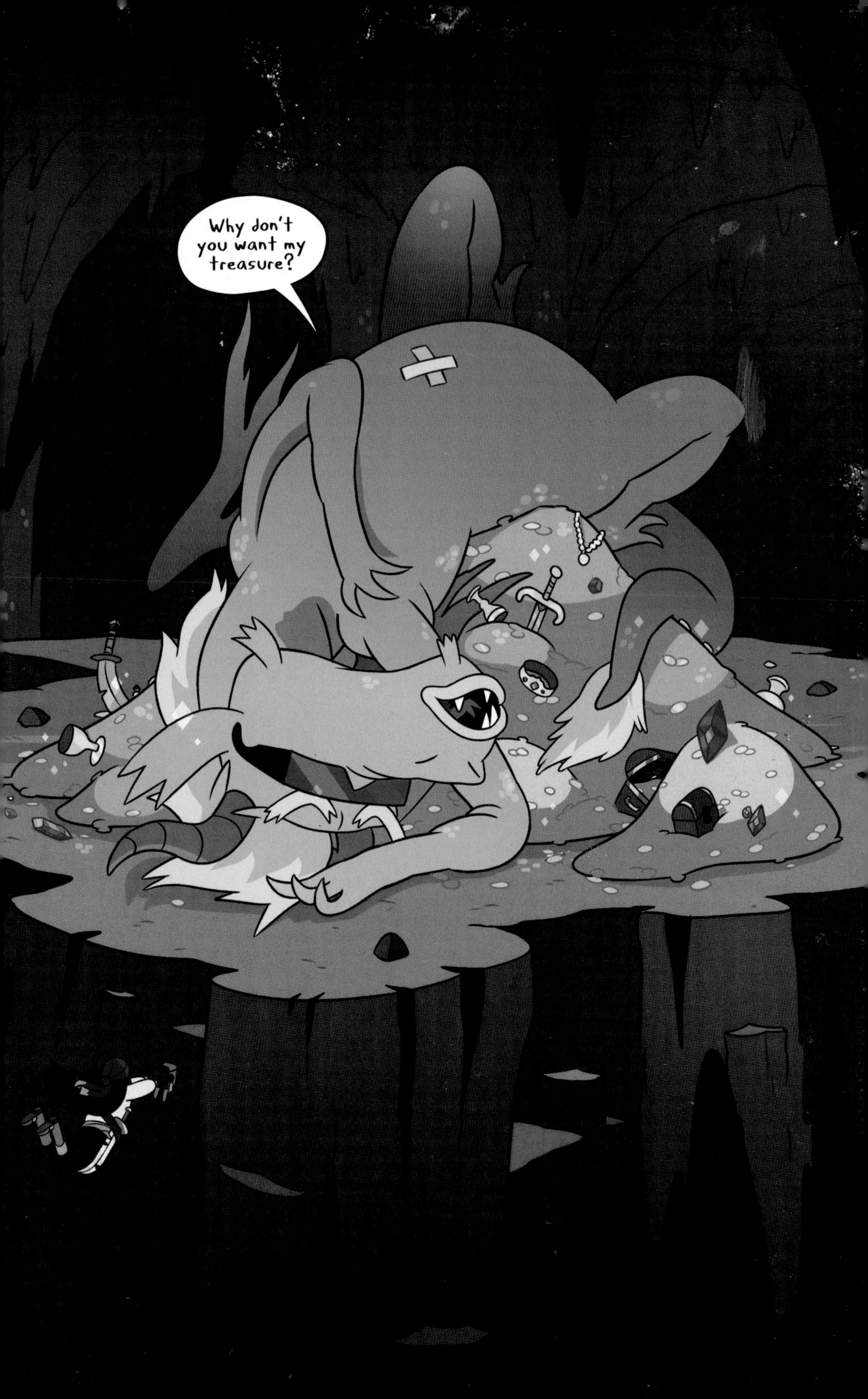
Why don't you want my treasure?

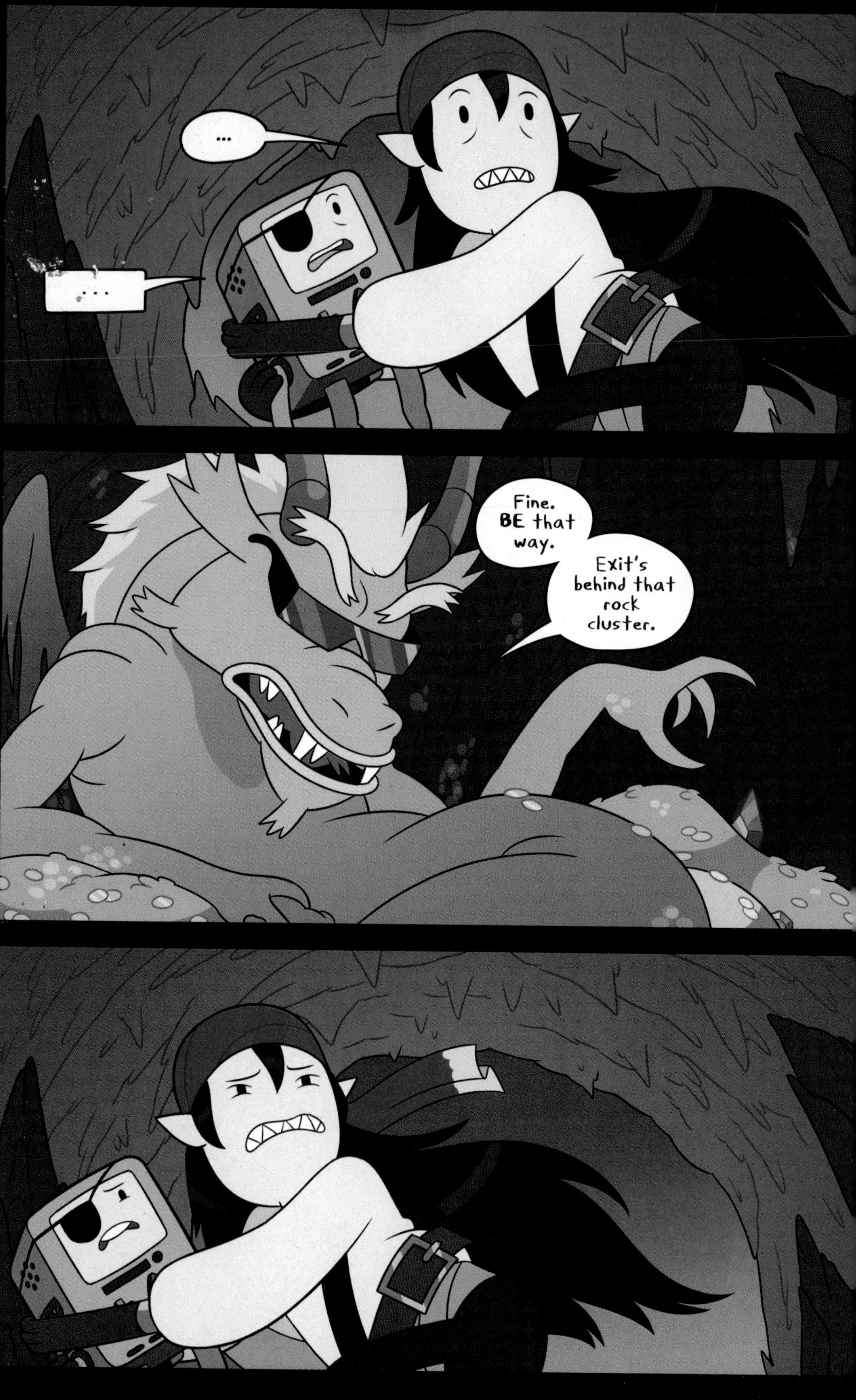
...
...
Fine. BE that way.
Exit's behind that rock cluster.

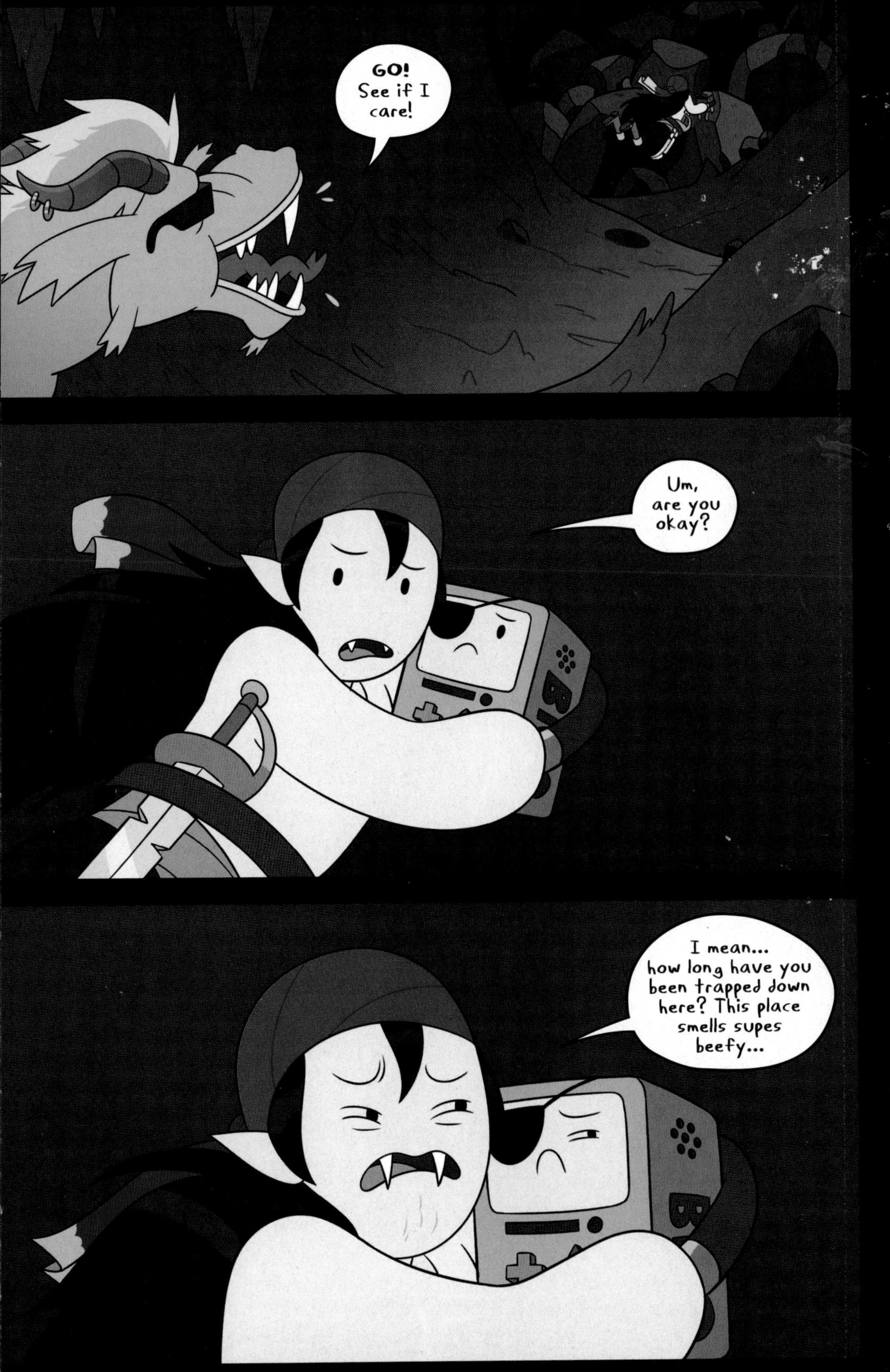
GO! See if I care!
Um, are you okay?
I mean... how long have you been trapped down here? This place smells supes beefy...

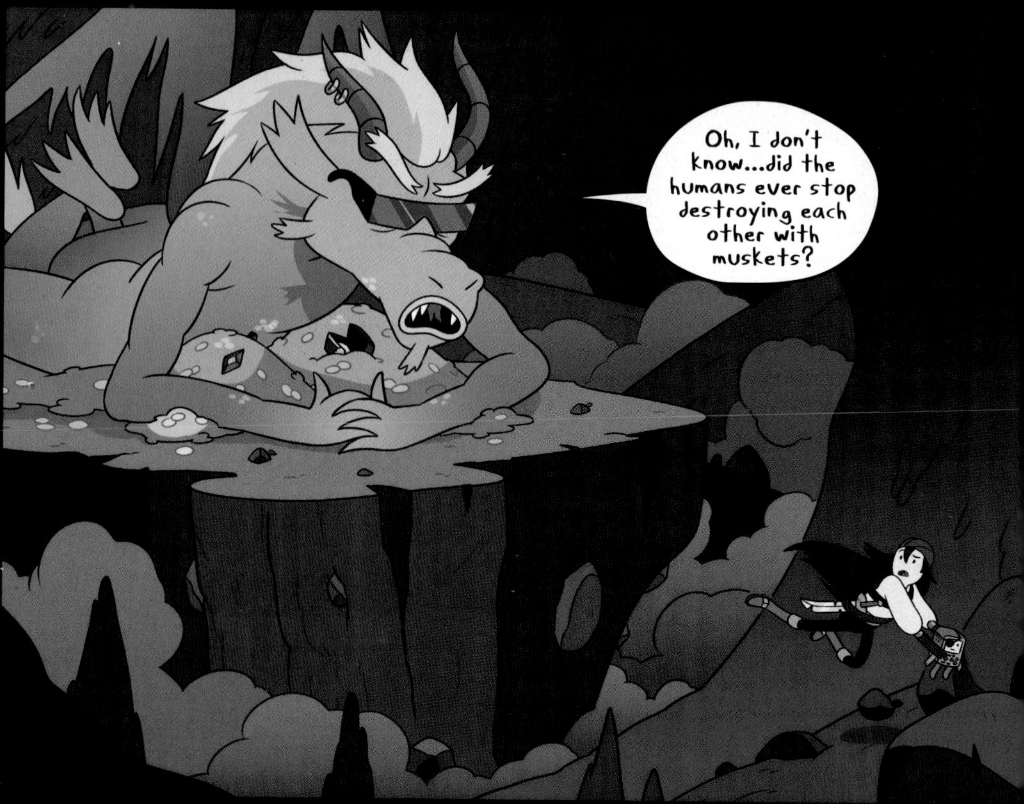
Oh, I don't know...did the humans ever stop destroying each other with muskets?

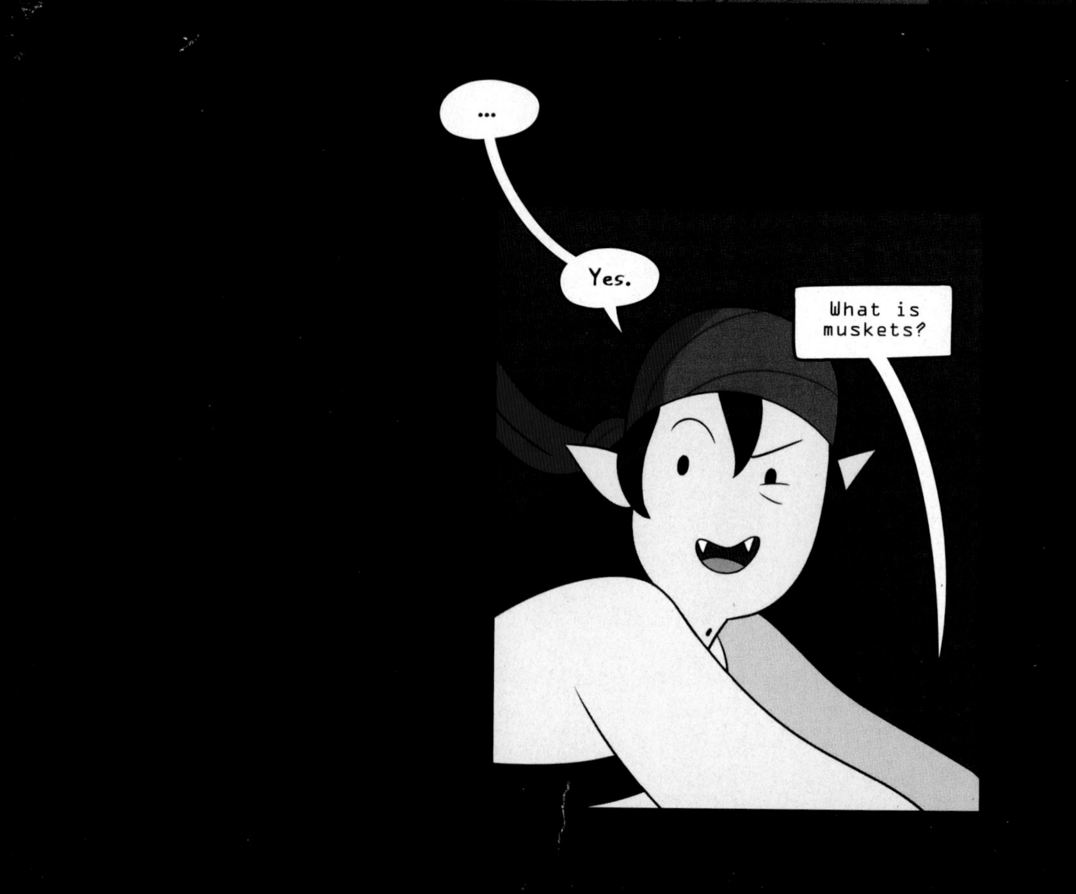
...
Yes.
What is muskets?

DEEP
BREATH

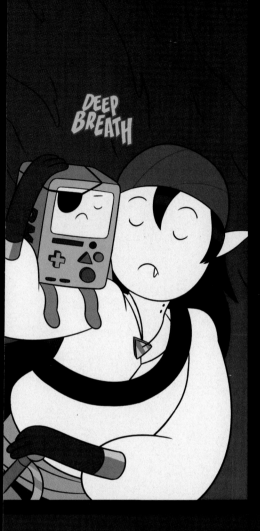

Look...

Do you
wanna come
with us?

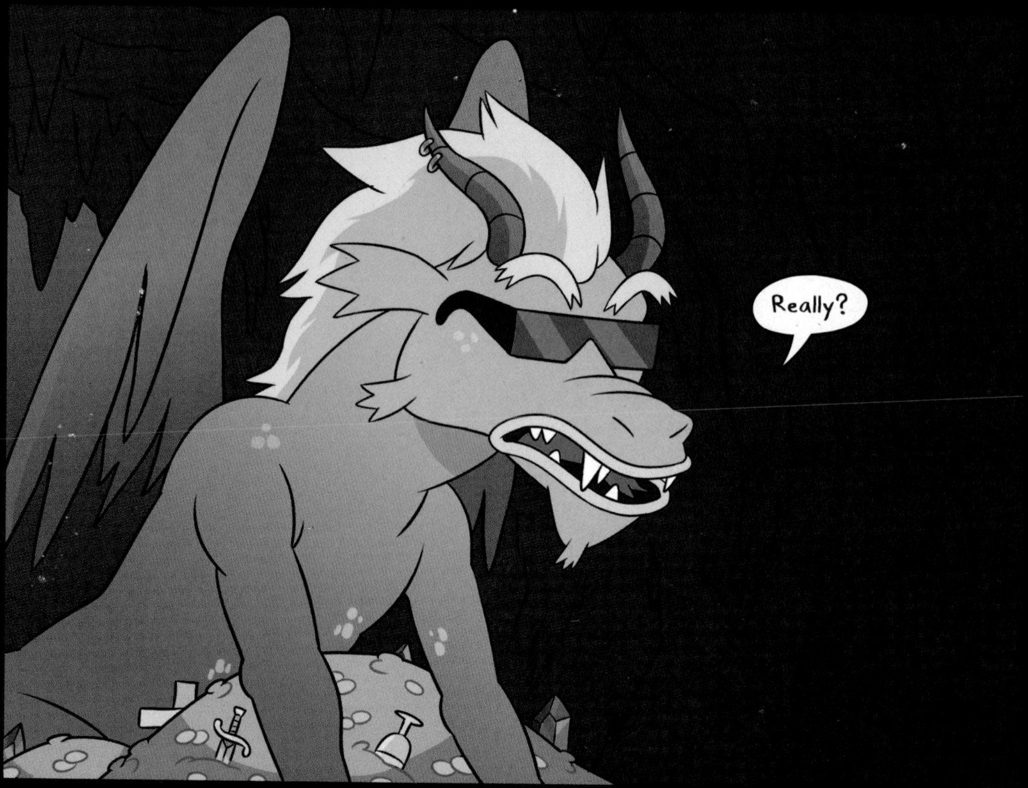
Really?

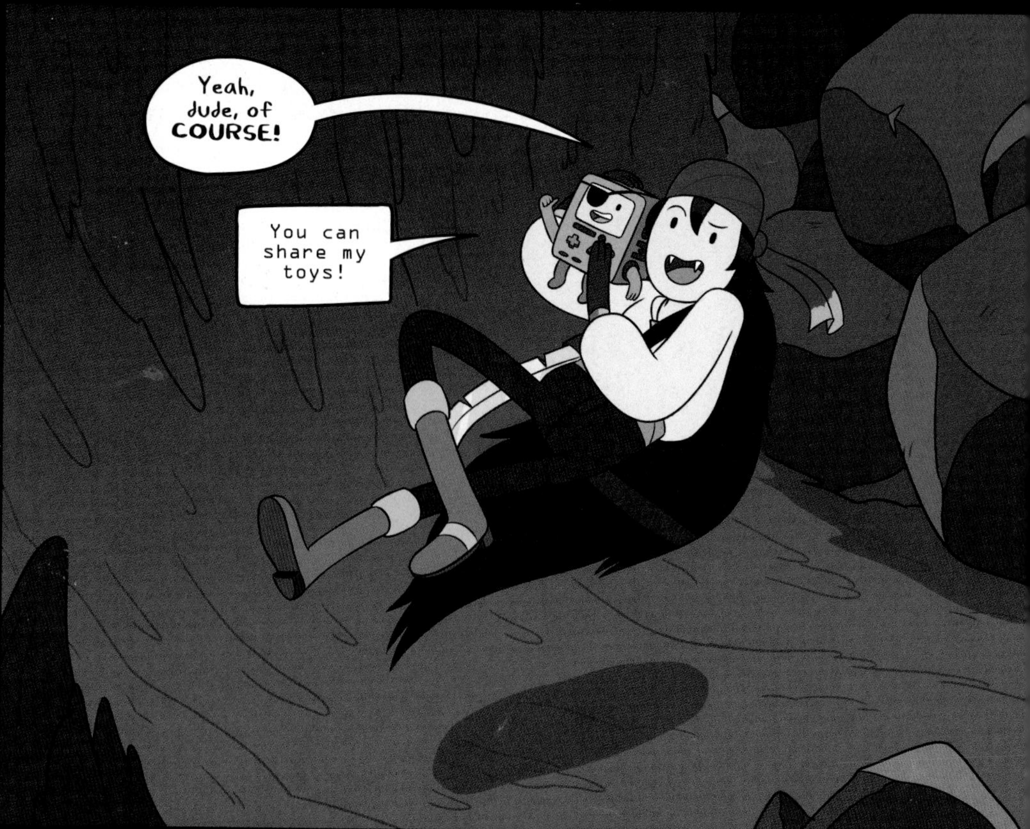
Yeah, dude, of COURSE!
You can share my toys!

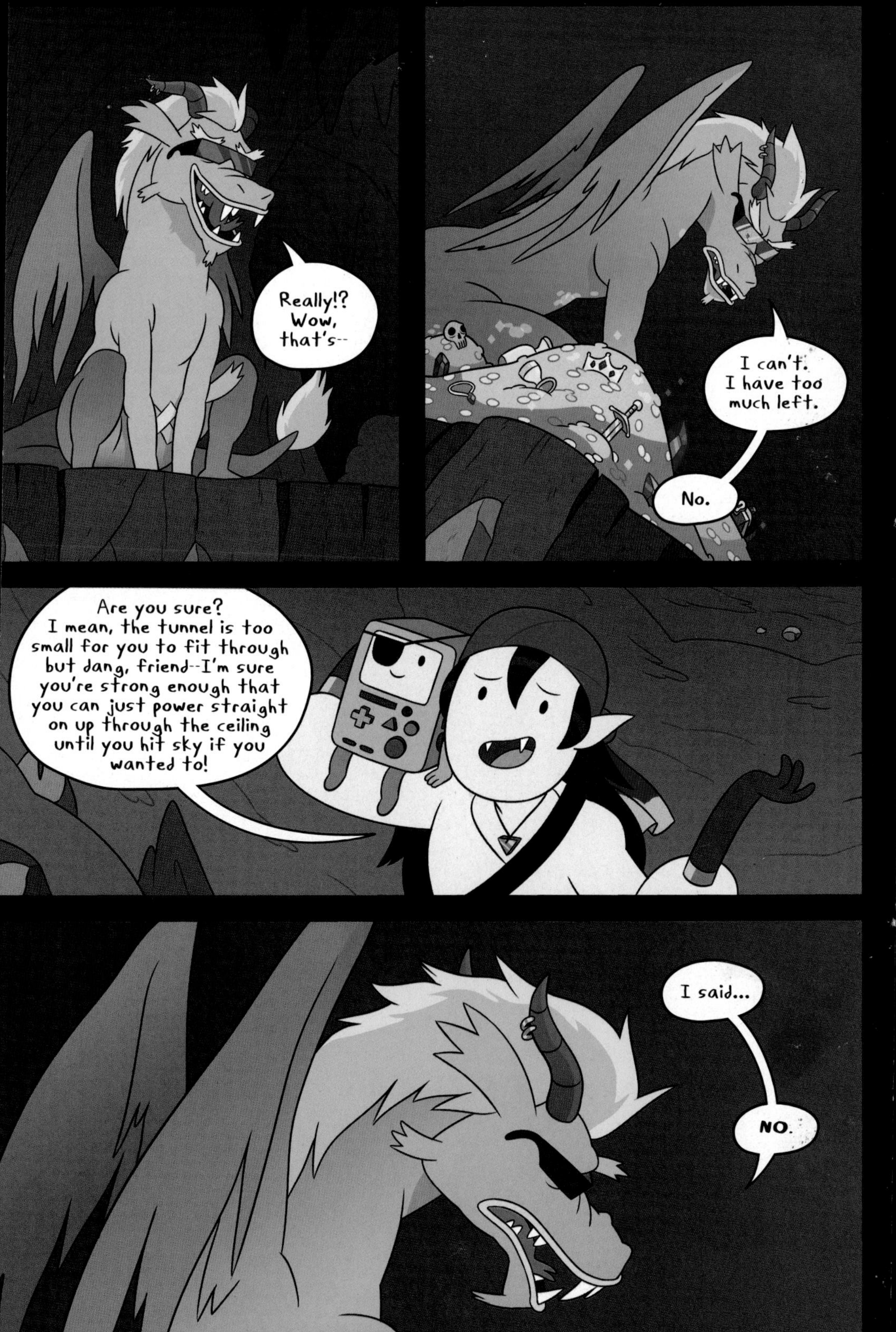
Really!? Wow, that's--
I can't. I have too much left.
No.
Are you sure? I mean, the tunnel is too small for you to fit through but dang, friend--I'm sure you're strong enough that you can just power straight on up through the ceiling until you hit sky if you wanted to!
I said...
NO.

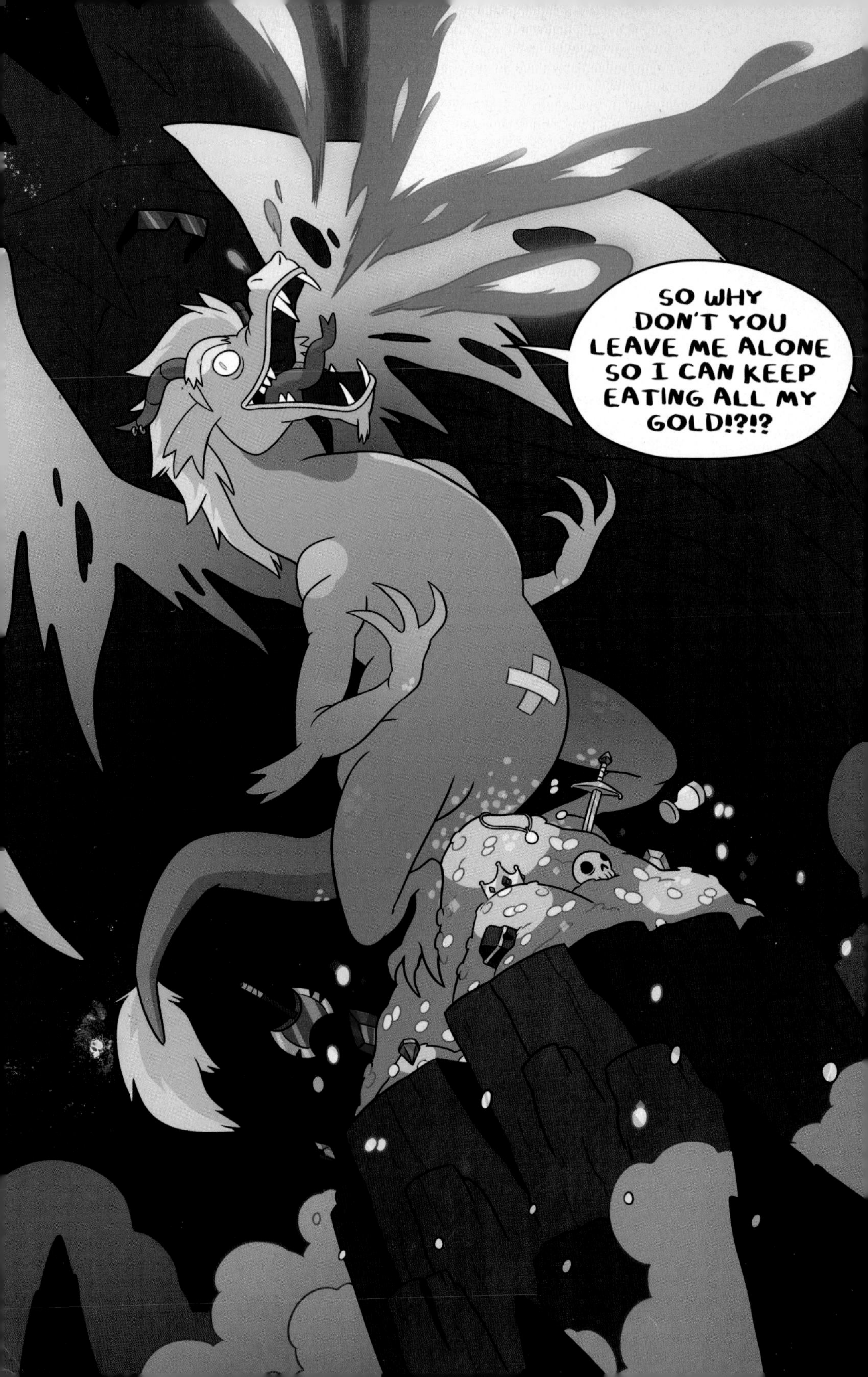
SO WHY DON'T YOU LEAVE ME ALONE SO I CAN KEEP EATING ALL MY GOLD!?!?

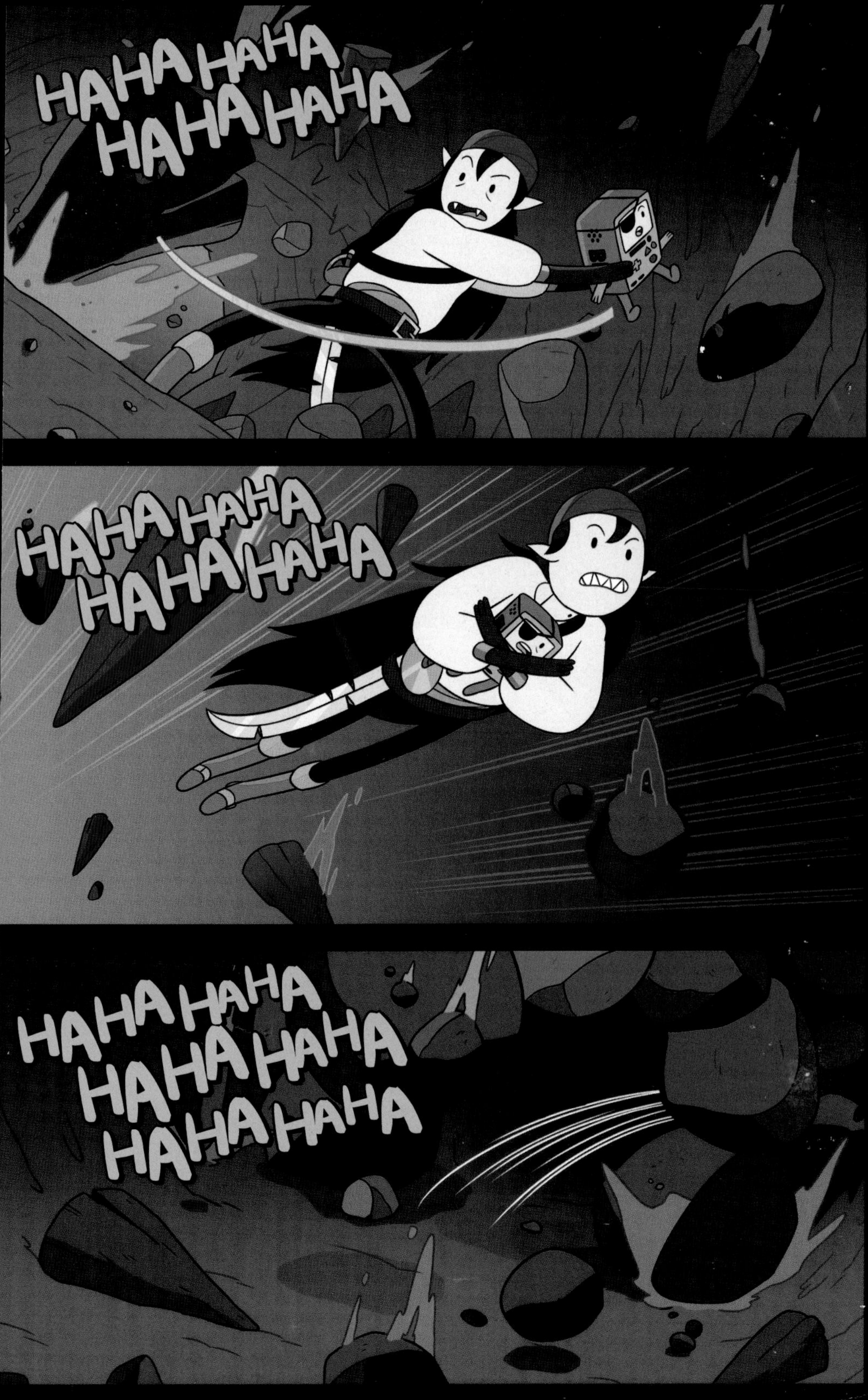

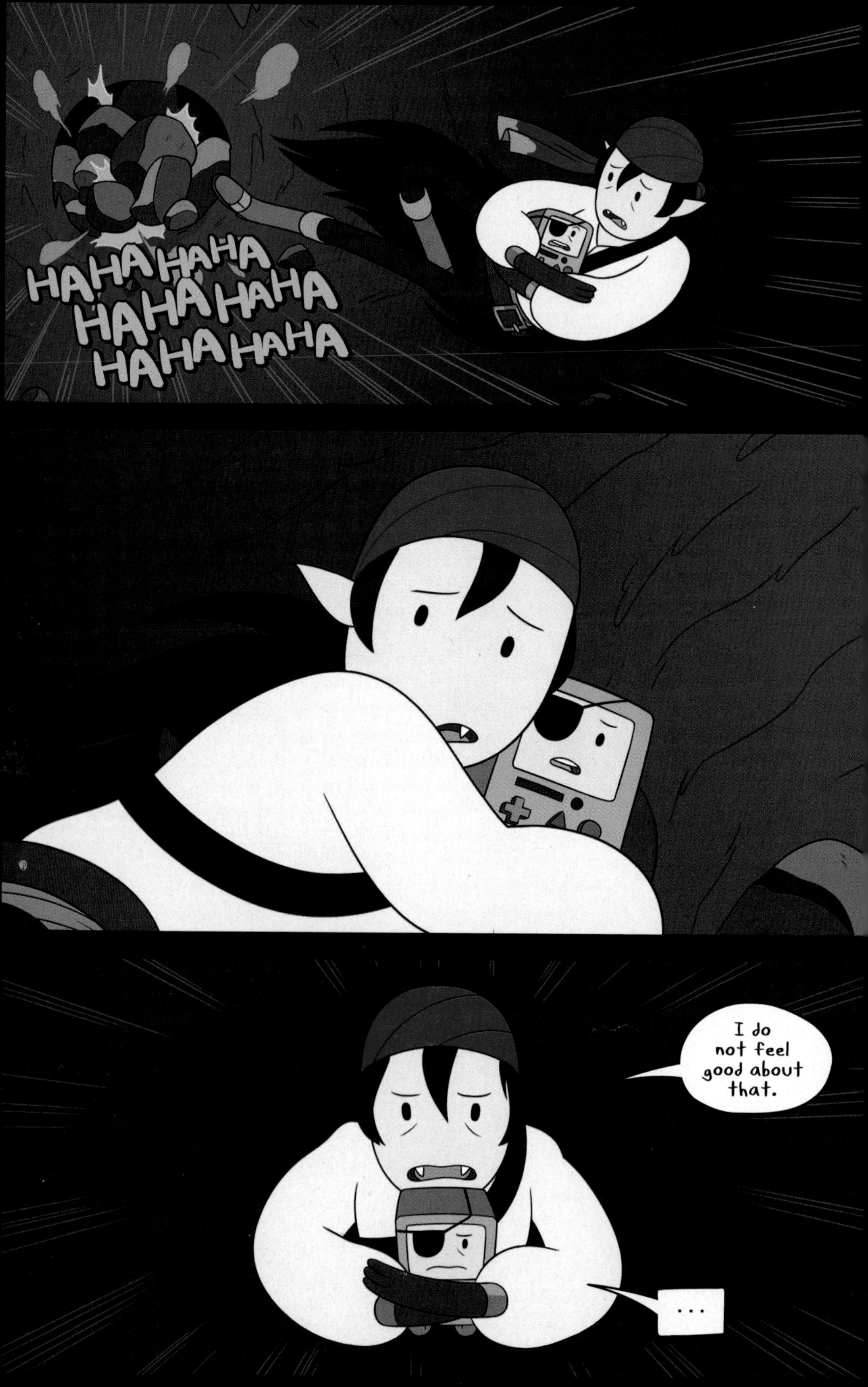
HAHA HAHA
HAHA HAHA
HAHA HAHA
I do not feel good about that.
...

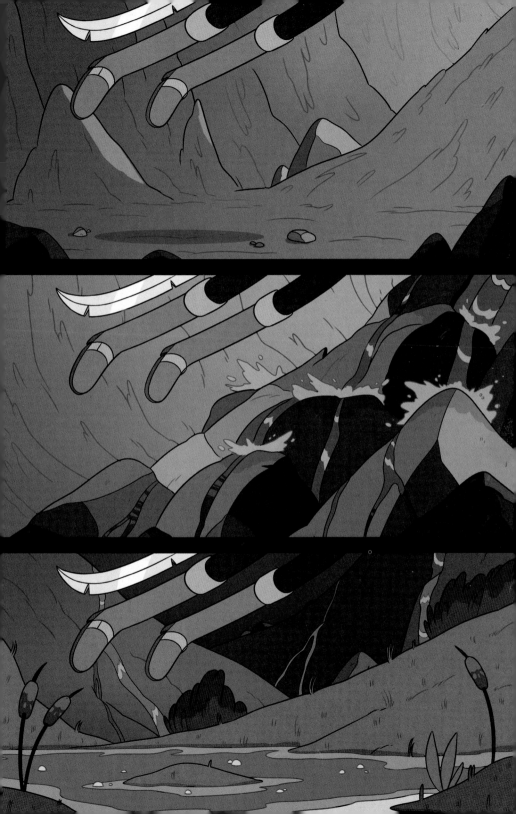

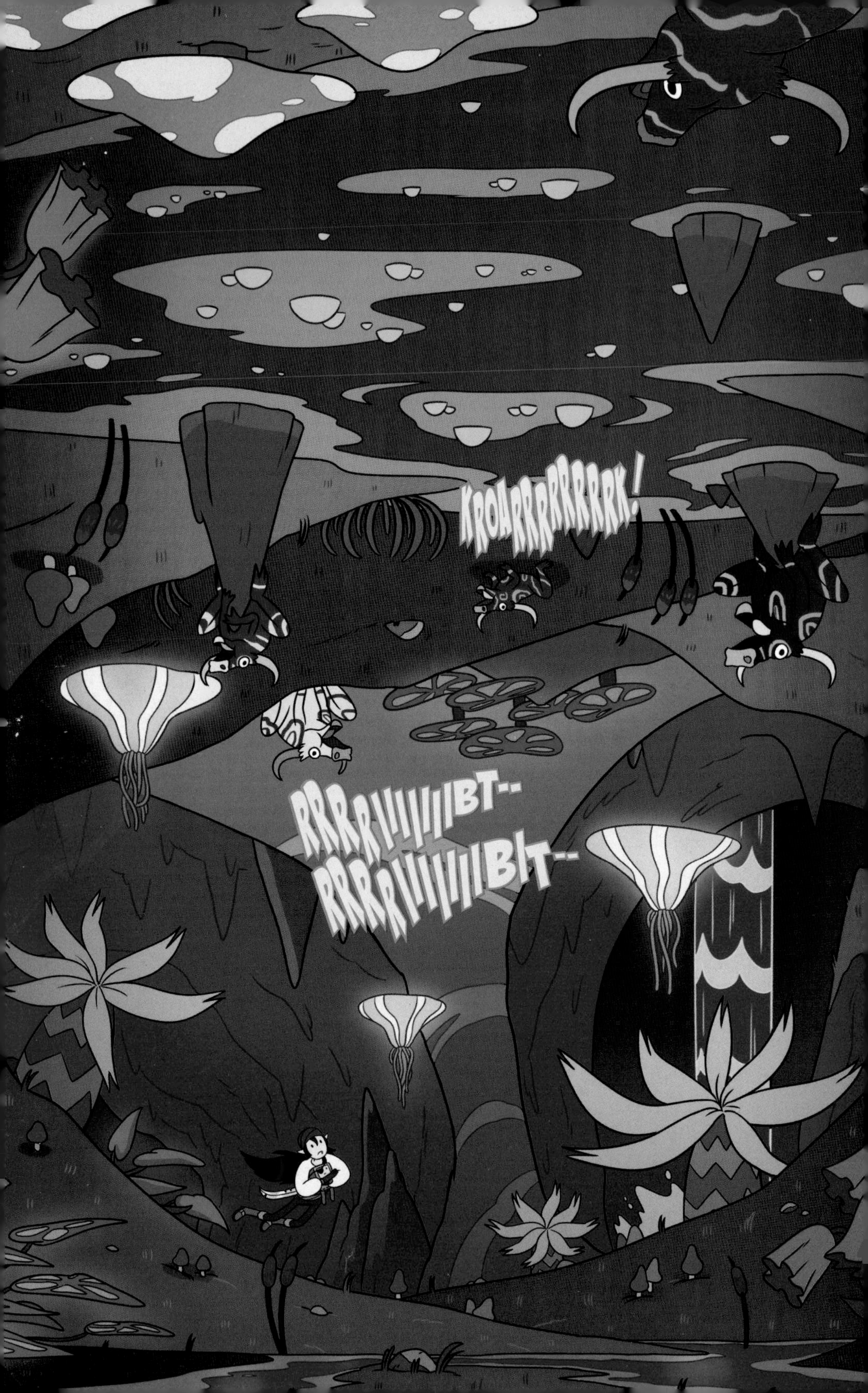
KROARRRRRRRK!
RRRRIIIIIIIBT--
RRRRIIIIIIIBIT--

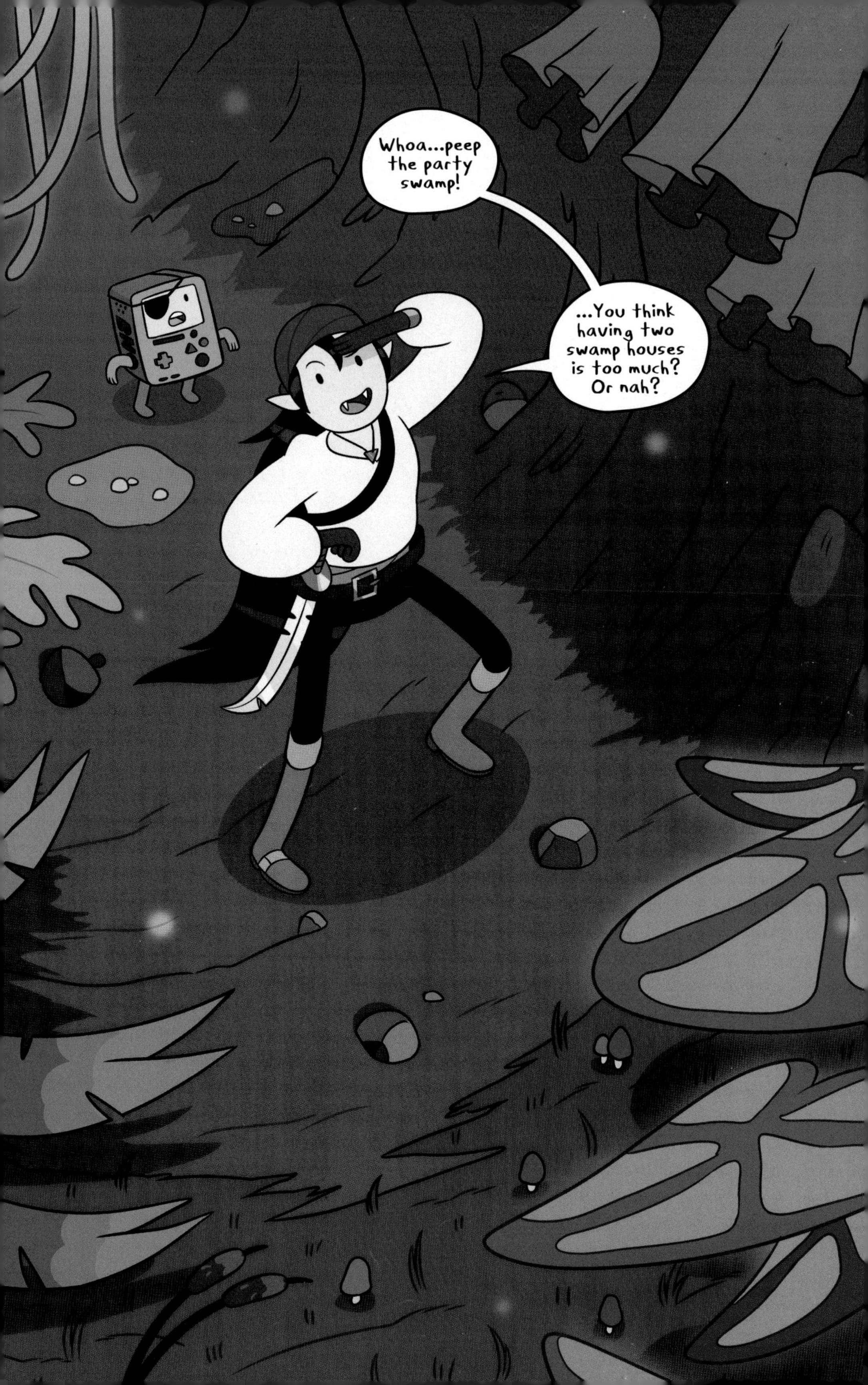
Whoa...peep the party swamp!
...You think having two swamp houses is too much? Or nah?

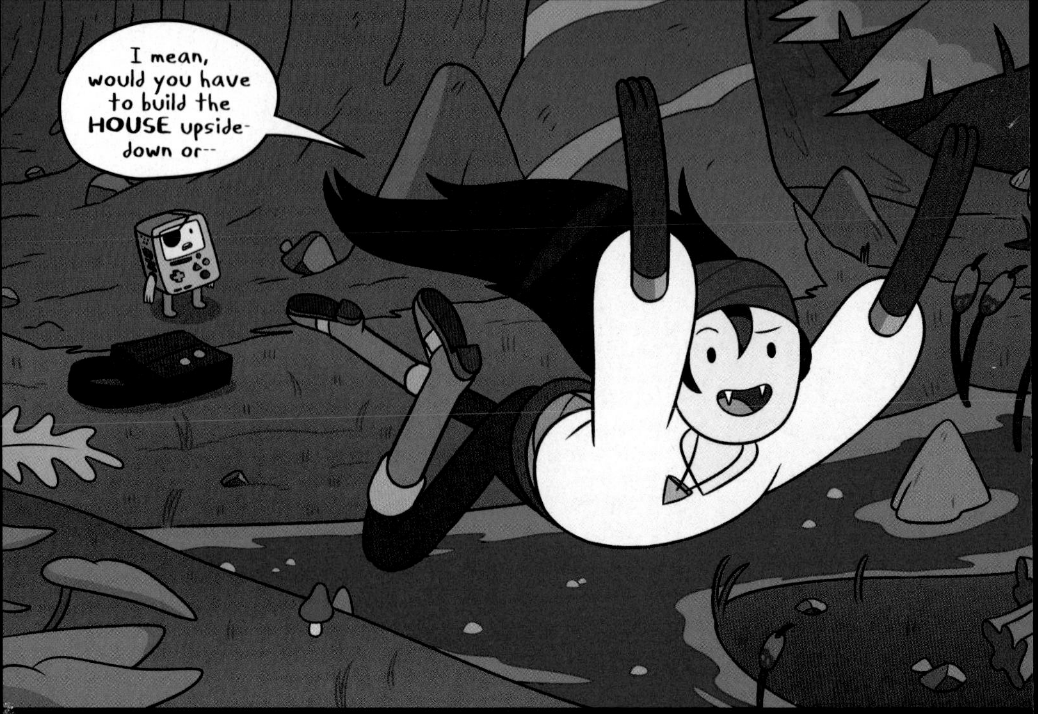
I mean, would you have to build the HOUSE upside-down or--

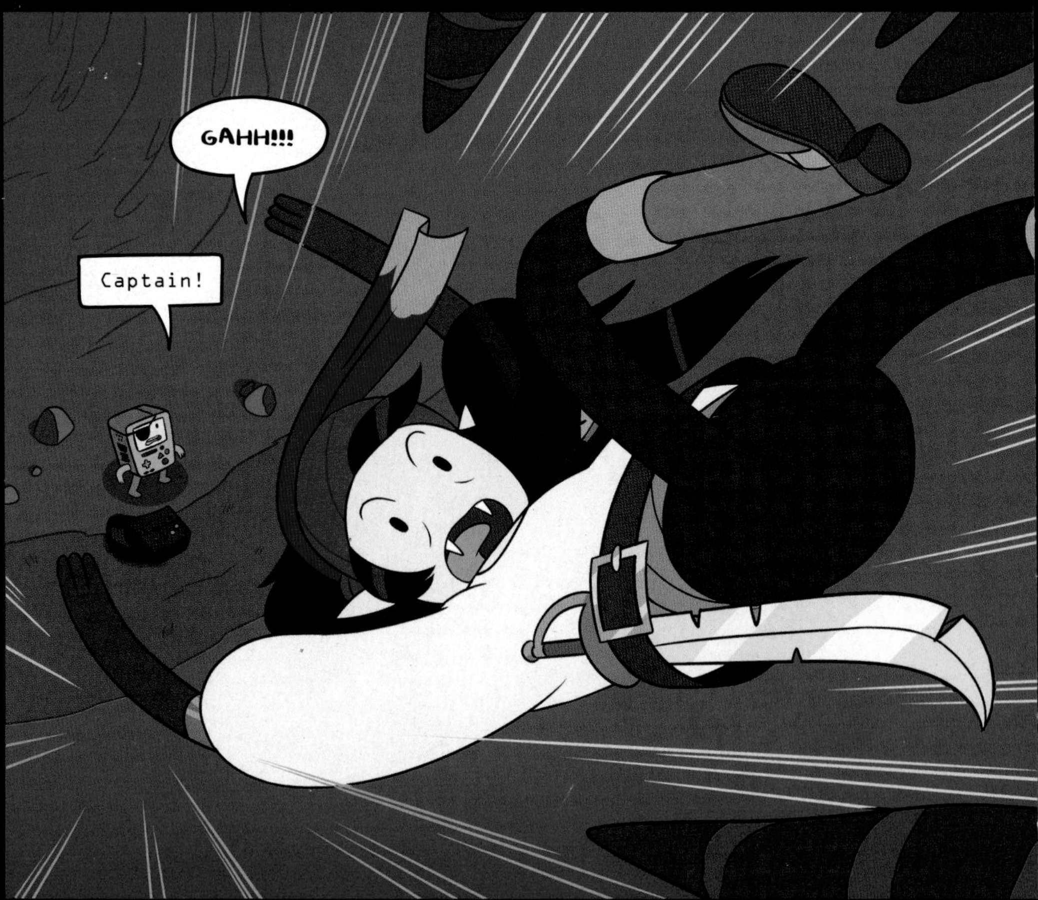
GAHH!!!
Captain!

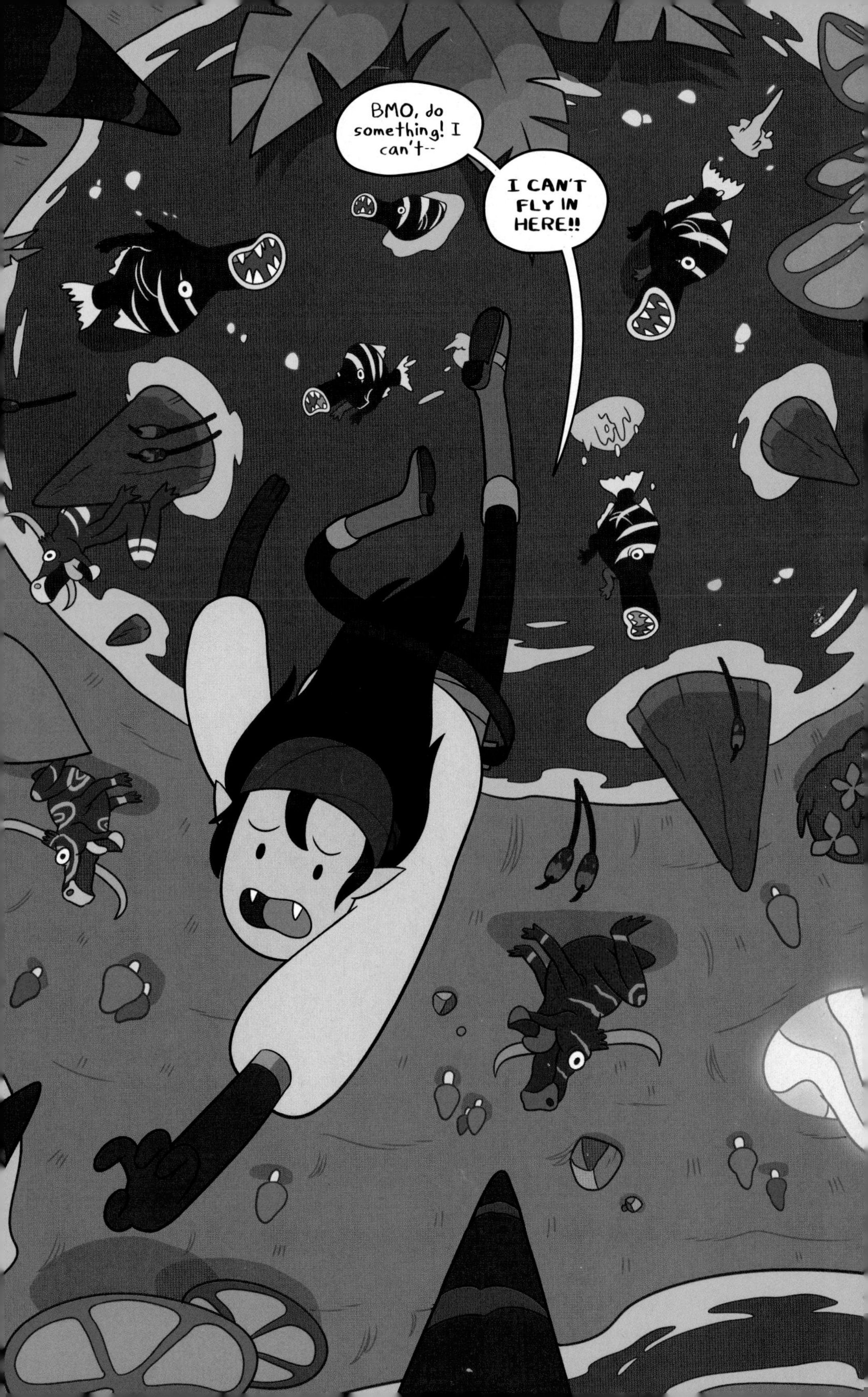
BMO, do something! I can't--
I CAN'T FLY IN HERE!!

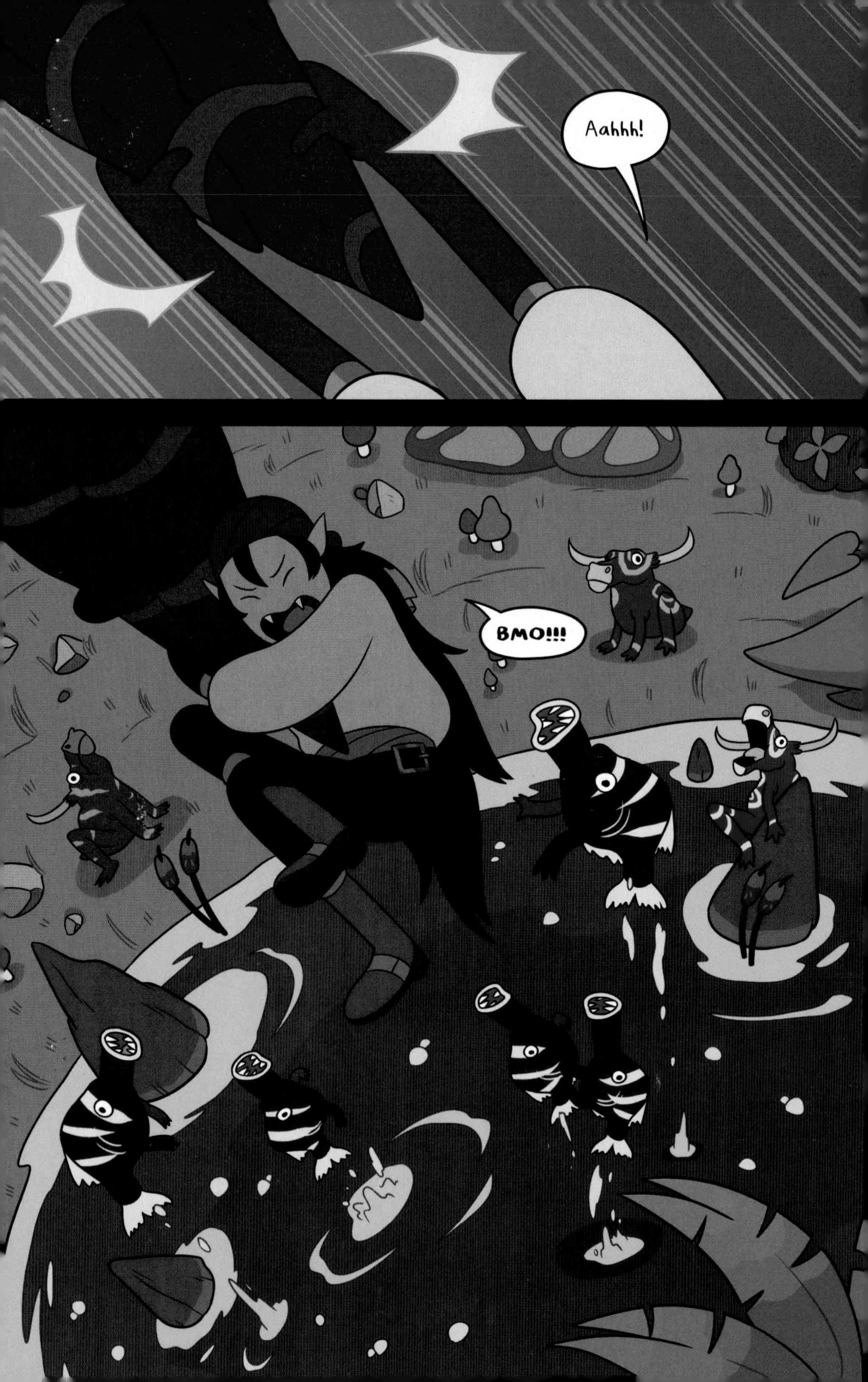
Aahhh!
BMO!!!

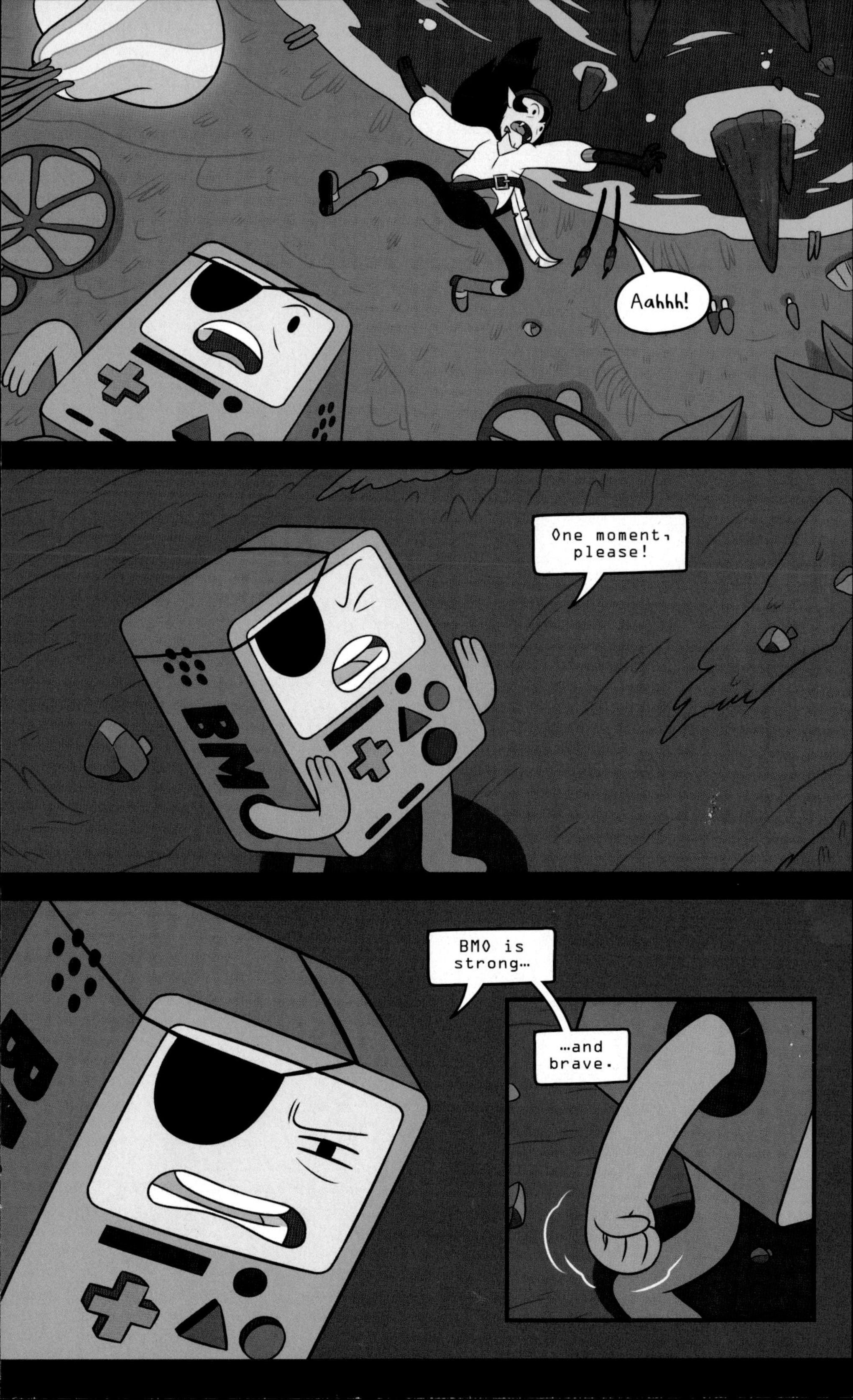
Aahhh!
One moment, please!
BMO is strong...
...and brave.

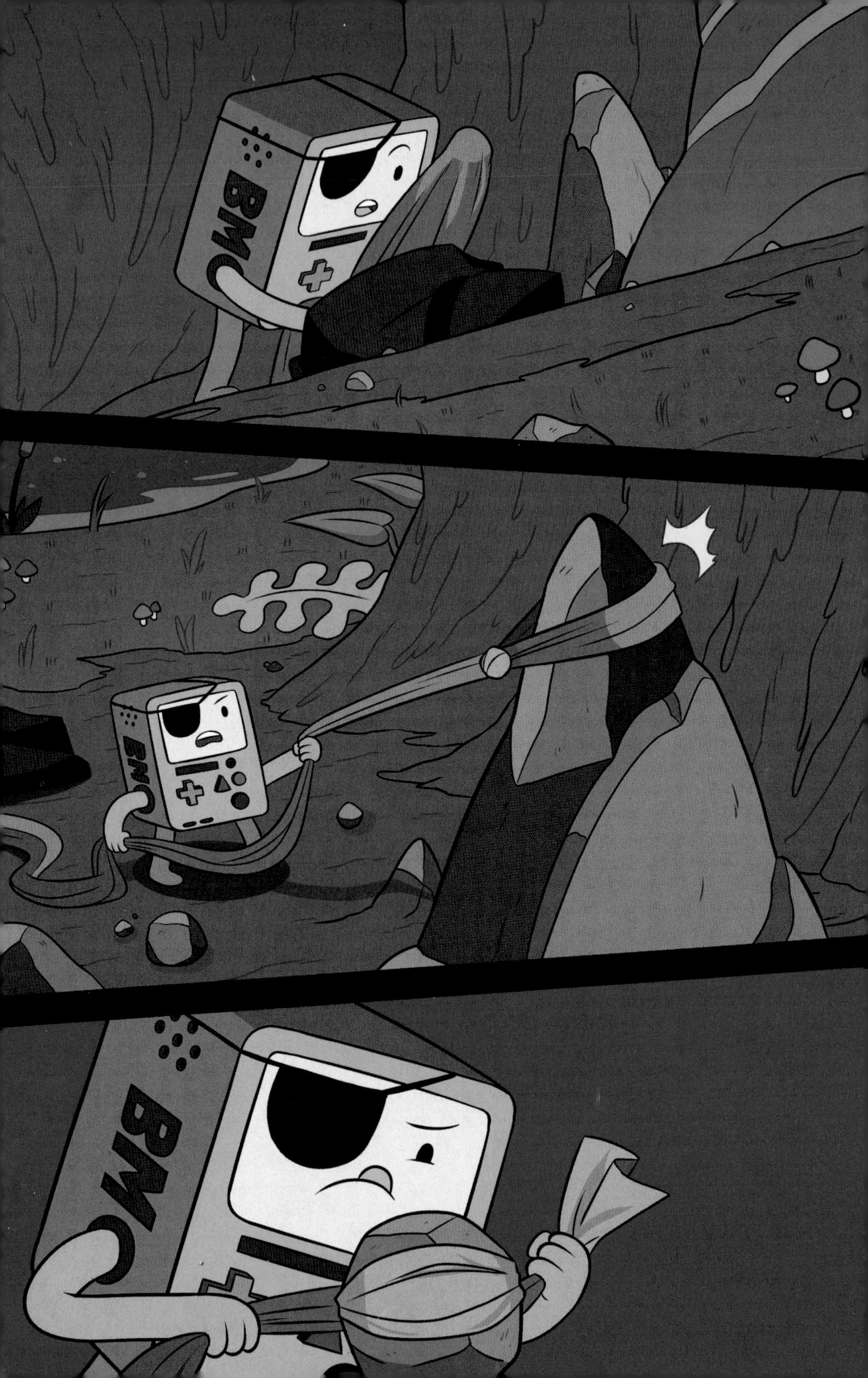
BMO
BMO
BMO

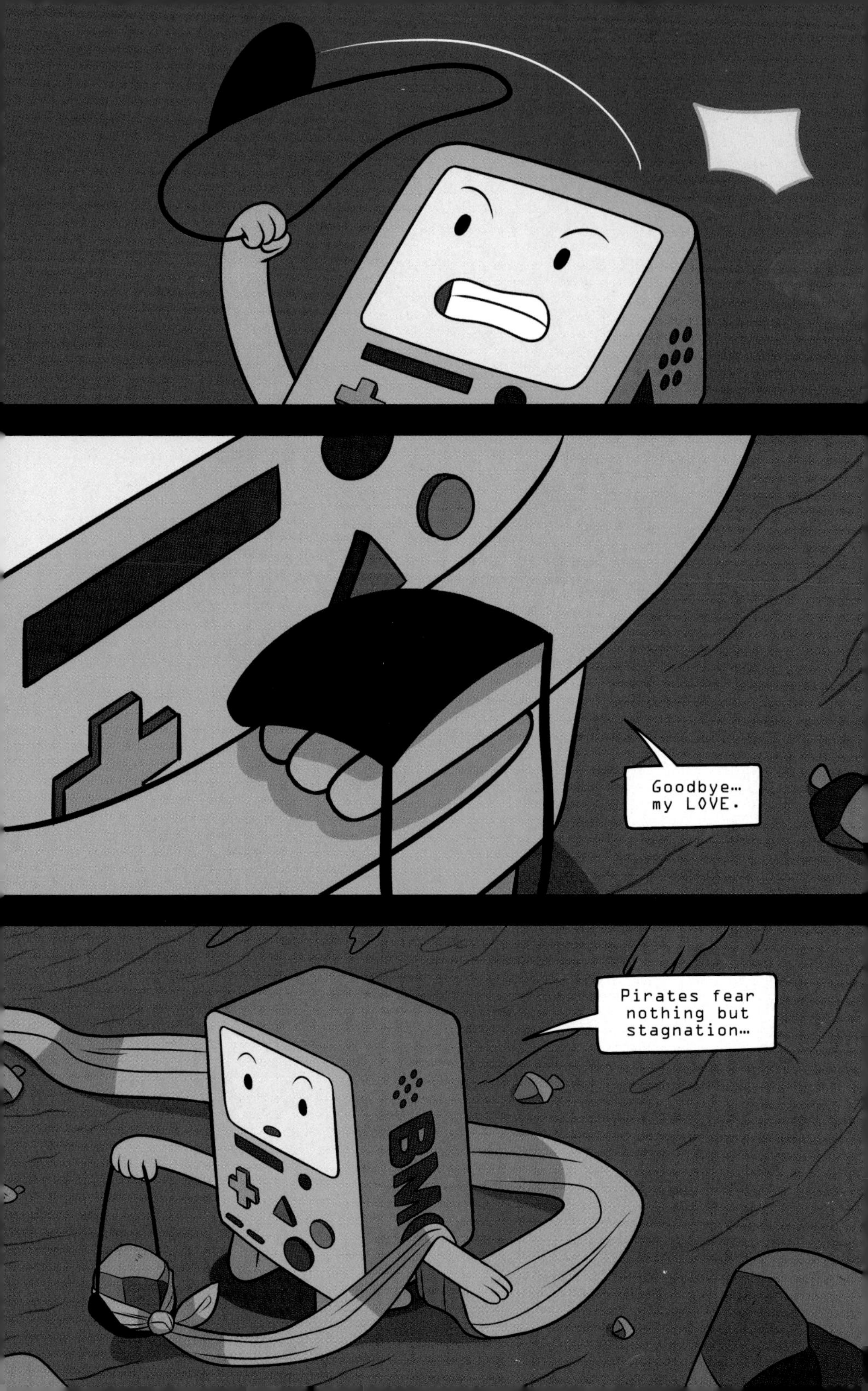
Goodbye... my LOVE.
Pirates fear nothing but stagnation...

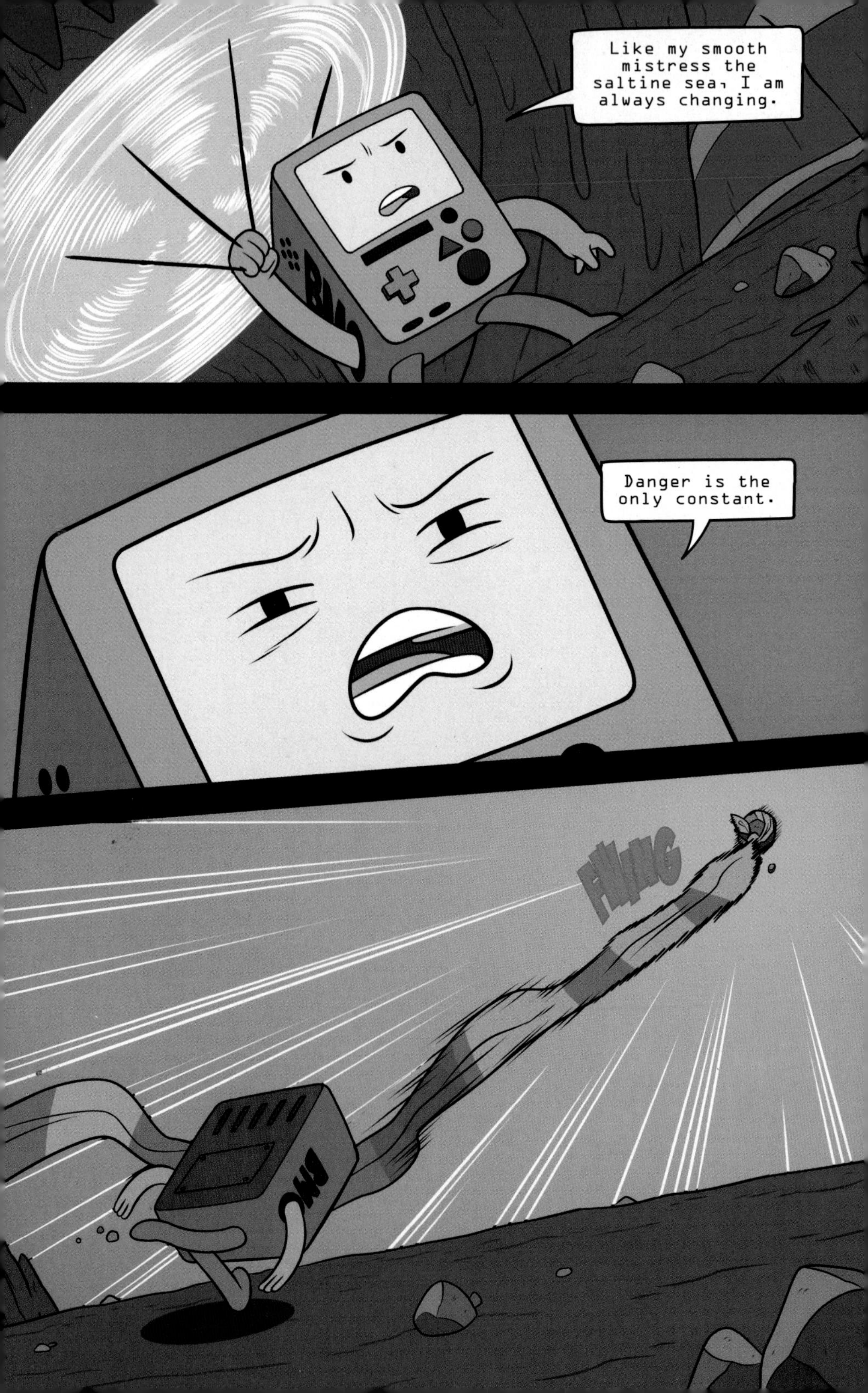
Like my smooth mistress the saltine sea, I am always changing.
Danger is the only constant.
FWING

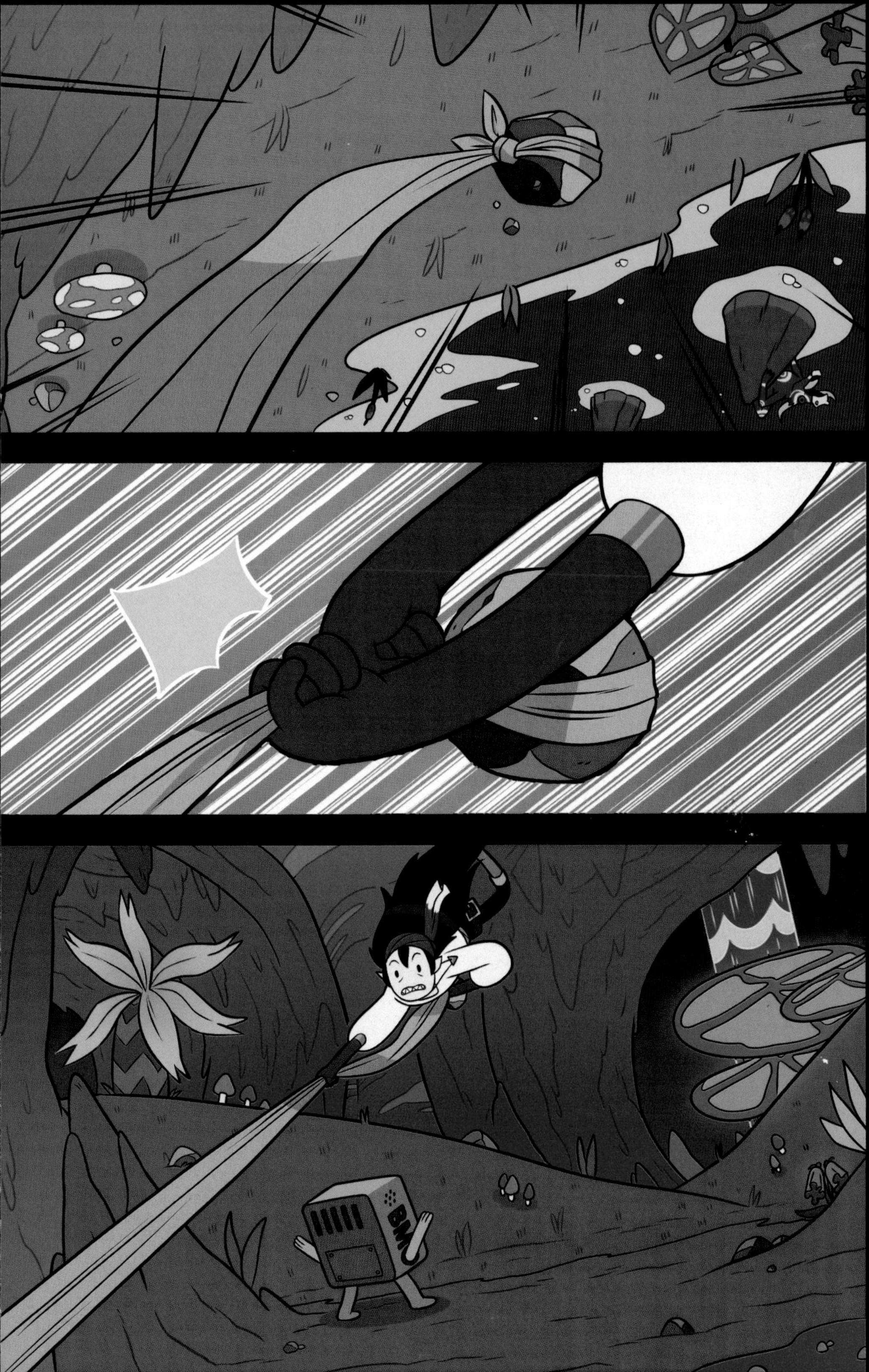
BMO

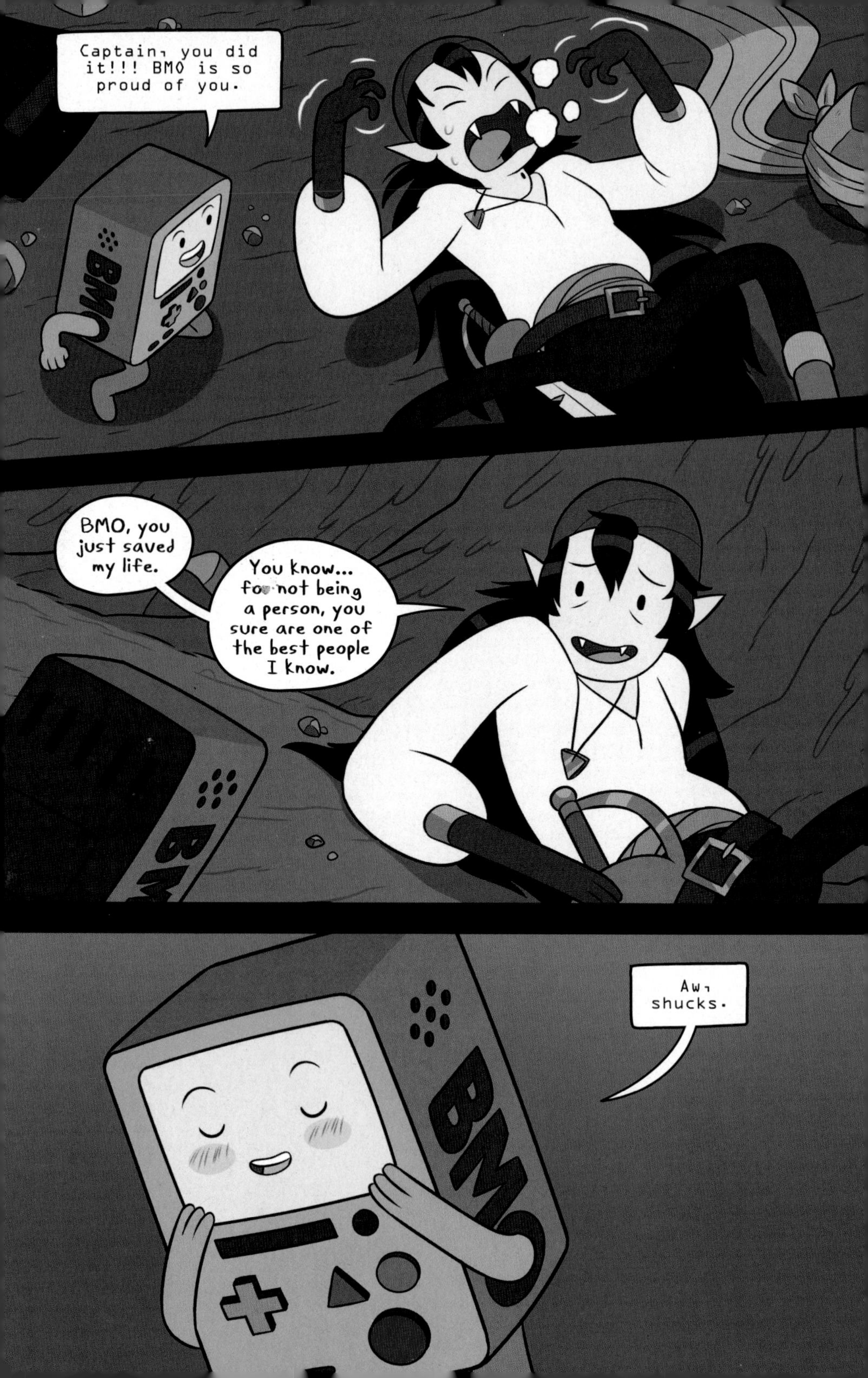
Captain, you did it!!! BMO is so proud of you.
BMO, you just saved my life.
You know... for not being a person, you sure are one of the best people I know.
Aw, shucks.

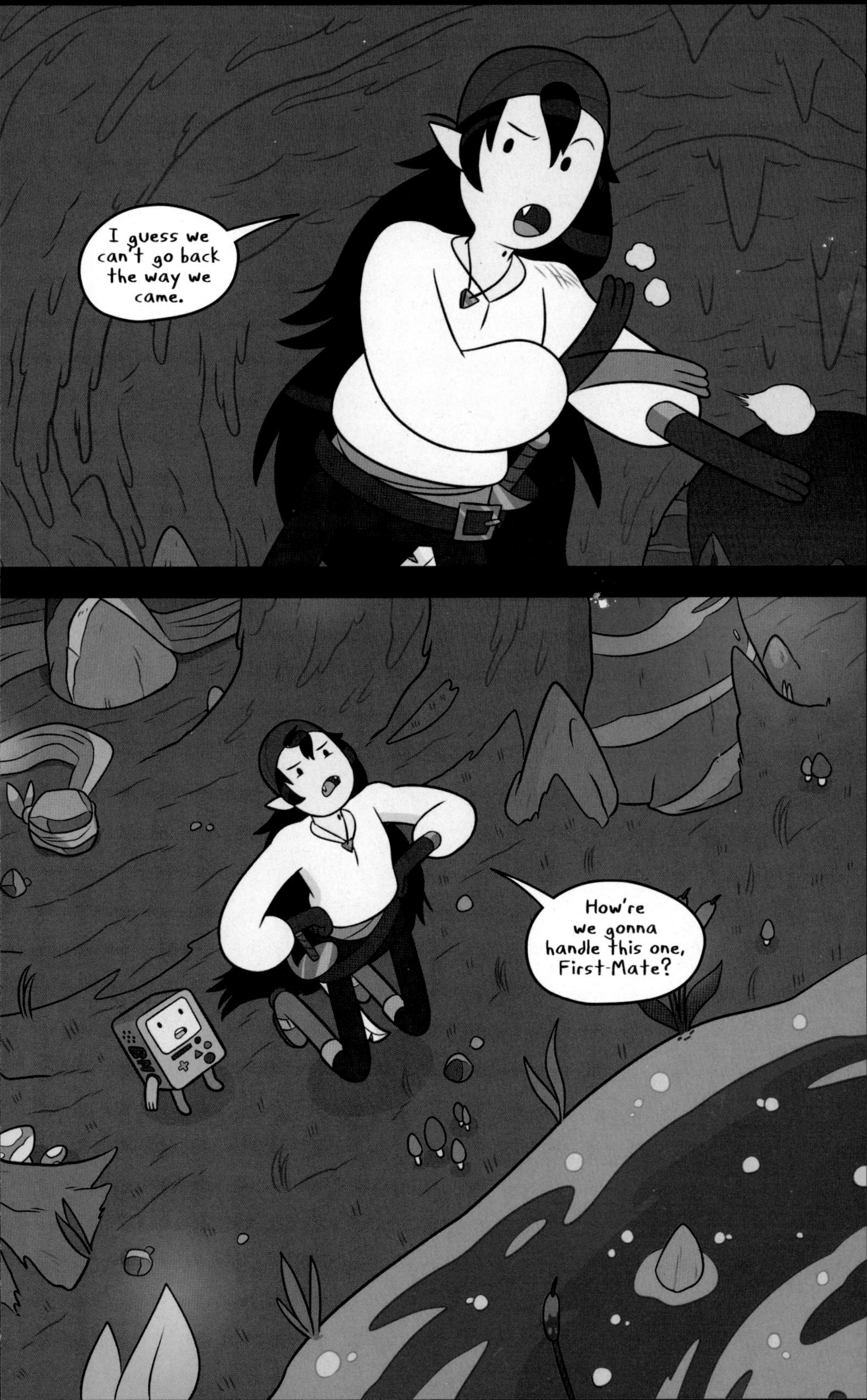
I guess we can't go back the way we came.
How're we gonna handle this one, First-Mate?

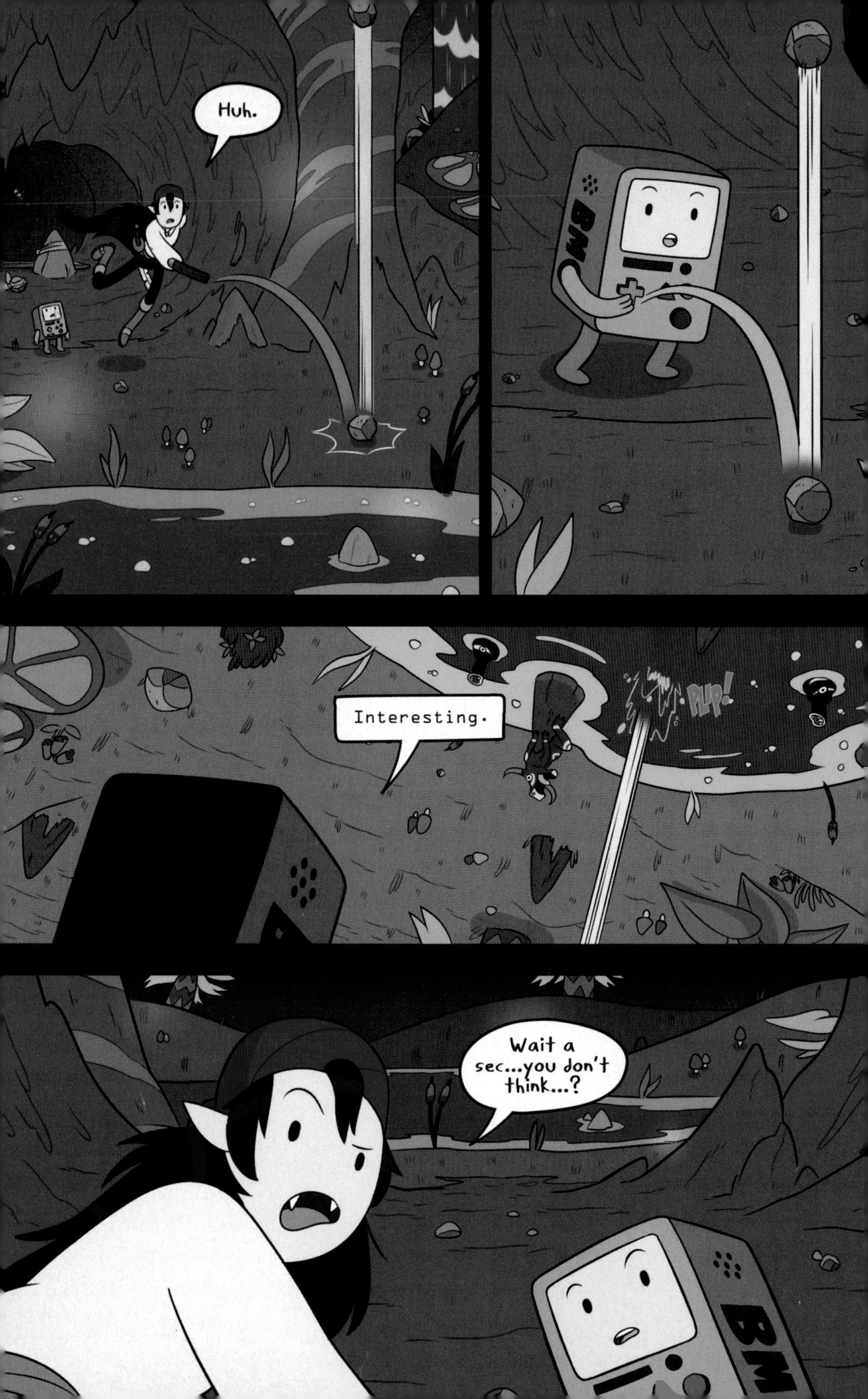
Huh.
Interesting.
PLIP!
Wait a sec...you don't think...?

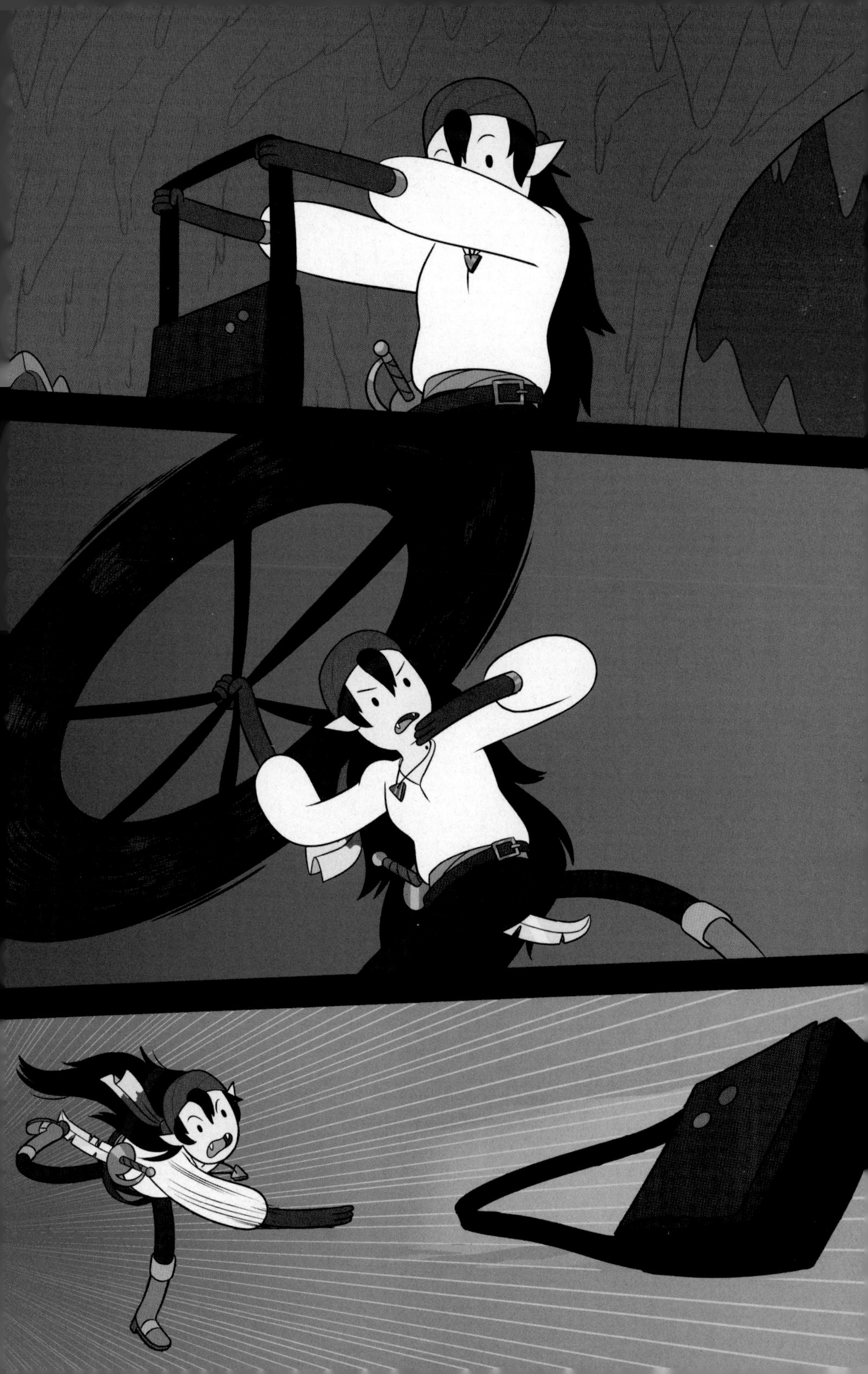

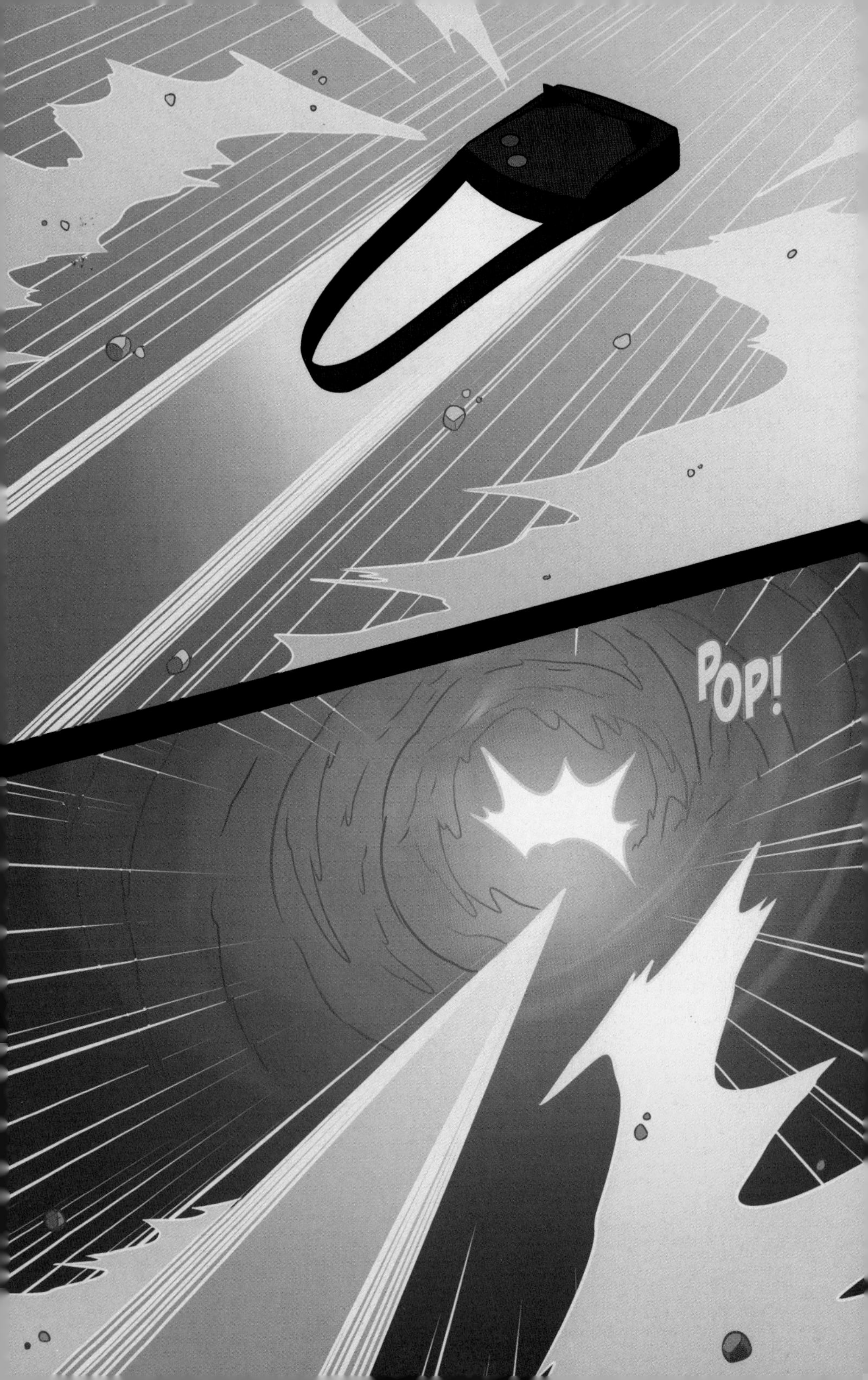
POP!

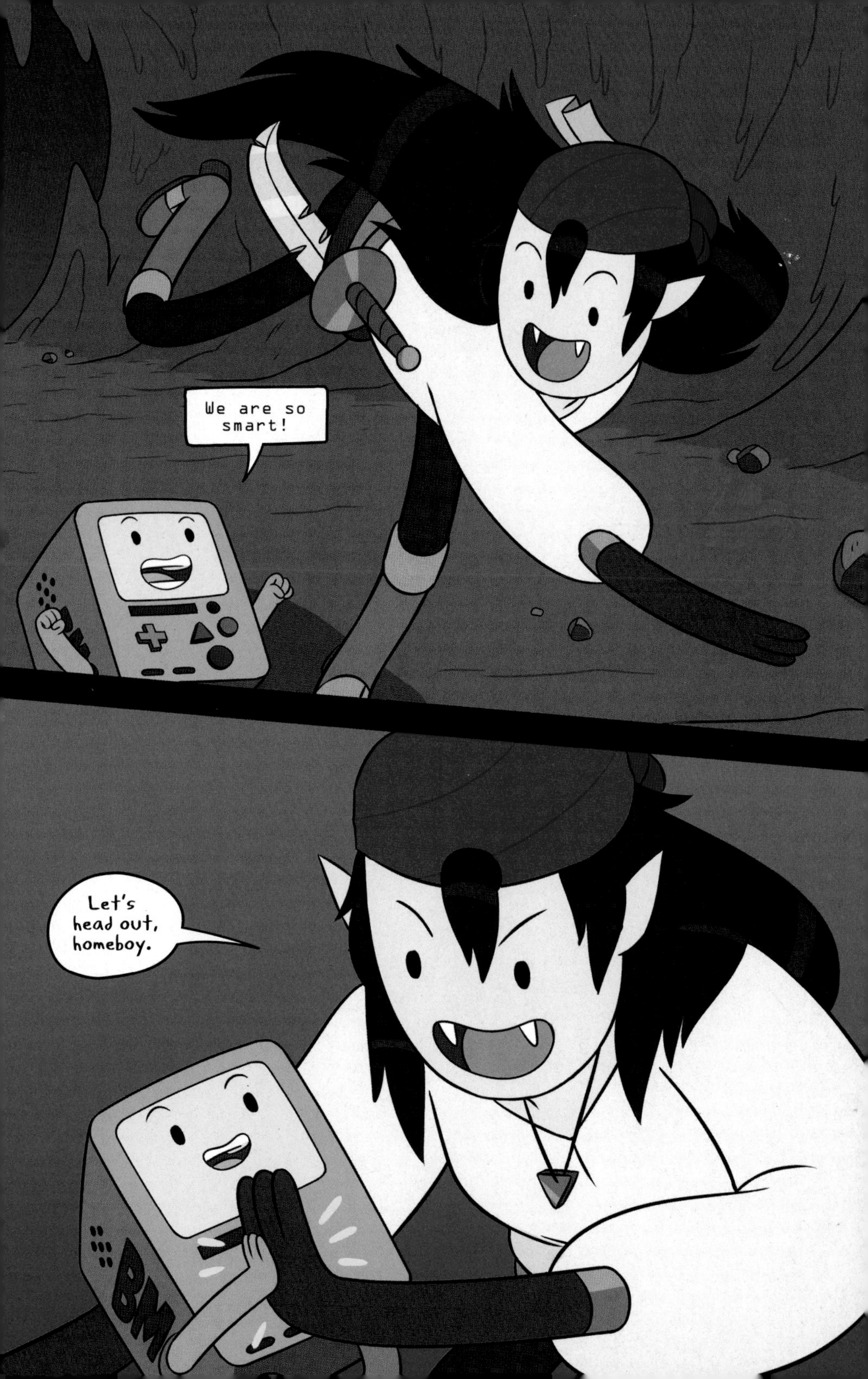
We are so smart!
Let's head out, homeboy.

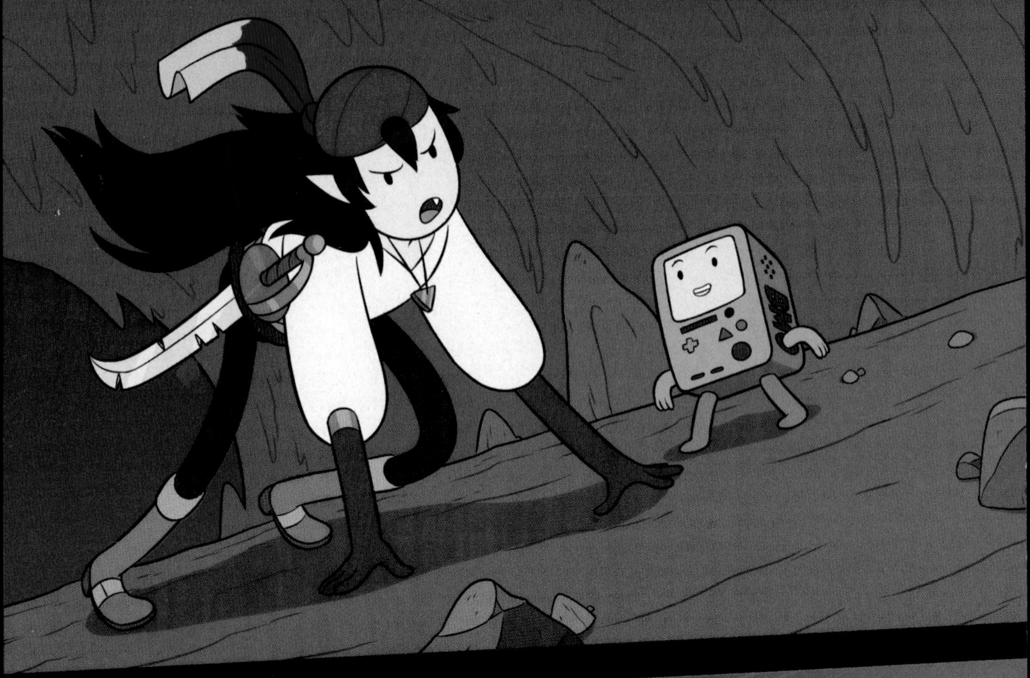

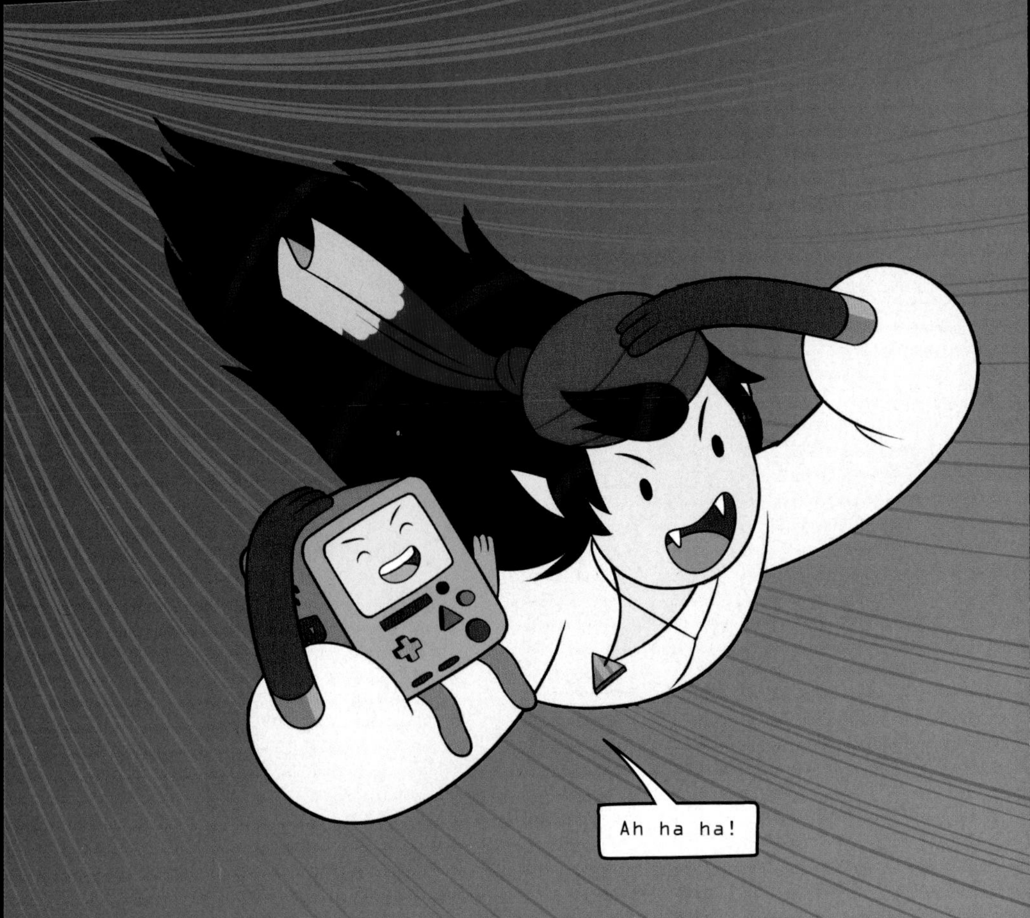
Ah ha ha!

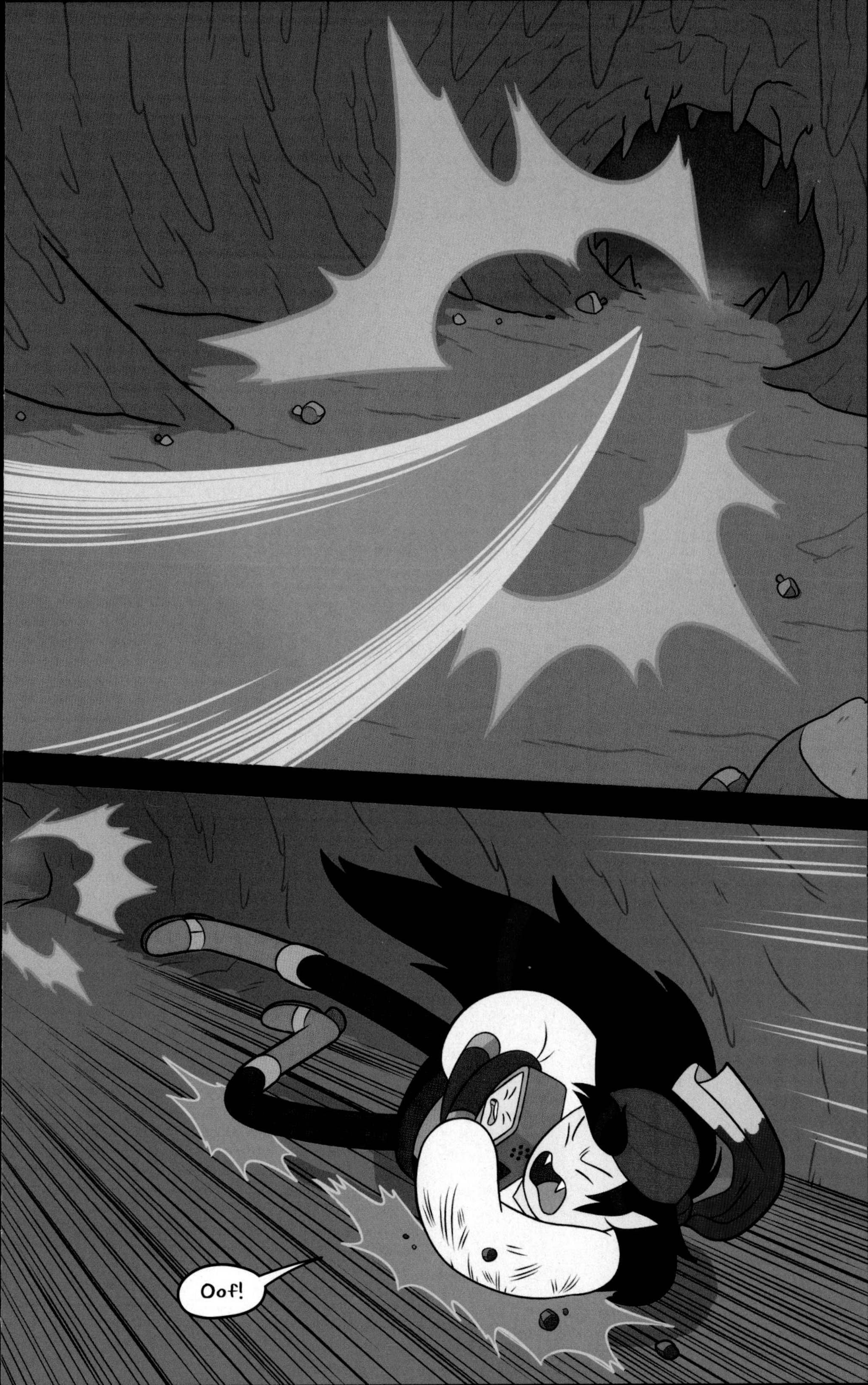

Oof!

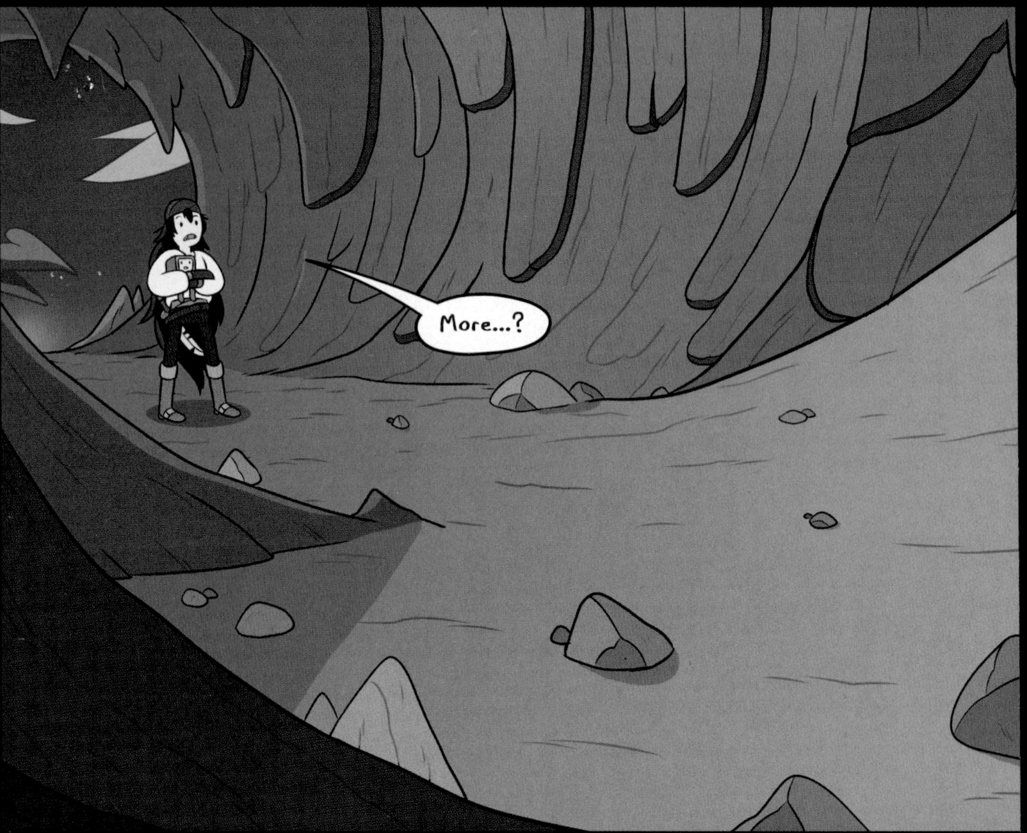
More...?

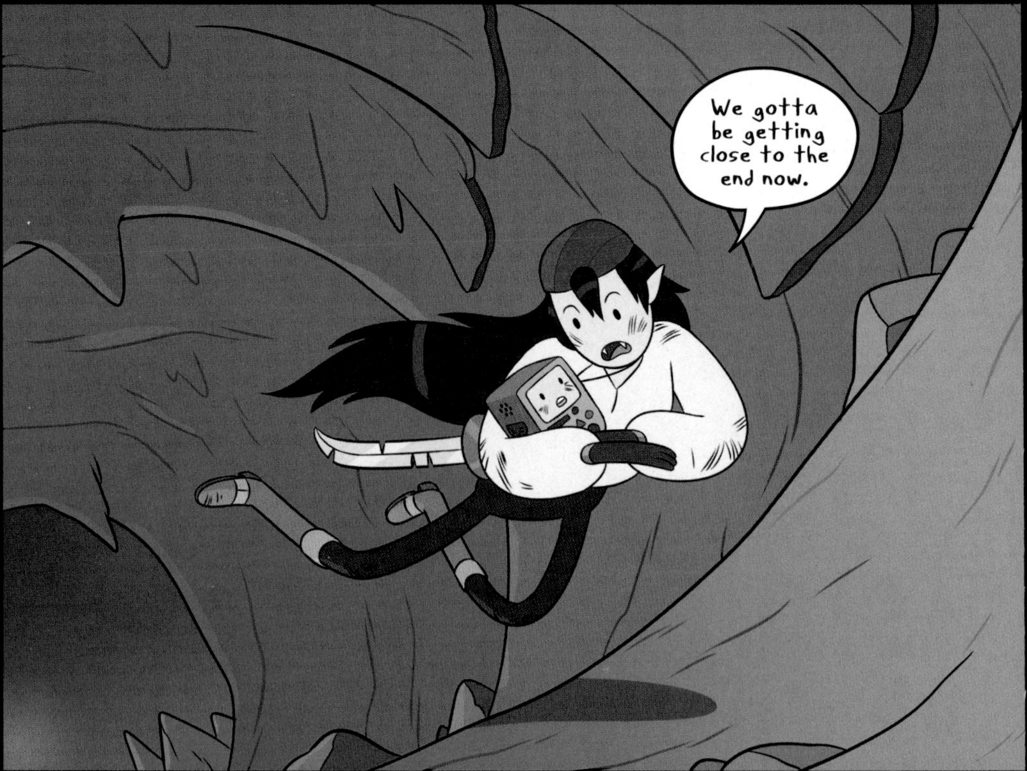
We gotta be getting close to the end now.

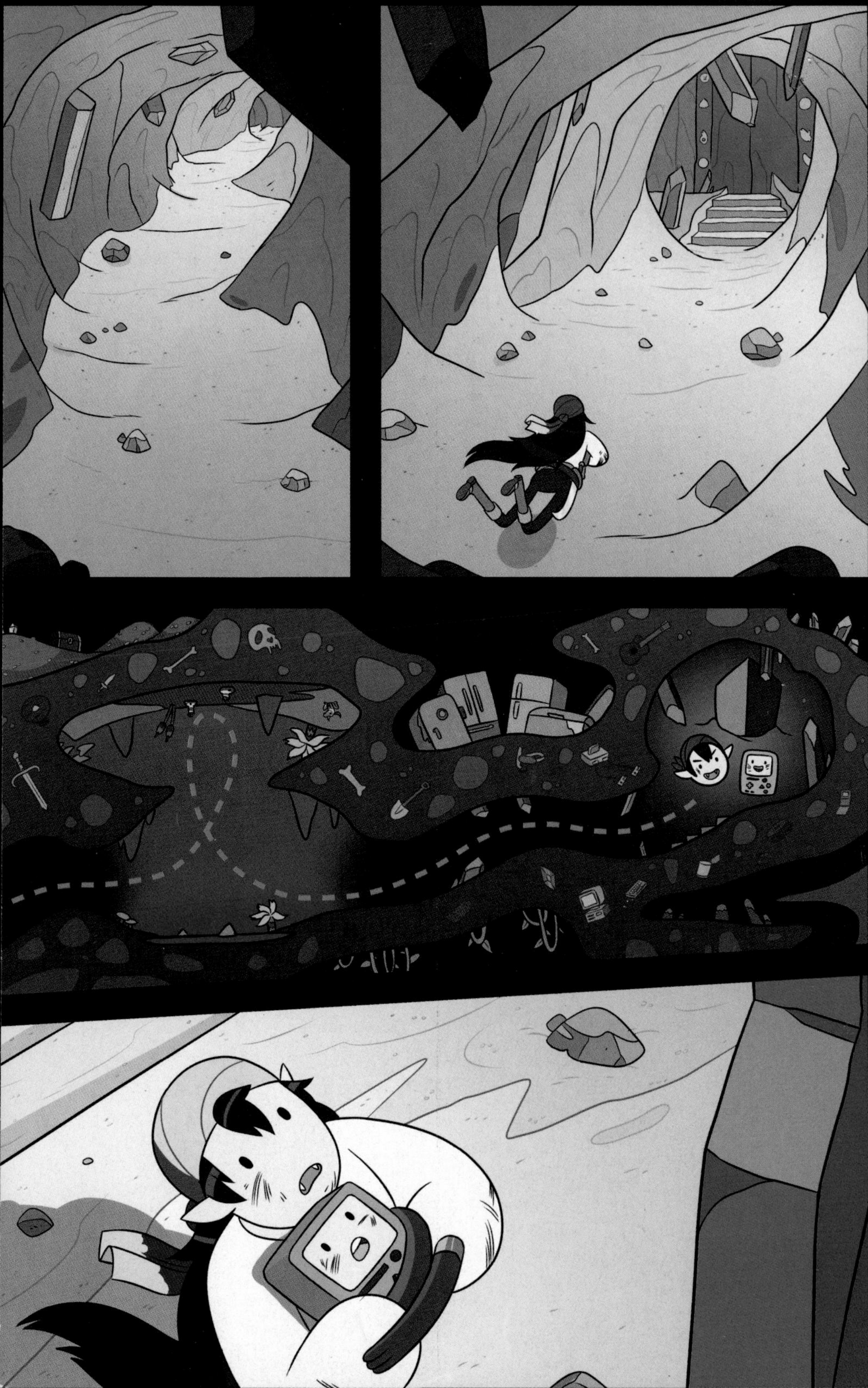

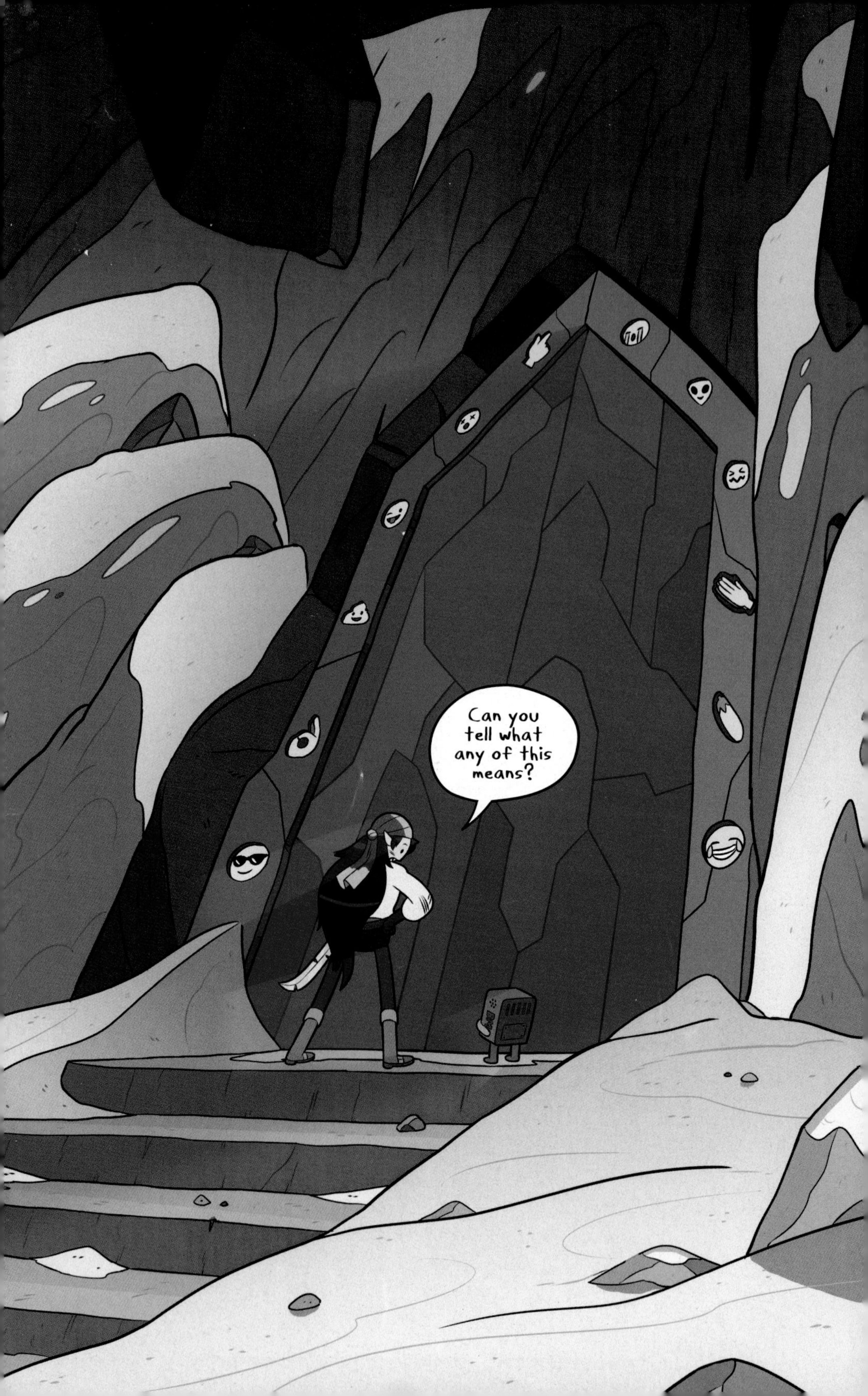
Can you tell what any of this means?

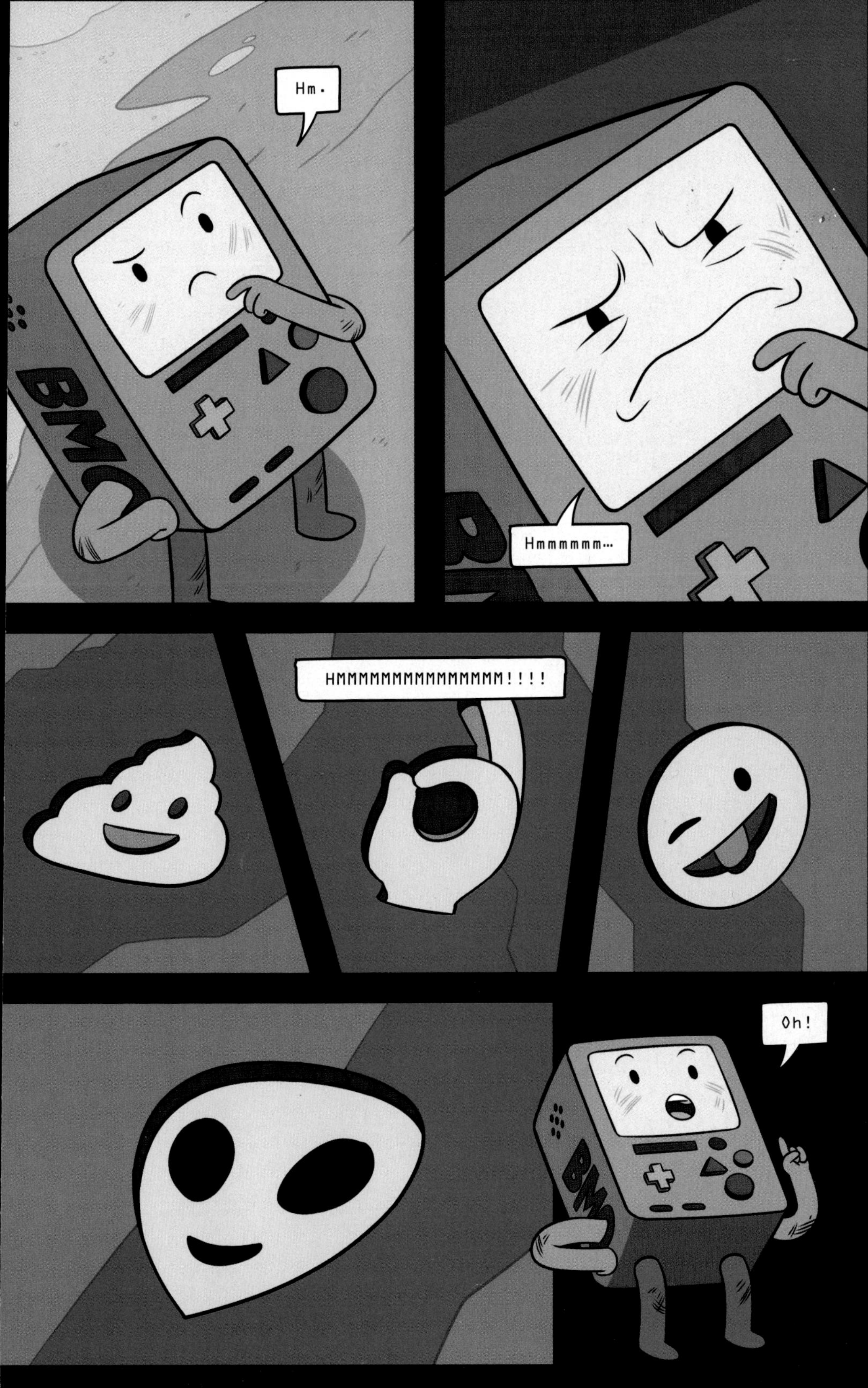
Hm.
Hmmmmmm...
HMMMMMMMMMMMMMMM!!!!
Oh!

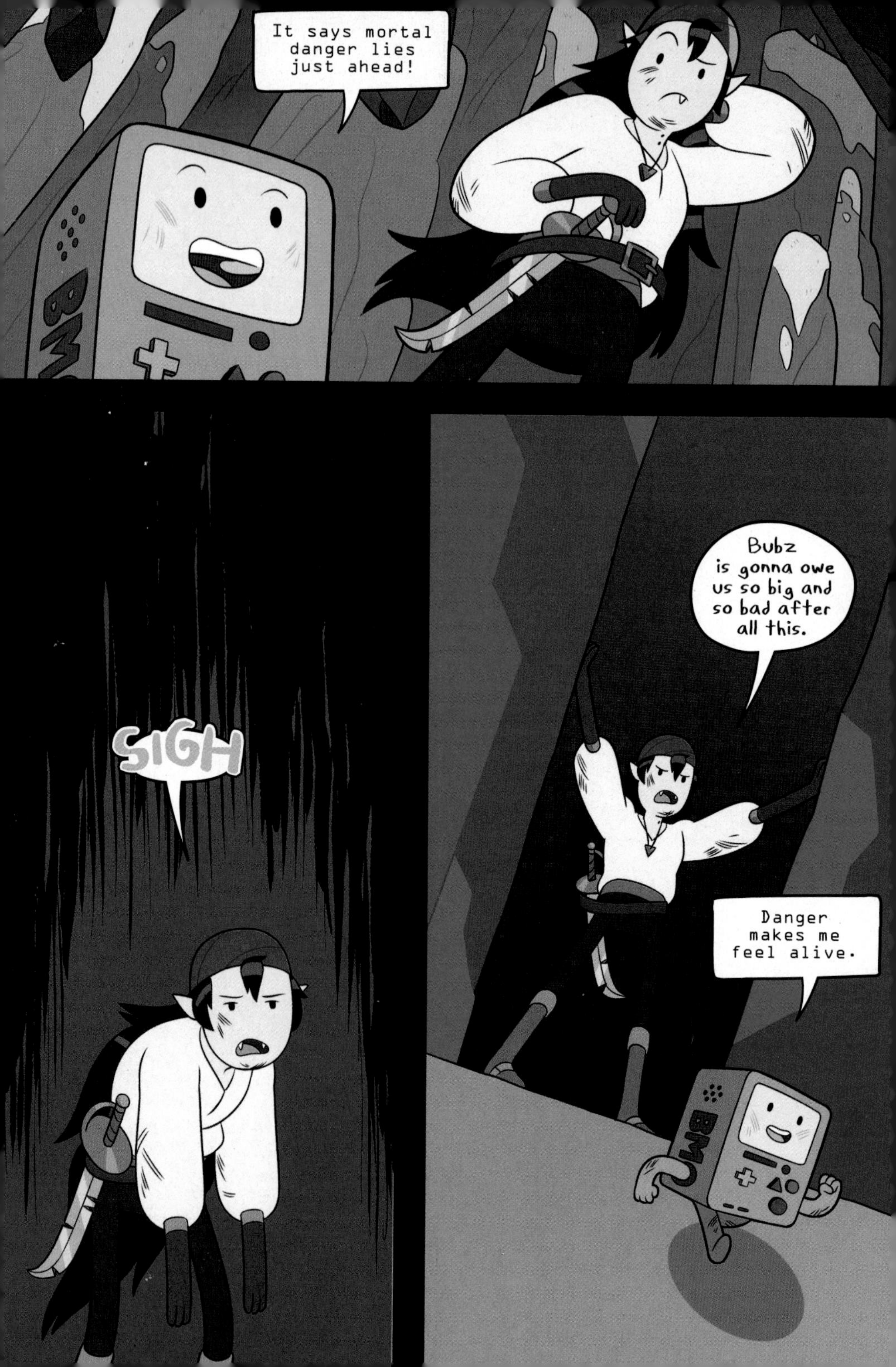
It says mortal danger lies just ahead!
SIGH
Bubz is gonna owe us so big and so bad after all this.
Danger makes me feel alive.

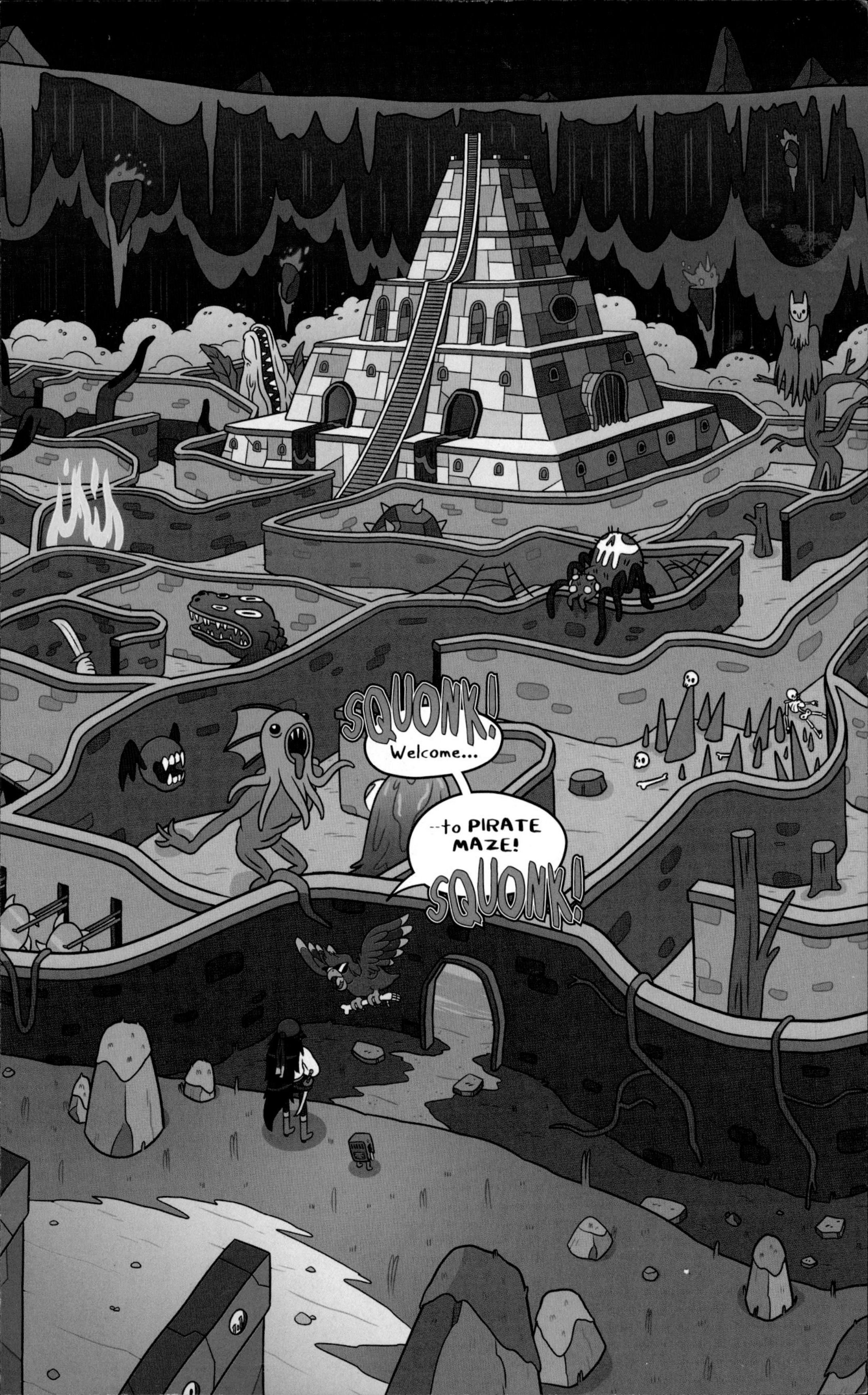
SQUONK!
Welcome...
--to PIRATE MAZE!
SQUONK!

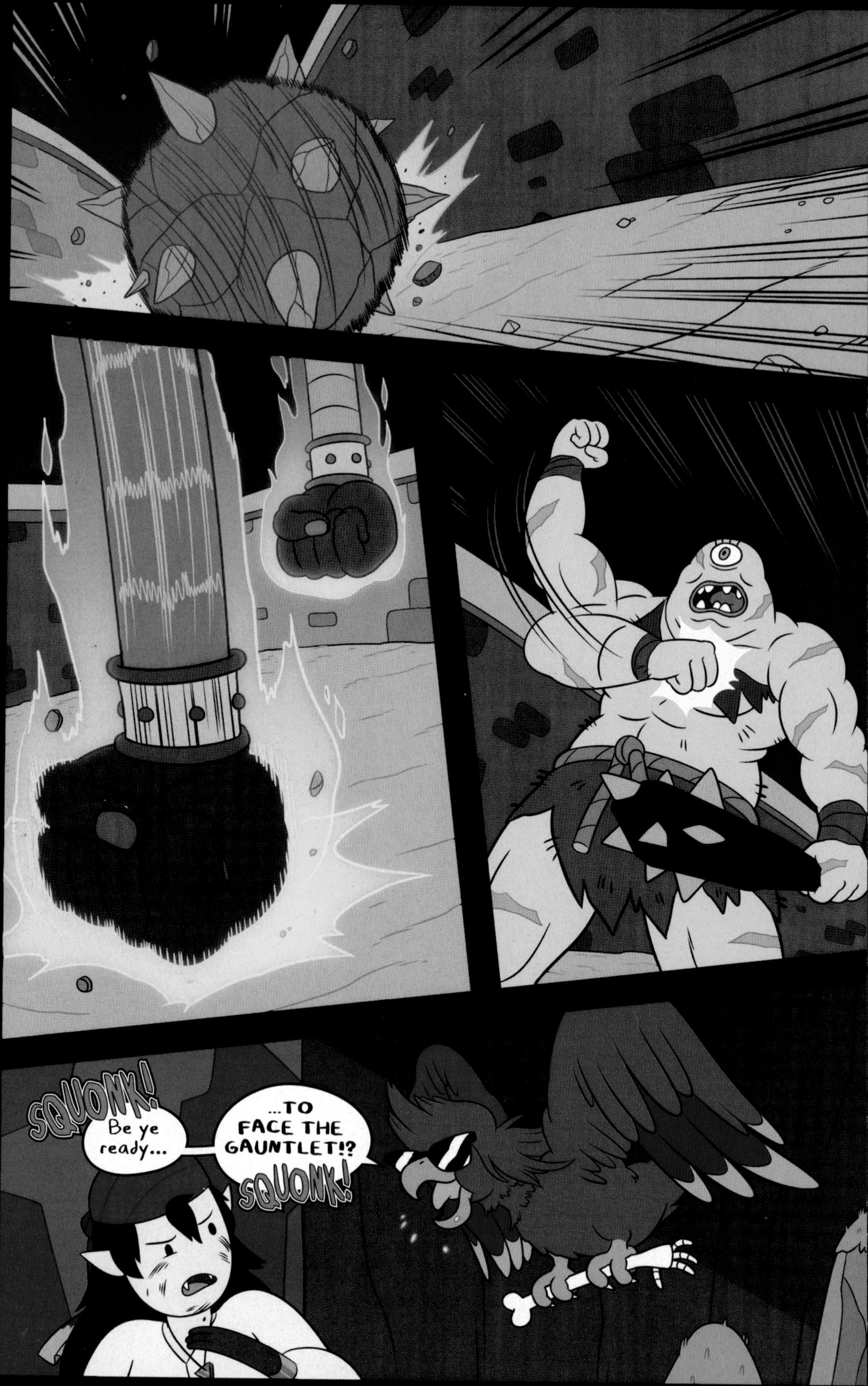

SQUONK!
Be ye ready...
...TO FACE THE GAUNTLET!?
SQUONK!

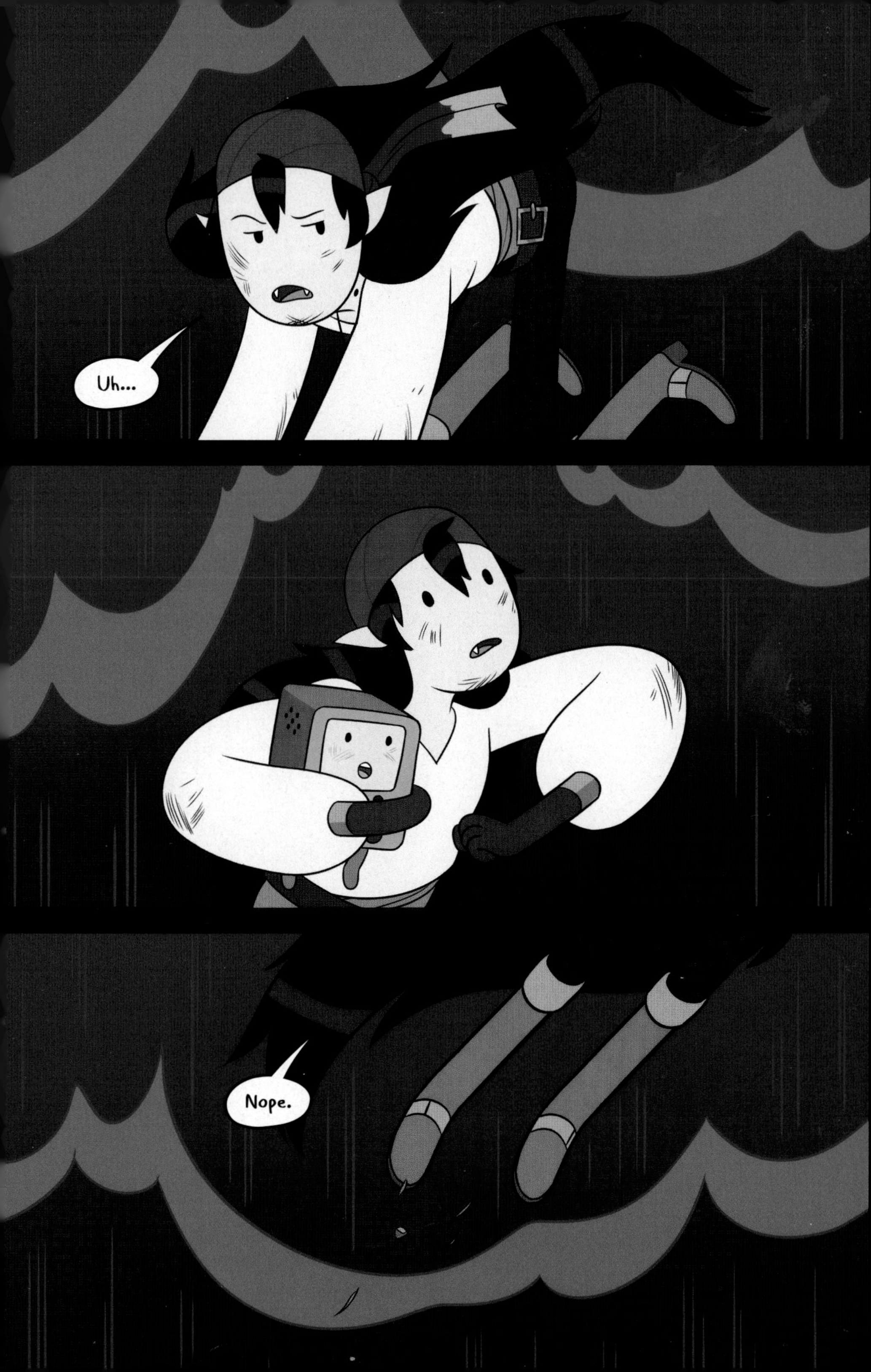
Uh...
Nope.

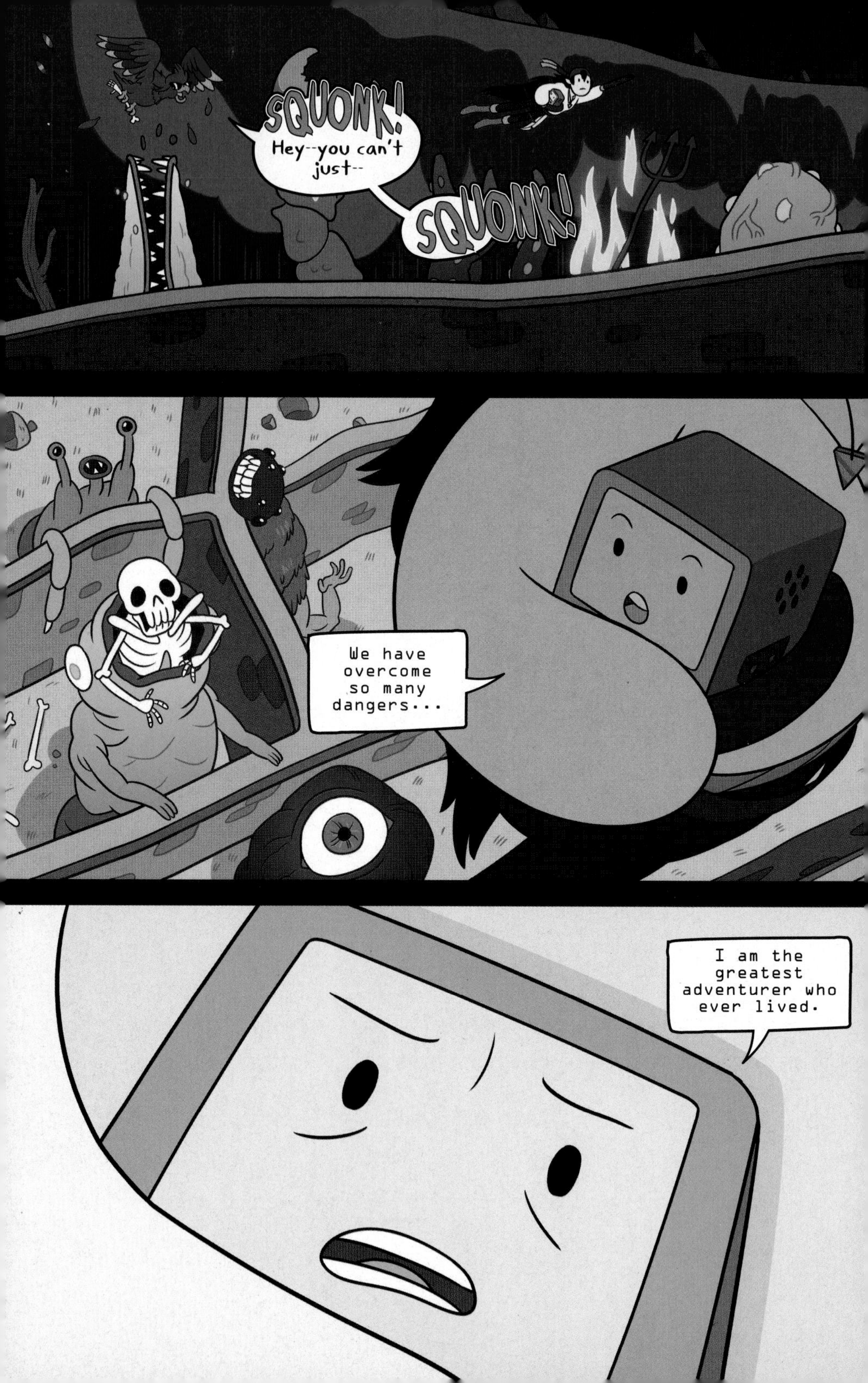
SQUONK!
Hey--you can't just--
SQUONK!
We have overcome so many dangers...
I am the greatest adventurer who ever lived.

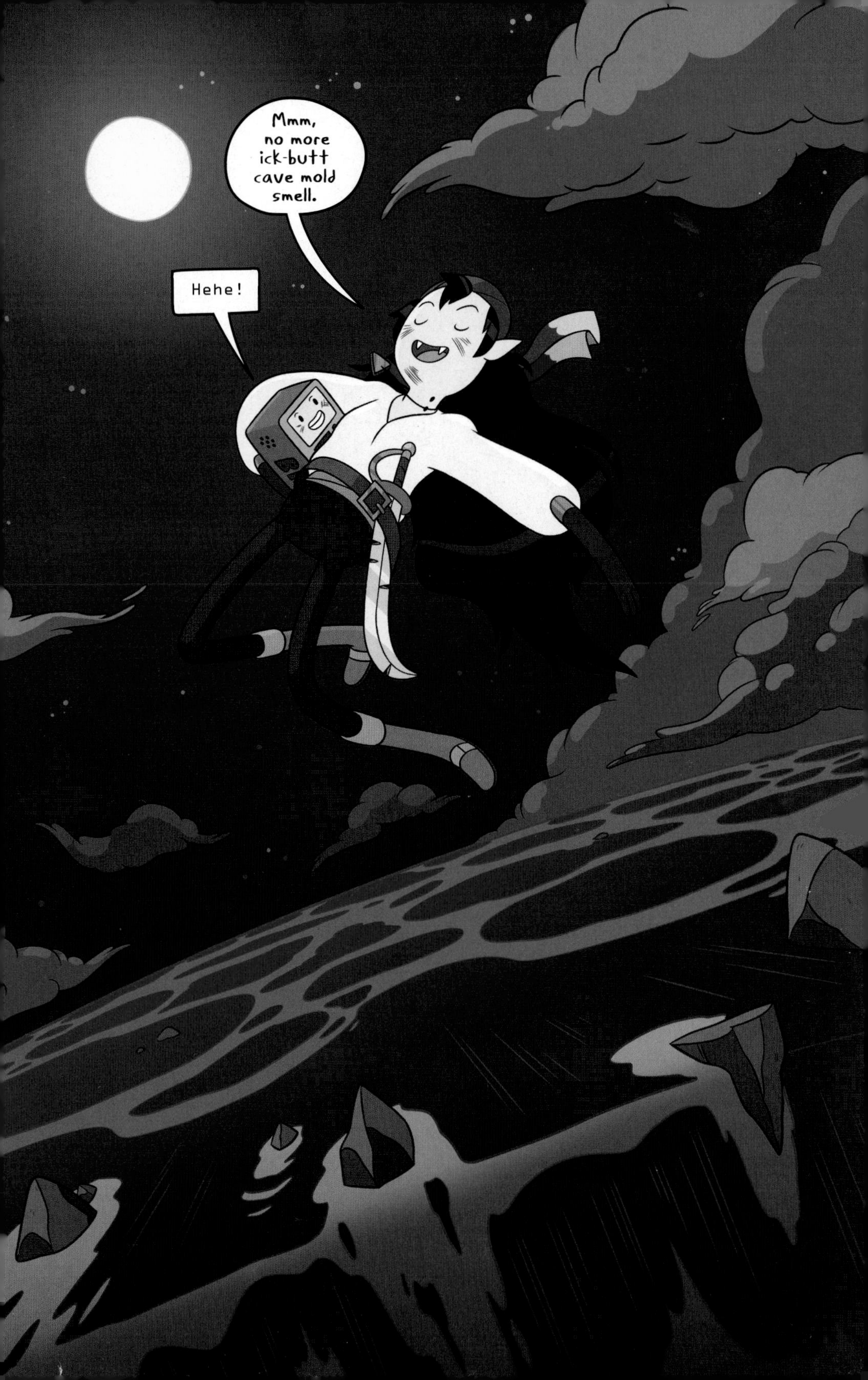
Mmm, no more ick-butt cave mold smell.
Hehe!

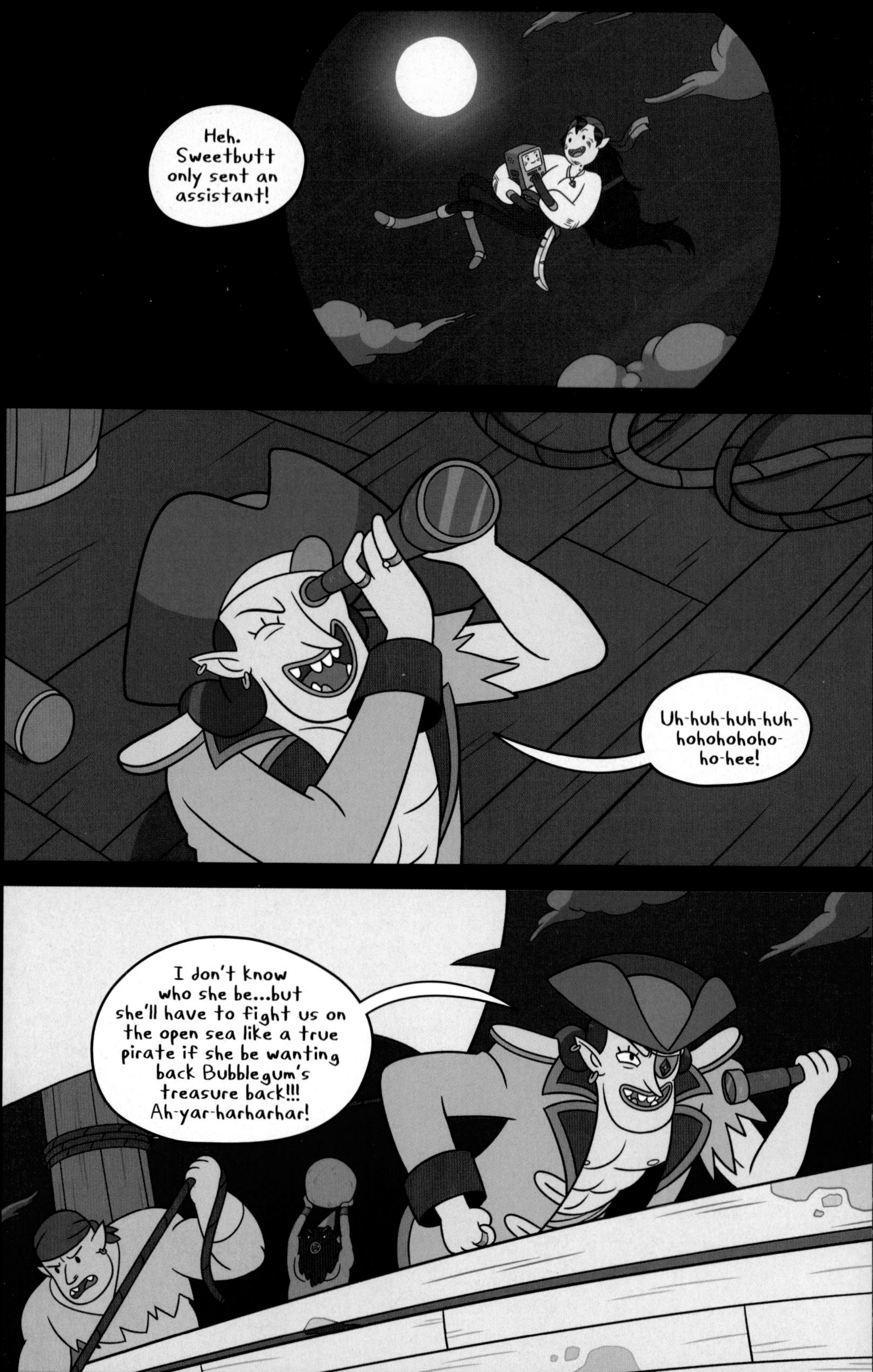

Heh. Sweetbutt only sent an assistant!
Uh-huh-huh-huh-hohohohoho-ho-hee!
I don't know who she be...but she'll have to fight us on the open sea like a true pirate if she be wanting back Bubblegum's treasure back!!! Ah-yar-harharhar!

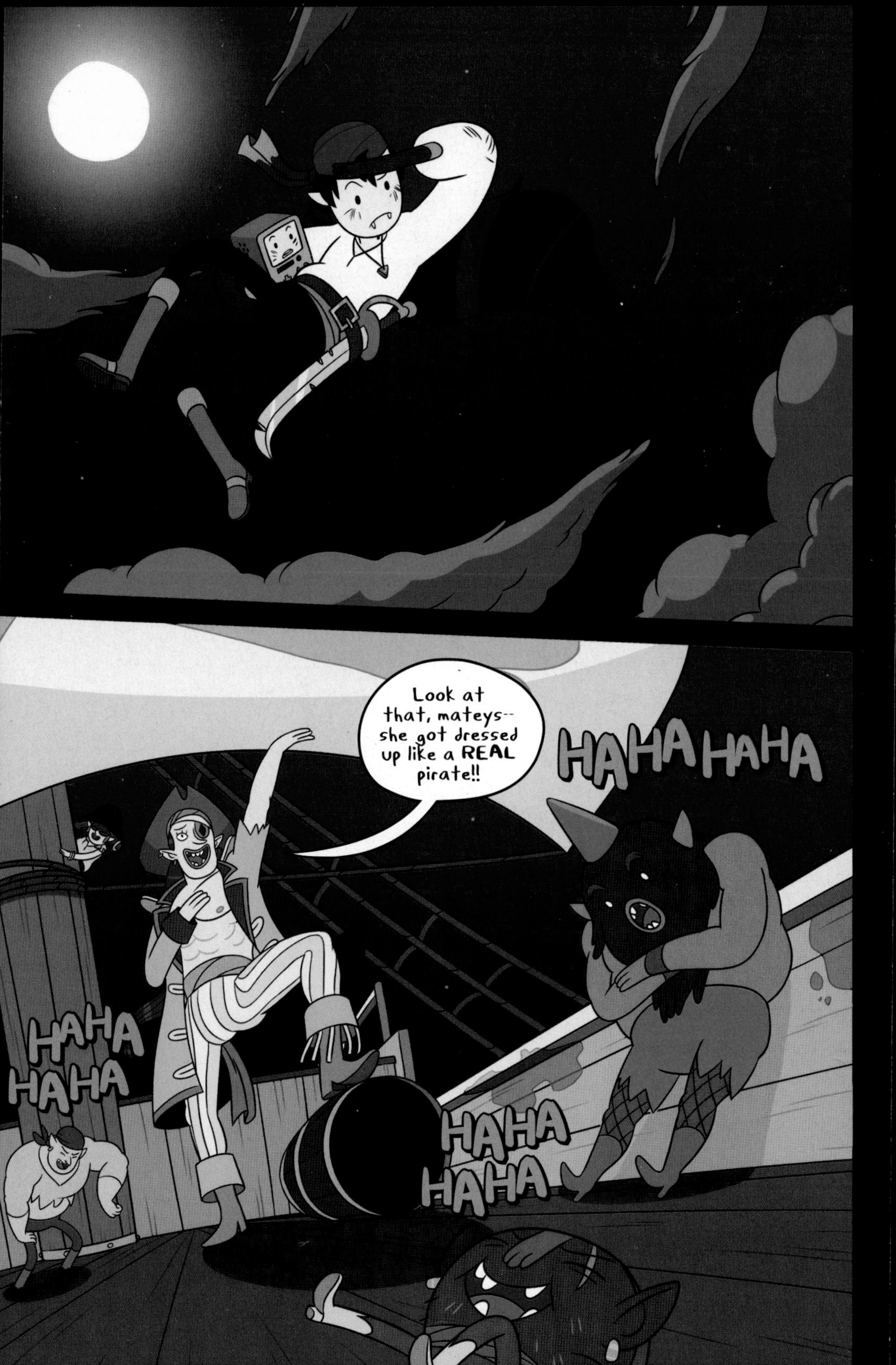

Look at that, mateys-- she got dressed up like a REAL pirate!!
HAHAHAHA
HAHA HAHA
HAHA HAHA

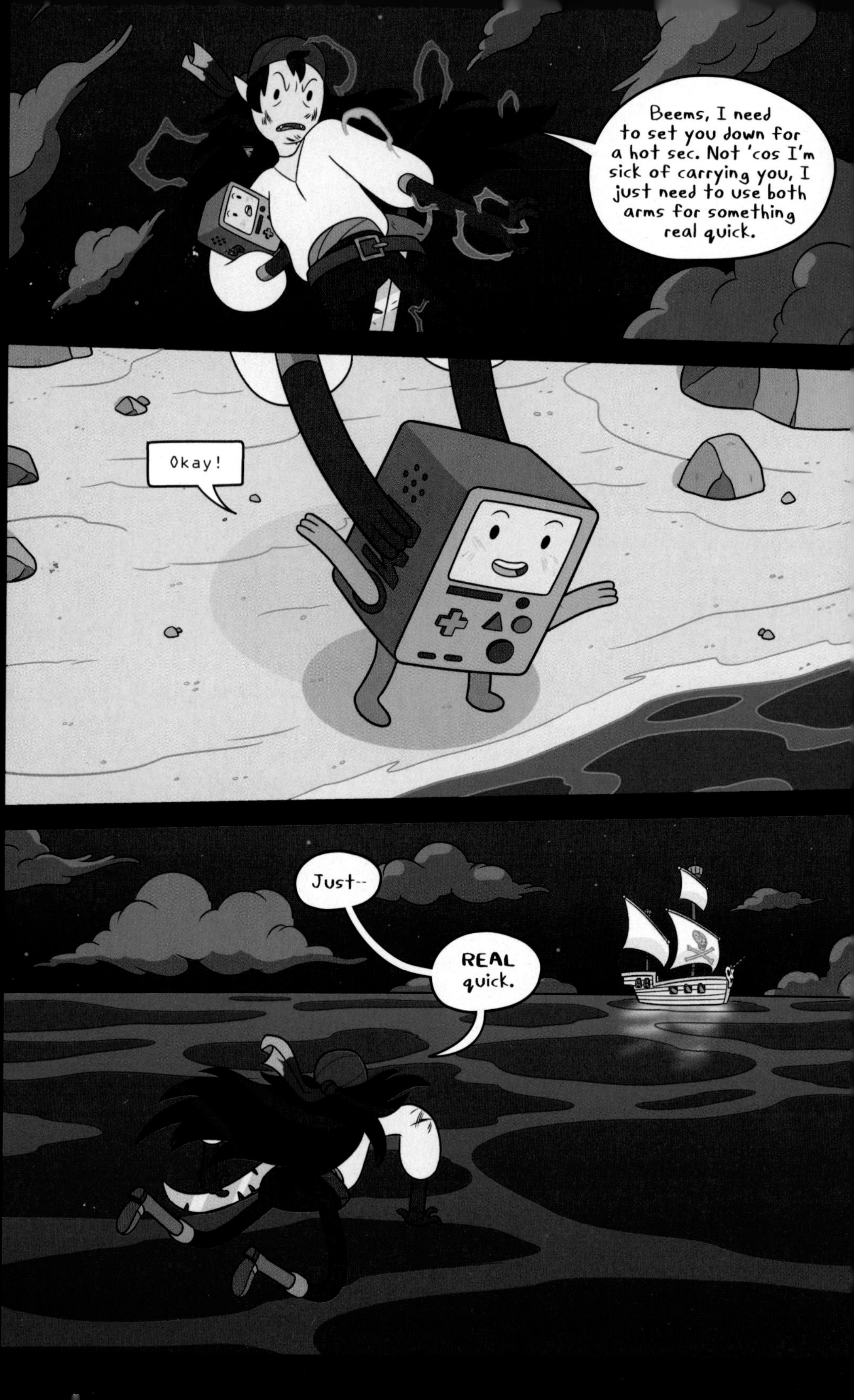
Beems, I need to set you down for a hot sec. Not 'cos I'm sick of carrying you, I just need to use both arms for something real quick.
Okay!
Just--
REAL quick.

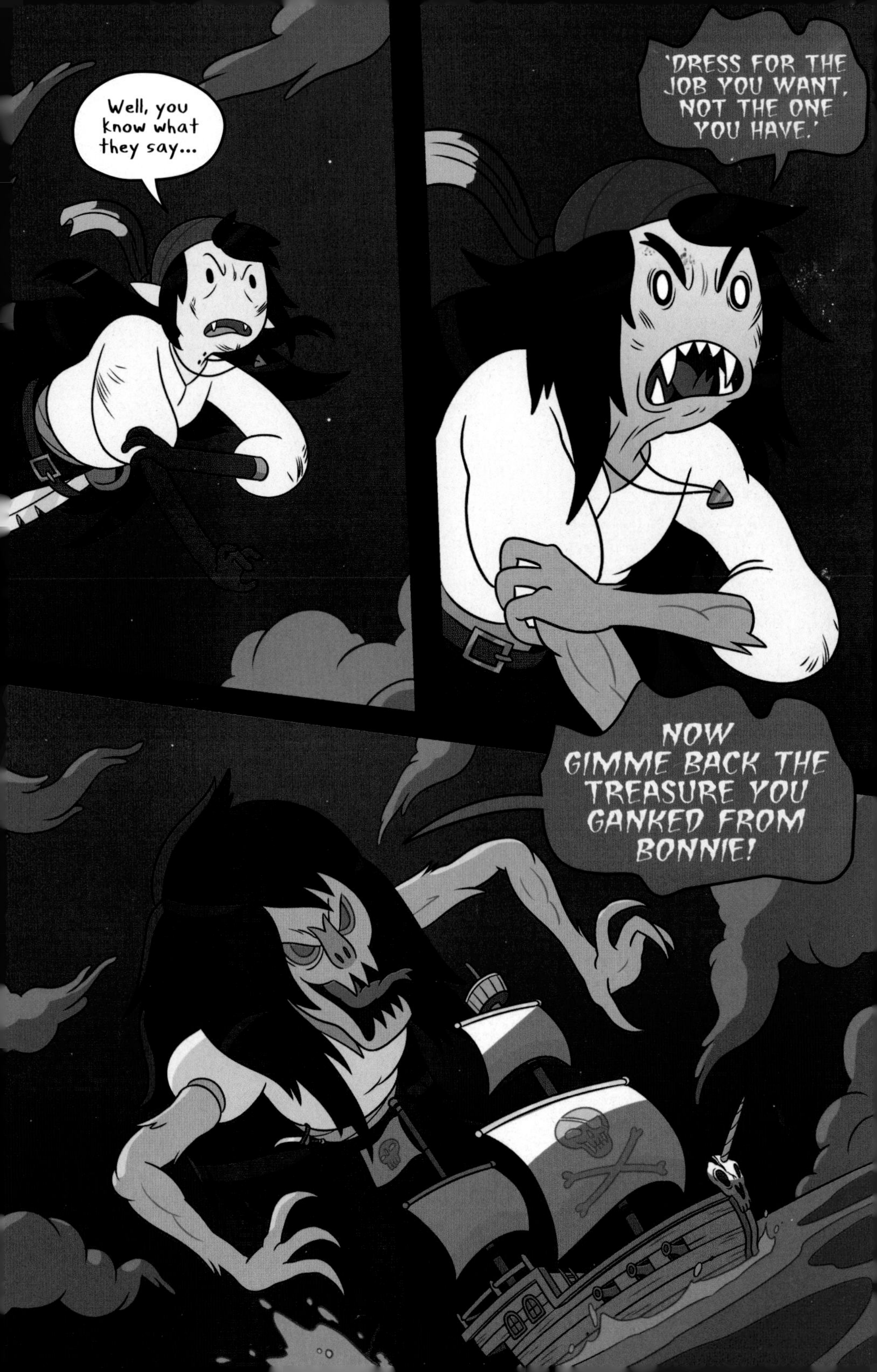
Well, you know what they say...
'DRESS FOR THE JOB YOU WANT, NOT THE ONE YOU HAVE.'
NOW GIMME BACK THE TREASURE YOU GANKED FROM BONNIE!

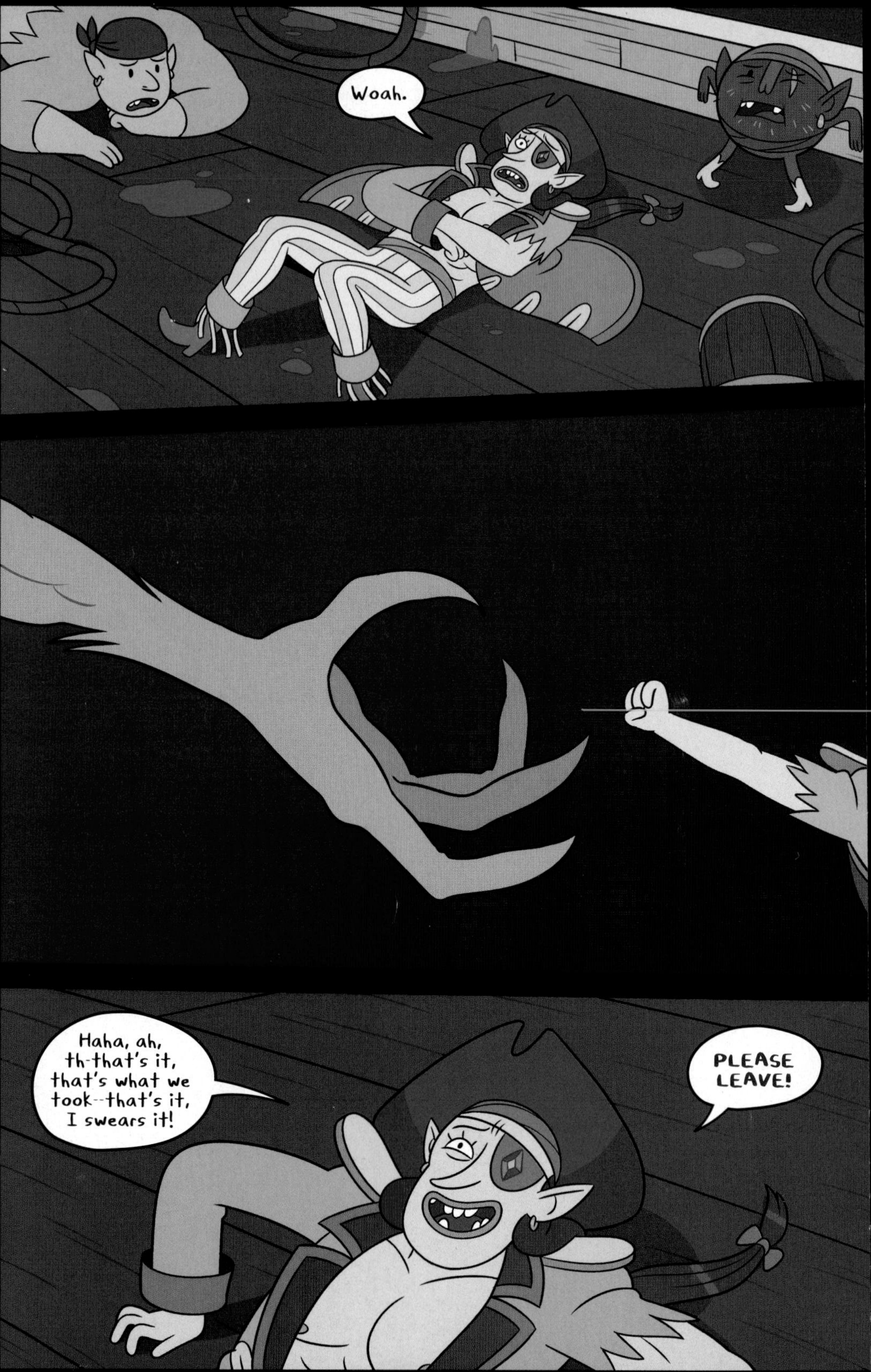
Woah.
Haha, ah, th-that's it, that's what we took--that's it, I swears it!
PLEASE LEAVE!

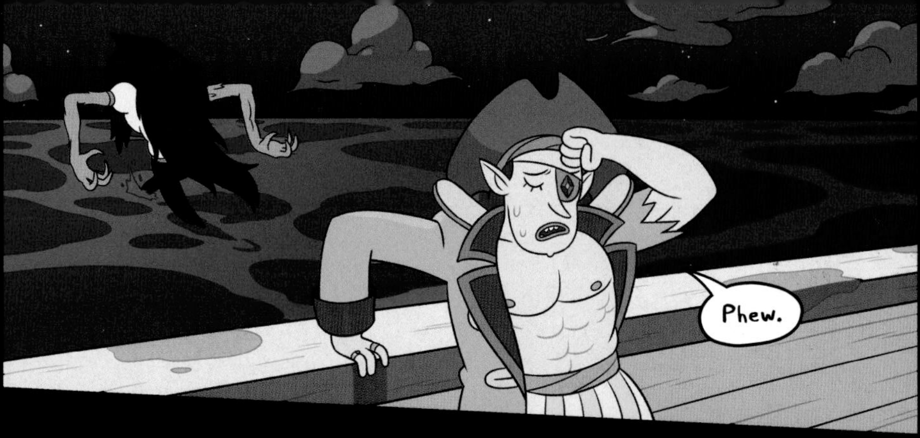
Phew.

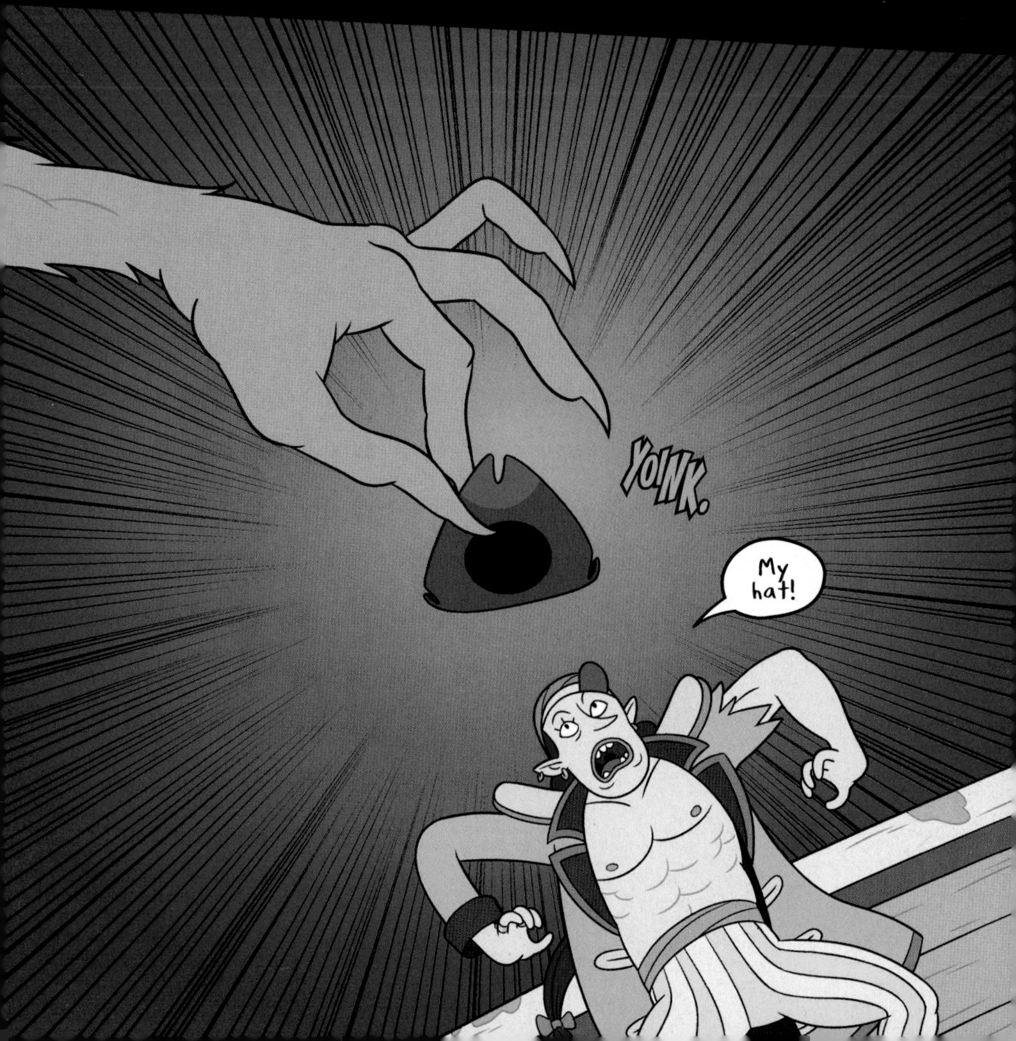
YOINK.
My hat!

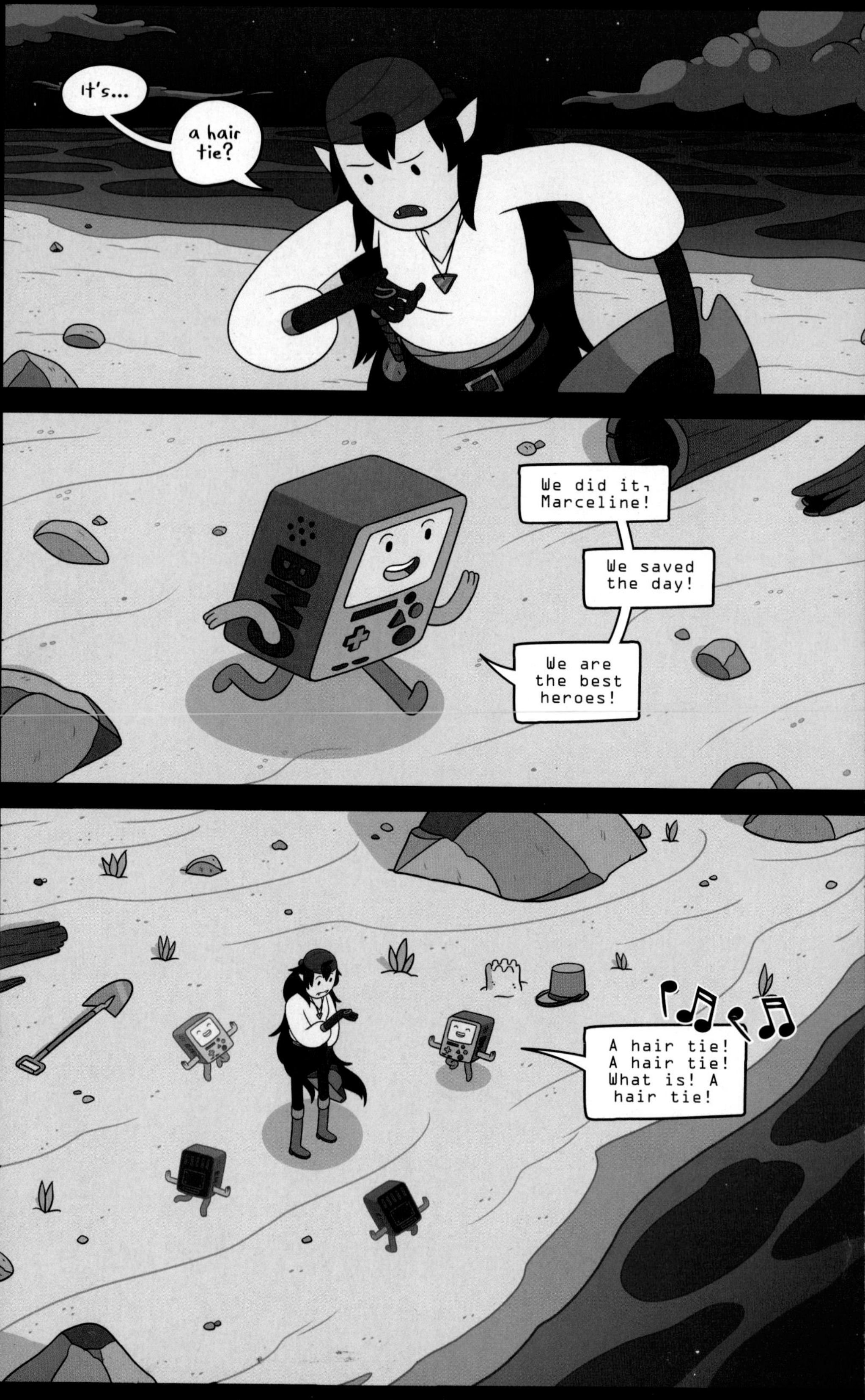
It's...
a hair tie?
We did it, Marceline!
We saved the day!
We are the best heroes!
A hair tie! A hair tie! What is! A hair tie!

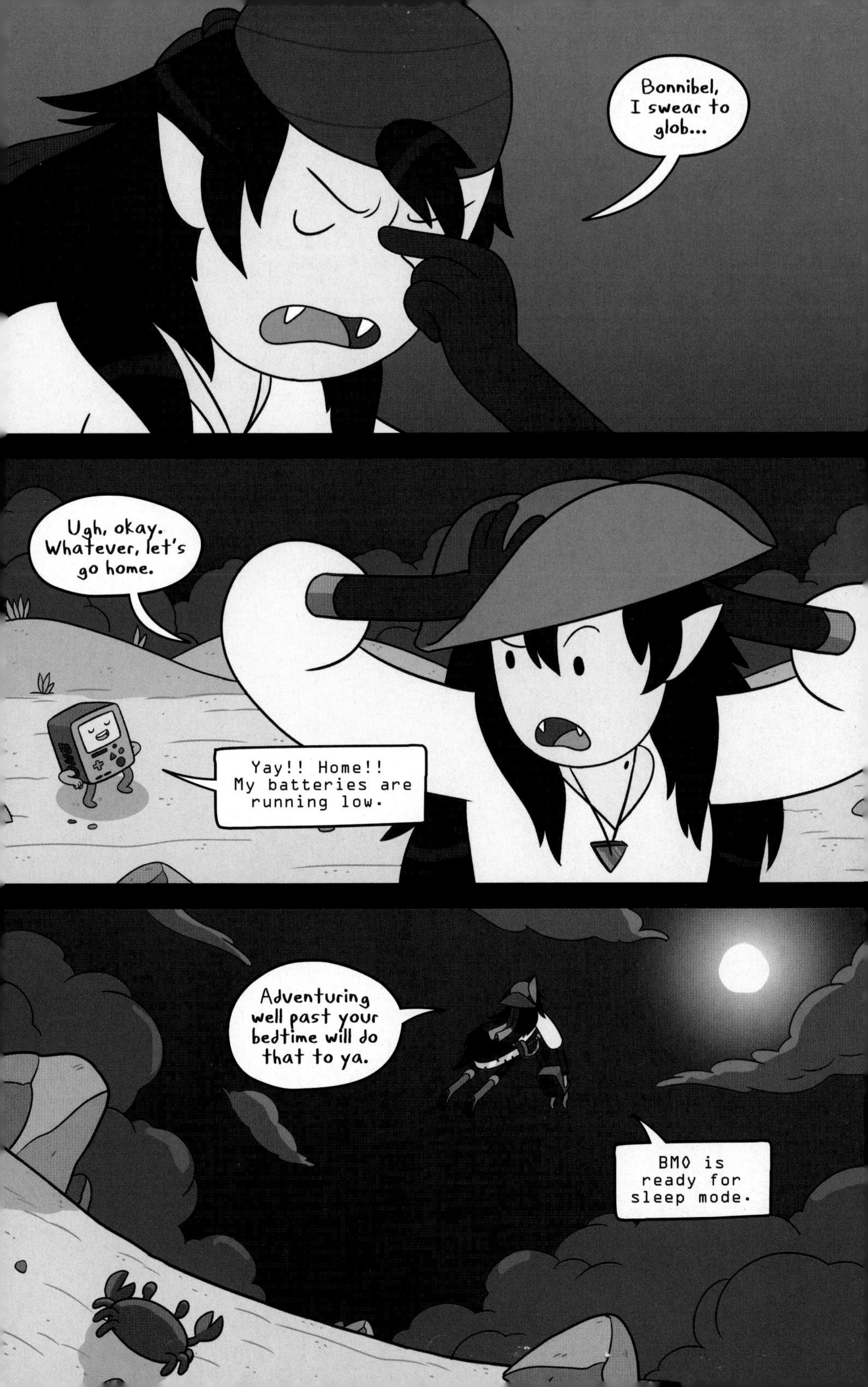
Bonnibel, I swear to glob...
Ugh, okay. Whatever, let's go home.
Yay!! Home!! My batteries are running low.
Adventuring well past your bedtime will do that to ya.
BMO is ready for sleep mode.

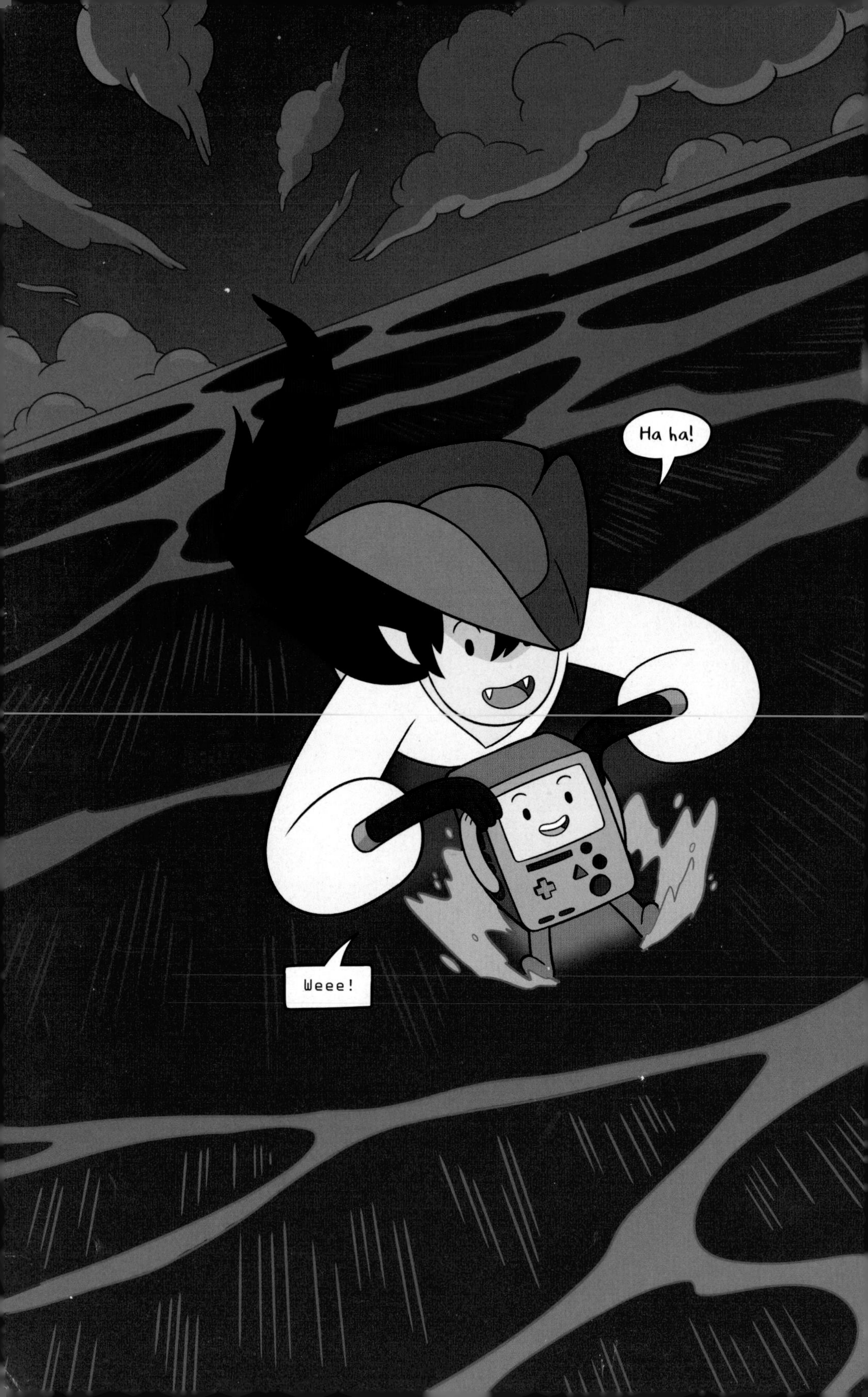
Ha ha!
Weee!

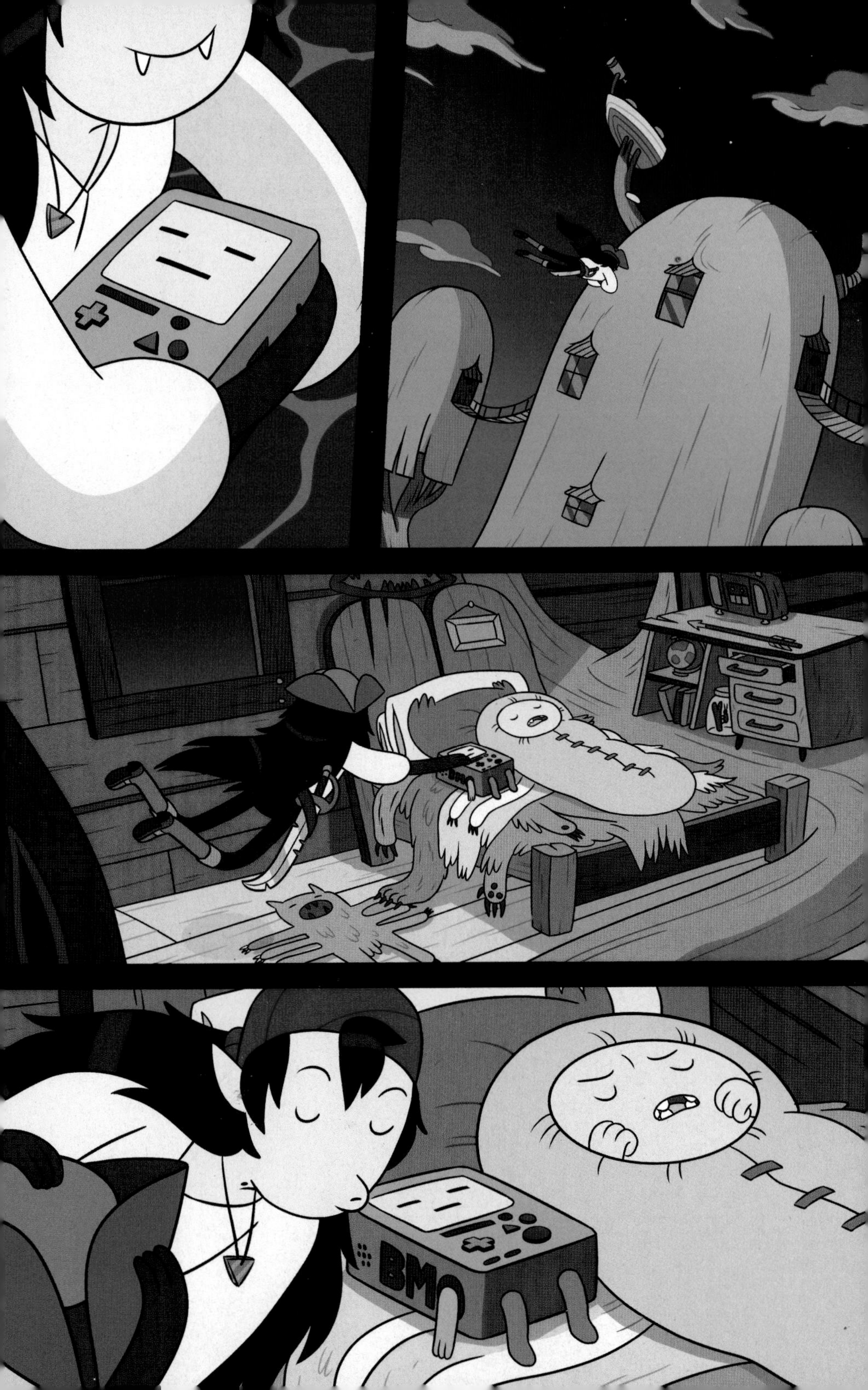
BMO

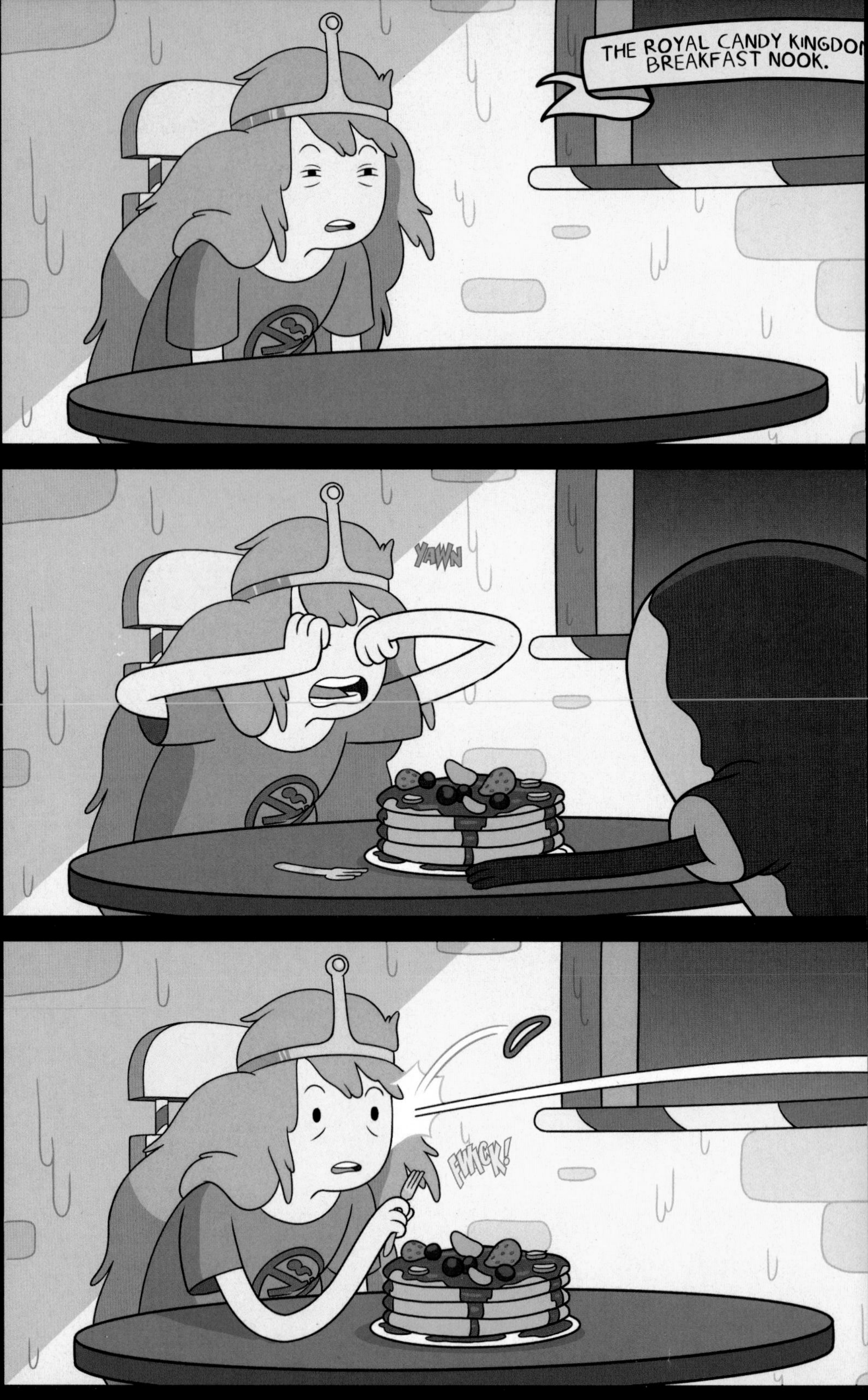
THE ROYAL CANDY KINGDOM BREAKFAST NOOK.
YAWN
FWACK!

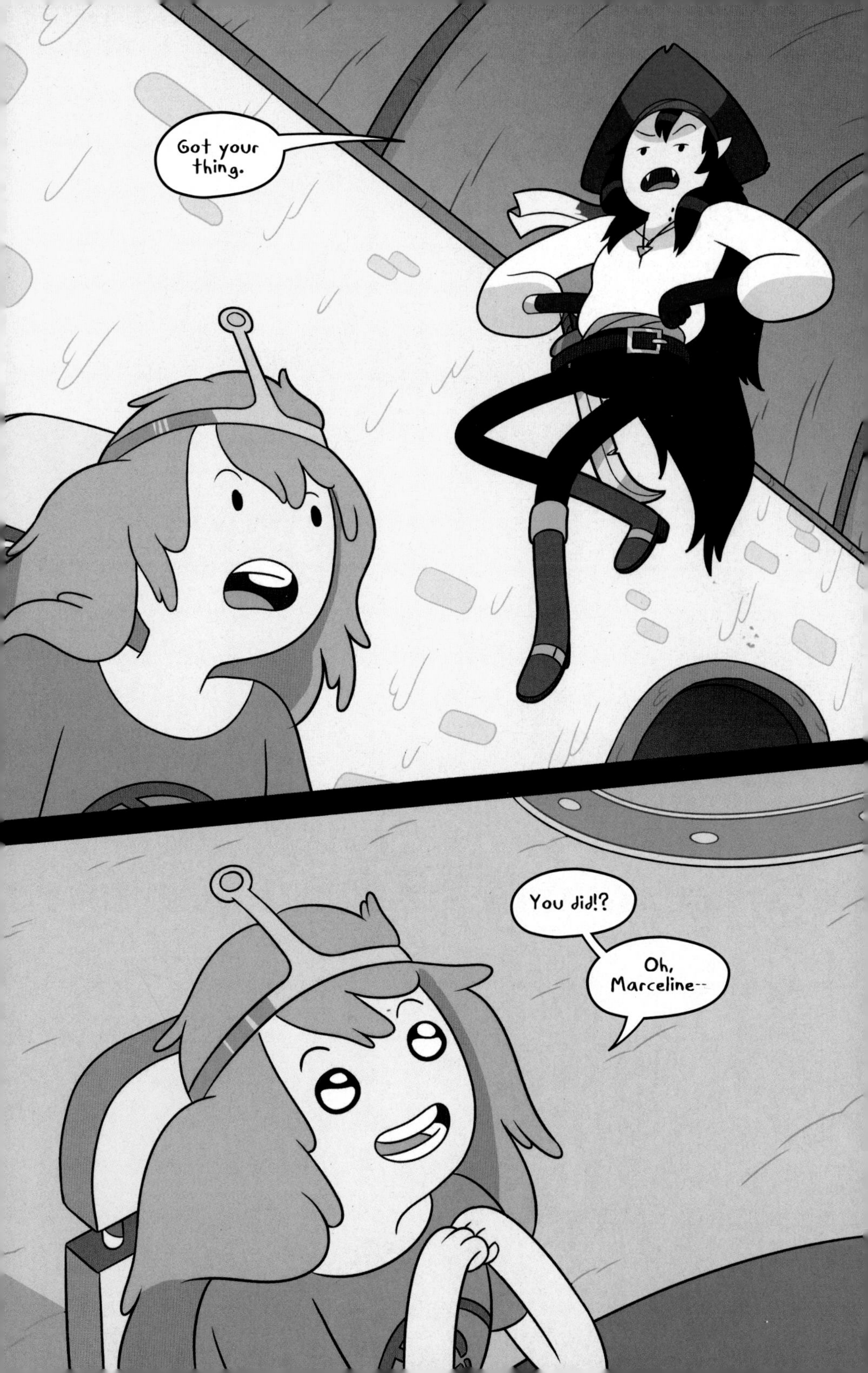
Got your thing.
You did!?
Oh, Marceline--

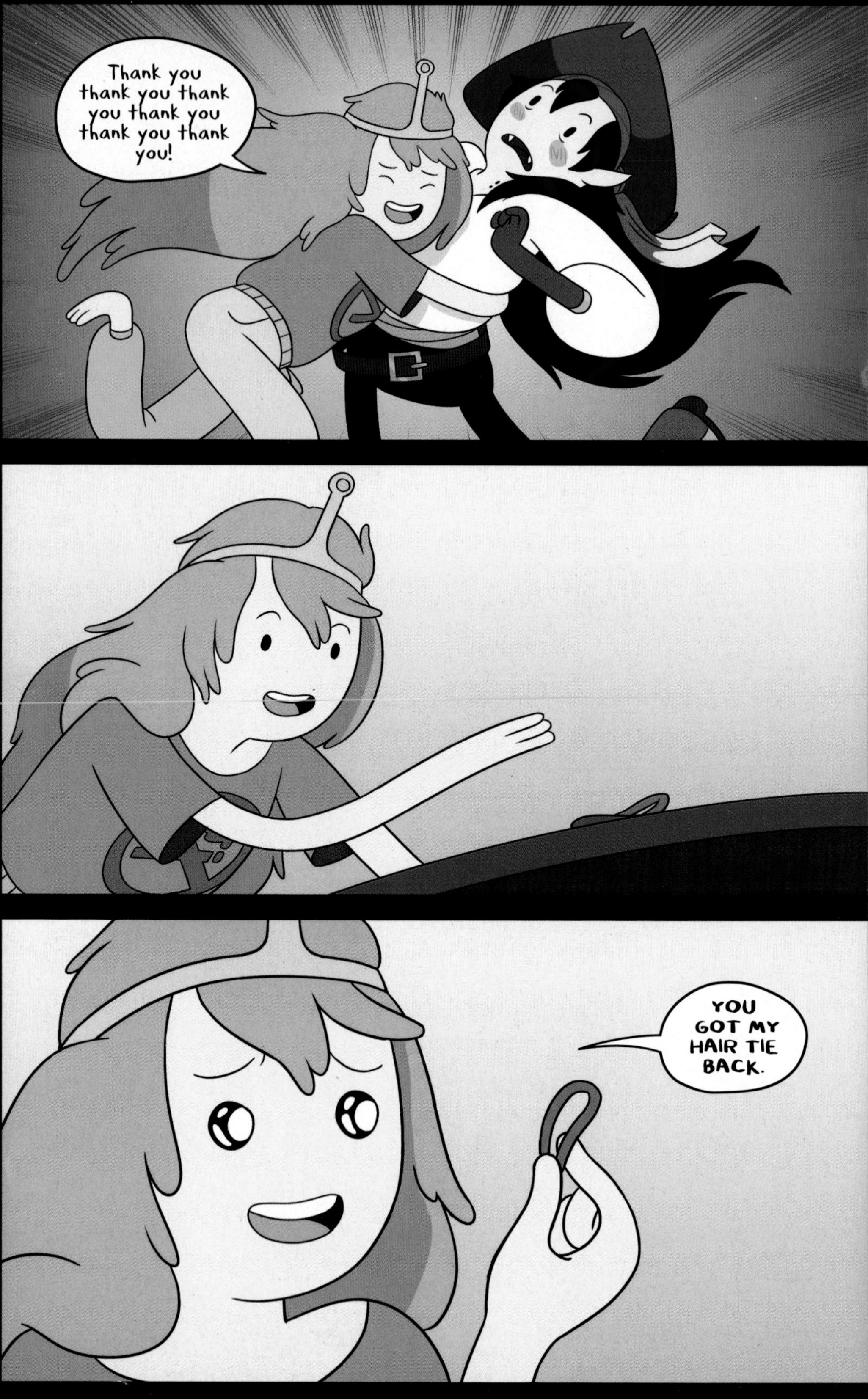
Thank you thank you thank you thank you thank you thank you!
YOU GOT MY HAIR TIE BACK.

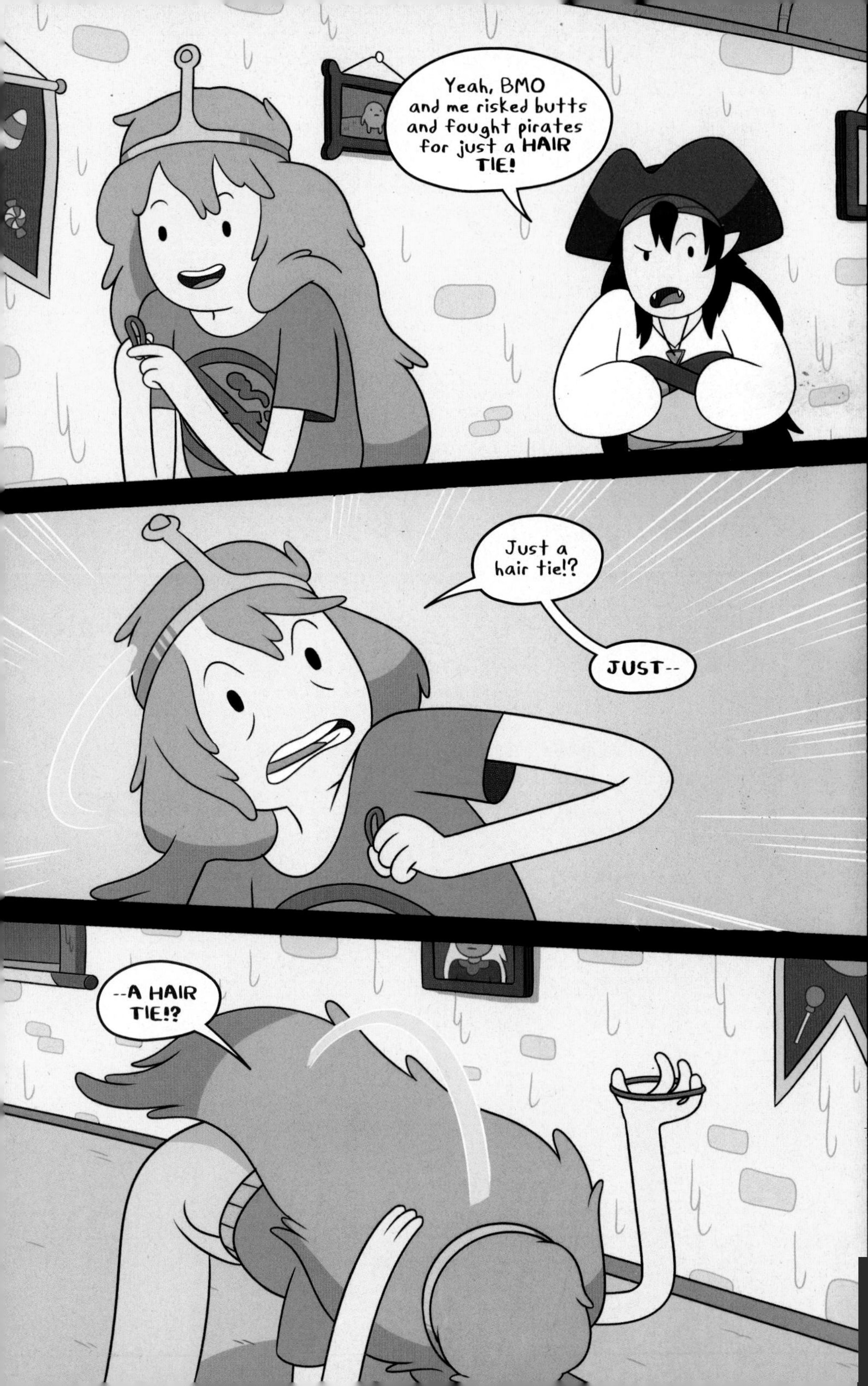
Yeah, BMO and me risked butts and fought pirates for just a HAIR TIE!
Just a hair tie!?
JUST--
--A HAIR TIE!?

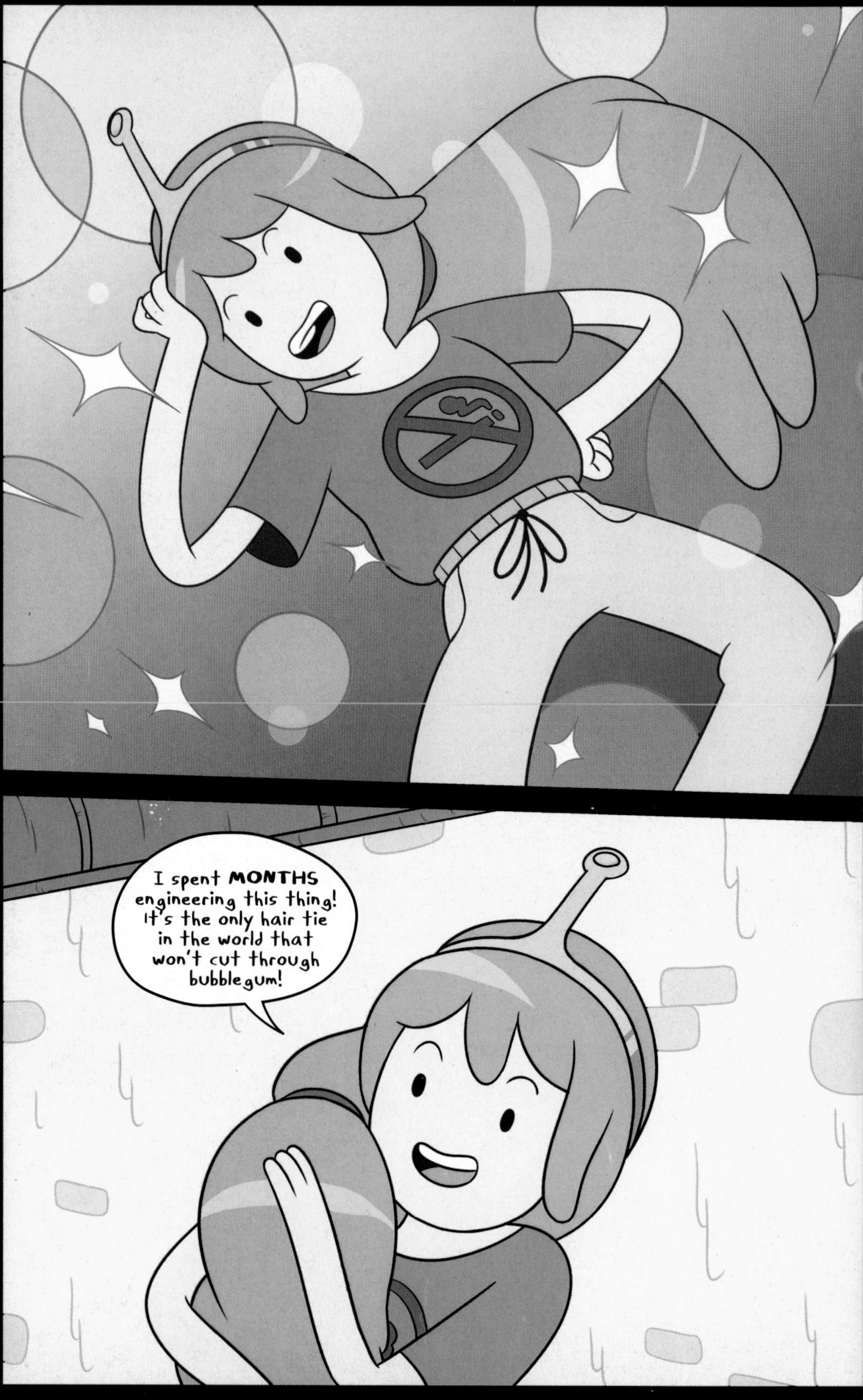
I spent MONTHS engineering this thing! It's the only hair tie in the world that won't cut through bubblegum!

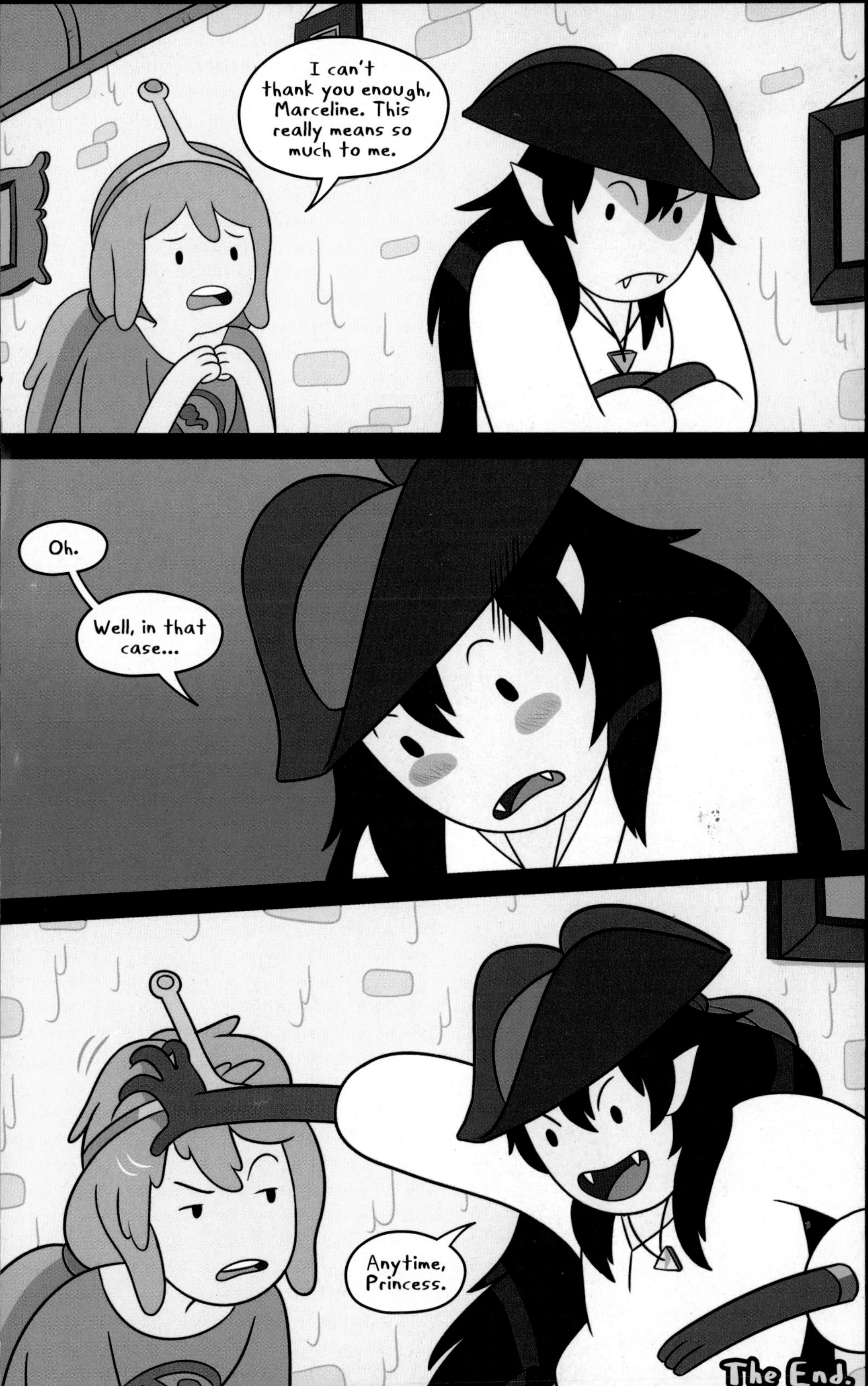
I can't thank you enough, Marceline. This really means so much to me.
Oh.
Well, in that case...
Anytime, Princess.
The End.

DISCOVER
EXPLOSIVE NEW WORLDS

ADVENTURE TIME

Sam Sykes · Selina Espiritu · Sarah Stern
Brave Chef Brianna

KELLY THOMPSON BRIANNE DROUHARD M. VICTORIA ROBADO
MEGA PRINCESS

THE NOT-SO SECRET SOCIETY
DALEY · CRAFTS · CLARK · BRUNI
KEEP OUT
CAUTION

OVER THE GARDEN WALL

STEVEN UNIVERSE
VOLUME ONE

Adventure Time
Pendleton Ward and Others
Volume 1
ISBN: 978-1-60886-280-1 | $14.99 US
Volume 2
ISBN: 978-1-60886-323-5 | $14.99 US
Adventure Time: Islands
ISBN: 978-1-60886-972-5 | $9.99 US

The Amazing World of Gumball
Ben Bocquelet and Others
Volume 1
ISBN: 978-1-60886-488-1 | $14.99 US
Volume 2
ISBN: 978-1-60886-793-6 | $14.99 US

Brave Chef Brianna
Sam Sykes, Selina Espiritu
ISBN: 978-1-68415-050-2 | $14.99 US

Mega Princess
Kelly Thompson, Brianne Drouhard
ISBN: 978-1-68415-007-6 | $14.99 US

The Not-So Secret Society
Matthew Daley, Arlene Daley, Wook Jin Clark
ISBN: 978-1-60886-997-8 | $9.99 US

Over the Garden Wall
Patrick McHale, Jim Campbell and Others
Volume 1
ISBN: 978-1-60886-940-4 | $14.99 US
Volume 2
ISBN: 978-1-68415-006-9 | $14.99 US

Steven Universe
Rebecca Sugar and Others
Volume 1
ISBN: 978-1-60886-706-6 | $14.99 US
Volume 2
ISBN: 978-1-60886-796-7 | $14.99 US

Steven Universe & The Crystal Gems
ISBN: 978-1-60886-921-3 | $14.99 US

Steven Universe: Too Cool for School
ISBN: 978-1-60886-771-4 | $14.99 US

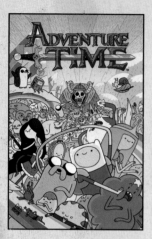

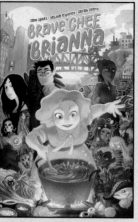

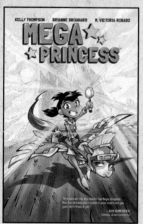

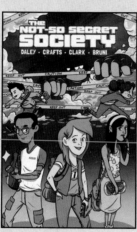

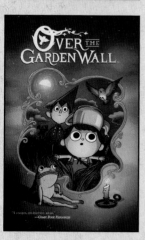

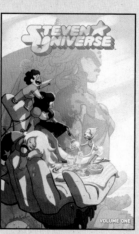

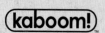